"I BELIEVE THIS DANCE IS MINE,"
HE SAID.

"Is it?"

"I'd like to make it my dance," he said softly.

Without a word she slipped into his arms to dance the waltz that tinkled off the keys of the piano. Immediately Christopher realized that touching her was a grave mistake on his part. She was warm and supple beneath the green silk. . . . He should end the dance and let her go, but he couldn't.

"You look lovely tonight." He looked down at her and smiled. She hadn't seen such warmth in his eyes for weeks. "You have a gift for being a perfect lady when you want to."

"You don't need to compliment me on manners—like giving a treat to a dog. By now I know what manners are and when they have to be used."

"I didn't mean any insult, Maggie."

His arms tightened around her, and her pulse leapt to the feel of his hard body moving in concert with hers. Maggie let herself be taken by the rare moment, let herself imagine that she could see herself reflected in his eyes, beautiful, desirable, beloved. For a moment she pretended that she and Christopher Talbot had a real marriage, not just a business arrangement. Perhaps if she pretended hard enough, the fantasy would come true. . . .

"From page one I became totally immersed in this book through research, feisty people, poignant situations, but above all, the witty, realistic, wry humor and dialogue made this one heck of a trek to California via the written word." —*Heartland Critiques*

Cactus Blossom

"This is a fast, enjoyable read with dashes of humor, adventure, and romance . . . read this one for the pure enjoyment of it." —*Rendezvous*

"Reading *Cactus Blossom* is like riding a bucking bronco: wild, untamed, exciting, and exhilarating. Maxie is an utter delight . . . Aaron is a hero to dream about, and their adventure will keep you in laughter and tears for hours of fun. Emily Bradshaw has written a splendid 'love and laughter' western—THE BEST OF THE SEASON!" —*Romantic Times*

"Maxie is a heroine you'll never forget. Hunter is a hero with all the right ingredients . . . including a wild streak that makes a walk on the wild side seem mighty appealing." —*Affaire de Coeur*

EMILY BRADSHAW

MIDNIGHT DANCER

A DELL BOOK

Published by
Dell Publishing
a division of
Bantam Doubleday Dell Publishing Group, Inc.
1540 Broadway
New York, New York 10036

ISBN: 0-440-21303-7

Printed in the United States of America

Published simultaneously in Canada

November 1994

10 9 8 7 6 5 4 3 2 1

RAD

I

The Wild West

One

If Magdalena Teresa Maria Montoya had a guardian angel, which she often contended, then that particular angel must have been asleep on that cold November night of 1882. It was not a night of good omens. A frigid east wind swept from the prairie into Denver's muddy streets, rattling the few dead leaves that still clung to the trees and sucking others into swirling eddies along the ground. To the west the mountains hid beneath a thick, low bank of clouds that seemed ready to pounce upon the town with the first real storm of winter.

"I have my doubts that this is a wise course of action, Magdalena." Luisa Gutierrez pulled a woolen cloak more closely about her shoulders and gazed regretfully after the retreating streetcar they had just exited.

"You didn't have to come. I can manage this alone."

"Indeed. You believe you can manage everything and anything alone."

Maggie flashed an impish smile that made her look much younger than her twenty years. "I've done all right so far, haven't I?"

Luisa lifted a skeptical brow.

"Not that I don't appreciate the company," Maggie admitted.

The older woman sniffed. "You're an investment, girl. If you insist upon flying off on such a foolish scheme, it's to my benefit to keep you in one piece."

"Whatever you say." Maggie gave her companion a fond glance. "We wouldn't want anyone to think you're getting softhearted, would we?" She laughed at Luisa's stern expression. "Come on. I've only got an hour and a half. If I'm late for work you'll dock my wages."

"You can be sure that I will."

The two women made their way through the half-frozen mud to the sidewalk. Magdalena glanced up at the street sign. Grant Street. Capitol Hill. She'd never before had occasion to visit this elegant section of Denver. People like Magdalena Montoya stayed in lower downtown, where they belonged. But Maggie wouldn't belong there forever. Someday she would wear silk dresses and drive out in a fancy carriage like the one passing just now on the street. The well-groomed horses gleamed in the light of the streetlamp. Maggie imagined a grande dame in silks and lace sitting behind the closed curtain, diamonds circling her throat and wrists and gold rings on her fingers.

"If you stop to gawk at every carriage that passes we'll never get this chore accomplished," Luisa said sharply.

Maggie hastened to catch up with her companion. "I wasn't gawking. I was just thinking of what kind of carriage I will have for myself when I'm the toast of the San Francisco stage. Or maybe New York. I've heard lovely things about New York."

"I doubt you even know where New York is."

"Of course I do. It's east. I'm not entirely stupid."

They walked on until they came to an imposing two-story brick house guarded by a wrought-iron fence. Luisa sighed. "Is this the house?"

"Sixteen eighty-two. This is it."

Steps led up to a broad veranda. An elaborately land-scaped garden adorned the base of the veranda and spread out like skirts on both sides of the house.

Maggie took a deep breath, opened the wrought-iron gate, climbed the steps, and knocked at the big oak door with its panes of expensive stained glass. She whispered a silent prayer to her guardian angel, the one who had kept her alive and safe through all the misadventures of her youth.

The latch rattled and the door swung open on well-oiled hinges. A black-clad woman with a starched apron confronted them with a stern countenance. "Yes?"

"We've come to see Mr. Stone," Maggie said boldly.

The woman eyed both Maggie and Luisa with ill-concealed scorn. "Who may I say is calling?"

"Two ladies of his acquaintance who wish to discuss a business matter." Maggie looked down her nose at the woman as best she could, but with her nose only at the level of the woman's collarbone, the task was difficult.

Starched as her apron, the black crow did not seem impressed. "I will inquire if Mr. Stone is at home."

"He's at home." The door closed in Maggie's face. She

sniffed. "The man is probably still hung over from last week. Lordy! I've never seen anyone drink so much and be so disgusting about it."

A spare smile touched Luisa's lips. "That's one of our best customers you're talking about, girl."

"He's still disgusting."

The door opened abruptly and Mr. Arnold Stone's florid face peered out. "Maggie! What the hell . . . ? And Luisa! What in blazes are you two doing here?"

Maggie hated the name that everyone but Luisa called her. It lacked the drama that a performer needed to be noticed. But she wasn't going to argue the point with Arnold right now. She had more pressing matters on her mind. She drew herself up to her full height of two inches over five feet. "I've come to discuss—"

Before she could finish he pulled them both into the house and away from the door.

"—business," she finished lamely as he pushed them into a dark room off the entrance hall.

"What the hell do you think you're doing, coming here like this?" He lit the lamps. Soft gaslight fell on a heavy oak desk, walls lined with dusty books, and a huge fireplace with a marble mantel. Over the mantel hung two rifles. "I've got a reputation to protect, y'know. I can't have a couple of tarts knocking at my front door and sashaying into my house like they were invited, for God's sake."

Luisa fixed him with a frigid glare. "We are not tarts, Arnold, as well you know. You've been escorted from my saloon more than once for making that mistake. As Magdalena said, she is here on business, and I am here as support."

Stone harrumped, exhaling a blast of liquor fumes.

"You owe me five dollars," Maggie reminded him. "It's

been a week since I danced for your roomful of business cronies, and you still haven't paid me."

"You came here for a lousy five dollars?" Arnold roared.

Maggie refused to be intimidated. "I need the money, Arnold. Now. I've got business dealings of my own, you know."

"I told you I'd pay you next time I came down to the Lady Luck."

"I would like my money now, please."

Stone's face darkened. He poured himself a whiskey from a bottle in the drawer of his desk. "You've got balls, little Maggie. Coming to my house like you were something other than a dirty little saloon dancer and demanding that I give you money."

Maggie felt her temper ignite. "I'd rather be a saloon dancer than a slobbering drunk who's known for beating up whores when he's had too much to drink—or a welsher who doesn't pay his debts."

"You little slut!" Stone tossed down another drink. "Who do you think you are to call me names? Get out of my house before I throw you out on your ass!"

"Not before you give me the money you owe me!"

"You'll get your damned money when I'm good and ready to give it to you!"

"Both of you calm down!" Luisa interjected, but her voice was drowned in a duet of bellowing as Maggie and Stone both unleashed their tempers.

Maggie almost matched Stone for sheer volume in the shouting match that followed. She knew she should cut her losses and beat a hasty retreat. Arnold Stone was drunk and deaf to reason. But reason had little to do with why she continued to argue with him. To be named slut and tart was guaranteed to set a match to her temper, and Arnold Stone used the words with great frequency. She'd teach him that she could trade insults with the orneriest muleskinner in town and turn as mean as the stray dogs that roamed Denver's streets. Arnold Stone would learn not to mess with Magdalena Montoya, and he wouldn't be the first man to learn the lesson.

Luisa once again attempted to intervene. "Arnold Stone, you'll have the whole neighborhood wondering if someone's being murdered in here! And, Magdalena, be quiet. You sound like a scalded cat."

"Stay out of this!" both combatants shouted at her.

"I'll give you one more warning to get out of here," Stone snarled. "I'll pay you when I'm damn well good and ready. No cheap saloon tramp prances into my house and demands money!"

"Give me what you owe me and I'll leave, you drunken skunk!"

"You need to learn your place in this world! Damn! I should have done this the first time you wiggled your ass in my face then taunted me that it wasn't for sale."

He reached for her. Startled by his sudden switch from words to action, Maggie was too slow to back off. Stone's meaty hands circled her neck and squeezed.

"Leggo!" Her words came out as a croak. She kicked at his shins, then shot her knee up into his groin.

Stone grunted in pain but held on, breathing whiskey fumes into her face. His mouth drew back from yellowed teeth. His reddened face gleamed with sweat. He squeezed tighter, ignoring her hands that clawed at his.

Maggie's lungs ached for air. Spots swam dizzily before her eyes. Faintly, as from a great distance, she heard Luisa shouting.

Suddenly, the pressure around her neck was gone. Sweet air flooded her lungs.

"Magdalena! Are you all right?"

Maggie was surprised to find herself on the floor with

Luisa bending over her. She coughed out an answer and massaged her throat. Then her eyes fell on Arnold Stone.

"Lord, Luisa! What did you do to him?"

"I hit him with the fireplace poker."

"Omigod!" Maggie crawled over to where Stone lay. The side of his face was scarlet.

"Is he dead?"

"I don't know." Gingerly, Maggie felt for a pulse. "He's dead."

Luisa was silent, her face pale and grim.

"He was going to kill me."

"You wouldn't be the first girl he's killed in a drunken temper."

Maggie's eyes widened.

"Carrie, last spring, in the Flower Garden. She didn't die of a fall down the stairs. She died of a beating from her customer. The law looks the other way when a rich gentleman forgets his manners on Market Street."

"What are we going to do?"

"Leave. Now. Come on."

"The servants saw us."

"They don't know our names." Face grim, Luisa helped Maggie to her feet. "As I said before, this wasn't a very wise course of action."

The Lady Luck Saloon was one of the few establishments on Market Street that was not a brothel. Its proprietor, Luisa Gutierrez, provided liquor and entertainment, cards and dealers for gambling, and food if the customer wanted it. But the upstairs rooms were strictly off limits to customers, and the women who worked in the barroom served only drinks. If a man wanted to spend his evening with a "sporting woman," there were plenty to be had on Market Street, but not in Luisa Gutierrez's saloon.

For the past year the Lady Luck had been home and

haven for Magdalena Montoya. Forced to make her own way since she was fourteen, Maggie had scrubbed floors, cleaned bedrooms, washed dishes, and laundered clothes in almost every brothel on Market Street. Once she had been promoted from scrubwoman to cook, but that job had lasted only until the "ladies of the house" tasted her bricklike biscuits, soggy flapjacks, and shoe-leather beef-steak. More than once the tarts she worked for urged her to take up the "profession," but Maggie wasn't about to whore for a living, even if the job did mean regular meals and a permanent place to sleep. She believed that life had to offer something better than whoring, and she was de-termined to find it.

Then a year ago Maggie's world had started looking up. She had talked her way into a job serving drinks at the Lady Luck. The high-class lady proprietor discovered that she could dance—not the rowdy high-kicking and bot-tom-wiggling that most saloon dancers passed off as danc-ing, but the Spanish dance that was grace and drama and seduction all in one. Maggie's mother had taught her the dance along with her first toddling steps. It had become her favorite entertainment, an exercise of mind as well as body that always made her troubles fade. But never had the dance earned her anything but pleasure until Luisa Gutierrez hired her for three shows a night in the Lady Luck—four on Fridays and Saturdays. The proprietor had raised her wages, given her a bed in a storeroom in the back of the saloon, and assumed a proprietary interest in her welfare.

The Lady Luck's customers loved Maggie. Conversa-tions stopped when she danced, poker games paused, drinks stayed on the table. And Maggie joyfully drank in the adulation and dared to dream that she would someday dance in surroundings more luxurious than a Market Street saloon. Denver's Tabor Grand Opera House would do for a start, and then on to exotic cities like San Francisco and New York, with silk dresses, a carriage of her own, and a haughty air that would tell everyone that she was the toast of the performing world.

Between such dreams, though, Maggie simply loved to dance. Dancing had always been her pleasure; now it was her life. There wasn't a time when she didn't want to dance.

Except tonight. The night's violence had stilled her dancing spirit. She didn't want to face the crowd or smell the fumes of liquor that would remind her of Arnold Stone. She didn't want to see the drunken faces or the fervent eyes following her every move. They would see her bruised throat, her flushed face, her guilt.

A knock on her bedroom door preceded the quiet inquiry of Luisa's voice.

"Come in," Maggie answered.

"Do you need help buttoning?"

Luisa's eyes communicated volumes that her words did not. Maggie wondered how she could be so calm after what had happened. Only fifteen minutes before they had been running like banshees through the back alleys trying to get back to the Lady Luck without being seen. Now Luisa looked as though this were an ordinary night where the only trouble came from rowdy customers in the saloon.

Maggie turned around and presented Luisa with her back buttons. "I don't feel much like dancing."

"We must often do things we don't feel like doing." Luisa paused. "Jack Morley is in the bar tonight."

"Figures." Jack Morley was the reason that Maggie had demanded her money from Arnold Stone. Three weeks past Jack had paid her in advance the enormous sum of ten dollars to keep him company at his favorite gambling house on Larimer Street. When the appointed night had come, he had tried to press her into duties more intimate than simply sitting with him at the card table and lending him her "luck," as he'd put it. When she'd refused to accompany him to a room upstairs, Morley had demanded his ten dollars back. Maggie had already spent it. He'd been hounding her ever since.

"I have two dollars I can give him." She cursed herself for not having had the presence of mind to take the money Stone owed her before they'd fled his house. After all, what was a little stealing when one had already committed murder?

"I can lend you the money." Luisa fastened the last button.

"I won't take your money to give to that bastard. God knows when I could pay you back." She brushed back the front and sides of the thick, curling mass of her hair and fastened it high on her crown with a silver barrette—one of the few things she had of her mother's. "I did what he paid me for. I don't see why I should pay him anything at all."

"Because he'll continue to make your life miserable until you do."

"What happened to your rule about taking care of yourself before looking after others?" Maggie gave the older woman a wry smile. "You're letting that slip a bit tonight, aren't you, Luisa?"

"Advancing you ten dollars on your wages is not going to put me in the poorhouse."

"Ten dollars isn't what I was talking about."

Luisa's mouth drew into a stern line. "Will you take the money or not?"

"And disappoint Jack Morley? Hell, no." Maggie grimaced. "I think he enjoys hounding me more than he'd enjoy getting paid."

"Be careful of him, Magdalena. He's not someone to

mess with. I warned you before and you didn't listen to me."

How could Maggie think about the problem of Jack Morley when she was still reeling from the lethal turn of events with Arnold Stone? Of course, if Morley weren't such a pest she never would have badgered Stone for her five dollars. One thing always led to another. Maggie sighed and slumped down onto the room's one straight-backed chair. "I really don't feel like dancing tonight."

She did dance, however. As usual, she ignored the smell of cigar smoke and sweat, the clink of glasses, the buzz of conversation and eruptions of raucous laughter. The chords of Hermano Gallegos's guitar washed over her, and her body responded, feet stepping in time, arms lifting proudly, hips and torso weaving in a declaration of innocent sensuality. After a few moments the room grew still as conversations trailed off and eyes turned to her performance. The music built. Her bright skirts swirled around her ankles and belled out to reveal trim calves and thighs. Only the guitar accompaniment broke a silence that had grown almost reverent.

Maggie tried to lose herself in the dance, but her eyes were drawn against their will to Jack Morley where he sat at a table close to the bar. His scowl was almost enough to make her break the dance's rhythm. Curse the man for an infernal pest. It wasn't as though she hadn't done what he'd hired her to do—at least what she thought he'd hired her to do. If he didn't have such an ugly temper, she'd have told him to go whistle for his damned ten dollars.

Her gaze pulled away from Morley's scowl to survey the other customers. In the haze of cigar and cigarette smoke familiar faces mingled with those of strangers. One stranger in particular caught Maggie's eye as she recovered from a series of graceful whirls and focused her eyes straight ahead. He was seated at an inconspicuous table in the very back of the room, but all the same he stood out in the rough crowd like a single towering pine on a hillside of scrub. Clean shaven, black hair neatly and stylishly trimmed, he had classically sculpted features set in an expression that showed neither appreciation nor disapproval of her dance. His mouth was a careful, noncommittal line, but his rapt attention to her at least indicated an interest.

Maggie decided that the stranger was a safer place for her attention than Jack Morley. She wiped all other faces in the room from her mind's eye and danced only for the stylish man with the black hair. The music enveloped only the two of them. Her smile, her arms, the sinuous language of her body, reached out only to the gentleman of her choice. As the music built and her dance climaxed, she let herself imagine that the tight line of his mouth relaxed and the slightly raised arch of one brow signaled masculine interest. She imagined his heart beating faster as his gaze was caught by the swirling of her skirts around her bare legs and ankles; she pictured his lips curving into a wry smile of admiration. Was it her imagination only, or had the stranger's carefully impassive face really softened?

This was a game Maggie had played more than once when she had become distracted from the dance. Narrowing her focus to one man and enticing him into her power brought back her concentration to center, and the dance became effortless once more. Jack Morley and Arnold Stone both faded from her new reality. Magdalena Montoya dissolved into the elemental female, proud, vital, dancing not on a tiny stage in a shabby saloon, but in the center of the universe, with the world looking on. The very earth seemed to beat to her rhythm as she executed a final trio of turns. The guitar strummed a final deep chord. She sank to the rough planks in graceful repose.

The dance had ended, and the real world intruded once again as applause and approving foot stompings broke around her and shook the precarious stage. Rising, she smiled and took a bow, but she refused to look at Jack Morley.

Maggie was sitting in her little bedroom sponging the film of sweat from her neck, face, and arms when a knock sounded on the door.

"Come in."

Luisa stepped into the room. Maggie smiled slightly. Probably no one but the saloon owner would have bothered with the courtesy of knocking. After all, the room was a storeroom as well as a bedroom, and Maggie was hardly a personage of such importance that she rated privacy.

"They loved you tonight." Luisa smiled. "Of course, the crowd out there always loves you."

Maggie detected the strain in Luisa's voice. "Are you all right?" she asked.

"Of course."

There was no need to speak aloud what fretted them both.

"Luisa . . ."

They both knew what Maggie couldn't put into words.

"He was going to kill you." The tone of Luisa's answer was lifeless.

Maggie slammed her fist down upon her dressing table of discarded wooden crates. "If I hadn't been so—so damned foolish, none of it would have happened. Sometimes I think I couldn't roll off a log without something going wrong while I did it."

Luisa abruptly changed the subject. "There's a customer who wants to talk to you."

A moment passed before Maggie could pull her mind

away from the night's lethal misadventure. "Morley?" she finally asked. "I'll talk to him when I get the money, not before. I don't need to listen to any more of his threats."

"Not Jack Morley. A gentleman I haven't seen before. And I do mean gentleman. He looks like he has more money than Horace Tabor, if that's possible."

Maggie glanced at her employer in surprise. "You know I don't go with the customers."

"I don't think he has whoring in mind."

"Why?"

Luisa shrugged. "The look of him. If he wanted a woman, I doubt he'd come to Market Street to find one. Men with that look about them can afford better."

Maggie had to agree when they went into the barroom and Luisa pointed out the man who had requested her company. He was the fellow she had picked out of the crowd while dancing, definitely not the sort to fancy a cheap whore. He could probably afford to buy his thrills at Jennie Rogers's House of Mirrors, the plushest parlor house between San Francisco and St. Louis and the pride of the sporting women who worked there. But then, he might have noticed Maggie's earlier attention and thought she had invited a rendezvous.

"He didn't say what he wanted?"

"You'll have to find out for yourself."

Maggie grimaced. "Okay, okay. But have Big John keep an eye on us. For all his fancy clothes, that fellow looks like a gent who might not like the word *no*." She hadn't survived alone on the rough streets of Denver for six years without knowing a tough customer when she saw one.

When Luisa introduced Maggie, the man stood, a courtesy a saloon dancer rarely received. The other man at the table stood also. Luisa gave Maggie an encouraging smile and left.

When Maggie had earlier singled out the black-haired man, she hadn't noticed that he wasn't sitting alone. Usually she wasn't so unobservant. The other man was almost as distinctive looking as Mr. Black-hair, though older and somewhat leaner. They were both dressed in sober, expensively tailored suits that seemed a good deal too fine for their surroundings. The older man's eyes crinkled pleasantly as he smiled a greeting. Black-hair smiled also, but the pleasantry didn't reach his eyes. He scrutinized her with a critically assessing gaze that made Maggie feel like a horse on an auction block—one that didn't quite measure up.

"Thank you for joining us, Miss Montoya," the older man said when Luisa had gone. He nudged Mr. Black-hair, who scowled slightly.

"Maggie Montoya, isn't it?" Mr. Black-hair asked.

"Magdalena. I prefer to be called Magdalena."

Mr. Black-hair cleared his throat. His eyes, Maggie noticed, were almost as dark as his hair and set so deeply that they seemed shrouded in shadow. Heavy black brows curved upward over his eyes in a naturally sardonic arch. The nostrils of his narrow, aristocratic nose flared slightly as if repelled by the stench of unwashed bodies mingling with smoke and stale liquor, and cleanly molded lips drew a tight line across a face that looked unaccustomed to smiling.

"Please sit down, Miss Montoya," Mr. Black-hair invited. His accent was clipped and strange, marking him as a foreigner.

Maggie sat. The gentlemen did likewise. For the space of two minutes she thought the two men were simply going to look at her. Feeling free to be equally rude, she examined them in turn. She confirmed her initial assessment of Black-hair. For all his fancy clothes, well-trimmed hair, and clean hands, he was a man she wouldn't want to

cross unnecessarily. Under the fine coat were broad
shoulders and a powerful-looking chest. A certain hardness stamped the features of his face and belied his civilized appearance. He took power for granted, Maggie
speculated—both physical power and the power that
comes with money and family—and wielded them both
effectively.

Black-hair's friend seemed to be a mellower soul. Gray
haired, lean, and well built, he could have claimed anywhere from forty-five to sixty years. His face reminded
Maggie of an owl's—round, inquisitive, intelligent. His
hazel eyes were bright with interest and a half-amused
smile continually played on his narrow lips.

In the face of their frank assessment Maggie suddenly
felt coarse. Usually she gave little thought to her appearance. She knew that her face and form didn't fit the current fashion of beauty. Existing from hand to mouth had
created a figure that was too hard and thin. Her hands
were rough from years of scrubbing floors and washing
dishes, and the peaches and cream in her complexion had
long since surrendered to the frigid winds of winter, the
hot sun of summer, and the smoke and dinginess of saloons and brothels where she worked. She hadn't led a
sheltered or proper life, and it showed. Her only claim to
beauty was the mass of black, naturally curly hair that
cascaded over her shoulders and down her back. Her eyes
also weren't bad. In fact, one fellow had gone so far as to
liken them to stars shining in a black, black night—but he
was drunk at the time, Maggie remembered, and probably
he didn't know half of what he was saying.

"Forgive our bad manners, Miss Montoya." Mr. Black-
hair broke the silence. "We've been waiting a long time to
meet you, and . . . well, I must say, you and your dancing make an impression that is . . . quite arresting."

Gray-hair's smile seemed to become even more amused.

"My name is Christopher Barrows Talbot," Black-hair said. "My associate is Mr. Peter Scarborough."

"I'm very happy to meet you, my lady," Scarborough said with the same clipped accent.

Another foreigner. Not only foreign but green as well. Anyone who would call Maggie a "lady" hadn't been in these parts very long.

"Luisa said you wanted to talk to me, but I'll tell you right up front, gents, that I don't go with the customers. You want that, there's plenty of houses around here where you can plunk down your money and take your pick. But I'm not your sportin' sort."

Talbot arched one brow fractionally upward. "*That* is a relief, at least."

Scarborough chuckled. "I assure you, my dear, we have no such dishonorable intentions in asking to speak to you."

"Is there someplace where we could talk privately?" Talbot looked around the crowded barroom, scowling.

"No, there isn't." Who did they think Maggie was— some naive miss who would fall for such a dodge? "Listen, gents, if you've got something you want to talk about, spit it out. I don't have all night."

"Spit it out?" Talbot repeated, his mouth twisting into a sardonic smile.

"Yeah. Say your piece."

Talbot shook his head, his expression both sad and amused. "I really think it would be to your advantage to listen to what we have to say, and this is not an appropriate place for our conversation. Be assured that we have no designs on your—your private services. You will be quite safe with us."

In a pig's eye. An unprotected female in a woman-hungry town, Maggie knew enough about desire to recognize the light in a man's eye. This uppity gent acted like she was beneath his interest, but she guessed he wasn't half as indifferent as he'd like her to think.

"You can tell me what you got to say right here."

"Really, Miss Montoya . . ."

The rest of his comment flowed unheard past Maggie's ears as she caught sight of Jack Morley making his way toward their table. The rotten pest. Rotten dangerous pest. She'd hoped he would let her be for a few more days until she could come up with part of the money he thought she owed him. But here he came, looking like a dog with a cactus spine up its tail.

Maggie stood so abruptly that her chair almost toppled. "Let's go," she told Talbot.

"What?"

"You wanted to go somewhere and talk. Let's go."

The men stood, looking perplexed by her sudden change of heart.

"Do you have a wrap?" Talbot asked.

"A what?"

"A cloak. A shawl. The night air is quite cold."

"No." Maggie started for the door. Morley was too close. "Let's go."

"You're going to freeze. We can wait long enough for you to get your wrap."

She grabbed an arm of each man and tugged them both out the door and into the chilly November night. "Don't worry about me. I'm tough."

"So I surmise," Talbot admitted, his tone dark.

Maggie was too preoccupied to be cold as they hurried across the muddy street and headed uptown. A glance behind told her that Jack hadn't followed them out the door. She'd been half afraid that he would. The way was clear, though. All she had to do now was dump the two foreign gents. If she missed the next show Luisa would dock her wages, friend or no. Not to mention that the older woman would worry when she realized Maggie had left the saloon. Luisa knew that Maggie could take care of herself in almost any situation, but tonight was a strange night, a weird twisted night where luck turned sour and nightmares became reality. Tonight almost anything could happen. It already had happened.

Before she could think of a plausible excuse to turn around, however, they had reached their destination, only a short distance from Market Street but a world away—the plush Windsor Hotel. As they stepped through the double doors of the main entrance, Maggie couldn't help but gape in astonishment. Her feet sank into plush red carpeting. The furniture looked too fancy to be sat upon, and the elegantly papered walls displayed the famous diamond-dust-backed mirrors. Through a partially open double door she caught a glimpse of the ballroom with its crystal chandelier and shining parquet floor.

The people in the sumptuous lobby were as elegant as the furnishings. On one settee a portly gentleman read the *Rocky Mountain News*. He was apparently dressed to go out, his snowy white shirt and starched collar providing starkly elegant contrast to a black cutaway coat and silk necktie arranged in a neat bow precisely below the points of his collar. Next to him on the settee sat a top hat of finest beaver. A short distance away a lady stood in evening finery, fiddling impatiently with her gloves while her escort brushed a speck from his coat. Several other impressively dressed and faultlessly groomed men and women stood or sat in the lobby in practiced elegance.

"Omigod!" was the only word that Maggie could think of to express her wonder.

"Come along." Christopher Talbot urged her forward. He spoke as though to a child.

Every eye turned their way as Maggie walked with her escorts into the lobby. Elegant brows rose. Nostrils flared in disgust. The lady with the gloves raised one hand to her mouth and nose as if to ward off a disagreeable odor.

"A word with you, sir." The desk clerk's face was carefully neutral as Christopher picked up his key. "Uh . . . Lord Talbot . . ."

Lord Talbot? Maggie blinked. An honest-to-God lord? What had she gotten herself into?

"The . . . uh . . . young lady is hardly the sort . . . to . . ." He trailed off as Christopher gave him a haughty look worthy of a real lord. "We must think of our reputation, sir," the clerk continued quietly. "This is a refined hotel. We can hardly permit just anyone to go in and out."

Maggie didn't catch Christopher's answer, but the clerk turned a shade paler. He nodded deferentially as they made their way to the stairs. Knowing she would never again be in a position to score such a victory, she looked down her nose at the poor clerk as she imagined a grand lady might do. Then she flashed him a mischievous grin that only served to deepen his disapproving scowl. Some people, Maggie reflected, simply had no sense of humor.

After climbing two flights of carpeted stairs, Maggie's escorts led her into a room that was easily ten times the size of her little storeroom. The furnishings were every bit as luxurious as those in the lobby.

"Geez," Maggie exclaimed. "You get this big room for just the two of you?"

"This is my room," Christopher answered. "Mr. Scarborough's is next door." He indicated a connecting door.

"Kind of a waste of space, don't you think?"

Christopher sighed. Peter Scarborough looked worried.

"Are you a real lord?"

"Lord Christopher's title is merely a courtesy title," Scarborough told her. "His father is a peer of the realm.

Duke of Torrington, to be exact. But Christopher is every bit as much a commoner as you are."

"I'm not sure I would go that far!" Christopher said with a twisted smile.

"What's a peer of the realm?"

"A nobleman, my dear." Scarborough's voice was patient. Christopher's expression was not.

"Which realm?"

"England, Miss Montoya. Do you know where England is?" Christopher sounded doubtful.

"Of course I do!" At least she had a vague idea. It was farther away than New York. She knew that.

Scarborough gave Christopher a worried frown. "I'm not sure we shouldn't have found somewhere else to talk, my boy. It's hardly the thing to bring an unmarried girl to a gentleman's room."

Christopher chuckled. "I don't think Miss Montoya's reputation is going to suffer too drastically."

"I have a reputation!" Maggie didn't like the way he'd pronounced the word—as though it were a joke of some kind.

"I'm sure you do." Christopher poured himself a brandy from a bottle on the bedside table.

Maggie still didn't like his tone. In fact, she was beginning to think that she didn't like him. She folded her arms across her chest. "Well, I'm here, and this is about as private as you can get. What is it you want to talk about?"

The English lord took a swallow of brandy and placed the glass quite deliberately on the table. Then he fixed her with another of those appraising looks that had intimidated her in the saloon. A smile touched his lips, and something in the shadowed depths of his eyes sent a shiver tingling down Maggie's spine. "Quite right, Miss Montoya. It's past time we got down to business."

Two

She sat gingerly upon a damask-covered chair, a scrap of a girl with wide luminous eyes and wild hair. The last of a noble Spanish family, she certainly didn't look the part. If Christopher hadn't seen the documentation himself, he wouldn't have believed it.

He sighed and began to pace back and forth in front of her chair. "Down to business, then, Miss Montoya. I'm the bearer of good tidings for you, as it happens. An exhaustive search on the part of Mr. Scarborough and myself has shown you to be the sole heiress to a considerable portion of land in New Mexico Territory— five hundred thousand acres, to be exact. It also happens that I have an interest in this land, making it to my advantage to help you seek your rightful title to the acreage."

The girl's face paled and grew blank for a moment, but in the blink of an eye she regained color and animation. She cocked her head and regarded him slantwise out of catlike eyes. Her mouth twitched up at one corner, impishly irreverent. "You expect me to believe this?"

"I am not in the habit of lying, miss. Certainly I expect you to believe it."

She chuckled, then laughed outright. Christopher felt a wave of irritation. The little minx wasn't the least afraid of him, nor even impressed—an unusual bit of pluck. Men were impressed by his size, and women by his title. Americans especially seemed to believe that a title in front of a man's name made him akin to God. But not this tattered little American. She had the nerve to laugh at him.

"Do you find something amusing?"

"I find *you* amusing!" she mimicked in a fair imitation of his accent. "Greenhorns and foreigners are usually strange, but you're as crazy as a horse that's eaten a load of locoweed." She stood abruptly. "It's been fun, gents. But I've got a show to do."

"Miss Montoya, please." Peter Scarborough spoke for the first time, his voice persuasive. "We've gone to a great deal of trouble to find you. You are indeed the only living heir to one of the largest Mexican land grants in New Mexico."

"Sure I am." The girl turned back toward them, her hand gripping the doorknob. "I'm the queen of England's cousin too. Listen, your lordships, or whatever you are. I've had a rough night already. Why don't you go pester someone else? There's plenty of girls in town who'd like to play your game."

"This most certainly isn't a game." Suddenly Christopher wished that they could choose someone else. Maggie Montoya was not what he had expected. He'd pictured her as a number of things—a quiet spinster, a young wife with children hanging on her skirts, even a broken-down, opium-addicted whore. But the reality was neither quiet nor broken down, and the only thing hanging on her garish skirts were the hot gazes of the patrons of the Lady Luck.

"Sit down, girl!"

To Christopher's satisfaction she jumped at his barked command, but then glared at him.

"Sit. Down."

She released her death grip on the doorknob and eased gingerly into the nearest chair.

"Believe me, Miss Montoya, you are not my ideal choice to present as an heiress, but unfortunately, you're the only Montoya heir we could find."

"There's plenty of Montoyas in this country."

"True, but *you* are the only Montoya who is the offspring of Alberto Montoya and Carmen Estada. Your mother was a saloon dancer as well, wasn't she?"

That got her attention. She frowned, puckering the fine line of her brows.

"Magdalena Teresa Maria Montoya." The grand name seemed much too large for such a small morsel of a girl. "Maggie. Isn't that what you're called?"

Her eyes flashed; the little pointed chin lifted a notch. "My name is Magdalena, not Maggie."

Enjoying her obvious vexation, Christopher smiled condescendingly. "Maggie fits you better."

She glanced toward the door, where Peter had moved to guard the exit. Then her little vixen's face turned back to Christopher. Her dark eyes seemed to weigh his worth and his motives. "So you know my name and who my parents were. That doesn't prove anything."

"Doesn't it?" he inquired, one brow cocked upward.

"No, it doesn't." She arched one finely drawn brow in mocking mimickry of his.

Christopher's mouth twitched. He fought to hold in a chuckle. "And how much do *you* know about your family, Maggie?" He emphasized the name just to see her eyes flash. They were, after all, very attractive eyes.

"I know enough."

Christopher smiled. She stared at him suspiciously. "Peter," he said, "I think Miss Montoya wants to hear the whole story. Since you did most of the research, why don't you tell her about her illustrious family?"

Peter picked up a sheaf of papers from the dressing table and shuffled quickly through them. "Yes, well, let's see. Birth records, family tree, witness accounts, governor's proclamation—ah! I knew the summary was here somewhere." He pulled over a chair and sat down opposite the wary girl. "We've documentation, miss, as you can see. You are welcome to look through it if you like."

She glanced at the papers and flushed. "I don't read much. Not words this big."

Peter smiled sympathetically. "Well, then, I shall just summarize. The land is a tract granted to your grandfather, Don Ramón Bautista de Montoya, a direct descendant of the second Spanish governor of New Mexico —Don Pedro de Peralta. Your grandfather was confidant and friend of the last Mexican governor of New Mexico, Manuel Armijo. The Montoya family had several grants of land from the Spanish crown, and Armijo granted Ramón even more land that brought their holdings on the Llano Estacado grasslands to five hundred thousand acres."

"Where's the Llano Esta . . . stad . . ."

"Llano Estacado," Christopher supplied. "The Staked Plains. Some of the best grazing land in this country."

"The Montoyas never really developed the land," Peter continued. "They were mostly military men, more interested in dashing about fighting Indians. It was the same with your grandfather. He died in Santa Fe shortly after New Mexico became a possession of the United States. His widow moved back to Mexico City with her children, one of whom was your father, Alberto."

The girl's face was blank. Christopher suspected that much of the family history was news to her.

"In 1859," Peter said, "Alberto returned to the United States to look at the family grant along with other land he was interested in. Passing through the newly settled village of Denver, he was smitten with a saloon dancer named Carmen Estada. They married."

If Carmen Estada looked anything like her daughter, Christopher thought suddenly, Alberto's having been smitten was understandable. That wild gypsy hair and little cat's face could probably grow on a man who was susceptible to such things. Fortunately, he was not.

"They married." Peter cleared his throat. "We assume that his family cut Alberto off for such an unconventional alliance, for the couple lived in poverty. You were born in 1862, and a year later Alberto died under questionable circumstances—"

"A saloon brawl," the girl said bitterly. "My mother said he got stabbed in a saloon brawl."

Peter flushed. "Quite. Yes. We could find nothing more on your mother other than she died on a ranch near here."

"Tony Alvarez's ranch. She was his mistress for four years while I worked my butt off on his place doing everything from punching cows to scrubbing floors." Maggie swung her level gaze toward Christopher as if challenging him to comment. He didn't. She had a pride that marked her as aristocracy in spite of her scruffiness. He didn't know whether that pleased him or worried him.

"When she died," Scarborough continued, "you were fourteen. You left the ranch."

"Damned right I left! Old Alvarez had me in mind for Ma's replacement."

"There was no trace of what had happened to you. We assumed you had returned to Denver, therefore we came here to search for you. Fortunately, your name is quite well known among the men who frequent the . . . uh . . . establishments on Larimer and Market Streets."

Christopher carefully assessed the girl's reaction. She had added to the seamier parts of the tale without hesitation or shame, almost with a challenge in her voice. Her chin was still high; her gaze was level and direct—no proper feminine meekness there. And her foot tapped impatiently on the rug. Maggie Montoya, he decided, was going to be damned difficult to tame and even more difficult to control. He found himself almost looking forward to a project that he'd dreaded for months.

"So my family's got this land. What's your interest in it . . . and me?"

"The point is, your family doesn't have the land at present." Christopher leaned against a post of the four-poster bed and folded his arms across his chest. "A good part of the grant—a hundred thousand acres—was worked as a cattle ranch by my brother Stephen. Last year a gambler by the name of Theodore Harley cultivated Stephen's friendship and then fleeced him of his holdings in a card game. It is my intention to see Mr. Harley ousted from his ill-gotten land."

"You found me so I could boot out the fellow who's on my land—is that the lay of the cards?" she asked boldly. "All this trouble because this poor hombre swindled your brother in a card game? Lordy, if everybody took after cardsharps that way, half the men from here to San Francisco couldn't earn a living."

Christopher broke his silence. "Two months after my brother Stephen lost his land to Theodore Harley, he took a pistol to his own head."

"Oh." She didn't give him the conventional words of sympathy. Her expression was guarded, but he could imagine what the tough little alleycat was thinking—anyone who couldn't take getting burned should stay away from the fire. Most times he would agree with her. But when it came to one's own brother, a man thought differently.

"How am I going to get all this land?" she urged warily.

"Under terms of the United States' treaties with Mexico, Spanish and Mexican land grants are recognized by the United States government. Working on behalf of my family Mr. Scarborough has put together more than enough documentation to establish your title to the Montoya grant."

She looked dubious. "If Harley has to give the land to me, how's that going to help you? The land would be mine."

Christopher proceeded carefully, feeling as though he were treading careful steps around a wild animal he didn't want to startle into a run. "Needless to say, I won't be satisfied merely with seeing Harley lose the land."

"If you would, you're stupider than you look."

Christopher cocked a brow. "I think you'll find that I'm not a stupid man, Miss Montoya. I'm also a man who takes care of those who serve him well."

Her mouth slanted into a skeptical smile. "And just how, exactly, do you want me to serve you?"

"I want you to learn to be a lady whom I can believably present as the heir of a noble Spanish family. Then I want you to take title to the land and toss Harley off on his backside."

"And . . . ?"

She wasn't dumb, Christopher observed with grudging respect. Scruffy, crude, uneducated, proud, but not dumb.

"And we can discuss the details later," he pronounced with finality.

"Or we could discuss them now."

"Let's see first how your claim progresses—Maggie."

Her eyes flashed quite appealingly when she was provoked, he noted.

"I will leave tomorrow to submit this documentation to the surveyor general's office in Santa Fe. You will stay with Mr. Scarborough and learn in a few months what most ladies learn in a good number of years. That should keep you busy, I would think."

She hesitated. For the first time he saw a shadow of fear in her eyes. "I get to stay here?"

"Mr. Scarborough will rent a house." Curiosity piqued, he wondered why she didn't want to go back to the saloon. He played a hunch, gambling to get her cooperation. "From now on," he said temptingly, "you can be a genteel lady. No one need know you were ever a saloon dancer. Once you are Magdalena Montoya, heiress, the Maggie Montoya who frequented the back alleys of Denver can be gone forever." If there was something back at the Lady Luck that she feared, he wasn't above using it to his advantage.

Her eyes narrowed thoughtfully, giving her face the look of a kitten conniving mischief. "I'd need a chaperone."

He tried not to show his surprise. "I suppose that could be arranged."

"Luisa Gutierrez." She said the name with the tone of a bargainer who was stating a bottom-line demand.

"And just who is this Luisa Gutierrez?"

"A friend."

"My dear," Peter chided, rejoining the conversation, "I hardly think that another saloon dancer would be an appropriate chaperone, though I fully agree that a reputable older female companion is very much in order."

"Luisa's not a dancer. Or a whore, if that's what you're thinking. She's a widow, and very old and proper."

Christopher noted the cunning slant of her lips. The chit was a gambler who knew when she held the winning hand. And Christopher was a man who knew when not to quibble over details. "Very well. Tell me where I can find this paragon."

"You've already met her—the owner of the Lady Luck. Tell her I need to see her. She'll come."

Saloon dancers rarely thought so highly of propriety. There was something more in the little cat's request than wanting a chaperone. When Christopher found out what it was, he fully intended to use it to his advantage.

"I'll send the lady over if she's willing," he agreed. "We wouldn't want you to fear for your virtue, now, would we?"

Christopher took his coat and hat from the rack beside the door. "Peter, my friend, Miss Montoya will be all yours until I return from Santa Fe. Do try to transform her into something that won't make my life hell. Won't you?"

He pulled the door shut behind him, blocking the dagger thrusts of her eyes. This little stray cat was going to present the entertainment of a challenge, he decided with satisfaction.

The fire in the library fireplace was hardly necessary, as the day was warm for March. Still, Peter insisted upon a fire. The English were peculiar in a number of ways,

Maggie had decided weeks ago. A particular fondness for fires and fireplaces was one of those peculiarities. England, she decided, must be a very cold place. It must be a very ostentatious place as well.

Ostentation. Ostentatious. Maggie had only learned the word the day before. She liked the sound of it, and it must certainly describe the place that Peter had told her was crowded with mansions and great, elaborate estates. She thought their rented house on Fourteenth Street was very grand, but Peter called it a "cottage." He staffed it with an army of servants and commented about the shortage of "proper domestics." Lordy, what did he want? They employed a cook, a gardener, a coachman for the elegant private coach that sat in the carriage house, a stableboy, a woman to help in the kitchen, a woman to clean the downstairs, another to scrub the upstairs, and another whose only task was to see that everyone else worked hard. In addition, Peter had tried to hire a maid whose only job was to help her and Luisa dress and arrange their hair, but Maggie and Luisa had both put a quick stop to that idea.

"Magdalena, you are not paying attention."

"What?" Maggie blinked and tore her gaze away from the window.

Peter sighed in gentle reproval. "Your reading has improved dramatically, but your discipline and attention still leave much to be desired. Now, shall we continue the recitation?"

Maggie grimaced. She loved reading, even though she still had to guess at some of the words. It had introduced her to a world she hadn't known existed. But *Oliver Twist* seemed a hopeless struggle, and deadly dull compared to the more exciting volumes in the library of the rented house. She had devoured *Tom Sawyer* and *Ben Hur*, amazed that Lew Wallace, the author of the latter, had been governor of New Mexico. Just recently she had finished *Little Women* and several stories by Bret Harte, her favorite being the "Luck of Roaring Camp." Those tales were much more entertaining than the dry English works Peter insisted she read.

"You may start with the beginning of Chapter Five."

Peter listened to Maggie's bored recitation, correcting her pronunciation now and then and occasionally helping her with a word she didn't know. He was amazed at how bright the girl was, and how difficult. She had driven away the tutors he had hired to teach her. One had left after she used the vocabulary he had taught her to concoct a particularly insulting description of his intellect. Granted, the fellow had been a bit slow. The second tutor she had injured most distressingly after he had made improper advances. Peter certainly didn't excuse the fellow's dishonorable behavior, but neither could he condone a lady taking such matters into her own hands—and quite violently at that—instead of properly calling for a gentleman's intervention.

After that incident Maggie would tolerate no other tutor. Peter found himself filling the roles of guardian, nursemaid, tutor, and occasionally, jailer. Neither his training as a barrister nor his sometime hobby of seeking adventure had prepared him for such tasks. He was grateful indeed that the girl had brought Mrs. Gutierrez with her, for the "chaperone" was at times the only person with enough influence to control the little imp.

His eyes strayed to where Luisa sat reading on the window seat. A smile gentled his mouth as he remembered how Maggie had described her lady companion. Very old and proper. Luisa was much more proper than one would expect of a female who owned a saloon, but Peter wouldn't describe her as old. Not at all.

Maggie finished a paragraph and stopped. "Can't we do something else?"

"If you wish." Peter's attention swung back to his pupil. "Your reading is excellent, Magdalena. I'm proud of how much your vocabulary and pronunciation have improved. Perhaps we should take this time to continue our discussion on values and standards of behavior."

Maggie rolled her eyes. "Why is it that all these damned rules of behavior apply to women and not to men?"

"Please discontinue your use of that word, Magdalena. It is most unsuitable."

"Which word?" Her eyes twinkled.

"You know very well which word," Peter said, trying to sound stern. The minx had a way of making him want to smile, but for her own good he shouldn't encourage her hoydenish ways by showing his amusement. "As to your question, both men and women have certain rules of behavior they must adhere to, but since women are by far more vulnerable and delicate, and since they are responsible for bearing and guiding the next generation, they in particular must ensure that their deportment is exemplary."

"Women aren't any more delicate than men," Maggie argued. "The truth is, I think we're a good deal better at taking care of ourselves."

"It's natural for you to be so deluded. You've endured a hard life and had to reach beyond the usual feminine capabilities. But in gentle society you'll find that women are protected by men. They don't bother themselves with such things as money, property, or politics so that they may concentrate on the gentler pursuits of raising their children and creating a pleasant haven and home for their husbands."

Luisa looked up from her reading. The hint of a smile softened the curve of her usually stern mouth.

"Women are the moral uplifters of society," Peter continued self-consciously. "They make this world a gentler, purer, more innocent place by cultivating their own virtue, purity, and innocence. In society a woman is meek. She does not push herself forward or intrude into matters where she is not competent. She abides by the advice of her father, husband, brother, or other male guardian. And by guarding her own behavior she maintains the high standards of our civilization for her own generation and the generation to come."

"Really?" Maggie's brows rose with amused disbelief. Peter sensed laughter bubbling beneath her mock seriousness, surfacing as a dance of light in her eyes. Only tightly sealed lips prevented the disrespectful mirth from escaping. How was he ever to teach the girl to be a lady when she had absolutely no reverence for propriety?

"Yes, really, Magdalena. That is the way the world works, except possibly in the lower strata of society where ill fortune unhappily threw you. Perhaps, since you do not seem to be in a mood for serious discourse, we should move on to a dancing lesson."

Maggie brightened. "Would you like to learn to dance?"

Peter felt his patience grow thin. "No. *You* are the one who must learn to dance."

"I know how to dance. My mother taught me almost as soon as I could stand."

"I do not refer to the sort of dance one does in a saloon. You must learn the socially acceptable dances that ladies and gentlemen perform at social gatherings."

"The Spanish dance is very socially acceptable. My mother said it has been danced for many years in a place called Andalusia in Spain."

Peter could point out a number of things developed in Spain that were not socially acceptable, but knew it was useless to argue.

"Let me demonstrate." He motioned her toward the sunroom, which had a polished oak floor. After sliding the furniture to the margins of the room, he gingerly took her right hand and placed his right hand lightly at her waist. "Now, count as you move—one, two, three, back, side, together." Humming an off-tune waltz, he guided her awkwardly around the floor.

Maggie labored with difficulty to catch the rhythm. It was painfully different from the one to which her body longed to move. The dance was awkward and bland, with no flair, no drama, no sensuality—perfect for these prissy Englishmen with their prim ideas of virtue and propriety.

Her foot landed directly on top of Peter's. His tolerance was stoic.

"Sorry," she murmured.

"Quite all right. Don't forget to count. One, two, three—ouch!"

"Sorry again."

Luisa's voice interrupted the dance. "Magdalena, are you trying to injure poor Mr. Scarborough? It's difficult to believe that someone with your grace in the flamenco could be truly that awkward."

"This isn't a dance; it's a funeral march!"

"The waltz is a beautiful dance, dear. Perhaps Mr. Scarborough would consent to demonstrate." She came onto their impromptu dance floor and offered her hand to the Englishman.

"You are too kind, madam."

Peter's face flushed scarlet, Maggie noted with interest. She dropped down into one of the rearranged chairs and watched.

This time Luisa's voice was the one that provided ac-

companiment. True and rich, it rose in a melody that
made Peter smile.

"Ah. Strauss."

"What else would one waltz to?"

They sailed off together in a motion that seemed totally
unlike the dance Maggie had just stumbled over. Possessed by the rhythm, they moved as though one creature,
Peter's hand firmly planted at Luisa's waist, his other
hand clasping hers, their bodies so close that her breasts
brushed the front of his shirt. Luisa's voice soared in a
warm contralto that pulsed with vibrance, and the Englishman's eyes crinkled in an entranced smile.

Maggie grinned as she watched. This was a socially
acceptable dance? She must have gotten the wrong impression about society's ideas of virtue and propriety.

Suddenly they stopped, stuttering to an awkward finish
as if only then aware of stepping past the bounds of their
heretofore distant relationship. Luisa's face colored in
girlish embarrassment, and Peter cleared his throat and
looked away.

"Yes," he harrumphed. "That is how the waltz should
be . . . uh . . . danced. Thank you, Mrs. Gutierrez, for
the demonstration."

"You're quite welcome, Mr. Scarborough. It was my
pleasure. When I was a girl in Mexico City, I loved to
waltz. Magdalena, you really should try harder to learn it.
It's a lovely dance."

Maggie had a quick vision of waltzing with Christopher
Talbot, his hand pressing her close to him, their bodies
brushing lightly as they moved together in fluid grace.
Her head scarcely reached his shoulder. He looked down
at her as they floated around the floor. In his eyes she
read his surprised appreciation of what a fine lady she had
become.

She frowned and shoved the vision out of her mind,

attributing it to the green apple she'd eaten an hour before. But she walked onto the floor more willing than she'd been earlier. "All right, Peter. Teach me how to waltz."

The days passed, each one much the same as the last. Maggie struggled through *Oliver Twist* and *Pamela* and flew through the adventurous romances and books of poetry in the library. She endured Peter's lectures on etiquette and virtue, dabbled in learning how to draw and paint, a useless exercise the Englishman seemed to think necessary to her brief education, and bore with Luisa's teaching her the finer points of needlework. Her friend and former employer had talents Maggie had never suspected, but Maggie's curious questions only got her admonishments to concentrate upon her lesson. Sometimes, Maggie reflected, Luisa was as bad as Peter.

As history, literature, music, art, and etiquette were stuffed willy-nilly into her brain, Maggie felt at times as though she would burst. Up until a few weeks ago she had been certain of her place in the world. That place hadn't been a grand one, to be sure, but it was her place. She had known herself, known her talents, and felt in command of the problems that beset her. She had gotten out of fearsome scrapes with cockiness as her only weapon— and the possible intervention of her guardian angel. Impetuosity and insolence had served her well. She had not only survived, she had been happy in her survival.

Now a brief taste of knowledge was robbing her of that cockiness. Her place in the world was not so certain, nor was the world such a familiar place; it had unimaginable places and strange people with even stranger ideas. Old notions of what was right and wrong, what was important and what was nonsense, were eroding. Confusion robbed her of self-confidence, and Maggie didn't like it. She wished Christopher Talbot would return so they could go through whatever process was needed to get her land and his revenge. Then she could go back to being herself. Maybe. If she could ever find herself again.

Maggie didn't know just when the foreigners' scheme had settled into her mind as something more than an opportunity for her and Luisa to lie low in the wake of Arnold Stone's death. Sometime over the past few months as she labored over her lessons and listened to Peter's reports of the English lord's progress in Santa Fe, the family they had told her of, the land in New Mexico, and the gambler-turned-rancher who now occupied it had become real. Christopher Talbot and his drive to avenge his brother were becoming more than just an excuse to get out of Denver.

Christopher Talbot. She had seen the man only once, and then for just a few stormy hours, but he occupied a much greater part of her mind than he deserved. His Most Arrogant Lordship was an impressive man, she supposed, if one were impressed by dark good looks and an aura of careless power. Not that he was so good looking. His nose was a bit crooked, she remembered. His lips were too thin and his brow a bit too high—probably to accommodate those devilishly arching brows that gave him such a supercilious air.

On the whole, Maggie remembered, Christopher Barrows Talbot was rude, condescending, arrogant, and generally unpleasant. During their interview at the Windsor he had regarded her one moment as though she were a piece of dung in the streets, and the next as he might a horse he was about to purchase. She didn't like him at all, and she was glad he had stayed away for three months.

Still, sometimes her mind slipped and she found herself thinking of the stranger who had barged into her life, changed it, and then rushed out again. She danced the waltz much better if she pretended that Christopher were holding her instead of Peter. She listened with rapt attention when Peter read her Christopher's letters. They always ended by instructing Peter to give regards to Maggie. She could almost see the sardonic twist of aristocratic lips as he penned that wretched name, the nickname she had always hated, and she tried to be angry. But if she was honest with herself, she had to admit that she was rather glad that he took the trouble to tease her.

Thus the days passed, with Maggie having too much on her mind, the uncertainty of change eating at her until the restlessness could be contained no longer. "Let's go for a walk," she suggested to Luisa one unusually pleasant March evening.

Luisa put down her book and glanced out the window. The sun rode a handspan above the mountains and the usually blustery March wind was calm.

"Where would you like to walk?"

Maggie shrugged noncommittally.

"I suppose it would do us both good to get some fresh air. And you'll go with or without me, won't you?"

Maggie grinned.

"Well, perhaps I can keep you out of trouble."

The evening was pleasantly brisk, the sky a brilliant vault of crystalline blue. The trees along Fourteenth Street swelled with green buds of new life, and for the first time in months the frozen ruts in the street showed signs of softening to mud. As they strolled along the walkway in front of spacious gardens and stately brick homes, Maggie was suddenly homesick for the narrow alleys and grimy buildings of Market Street.

"Let's walk down to the Lady Luck and make sure John Travis isn't cheating you," Maggie suggested.

"Travis isn't cheating me. He probably does a better job running the Lady than I do."

"Don't you miss the saloon?" Maggie asked a bit wistfully.

"No, I don't. Not at all. The Lady Luck is my livelihood, the only worthwhile thing my husband left me out of twenty years of marriage. But I can't say I enjoy dealing with drunks, gamblers, and lechers every night—men like Jack Morley and . . ."

Luisa's voice trailed off, but Maggie knew the name left dangling. Arnold Stone. The day after that terrible night every paper in Denver, the *News*, the *Times*, the *Tribune*, had printed stories of the "wanton murder." Luisa had read Maggie the account in the *Rocky Mountain News*, a particularly lurid description that quoted the housekeeper as laying the heinous crime at the feet of two women. Unfortunately for the police, the suspects had been cloaked and hooded. The housekeeper was able to give only a very vague description.

Neither Luisa nor Maggie had spoken Arnold Stone's name since that night, but Maggie knew what kept them both holed up on Fourteenth Street. Someday that housekeeper might remember how the wind had whipped strands of Maggie's distinctive almost-kinky black hair across her face when she greeted them at the door. Someday the pair of drunks that they had encountered two blocks from Stone's house might remember two women fleeing as if the very devil pursued them. Maggie's hood had blown off in the wind, exposing her face to clear view in the streetlamp.

When someday came, both of them would be better off in New Mexico. Maggie couldn't go back to her old life even if she had wished to, and neither could Luisa.

They crossed Broadway and continued west toward lower downtown. The brick mansions of Capitol Hill gave way to shops and businesses. The nearer they got to Market Street the more Maggie longed for one more look at the rowdy, disreputable thoroughfare where she'd spent a good part of her youth.

"Magdalena, we really should be getting back. Mrs. Colby will have supper laid out, and Mr. Scarborough will wonder where we are."

"The devil take him. It'll do Peter Scarborough good to realize that we don't always move to his beck and call. Oh, look! There's old man Sandoval's bakery. Wouldn't a roll taste good?"

"We haven't a single coin, Magdalena."

Maggie laughed. "When did that ever stop me? Besides, Sandoval gave me a load of trouble last summer in the saloon. Remember that? He owes me more than a roll."

"Magdalena!"

Maggie scarcely heard the warning in Luisa's voice. The imp in her soul was unleashed and running. It had been suppressed too long.

"Come on." Maggie looked in the bakery window. "Sandoval's in the back room."

"Magdalena! Don't you dare!"

Maggie tiptoed into the shop and inhaled the warm aroma of baked goods. Display counters stood along two walls, and thereon sat trays of cookies, rolls, and loaves of bread. For a moment Maggie couldn't make up her mind which she wanted. Sandoval thumped around in the back room.

"Be right with you!" he called out.

"Magdalena, come out of there this instant!" Luisa whispered urgently.

A roll, Maggie decided. What she really wanted was a nice, soft, fat, golden-crusted roll. She reached out and picked one up just as the pudgy little baker came out of the back room. For a single second of delicious terror

Maggie's eyes grew wide. Then she bolted, grinning with larcenous joy.

"Hey, there!" Sandoval shouted. "Come back!"

Roll in hand, Maggie sprinted down the street. Sandoval pursued, white apron flapping. He puffed like a steam engine climbing a hill. Maggie paused in her flight and waved back at him, bouncing with an energy she hadn't felt in months. "You owe me this one, Sandoval!"

"Maggie Montoya, you tramp!" Sandoval labored to a halt and shook his fist. "If I see you in my store again I'll —I'll . . ."

Maggie didn't stay to hear the rest of his threat, for the baker had regained his wind and was coming toward her. With a bounce of joy she was off again. Before Sandoval had worked up a full head of steam she'd turned down Larimer Street, where the respectable businesses in the Tabor Block were closing and gambling dens across the street were just beginning to hit their pace. Immediately she ducked into an alleyway between two of the noisier gambling halls. Sandoval had given up the chase, she suspected. But it never hurt to be safe.

Leaning back against a brick wall, Maggie happily took a bite of her purloined treat. Nothing tasted quite so good as food spiced with danger. When she had first lived on the streets of Denver, fourteen years old, recently orphaned, and too proud to turn to whoring for money, she had lived mostly off pilfered food. After the confusion of the last few months, it was a comfort to know she hadn't lost the touch. Even the thought of facing a furious Luisa and probably even more furious Peter Scarborough didn't diminish the pleasure.

Maggie was about to take another bite of roll when a scuffle and angry voices made her crowd back into the shadows. Two men tumbled into the alley.

"I'll teach you to stack the deck with me, you bastard!"

The meaty sound of a fist plowing into soft flesh was punctuated by a groan.

Silent and still as a mouse, Maggie huddled tightly against the wall. But the shadows weren't deep enough. As the battling pair swung around, one straightened. He let his limp victim slip to the dirt.

"Well. What have we here?"

In the gathering dusk Maggie couldn't make out his face. It was his voice that she recognized. Jack Morley.

Three

Christopher stepped out of the hired carriage and double-checked the address on the house in front of him.

"This is it, Yer Honor."

"So it is." Christopher paid the hack driver, unlatched the iron latticework gate, and strolled up the walkway to the porch. These Americans could certainly never be accused of having good taste in architecture, but at least they weren't dull. Elaborately turned posts supported the roof of the porch. Farther up, gingerbread woodwork decorated the eaves, the window shutters, and the hexagonal turret on one corner of the house that started at garden level and rose above the adjacent roof.

A graying, pudgy woman answered Christopher's knock. "Yes sir?"

"I'm—"

"Christopher! You're back!" came Peter's shout from the entrance hall. "Marvelous! I'd just begun to wonder if the bandits or Indians or some such barbarian menace had done you in."

Christopher handed his hat and coat to the housekeeper. "I thought about writing you that I was on my way, but this country being what it is, I judged that I would arrive here faster than a letter. So here I am."

"Come into the parlor. The place isn't much, but it's acceptable. The best I could do, unfortunately. How was your trip?"

Christopher looked around. The room was cluttered with heavy walnut furniture, Oriental rugs and hangings, oil paintings of dubious quality, an ornately framed mirror, and a heavy crystal chandelier. "I assume it came furnished."

Peter grimaced. "Obviously. Sit down and tell me what you've found out. Would you like a drink? Supper is in about thirty minutes."

"I can wait, thank you." He selected the least uncomfortable-looking chair and sat. "The news is good. This country is ripe for investment. All that is needed are the funds. I looked at properties in Oregon and northern California as well as New Mexico. Someone with the capital could make a fortune out here, not only in ranching but logging, farming, import/export. There are opportunities by the hundreds. If my brother had not been such a featherbrain . . ." He trailed off, pain that was a year old but still sharp stealing his words.

Christopher saw a reflection of his own emotions on

Peter's face. The barrister had been a friend and associate of the Talbot family for years, and he had actually been much closer to Stephen than Christopher was. Christopher had spent most of his adult years in the army, first in Africa, then in India. Having known his younger brother so slightly made the loss all the worse.

"Speaking of Stephen," he continued grimly, "I placed the Montoya claim with the Office of the Surveyor General in Santa Fe. The case seems to be fairly cut and dried, but the disposition will undoubtedly take a while. Some cases, I'm told, have been filed for years without settlement, but the official with whom I had the most conversation indicated that the documentation in our claim is much more complete than most others. As usual, Peter, you did a commendably thorough job. If you regularly applied your talents to your profession you would no doubt become rich in a very short time."

Peter shook his head and smiled. "The law is a fine enough endeavor, I suppose, but being a barrister's deadly dull."

Christopher flicked a brow upward. "Has your labor here been more interesting?"

"At times."

"How is our little heiress?" Christopher was almost afraid to open the subject. Maggie Montoya, scruffy little hoyden that she was, would make any man question God's wisdom in creating the opposite gender, he reflected. Worse still, even his brief encounter with her made him suspect there was an appealing bit of seductiveness beneath her coarse exterior, and that appeal could be more dangerous than her rough edges. It was almost a shame that they were obliged to transform the little scruff ball into a lady, for doubtless she would become as boring as most other ladies of his acquaintance.

"Miss Montoya is doing well," Peter said. "I think

you'll be pleasantly surprised, my boy. She's very bright. Very bright indeed. Picked up reading and writing so quickly, I had difficulty believing it myself. She's less quick at her numbers, but still is progressing quite nicely. As to the social graces . . ."

Peter hesitated, and Christopher steeled himself. Creating social graces in that girl would require a miraculous hammer stroke indeed.

"She is really quite a warmhearted and decent girl," Peter continued, obviously choosing his words with care. "Given time, I'm sure she'll come to understand the subtleties of proper behavior. Unfortunately, in spite of possessing some very fine qualities, she has a stubborn streak that is remarkable in a female. At times she forgets herself in a fit of irreverence and mischief."

Christopher sighed. "I feared you were going to say something like that."

"One must consider that she had a most irregular upbringing, and up until several months ago she was living in very low circumstances."

"So much for the theory that breeding will tell. Two generations ago the Montoya family was one of the bluest Spanish bloods in Mexico. Ah, well, I suppose Miss Montoya and I can put up with each other for a few months, at least."

Peter gave him a considering look. "Christopher, my boy, are you positive that you've thought this situation through? This seems a great sacrifice you're making, and have you considered the consequences to Miss Montoya? She might balk if she knew what is truly required of her."

Christopher massaged his brow with one hand. "I appreciate your concern, Peter. Truly I do. But there's not only family honor to consider—strange, isn't it, how honor is so often a synonym for revenge? The family finances require that drastic steps be taken; the agricultural slump hit us rather badly, you know."

"And Miss Montoya?"

There was the rub, Christopher admitted to himself. His conscience did prick at him on her account. He tried to bolster his own doubts at the same time he reassured Peter. "Miss Montoya is an alleycat who's landed face first in a tub of cream. She'll never have to go back to dancing or whatever other unsavory occupations she pursued to make a living. I don't think you need to trouble yourself about her." He glanced toward the stairway. "Speaking of little Maggie, where is the chit?"

"Most probably in her room or chattering somewhere with Mrs. Gutierrez." Peter's expression warmed. "Mrs. Gutierrez, by the way, has proved of inestimable value. I do hope you'll see that she's rewarded."

"I take care of the people who serve me. You should know that, Peter."

Peter smiled. "Just thought I'd mention it."

He pulled the cord for the housekeeper, who appeared with enough alacrity to have been on the other side of the door. No doubt her ear was pressed against it, Christopher mused. American domestics were an ill-mannered lot.

"Mrs. Colby, would you fetch Miss Montoya, please? Tell her that Lord Christopher has returned and wishes to speak with her."

"The miss ain't here, sir. Her and Miz Gutierrez went out walkin' some time ago."

Peter looked startled. "How long ago, Mrs. Colby?"

The woman shrugged. "An hour. Mebbe longer. Mrs. Gutierrez said they'd be back for supper. Speakin' of supper, its almost on the table, Yer Grace."

Peter sighed as the housekeeper closed the door behind her. "I do wish the ladies had told me they were going out. I'm sure they're quite all right, though. Crude as this town is, a virtuous woman is treated with courtesy by even the rougher elements."

"That may be true for virtuous women." Christopher strode into the entrance hall and grabbed his coat and hat. He had a bad feeling about this situation. "What you forget, my friend, is that the woman we speak of is scarcely one whom I would call virtuous."

"Hullo, Jack." Maggie tried to avoid looking at the body slumped in the dirt of the alley.

"Maggie. Little dancin' Maggie. I thought you'd skipped town without payin' yer debt. Where ya been, girl?"

Maggie looked him in the eye. "I've been where I want to be, and that's none of your business. You'll get your money when I get it."

"I'm not sure I like your attitude, little Maggie."

The normal evening traffic rattled past the mouth of the alley a tempting fifty feet away. If she were just fast enough . . .

"Did ya hear me, Maggie? I don't like your uppity attitude."

He came toward her, blocking even that slight chance of escape. Maggie caught a whiff of liquor fumes. His gait wasn't a stagger, but it was shaky enough to tell her he'd been drinking. Not good. Jack was mean when he'd been drinking—meaner even than he usually was.

Maggie pressed more tightly against the wall. "You hurt me, Jack, and you'll never get your damned money."

"I ain't gonna hurt you, Maggie girl. The thought just sprung into my head that with you havin' such trouble payin' what you owe, maybe I'd just better take it out in trade. I'm a reasonable man, after all. We can do a deal.

You just deliver the goods I paid you for and we'll call it even."

"I never agreed to sleep with you, you big lout."

"When a girl keeps me company at the gamblin' tables, that's just understood."

"Not by me it isn't. You know well and good that I don't sell myself for bed-sport. And if I did, I'd charge a hell of a lot more than ten measly dollars. Especially if it was you doing the buying."

"Don't make me mad, Maggie girl." He nodded to the limp body in the dirt. "He made me mad, and look what it got him."

"Back off, you bastard, or I'll scream my bloody head off."

"And who's gonna hear that cares?"

She screamed. Morley jumped, looking surprised that she would actually do it. He slapped her, hard. Then his hand clamped over her mouth before she could dodge away. Liquor fumes assaulted her. His free hand found her breast and squeezed. She bit down viciously on the dirty palm that covered her mouth.

"Shit!" He lurched back. "You little bitch! Goddamn if I don't make you sorry for that! I'm gonna make you bleed, girl. After I'm through with you, my knife is gonna carve your face so that no man is ever gonna look at you again."

Morley agilely avoided the knee she sent toward his groin. Pinning her shoulders to the wall, he attacked her mouth with his own. Maggie gagged and almost choked as the taste of sour liquor and cigar smoke invaded her mouth with his tongue. Futilely she pushed against him and kicked. When that didn't work, she clawed at his face. Spots swam before her eyes, and the world began to spin. . . .

* * *

"Where is the little minx?" Christopher fretted aloud. The evening shadows had merged into night, and the electric lights along Larimer Street illuminated the muddy street, locked shops, and gambling parlors that were just hitting their stride. But the light revealed no small female with wildly curling hair, nor an irate baker with retribution in his eyes. "When we find her, I vow—"

A woman's scream pierced the air, then ended as if cut off cleanly by a sharp knife.

"This way!" Christopher ran toward the source. Dodging around a trolley and jumping out of the path of a carriage, he headed for the entrance to a dark alley. Cautiously, he stopped just inside. Panting, Peter halted beside him.

Here, the modern electric lights didn't alleviate the darkness. For a moment Christopher saw only solid black within. Then, dark shadows resolved into something that heaved and struggled obscenely. Somehow Christopher knew it was Maggie. The little alleycat had finally gotten herself trapped by a cur dog. Sudden rage brought his blood to a boil.

"Stay here!" he ordered Peter.

"Gladly."

Christopher charged into the alley, anger fueling his strength. He grabbed the topmost of the struggling pair and plucked him off his victim. Before he could lay the blackguard out with a blow, the man twisted free and bellowed like a bull. Out of the corner of his eye Christopher saw Maggie slide down the wall until her bottom hit the dirt. She spat and scrubbed frantically at her mouth.

"Whaddya think yer doin'?" the man roared. "Nobody gets away with layin' hands on Jack Morley!"

"If you've hurt her, you blackguard, I'm going to do a great deal more than lay hands on you."

Morley cursed and pulled a knife. Christopher was too

fast for him. His hand shot out like a striking snake and grabbed Morley's wrist. For a moment they struggled. Morley opened his mouth in a silent scream of pain as Christopher squeezed. Wristbones gave, then cracked. The knife dropped to the dirt. Christopher picked Morley up by his jacket lapels and shook him so hard that his head whipped back and forth with an audible crack.

"Okay, okay," Morley gasped. "You win. Enough."

Contemptuously, Christopher set Morley on his feet.

"Stupid ass!" Morley made a lightning jab for the gut.

Christopher bent double, but the pain was quickly absorbed into the red haze of his rage. He recovered in time to deliver a right hook to Morley's jaw.

Morley bounced back against the wall inches from Maggie, who scrambled to her feet and joined the fun. She kicked Morley in the shins.

"You slime-eating toad!" Her fist landed with a solid and satisfying thud in his stomach. "Snake! Skunk! Woman-beating dog!"

A strong hand caught her arm as she swung back for another blow. "Enough, Maggie!"

She stomped on Morley's toe. The attack had little effect on his booted foot, but made her feel better all the same.

"I said enough!"

Maggie growled as Christopher pulled her away from her victim. She whirled angrily to face him, and froze, her face inches from his.

"You!" Her mouth fell open in astonishment.

Christopher placed a finger beneath her jaw and snapped her mouth shut. "Yes. Me." He nodded toward Morley. "That's a baker?"

"What? How . . . ?"

"We met Mrs. Gutierrez on her way back to the house.

She told us you had pilfered some baked goods and were being pursued by the baker."

"Sandoval? Oh, no. I lost him. That's Jack Morley."

"And the other fellow on the ground?"

"Just someone Jack was beating up."

"Pleasant friends you have, Maggie."

Morley slumped against the wall, his eyes threatening to cross. He made a halfhearted attempt to lurch toward the street, but Christopher reached out and slammed him back against the wall. "Stay where you are, if you please."

Just then Peter Scarborough stepped out of the shadows. "Good show, my boy. Always knew those years in the army were good for something, despite what Lady Torrington believes."

"Why didn't you help him?" Maggie demanded.

"My dear, two-to-one odds is hardly sporting. I never doubted that Lord Christopher could deal with this villain." He gave Morley a contemptuous glance. "How disappointing. I believed that even the ill-mannered louts of this town respected the sanctity of virtuous womanhood!"

Maggie explained. "He thinks I owe him ten dollars, the bas—"

A sharp look from Christopher made her curb her tongue.

"Do you owe him money?" Christopher asked coldly.

"Not really. He just thinks—"

"The fuckin' tart got paid for goods she didn't—oof!" Christopher's elbow drove into Morley's ribs and put an end to the comment.

"Mind your mouth, Mr. Morley, or I'll be obliged to give you another lesson in manners. Now"—he turned back to Maggie, who stared at him with wide eyes. Her assessment of the man when she'd first seen him in the Lady Luck had been correct. He might look like a greenhorn, but he wasn't a fellow to rile—"how much do you owe this man?"

"Nothing!" For some reason Maggie desperately didn't want Lord Christopher Talbot to believe she was a whore. "He paid me to keep him company at his table, not in his filthy bed!"

Christopher sighed. "Ten dollars? Is that it?" He took a money clip from his vest, peeled off a few bills, and stuck them into Morley's pocket. "That should settle the matter."

Maggie wiped her hand across her mouth. "You shouldn't pay him. He's a snake."

Christopher ignored her objection. "Now, Mr. Morley, you have your money. If you attempt to bother Miss Montoya again, I'll make sure that it's the last time. Do we understand each other?"

Maggie wondered that calm, quiet words could carry such menace.

Morley stared at the Englishman for a moment, then grunted. "She ain't worth the trouble."

"Just keep that in mind." Christopher turned his chilly gaze on Maggie. "As for you, I believe that once we get back to more appropriate surroundings, we have some matters to discuss."

"I can see that the time and labor Mr. Scarborough has devoted to your education has been mostly in vain." Christopher paced back and forth before the parlor fireplace, his expression as cold as the marble of the mantelpiece.

Maggie sat in a wingback chair that dwarfed her. Her feet dangled an inch off the Oriental rug. Hands folded in her lap, her gaze fixed straight ahead, she looked like a child called up before a school headmaster. Her eyes, however, blazed with defiance. How the little culprit could look so totally unrepentent Christopher didn't know.

"It wasn't my fault."

"Walking out where you had no business to be wasn't your fault? Stealing from a shopkeeper wasn't your fault?"

"Oh, bosh! That was just a bit of fun. Old Man Sandoval wasn't serious about chasing me."

"And why wouldn't he be after you'd stolen from him?"

"He knows he deserves it. He can't hold his whiskey, and more than once he's given me trouble when I dance."

"You are no longer a saloon dancer. Ladies do not pilfer from shopkeepers like street urchins. As for Mr. Morley—"

"*That* wasn't my fault! You can ask Luisa. He hired me to keep him company while he gambled. Then the bastard tried to . . ."

Christopher raised one brow in chilly disapproval. Maggie rolled her eyes.

"Well, he is! The rotten dirty dog tried to . . . well, he tried to . . ."

"I can imagine," Christopher assured her in a cold voice.

Maggie frowned rebelliously. A quick, pleading glance toward her chaperone sitting on the settee garnered no support, for Luisa sent her back a look of stern censure.

"Talbot, don't be so hard on the girl." Peter Scarborough leaned on the mantelpiece, looking more amused than displeased. "You can't expect a wildcat to turn into a kitten overnight, or even in a few months. This is partly my fault. I kept her in the house, expecting her to be satisfied with ladylike pastimes when she's accustomed to—"

"We know what Miss Montoya is accustomed to."

"She's accustomed to a more active life," Peter said

gently. "Give her a chance and I think you'll be pleased by what you see."

Being pleased by what he saw was not the problem, Christopher acknowledged to himself. Once they had gotten back to the house and he had seen Maggie in the lights of the parlor, he'd been surprised to note that with proper care, the coarseness of her complexion had smoothed into fine ivory. The hair that cascaded down her back in tight curls shone with a healthy luster. The defiant eyes were large and luminous, and if her face, with its wide mouth, firm jaw, and unfashionably uptilted nose, didn't meet the standards for beauty, it certainly was striking for its strength and its clean, aristocratic lines. Maggie Montoya might still behave like a saloon dancer, but she no longer looked like one.

Her behavior was quite another story, however. To do justice to her ancient family and justice to the claim he'd submitted in her name, Magdalena Montoya must at least present the appearance of a lady. No matter how blue her blood or how convincing the documentation that he and Peter had assembled, no one of influence in Santa Fe was going to believe Maggie was the last of a distinguished family if she behaved like a tramp fresh from the gutter.

"Peter, why do you allow the chit to dress like a guttersnipe? Are there no decent clothing shops in this town?" The Mexican-style bodice the girl wore—flimsy cotton with a loosely gathered scoop neck and an embroidered ruffle that fell over her breasts and shoulders—was too enticing for Christopher's comfort. Her plain gathered skirt scarcely reached past her ankles. A decorative corset, laced in front, over the chemiselike bodice and under the girl's breasts, pushed them into high, round globes that, while adequately concealed, were an invitation to any man's eye.

"She's been provided with more suitable clothing, but

she prefers that . . . uh . . . more casual costume. Short of dressing her myself, I didn't see any way to change her mind."

"Peter, my friend, you're much too chivalrous." He stabbed a finger in Maggie's direction. "Tomorrow, little alleycat, you will appear in proper ladylike attire, or I myself will discard your old attire and dress you in the new."

"You wouldn't!" Maggie's tone was confident, but Christopher was gratified to see the beginnings of doubt shadow her eyes.

"You may easily find out by appearing tomorrow morning in a costume similar to what you have on."

Their gazes locked in battle for a moment, and Christopher felt almost as though he were sinking into the dark, luminous eyes that gave her small face such life. Then her thick lashes dropped like a veil.

Peter sighed. "It's late, and I think we're all a bit cross. We may thank kind fate that Mrs. Gutierrez found us so quickly to tell us that Magdalena needed help. You have our gratitude, Luisa . . . uh, pardon me . . . Mrs. Gutierrez. Now perhaps we should all retire and continue this discussion in the morning."

Christopher watched as Maggie and her "chaperone" walked from the room. Mrs. Gutierrez, the taller of the two, leaned down to speak quietly in her charge's ear. Apparently not pleased, Maggie drew herself up, her spine stiff. Reeking of injured dignity, she left the older woman in her wake and ascended the stairs with royal composure.

Arching one dark brow in wonder, Christopher shook his head. "What does one do with a woman who acts like a tart one moment and a queen the next?"

* * *

After spending an hour debating the wisdom of calling Christopher's bluff, Maggie appeared in the breakfast room the next morning clad in a most proper dress of green silk trimmed with black ribbons. The tightly fitted bodice plunged to a deep V at her waist, emphasizing her slenderness. The skirt was flat and smooth in front, drawn back by ribbons over a small, shelflike bustle in the back. The modest train dragged at her like a lead weight.

Maggie felt pressed, pinched, and confined. Her own clothes (she didn't quite think of the dresses Peter and Luisa had chosen for her as *hers*) were much more comfortable, but something about the image of Christopher Talbot peeling off her old clothes and dressing her in the new ones was particularly unnerving.

As Maggie sat down at the dining table, Christopher eyed her costume with amused approval. Luisa smiled her sympathy. She had spent the last hour listening to Maggie's complaints, then bore with squeaks, grunts, and curses as she laced the corset that allowed Maggie to fit so nicely into her new finery.

"You look very nice, Magdalena," Luisa complimented her.

"Very fetching!" Peter added his approbation to Luisa's. "Don't you agree, Christopher?"

Christopher smiled. Maggie felt warm as his eyes roved over her in an unnervingly possessive manner. "A definite improvement," he said. "Now if we could just put her on a leash and put a gag on her mouth, we might be able to pass her off as a lady."

Maggie's knife grated across her plate as she stabbed too deeply into her slice of ham. "I see that ladies are the only ones in society required to watch their manners." She sliced him with a sharp glare. "It's plain that gentlemen don't."

Peter intervened. "Magdalena, please. We've had discussions before about your overly forthright manner of speaking. And, Christopher, don't look so cross, my boy. I've come up with the perfect setting to display Miss Montoya's new social skills."

"Indeed."

Maggie didn't like the sardonic twist to Christopher's reply. She had no wish to put on an exhibition for His Wretched Lordship. All the time he'd been gone, she had looked forward to his surprise at what a lady she'd become. And now, because of one tiny, innocent escapade, he was treating her like something he'd picked out of the gutter.

Peter continued. "Senator Tabor has returned from Washington, D.C., with his bride, Elizabeth McCourt Doe."

"Um, yes." Christopher sounded only mildly interested. "I've heard. Quite a scandal, I understand."

"These Americans do have a flair for scandal, don't they?"

"No more than the English, I suspect. We're simply less open about it than they are."

"Yes, well, Tabor is giving a banquet to celebrate his return, and I've obtained invitations. Once the senator learned that the son of a duke was in Denver, he was most insistent that you attend."

Maggie surfaced from her sulk. "Baby Doe? Horace Tabor finally wed Baby Doe? Oh, how romantic!"

"Most of Denver society certainly doesn't think so." Christopher took a sip of his coffee. "I suppose they'll all be there, though."

"Indeed they will," Peter agreed. "What better experience could there be for our young lady than to test her skills on what passes for society in this town? After all, she'll never have to come up to snuff for anything more demanding, I'd think. It's not as if she'll ever be doing the Season in London."

"Oh, I'd love to go!" Maggie could scarcely restrain herself from jumping up and down in her chair. "To meet Baby Doe and Horace Tabor—and all the rest. I'd be on my best behavior, I promise!" The prospect of such an exciting adventure wiped clean the last shred of her anger. She'd heard stories of Baby Doe from whores in the cribs on Market Street, from customers in the Lady Luck, from shopkeepers on Larimer Street. Almost all of Denver called Elizabeth McCourt Doe a whore, but Maggie found the story more romantic than wicked—how the most beautiful woman in Colorado, deserted by her husband, had attracted the love of the wealthy Silver King, himself trapped in a loveless marriage with a stern wife who despised his rich style of living. Maggie couldn't label Baby Doe a whore because she'd fallen in love, nor could she blame Baby Doe for allowing her lover to keep her in style in his Windsor Hotel. And now they had married—a triumph of love over the seamy realities of life. Maggie was entranced.

Christopher peered at her from beneath raised brows. "If we go, Maggie, you'll do exactly as I tell you the whole time we're there. Without question."

"Of course I will!"

The suspicious Englishman looked as though he didn't trust her.

"I will! I really will!"

"Don't get your hopes up, Maggie. I hate to see such high expectations disappointed." Luisa yanked the last little bit of give out of the whalebone corset as Maggie obediently exhaled. The younger woman inhaled in short, cautious breaths; her face pale.

"This is stupid."

"No, dear. This is fashion."

"I suppose it's worth it." Maggie grinned. "If I'd thought His Mighty Lordship was going to take me to a grand do like this, I would've paid more mind to my lessons. I thought we were just going down to some ranch in New Mexico."

"Try not to be too impressed. These society people are just like you and me. In fact, some of them I wouldn't let cross the threshold of the Lady Luck. As I said before, dear, don't set your expectations so high. This isn't a fairy tale you're stepping into."

Luisa lifted the evening gown over Maggie's head. It slipped over the tight corset and multilayered petticoats in a shimmer of rich blue silk. The low-scooped neckline was trimmed with fur. Half sleeves draped over her upper arms in graceful folds of silk. The bustle, larger than for daytime wear, made Maggie feel rather like a deformed duck, but if it was fashionable, she supposed it must be beautiful.

"I wish you would come with us. Mr. Scarborough said he'd escort you."

"I've no wish to mingle with the snobs, dear. I had enough of that when I was a young woman in Mexico City. I'd rather deal with the drunks at the Lady Luck. At least they admit who they are and where they came from."

Maggie's eyes twinkled. Her smile turned impish. "You're becoming a cynical old woman, Luisa."

"Not cynical. Sensible."

"Well, *I'm* not sensible at all! I've always wanted to see what the rich ladies and gents did for fun. Now I'm going to be hobnobbing with the best of them."

"If you behave yourself and do what Lord Christopher tells you, you may be rich yourself someday."

"And then I can do whatever I want." Maggie grinned and spread her arms. "Do I look presentable?"

"You'll catch the eye of every man there."

"Really?"

"And the ire of every wife."

Luisa was right. Maggie did catch the eye of almost every man in the Windsor Hotel's lavish banquet hall, and wives regarded her with polite faces but eyes sharp as daggers. Maggie was not the primary target for the women's dagger-eyed glances, however. Baby Doe Tabor, looking exquisite with her red-gold hair fashioned into a mass of tight curls and wearing a gown that was the height of fashion, would have been bruised and bloody if those looks had had physical force behind them. Denver's elite society wives had not forgiven her illicit affair with the Silver King. The fact that she was now Mrs. H.A.W. Tabor, even the fact that President Arthur himself had attended the wedding in Washington, D.C., could not buy Baby Doe's way into Denver society. The covertly admiring glances that the men directed toward the new Mrs. Tabor only crystallized the ladies' animosity.

Dinner was the most sumptuous affair Maggie had ever seen or tasted. Surely no one person could do justice to the various courses that were served, though she did try. Years of living on meager fare made her loath to waste such bounty when it was offered. Sitting next to her, Christopher regarded her attack upon each and every dish with amazement. Maggie got the idea that perhaps such an eager appetite was one of the many things in the world that were not ladylike. She was beginning to think that nothing involving fun or pleasure was ladylike.

Gossiping definitely was ladylike, however—at least if she could judge from conversations going on around her. The ladies at the table ignored their husbands, who discussed with great fervor the chances of Senator Tabor running for U.S. President. The subject of feminine conversation was, of course, Baby Doe, how "the tart" had followed Tabor from Leadville to Denver when Tabor became lieutenant governor to Governor Pitkin, how she had beguiled Tabor into traveling to Durango to obtain an illegal divorce from his wife, Augusta, how they were married in a civil ceremony in St. Louis, and how a humiliated and tearful Augusta, faced with a bigamist husband and forced finally to seek a legal divorce, had wept in the courtroom and declared to all within hearing that she never would willingly have sought a divorce.

"And to think that after all that, those two sinners were married in a church!" one lady said as she picked at her food. "I wonder that they dare to show their faces, much less expect to be received by decent society." Eating the sinners' food and sitting at their table did not seem much to bother the ladies, however.

Maggie looked to the head of the table, where Baby Doe Tabor sat with her husband. The beauty with the red-gold curls didn't look like a tart, Maggie decided. The looks the bride gave her husband were full of love, though her expression hinted at a deep-seated sadness. What did Baby Doe Tabor have to be sad about? Maggie wondered. With all she had—riches and a devoted husband—what did she care about the wagging tongues of these sour old biddies?

When the dancing began, Maggie found herself the object of scrutinizing glances from those same sour old biddies. They fawned over Christopher as though his English accent and a title in front of his name made him something more than a mortal man, but his golden aura did not extend to Maggie.

"I haven't seen you before, my dear." One matron raised a lorgnette to observe Maggie in greater detail.

"Miss Montoya's family is from New Mexico," Christopher explained calmly. "She has been living with family friends in Denver, but they haven't been out much in society. Fortunately for me, we met through the good offices of my brother when he purchased a large tract of land near Santa Rosa."

The matron's attention shifted to Christopher, and she smiled. "How lovely to have you with us, Your Lordship. How do you find our city? Accustomed to London as you are, I imagine you must think us quite dull."

"Not at all, madam. This whole country is quite fascinating. I hope to learn much more of it."

The woman simpered.

"The ladies in particular are enchanting."

"Oh, my, Your Lordship! Surely you flatter us!"

Maggie choked back her laughter as Christopher moved her out onto the floor for a dance. "What a load of horsefeathers! Why do you say things like that?"

"There is a certain formula in social conversation, Maggie. Particularly with women. Honesty and the truth have nothing to do with what one says. As long as one realizes that everyone else is prevaricating as well, no harm is done."

"Seems awfully complicated to me."

"Your dancing is very nice, by the way."

"Another social prevari . . . prevar . . ."

"Prevarication."

"Right. Another one of those?"

"No, actually, my compliment on your dancing was sincere."

Maggie's face grew warm. "Mr. Scarborough's feet still haven't recovered from the first lesson he gave me. I'm used to dancing alone, not with someone else."

"You're doing very well."

"Dancing with someone else isn't really so hard," Maggie admitted.

Not hard, but very distracting—more distracting than Maggie had imagined in her fantasies of whirling around the floor in Christopher's arms. She was too conscious of his hand firmly holding her waist and the other hand grasping hers. Even through her gloves she could feel the heat of his flesh. His closeness made her lose concentration and fumble with her feet more than once. Worse still, she couldn't find a comfortable place for her eyes. Straight ahead they measured the masculine breadth of his chest. Turned upward they traced the firm line of his jaw or looked into the shadowed depths of his eyes. His face filled her vision. It was an abrupt face with harsh planes and sudden angles—not really handsome to Maggie's way of thinking. But having it so close above hers disconcerted Maggie so that she could scarcely remember the steps to the dance.

The music ended. Christopher smiled, a genuine smile without the usual sardonic twist. Unbidden, a warm glow softened Maggie's heart.

"You really do look very lovely tonight."

She could see from the masculine appreciation in his eyes that his words weren't a "social prevarication." More than once during the evening she had seen a flash of male hunger cross his face when he looked at her. Tonight he didn't think her a scruffy alleycat, Maggie realized. The knowledge gave her a feeling of power.

Almost nightly in her former life she'd seen sexual hunger in men's eyes, and she had felt disgust, or sometimes tolerant amusement, at their cravings. But Christopher Talbot was a horse of a different color. His desires were so well disguised, she could only guess at them. Perversely, his self-control made her want to break through his reserve and have him frankly slobbering after her. Tonight, at least, his guard had weakened enough to reveal he had the same desires as other men.

"Would you like to sit the next one out?" he inquired. "I can get us something to drink."

"Yes, please."

"I'll only be gone a moment."

Maggie made her way toward the row of chairs along the wall. Her fancy slippers pinched her feet and the silk stockings were hot. How nice it would be to take off her shoes and walk barefoot on the cool parquet floor, but Maggie supposed that such behavior would indeed be unladylike. His Prim Lordship would not forgive her if she broke her promise to behave at this affair.

She was still determined to behave when a draft of cool, fresh air momentarily relieved the stuffy warmth of the ballroom. Maggie looked around. Someone had come into the room, but not from the lobby entrance. Only now did she notice the glassed double doors along one wall. She could see a hint of foliage beyond.

Curious, Maggie crossed the room to look out into a walled garden where a tiny expanse of lawn spread between small flowering trees. She opened one of the glassed doors. The fragrance of cherry blossoms floated in with the fresh, cool air. New spring grass poked soft blades above winter's brown thatch.

Maggie glanced around the room, looking for Christopher. He had apparently been diverted from his mission to fetch drinks and was deep in conversation with Horace Tabor himself. She looked longingly back at the garden. Her shoes pinched; her feet ached; a single drop of perspiration trickled down the back of her neck from beneath the heavy mass of her hair. The cool, fragrant air from the garden curled around her like the teasing arms of a siren. Surely there could be no harm in a moment's relaxation away from the stuffiness of warm air crowded with too many bodies. No harm at all.

Four

Maggie slipped through the glass-paned door and closed it behind her. She didn't hesitate to rid herself of shoes and stockings. The night was warm for early April, and the tender new grass fairly called to her aching feet. Shoes in one hand, stockings in another, she gratefully padded onto the lawn, sighing as the cool blades of grass hugged her toes and tickled her ankles. Suddenly she was very tired, more tired than she would have been after dancing four shows at the Lady Luck. Pretending to be someone you were not certainly took a toll.

She gratefully sat down upon the grass, wriggling her toes among the cool blades. Only a single light illuminated the little garden; Maggie was certain that no one in the ballroom could see her where she sat in the shadows. She would stay just a moment, then she would put on the hot silk stockings and the pinching shoes and be a lady again. For a moment she felt sorry for His Most Proper Lordship. He had probably never had the pleasure of digging bare toes into new grass; with all his schemes he wouldn't have the time to sit back and sniff the perfume of cherry blossoms in the air.

Still, despite his starched propriety, cutting tongue, and somewhat twisted humor, Christopher Talbot wasn't bad, as men went. He'd been remarkably polite the whole evening, and more than once the slant of his smile combined with a certain warmth in his eyes to make her feel all goosey inside. When the man chose to be charming, he was very charming indeed. Maggie was hard-pressed not to like him.

And why shouldn't she like him? Maggie asked herself. At times the Englishman was a jackass, true. But he and Peter had given her a future, shown her an exciting new life. He'd even been honest about his motives.

Maggie had always considered men adversaries. They were crude, violent, deceitful creatures who had only one purpose for a woman like her. Sometimes a man was good for a laugh. One or two had been friends—up to a point. She didn't trust any of them very far, though.

Of course, she didn't trust Christopher Talbot either. But damned if he wasn't appealing in some ways. She'd been impressed when he tore Jack Morley off of her. Maggie had never been rescued before. What's more, dancing with him tonight she'd felt almost giddy as she whirled around the dance floor in his arms. Small though she was, Maggie rarely felt small. But she had felt tiny next to Christopher—pleasantly tiny, dainty, feminine, and very oddly inclined to lay her head against his broad chest and relax in perfect trust. It was a new sensation, and Maggie decided to savor it for a while before admitting what a ridiculous and dangerous feeling it was.

"Well, look'ee here! Miss Montoya, isn't it?"

Startled, Maggie looked around as a young man stepped from behind one of the cherry trees. His coat was rumpled, his dress trousers only half buttoned. Even halfway across the garden Maggie could smell the liquor fumes and sour sickness that he breathed. Her mouth pulled into a half smile. She had apparently intruded upon one of Denver's society gentlemen being sick in the bushes.

She pulled her bare feet in under the cover of her skirt.

"Oh, don't mind me. You got pretty feet," he slurred.

"Had a few too many?" she asked amiably, then instantly regretted it. Ladies didn't ask such questions. Ladies were deeply offended if a gentlemen was sloshed in their presence.

"Jus—just a few." Uninvited, he dropped down beside her on the grass. "Feels good to sit down. You have the right idea. Maybe I'll take off my shoes too." He hiccuped. "Hot as Hades in there. Makes my head go all . . ."

Even in the half-light she saw him start to turn green. She fanned his face with her open hand. "Breathe deep."

He sucked in a gulp of air.

"That's right. Better?"

"Yeah. You're okay, you know? Most ladies'd either faint or have a hysterical fit when a gent belches, much less tries to puke in their lap."

"Well, I haven't been a lady very long," Maggie answered truthfully.

"Ya don't say." The drunk grinned. "Well, ya done well for yourself, snaring that English fellow who has all the females in Denver drooling." He stared at her until his eyes threatened to cross. "Course, looking at you close like this, I can see the poor fellow didn't have a chance."

"What?"

"You know." He hiccuped again. "Your grand fiancé with the lord in front of his name."

"My fi-an-cé?" Maggie didn't know the word.

"Yeah. Everybody knows. Was it supposed to be some kind of secret? If it was, then His Lordship shouldn'a told Millicent Pottsdam. She's the old gal in the pink. Can't miss her—the lady who's sixty trying to look sixteen. That woman's first love is spilling other people's secrets."

Had Christopher told this woman about the New Mexico scheme?

"What does *fiancé*—?"

"Maggie!"

A man-shaped shadow fell across the grass. Maggie looked up to see Christopher blocking the light from the garden's one lamp. He looked like a thundercloud about to spit lightning.

"Speak o' the devil," the drunk said, then belched.

Christopher almost exploded as Maggie gave him a tentative smile. The jade didn't even have the grace to look chagrined. His eyes traveled from her shoes and stockings carelessly tossed in the grass beside her to the bare toes peeking from beneath her skirt to the rumpled, half unbuttoned state of the man beside her.

"Get out of here while you still can," he told the drunk in a level, dangerous voice.

The drunk wasn't so far gone that he couldn't recognize imminent peril. He struggled to his feet and stumbled toward the door to the ballroom.

Maggie looked peeved. "You don't need to be such a bully. He was a nice fellow."

"I'll bet. Earning a little cash on the side tonight?"

Her eyes grew wide. Her face paled. She looked as though he'd slapped her. "What did you say?"

"You heard what I said." Her betrayal—yes, that was how he thought of it, betrayal—hurt all the more because tonight she'd shown that she could act the part of a lady. Her conversation at the table had been reserved and refined, her dancing delightful. The gown Luisa had selected for her was in the height of good taste. In it she looked like an angel. A black-haired, cat-eyed, barefoot angel who'd lain down with the first lecher who crossed her palm with enough money.

He reached down to pull her to her feet. She slapped his hand away. He grabbed her upper arms and hauled her up. She twisted, but he was too strong for her. "We had a bargain, Maggie Montoya! I was going to help you become rich, and you were going to learn to play the role of a lady."

"Let me go!"

He pushed her back into the shadows, not wanting an audience of banquetgoers looking out the doors.

"I *am* learning to be a lady!" she declared.

"Ladies do not steal, they do not consort in dark alleys with villains who would kill them for lack of a sum of ten dollars, they do not leave a ballroom to walk barefoot in a dark garden, and they do not lie in the grass with drunken gentlemen whose trousers are conveniently unfastened.

"I wasn't—"

"Is your price still ten dollars?" Christopher felt his temper slipping from control.

"You jackass!" she hissed up at him. "You're jealous." She seemed to brighten as the idea took hold. "That's why you're so mad. You're jealous!"

Maybe he was jealous. She'd been soft and warm in his arms tonight when they danced. Her eyes had been bright, her smile animated as a child's at Christmastime.

She'd taken in everything around her with untrammeled delight, but her warmest smiles had seemed to be for him. Desire had knotted within him until he'd known that to dance so closely with her once more would be a disaster.

But apparently little Maggie didn't care whose fires she stoked. "I asked if your price was still ten dollars." His voice was hoarse.

"My price?" Her voice simmered with indignation. "My price is more than *you* can afford, you damned bas—"

His mouth covered hers and cut short the curse. Ruthlessly he forced her lips apart. Her startled acquiescence encouraged him. He deepened the kiss, pressing her back against the cherry tree in whose shadow they were hiding. When he came up for air she stood perfectly still for a moment, then pushed frantically at his chest.

"Be still!" he commanded softly. Again he lowered his lips to hers, more gently this time. She obeyed, immobile as an ice carving under his seeking mouth. Slowly the ice thawed. Her lips moved. Her tongue tentatively, sweetly, met his. She was warm honey and cherry blossoms, soft velvet and cool, wet silk. Christopher ached with his arousal and a strange tenderness that the chit didn't deserve. Maggie Montoya was indeed an alley cat, sleek and aristocratic one moment, padding through the gutter the next. One part of him wanted to hold and protect her, and another part wanted to lift up her skirts, unbutton his trousers, and finish what the drunken lout had started.

The thought of Maggie on the grass with the foul-smelling drunk chilled Christopher's desire to the point where he could thrust her away, but still he kept a tight hold on her arms. "You can put that on my account," he taunted her.

She looked stunned, her usually sharp, bright eyes unfocused.

"And from now on, little Maggie cat, when you have the itch to ply your old trade, you can limit yourself to one customer—me. I can see now that you'll never learn to be a lady, but at least we can keep the rest of the world from knowing what you really are." She didn't answer. For once he'd stunned her into silence.

"Now, put on your shoes and stockings so we can go say our good-byes. I think we've seen enough of your social skills for one night."

Maggie thundered down the stairway and stormed into the parlor. Luisa trailed in the storm's wake, wringing her hands with uncharacteristic helplessness. She scarcely brushed through the double doors as Maggie slammed them behind her.

"Do you know what *fiancé* means?" Maggie demanded.

Both Christopher and Peter looked up from reading in the morning sun that streamed through the windows. Peter flushed. Christopher's face settled into a carefully blank mask.

"Luisa just told me. *Fiancé* means *marriage!*" Maggie all but shouted. After being hustled home in disgrace and spending the night and most of the morning fuming in her room, she'd finally asked Luisa what the strange word meant. "Marriage! You never, *never*, said anything about marriage being part of this bargain!"

Christopher looked unperturbed. "If I remember correctly, I told you we would talk about the details of our bargain later. At the time you seemed satisfied with that approach."

"And just when were you going to tell me about this? You snake! You skunk! You miserable, deceitful, a low-down, stinking cur!"

"Since apparently someone at the Tabor banquet mentioned the subject to you, I suppose I'm going to tell you about it now."

To think that she had begun to almost trust the man! She'd even begun to like him, to see something other than coldness in those shadowed eyes, a hint of sensitivity and humor in his smile. But all along he'd thought her a whore, a strumpet not worthy to kiss his polished boots. He'd called her a whore to her face, and then kissed her as though she were a whore, with no by-your-leave or sweet words or wooing. Just a brutal, searing kiss that had sent a flash flood of unfamiliar sensations racing through her body, turning her spine to jelly and her mind to mush. She had wanted to fight, but while her pride had rebelled, her body had succumbed. The man had proven her weakness and confirmed his own power. How superior he must feel!

"Yes! Do tell me about it now," Maggie advised sarcastically. "And be sure to include any other little details that you've kept secret."

Marry her, indeed! Maggie didn't flatter herself that it was Magdalena Montoya that the wretched Englishman wanted. Five hundred thousand acres in New Mexico was what he craved. Maggie was nothing—worse than nothing, she was a scruffy saloon dancer. Her feelings were nothing, her wants and needs were nothing. She was a title to a parcel of land, nothing more.

"Suppose we discuss this in private," Christopher suggested.

Peter started to leave, relief plain on his face, but Maggie pulled Luisa up beside her and clung to the older woman's arm. "No. I want everybody to hear exactly what you have to say."

"Magdalena," Luisa cautioned quietly, "don't go flying into a temper. I'm sure Lord Christopher didn't mean to deceive you."

"Actually, I did." Christopher stood and walked to the window, where he stood for several moments looking out at the bright morning. When he turned and met her eyes, Maggie noted indignantly that he didn't look the least bit guilty. Nor could she detect any of the anger or passion that had burned in his gaze the night before. "When we first found you, Maggie, I had no notion if our scheme was truly plausible. The officials in Santa Fe might have dismissed the claim, or you might have turned out to be entirely unsuitable. Besides, if I had told you that first night that I intended to marry you to keep my brother Stephen's land in the Talbot family, you would have thought me quite mad."

"I still think you're mad," Maggie said darkly. "Mad as a hydrophobie skunk."

Christopher smiled tolerantly. "I'm not mad at all. In my country marriages made for the purpose of obtaining land are quite common, and I suspect they are more common in your country than you think."

"What do you need with Magdalena's land?" Luisa asked. "Surely an English lord, the son of a duke, doesn't need a paltry piece of ranchland in New Mexico."

"On the contrary, Mrs. Gutierrez, due to economic reasons, my family needs new sources of income. That was one of the reasons my younger brother Stephen came to your country in the first place. Maggie's land is some of the richest ranchland in New Mexico, and the market for cattle is good and growing even better. Income from that land can be used to invest wisely in other pieces of property. An astute man could build himself an empire, starting with one large cattle ranch in New Mexico."

"*My* ranch," Maggie reminded him sharply.

"The ranch you would never have known about if not for me. The ranch you'll never get without my help."

"So it isn't only revenge you're after."

"Vindicating my family's honor is certainly a big part of what I'm after."

"Well if *you're* any example, Your Mangy Lying Lordship, your family doesn't have any honor. It was nice not having to scrape for a living for a while, but even I've got some pride. No matter what you think, I've never sold myself on the street, or in a crib or a parlor house, and I'm not selling myself for a piece of land!"

Peter chimed in anxiously. "Magdalena, you shouldn't regard this as 'selling yourself.' No wonder you're upset if you think of this situation in such crude terms. The marriage is merely a formality. You'll be secure for the rest of your life. You'll have an honorable name, a good home—"

"And I suppose you have a cut in this?"

"Lord Christopher has paid me for my services."

"With what? Are you getting a wife out of the deal too?"

Peter flushed, and Maggie had an instant's regret at the hurt on his face. Peter Scarborough had never treated her any way but kindly. "I'm sorry, Peter. I didn't mean that."

"Maggie, calm down." Christopher used the tone he might have used with a recalcitrant child. "Obtaining a wife is certainly not my purpose in this project. Circumstances have dictated the necessity of marriage, not my own desires. We need to put up with each other for only a few months. After that I will return to England and you will remain in New Mexico to do whatever pleases you. You needn't feel that I've concocted the whole situation merely to bring you to the altar."

"Of course you didn't," Maggie sneered. "You're sacrificing yourself for your damned family honor and thinking yourself very noble to marry a—a . . ." She couldn't bring herself to call herself whore, not after all the years avoiding that very trap. "Well, you can just pack up your family honor and take it back to England. I'd rather go back to living in the streets of Denver than live with you."

"That's just where your stubborn foolishness is going to take you!" Christopher told her.

"I suppose stubborn foolishness is on your list of unladylike behavior along with everything else." She turned and marched stiffly toward the door. Luisa glanced at Peter, shook her head slightly, and followed.

"Unfortunately," Christopher concluded as the doors shut behind them, "stubborn foolishness seems to be a universal feminine trait."

Peter dropped heavily into a chair. "Well, my friend, you handled that with your usual tact. There goes almost a year's work, exploded in a fit of feminine fury."

"The girl's simply being difficult."

"Of course you couldn't trouble yourself to woo her a bit."

"Woo her? Then she would be correct in labeling me deceitful. This is not a romance, Peter; it's merely a business arrangement."

"Only whores jump into a man's bed for a business arrangement. Most women want at least the pretense of affection, if not love."

Christopher was silent. Peter regarded him suspiciously. "Just what happened last night at the Tabor banquet? I heard you pacing your room in the small hours of the morning. You sounded like an army stomping back and forth. I expected cannon to explode from the window at any moment."

"Nothing happened," Christopher said tersely. "Your pupil simply confirmed what an accomplished actress she is, and then proved what I have suspected all along."

"Which is?"

"That a tiger—or an alleycat—seldom changes its stripes."

"I see."

"I doubt that you see, Peter. You're much too good hearted. But I don't think you need to be concerned about Maggie's sensibilities. After spitting and hissing for a bit to salve her pride, our little cat will sheathe her claws and come purring back. She's smart enough to realize that this marriage is as much to her advantage as it is to mine."

"Most women want love as well as advantage."

Christopher chuckled. "You are more idealistic than I thought."

"And I suppose you aren't interested in any part of Maggie other than the land."

Christopher felt his face grow warm.

"I've seen you look at her, my boy."

"She's a damned attractive woman! How do you expect a healthy man to look at her?"

"Why don't you tell her she's an attractive woman?"

"That's not what this marriage is about. Why should I lead her to expect romance when that's not what I'm prepared to deliver? That would be unfair to her. Do you think I could take her to London with me? Can you envision what a disaster that would be for both of us?"

Peter shrugged. A half smile crinkled his eyes and twitched at his mouth. "It's a curious thing, my boy. I've known you since you were in the nursery, and yet I've never seen you get the least bit ruffled over a woman. I wonder what our little Maggie has that all the rest have not?"

Christopher gave him a bleak look but held his silence. He wasn't up to admitting that all through a sleepless night, he had wondered the same exact thing.

Meanwhile, in an upstairs bedroom, Luisa lectured a tearful Maggie along the same lines. "Calm down, Magdalena. I've never known you to be such a fool. Instead of crying you should be talking yourself around to some reason."

"Reason? Bosh! The man's impossible!"

"Men are quite frequently impossible. You should be used to that by now."

"Can you believe I'd almost begun to trust him? I thought that of all the men I knew, Christopher Talbot was the most . . . the most . . ."

"The most what?" Luisa asked with a twisted smile.

"He's the—the worst lying polecat I've ever seen. The low-down, ornery cur!"

"Of course you've been such a prize yourself—and completely honest with him."

I was! Well . . . I was up to a point. I didn't tell him about Stone."

Luisa's scrutiny was unmerciful.

"Okay. Okay. I've sometimes been a brat with Mr. Scarborough, and that night in town I slipped a cog or two and caused a lot of trouble." She grimaced. "And I suppose last night I really shouldn't have been sitting barefoot on the grass with a fellow who was drunk and halfway to being undressed."

"Do tell."

"But that didn't give His Wretched Lordship the right to say the nasty things he said! And it certainly didn't give him the liberty to kiss me like he did."

Luisa lifted a brow. "This is getting more interesting by the minute."

"It isn't interesting! It stinks! He lectures *me* on manners and morals, and then he has the raw nerve to grab me and kiss me where anyone walking out the door could see, without so much as a 'May I?' He thinks I'm a whore. Can you imagine that? He acts as though I'm worthless!"

"I think you're worth more to Lord Christopher than you know."

"I'm worth a few acres of land and revenge on this Harley fellow. And he gets a convenient bed-warmer into the bargain. What a deal!"

"I fail to see why you're upset, Magdalena. Does Lord Christopher repel you?"

Maggie tried to freeze her face into indifference. It wouldn't do to admit that at times she found the worm attractive, or that with one contemptuous kiss he'd reduced her to jelly. Magdalena Montoya was too smart to get sucked in by a set of broad shoulders and a striking masculine face. She didn't need a man, and she didn't let men take advantage of her.

"Or perhaps you do like him . . . a little too much?"

"Of course I don't like him!"

"Maybe you wouldn't be so upset if he'd told you what a lovely, gracious lady you'd turned out to be and declared that he had to have you for his one and only love."

"That's stupid!"

"Indeed?"

"He's a damned foreigner!" And she loved the way he spoke. "A know-nothing greenhorn!" Who'd bested one of Denver's toughest bullies with ease. "He's sneaky. And he thinks I'm a whore."

"He'll find out you're not soon enough."

Maggie puzzled out Luisa's comment, then flushed. "I don't care what His High-and-Mighty Lordship thinks. I'd rather stay just like I am. Free . . ."

"Poor," Luisa reminded her.

"Unmarried."

"Unprotected," the older woman countered. "Magdalena, you're not thinking with your head. Without Christopher Talbot you have no future."

"I'm going to dance in San Francisco or New York. That's a future."

"That's a child's dream. With no money and no name you'll be dancing from seven until midnight at the Lady Luck until the men are so tired of the show that I'll have to get some other entertainment to please them. And then what will you do? Will you give in and become a whore? Or maybe you'll get lucky and marry some miner who'll keep you in a shack in the mountains to wash his dirty clothes and bear a dozen children who'll have no chance to grow up any better than their father and mother."

Maggie lowered her eyes. Luisa had just eloquently vocalized the worst of Maggie's nightmares—the black thoughts that were so frightening that she seldom dared to acknowledge them.

"Magdalena, there are good reasons why you can't go back to what you were before."

"Yes, I know." Luisa hadn't mentioned Arnold Stone, but they both knew that the dead man lay like a bleak windfall across the paths of both their lives, forcing a change of course that perhaps neither would have chosen if that horrible night in November had never happened. Maggie had seen nothing in the newspaper other than the one account of his murder. Perhaps the police investigation had gone nowhere. Then again, maybe they were still pursuing the crime. In New Mexico she and Luisa would be safe. No one would connect the propertied young bride of an English lord with a saloon dancer who'd visited Arnold Stone to collect a debt. No one would dream that her female traveling companion had been a saloon keeper on Market Street—a woman who had clubbed a man dead to save a friend's life. Even John Travis at the Lady Luck didn't know exactly where Luisa had gone.

"I suppose that I don't have much choice," Maggie admitted quietly. Her heart gave a lurch as she realized that she'd been backed into a corner. She had to go along with the scheme and give her life and her body over to a cold-blooded Englishman who thought of her only as the price he had to pay to recover his brother's land. By all appearances Christopher Talbot had all the warmth of the South Platte in January. He bounded his life by rules that took the fun out of living and expected her to do the same. He expected her to act the lady in public while he ridiculed her morals in private. Living with him was going to be about as entertaining as walking through a cactus patch barefoot.

If only his smile didn't give her goose bumps and his voice make her heart race. Life would be less confusing if she could really, truly hate him.

"Don't look so tragic, Magdalena. There's plenty of girls on Market Street who would be more than happy to take your place. It's not as if the man has warts and bad breath."

"No. He doesn't." Maggie might have felt better if he had.

A short week later Maggie said good-bye to Denver. Her emotions were jumbled as Christopher handed her into the private railroad car that Horace Tabor had insisted they use for the trip to Santa Fe. She'd lived all but three years of her life in Denver. Here she had been an innocent child, a scavenging orphan, and finally, a woman who earned her own living in the world—not a wealthy living, to be sure, but just the same it was hers. Denver had not always been kind to her, but the problems and dangers there were old, familiar enemies. The life she faced in New Mexico was an unknown.

"Excellent," Christopher said as he followed her into the car. "It appears at least that the trip will be comfortable."

Peter exhaled a wondering breath as he handed Luisa

through the door and climbed in himself. "These mining chaps certainly know how to travel. Don't tell young Rodney about this, Christopher, or he'll want one of his own. Except your brother would need a gaming table or two to keep him suitably entertained."

Maggie turned slowly around and filled her vision with the luxury. The car seemed like something out of one of the more exotic adventures on the library shelves of the Fourteenth Street house. What delightful wickedness for four people to lounge in a space that could have seated forty. The car was stocked with liquor, playing cards, and books. Plushly upholstered chairs and couches would have made the longest journey a joy.

"It looks like one of the rooms in the House of Mirrors," she blurted.

Three sets of eyebrows rose.

"Not that I've ever been there! But I've heard stories. It's supposed to be the fanciest whorehouse ever."

"Indeed!" Christopher said caustically.

"Yes, I know. Ladies don't even know there is such a thing as a whorehouse."

The look Maggie slanted toward Christopher was more puckish than apologetic. Six days ago when she'd calmly informed him that she would consent to be his wife, she'd vowed that she wouldn't let herself be intimidated by him. Nor would she let herself be crowded into his narrow rules. If he wanted her land, he would have to take her with it—just as she was. And to hell with what he thought of her. She couldn't fight it; there seemed no way out of the trap she had stepped into, so she had decided simply to make the best of it.

"You English gents must be good at keeping secrets from your ladylike wives to keep them so ignorant of the real world," Maggie observed irreverently.

"I can see that won't be a problem in this marriage," Peter commented, his eyes twinkling.

Christopher glared at him. Maggie grinned. The longer she knew Peter Scarborough the more she liked him.

Christopher was quiet during the day-long journey, though now and again Maggie caught him giving her speculative looks that belied his apparent indifference to her. The last week had been a contest as to which of them could be the most distant. They had played the happy engaged couple at the social functions of the last few days —after their engagement had been formally acknowledged and their departure plans announced, invitations had poured in. Every Denver hostess had wanted a turn at the English lord before he left. Maggie had put on her best ladylike behavior, and Christopher had played the considerate gallant for the benefit of their audience.

But privacy bred a silence between them. Maggie had discovered a certain joy in sending small annoyances Christopher's way—such as appearing in the parlor barefoot or wearing her old clothes around the house. In turn, he lost no opportunity to remind her of the devil's bargain that she'd made. His silent assessment of every aspect of her manners and bearing rattled her, and he knew it. He sat in judgmental silence as Peter continued to instruct her in literature, philosophy, deportment, and numbers. His presence made her feel awkward and inept; she was sure that he planned it that way.

But to her relief there had been no more kisses, no more banquets that had required them to dance in each other's arms—nothing to remind her of how weak she could be when Christopher Talbot chose to really assault her defenses.

Of all the aspects of her new life it was Christopher's masculine magnetism that Maggie feared the most. For the entire week since the Tabor banquet she had watched him carefully, studying his strengths and weaknesses as a fugitive Indian might scout a pursuing cavalry. She gauged the depths of his moods, the quickness of his temper, the extent of his patience; she watched the camaraderie with which he treated Peter, though Peter had once told her that he was not really of the Talbots' social class. She envied the relaxed smiles he gave Luisa and wondered at his courtesy with the servants. When the downstairs maid adopted one of the hundreds of stray dogs that plagued Denver, Maggie was amazed at His Prim Lordship's tolerance when he found the pup in the kitchen gnawing at a beef shank the cook had thrown it.

If Christopher had treated Maggie with the same regard he gave even the stray dog, she might have been tempted to let down her guard, to forget bygones and make a new start. The maid's dog, however, rated more warmth than she did. Too often Christopher looked at her as though she were a piece of merchandise he had purchased without fully appraising. Those looks reminded her that she was merely an addendum to a land title.

They rolled steadily south, the mountains rising to their right and the plains spreading like beige and brown carpet to their left. The wheels of the train sang a song that over the hours grew into a lullaby. Maggie yawned and set aside *Ben-Hur*, which she was reading for a second time—Christopher had unbent enough to buy her a copy of her own. He had seemed surprised at her request, but had bought her *Ben-Hur* and several other books as well —two adventures by Jules Verne and a collection of Bret Harte stories. He had left the books in her room two days ago with a terse note that she might find them entertaining. The gift had surprised her. High-class men were certainly a mystery!

"Is the book that confusing?" Luisa, who had spent

most of the trip conversing with Peter Scarborough, sat down beside Maggie on the damask-covered settee.

"What?" Maggie asked.

"That puzzled frown on your face. Is the book so confusing?"

Maggie grimaced. "I wasn't reading. I was thinking about"—she glanced at Christopher, who had his nose in the newspaper—"men."

"One in particular?"

"Probably every one of them is equally annoying."

"Mm."

"You seem to be mighty friendly with Mr. Scarborough."

Luisa smiled tightly. "Do I?"

Maggie knew better than to probe further. When Luisa closed her mouth into such a line, she couldn't be persuaded by Indians pulling out her fingernails to utter a single word on a subject she didn't want to discuss.

"I'm glad you're coming with us," Maggie said to her friend. "I'd be lonely without you."

Luisa smiled. "I doubt that you'd be lonely for long, dear. After all, you're about to be a bride."

Maggie sniffed contemptuously.

"He'll come around," Luisa assured her, glancing at Christopher. "You simply frightened him by saying yes. Men tend to act like jackasses when they're frightened."

"I frightened him? This whole thing was *his* idea, you know."

"You've a lot to learn about men, Magdalena."

Maggie grimaced. "I know plenty about men. I'm not sure I want to learn any more."

"You don't know anything about men, you stupid child. But don't worry, once you're married, you'll learn. Most women do."

The song of the train suddenly sounded like mocking

laughter to Maggie. She felt rather than saw Christopher look up from his paper and glance at her with enigmatic regard. Sighing, she mused that life got more complicated every day.

Five

Santa Fe was not what Maggie had expected. Unlike Denver, which was raw with newness, Santa Fe had the maturity of almost three centuries of history. Set in a high mountain valley, bordered by cultivated fields, pine-clad mountains, and high desert, the town was a battleground between the stately old and the gaudy new.

Looking at the sights from the hired carriage that took the four travelers from the train depot, Maggie delighted in the brash youth and the stirring antiquity. Old St. Miguel Chapel shared the town with the new St. Francis Cathedral, which was itself built around the old Spanish church La Parroquia. The Palace of the Governors, an unpretentious one-story adobe building, had housed the rulers of New Mexico since the beginning of the seventeenth century, and the businesses and hotels along the Plaza looked as though they had stood since the Spanish conquest. Elsewhere, Victorian mansions and commercial buildings intruded upon the stately Spanish architecture. Likewise, the names on many business establishments bore witness that like newer American cities, Santa Fe had become a conglomeration of cultures. Signs bore almost as many English, German, Jewish, and American names as Spanish, and though the town was dominated by the Catholic St. Francis Cathedral, the Episcopalians, Methodists, Baptists, and Presbyterians were also well represented.

Christopher directed their driver to a sprawling adobe house east of the busiest part of town. The house sat atop a juniper-covered hill that sloped down to the Santa Fe River and had an impressive view of the mountains to the northeast and east and the high desert to the south and west. Maggie was instantly delighted by a set of three pottery bells that hung from the veranda roof and tinkled with every breath of breeze. Christopher watched as she tapped one of the bells with her finger and listened to the pure tone. Her peal of laughter was bright and pure as the chime of the bell.

"There's a man up the road who makes them," he explained, wondering that he should take such pleasure in her childlike joy.

Maggie started as the massive oak door opened and a stout, gray-haired Mexican matron bobbed her head in deference. "Oh! Hello there!" she greeted the housekeeper with entirely too much familiarity. "Did we wake you up? I'm sorry."

Christopher stifled a smile.

"*Buenas noches, señorita.*" The housekeeper, a well-trained domestic who'd served upper-class families most of her life, regarded Maggie with a proper amount of reserve. "We have been waiting up for your arrival."

"*Buenas noches*, Isabel." Christopher's English accent mixed strangely with the Spanish.

"*Señor.*" Her head bobbed again. "We received your letter that you would arrive tonight. Juan has supper for whenever you're ready."

"Thank you, Isabel. Is Pedro about?"

"He is in the kitchen."

"Please ask him to bring our trunks from the carriage."

"Yes, señor." With a curious look at her new mistress, Isabel nodded and left.

Maggie stepped into the big, open room that served as both parlor and entrance hall and turned in a slow circle to examine the emptiness. The walls were whitewashed adobe trimmed with dark wood. Only the large windows, shuttered for the night, alleviated their starkness. Polished wooden floors gleamed in the gaslights, unrelieved by rugs or carpeting.

"There are four rooms in this wing," Christopher told them. "This room, a library, dining room, and breakfast room—and five bedrooms across the courtyard."

"A bit bare, wouldn't you say?" Peter commented.

"The bedrooms are furnished—somewhat, though they're quite Spartan. I thought Maggie might want to furnish the house to her taste. I plan to keep it indefinitely. We'll need a place that's closer to civilization than the ranch."

"I get to furnish it to my taste?" Maggie exclaimed. She looked like a child who had just been handed a present. Her eyes were luminous, and her smile was almost too wide for her face. "But I've got no taste! The only furnishing I've ever done is drag a cot into a storeroom."

Christopher schooled his face to solemnity. He shouldn't be so tempted to smile at the little tart's fresh sauciness. "I'm sure you have taste of some sort, Maggie. You just haven't found it yet. Mrs. Gutierrez can help."

"Do you have enough money? You said your family was strapped."

"I'm sure we have enough to furnish a house as small as this one."

"You think *this* is small?" Maggie twirled around with her arms spread wide.

"It's small enough."

He watched Maggie dart from window to window. At one she opened the shutter and sniffed the cool air, wondering aloud at the clean smell of the river. At another she paused to look out and smile at the moon.

"The door over there opens into what the locals call a *placita*—a courtyard. The whole house is built around it. The bedroom wing is on the other side of it."

Maggie opened the door and exclaimed with pleasure at the small fountain, trees, and shrubbery of the little courtyard. Then she turned back to the room and measured it with her eyes. As her head tilted thoughtfully, Christopher pictured her imagination churning with the possibilities of how to spend his money on rugs, wall hangings, tables, chairs, and couches. He desperately hoped the house didn't resemble a bordello when she was through, but it didn't really matter, he told himself. She would have to live with the house much longer than he would, so she should be comfortable in it. Once things were running smoothly and he left for England, he needn't be much concerned with Maggie's manners, taste, sauciness, or familiarity with the servants.

A pang of regret caught Christopher by surprise. His task would have been much easier if Maggie had been unlikable, unpleasant looking, or even conventionally beautiful. Christopher had always found beautiful women rather boring. They thought too much of their looks and too little of the world around them, a common feminine foible shared even by ladies who didn't have enough looks to be concerned with.

Maggie Montoya was not like any other woman he'd known, however. In spite of her blue blood, she had little gentility. She was devilishly unpredictable, unconventional, at times crude, frequently ill mannered, and seemingly unconcerned with her looks or mode of dress. She was also refreshingly candid, Christopher admitted, disarmingly eager to learn about everything from history and politics to poetry, and appealing in ways that ranged from impish to sensual, depending upon her mood. Her hidden noble blood kept her from being hopelessly coarse, in spite of the raw life she'd led. Her aristocratic ancestors had stamped her with fine features, a bright, curious intelligence, and a pride that outstripped the bounds of reason.

Maggie was unique, in ways both vexing and captivating. She defied classification. But at least she wasn't boring. Christopher almost wished that she were.

Supper was a quick affair in the kitchen, the only room with a table. In spite of the luxury of the private car the journey from Denver had been tiring. They'd started at a very early hour and arrived very late. The four of them consumed the cold beef, cheese, and vegetables with little conversation. Christopher dismissed Juan and Isabel to their beds as soon as the servants had laid out the meal.

After dinner he showed Maggie and Luisa to the bedroom—furnished in his own rather Spartan taste—that the two women would share until the wedding ceremony a week hence. Peter had a room on the opposite side of the wing, and for propriety's sake Christopher would stay at the Exchange Hotel until the wedding. He wanted no one in Santa Fe to doubt the propriety of the arrangements. Any shadow on Magdalena Montoya's honor could only hurt the favorable disposition of her land claim. To that end, after showing Maggie her room, Christopher asked politely to talk to her in the parlor.

"Why are you staying at a hotel?" she asked with unladylike directness.

"My staying here before our wedding would be quite improper."

"Peter's staying."

Peter is not the one who is engaged to be married. Besides, he is staying in the opposite side of the house."

"You could stay there with him."

"It's simply much more proper for me to stay elsewhere, Maggie. After the wedding we may both move into the master suite and everything will be quite proper."

"By all means let's be proper!"

In spite of her impish grin Christopher thought she looked a bit uneasy at his mention of their occupying the same bed. He wondered at the brutalities she must have endured in her sordid life, and for a change he felt pity instead of contempt.

"It's propriety I wish to speak to you about, Maggie."

She sighed.

"Bear with me a moment, please. I've discarded the hope that you will ever behave as a lady brought up in genteel society. I was unreasonable to have expected it of you."

"I can act the lady with the best of them."

"No doubt about it. You're quite a talented actress. But it doesn't exactly come naturally to you, does it?"

She shrugged. "I think prissing around in fancy corsets and a bustle is silly. So is all that polite small talk and pretending that just because you're a lady you don't know about things that anyone with two eyes and two ears couldn't miss. But don't worry. We struck a bargain. I'll keep my part."

"I have no doubt you'll try, Maggie. What I wish to impress upon you is that until your claim is settled, you must strive especially hard to live up to your family name. We want no one to doubt that you are truly the grand-daughter of Ramón Bautista de Montoya. We know the truth of it, but some might question it if they were aware that the woman who claims one of the largest grants in New Mexico was a saloon dancer in Denver."

"I'm not ashamed of what I am." Her face grew thoughtful. A twitch of worry puckered her brows and recalled to Christopher just how he had tempted her the first night they'd met. He'd lured her into this bargain with the promise that the saloon dancer from the Lady Luck would be gone forever and no one need know that the woman he brought to New Mexico had once kicked up her heels in a Denver bar.

"It's not a matter of being ashamed," he told her, woo-ing whatever concern bothered her. "We're playing a deli-cate game, Maggie, and we wouldn't want to give the opposition any advantage that we don't have to."

"What opposition?"

"I'm sure Harley will do his best to keep the land he took from my brother."

She was silent.

"I've let it be known that you lived in Denver with friends after the death of your mother—not entirely the truth, but close enough."

"And Luisa?"

"A distant cousin who is your companion."

Suddenly, a wicked smile illuminated Maggie's face and banished the shadow of her worry. "You know, Chris-topher, for all your talk of honor and morality and such, you don't really have much more than I, do you?"

Her tone was complimentary rather than judgmental. Still smiling, she turned and waltzed out of the room, stepping to a tune that rose quietly from under her breath.

Christopher watched her go. He had never understood women, and he would never try. Particularly this one.

The wedding was scheduled for April sixteenth at the Episcopal Church. Maggie had scarce time to think about the coming event. Her wedding dress had to be chosen, fitted, fitted again, and yet again. The downstairs of the house had to be furnished, shops visited, and catalogs perused for chairs, tables, couches, a buffet, draperies, rugs, and paintings. Christopher gave offhand approval for anything she wanted to buy. At first Maggie was flattered that he trusted her, but then it occurred to her that he simply didn't care. To Christopher the bright, sunlit house with its banks of windows, its cozy courtyard, and its rugged, juniper-covered grounds sloping down to the Santa Fe River would never be home. His home was England, a place crowded with beautiful mansions and genteel, well-mannered ladies and gentlemen.

Two days before the wedding the territorial governor hosted a reception for the duke's son and his bride-to-be at the Palace of the Governors—the building that took up the entire north side of the Plaza and served as both the governor's residence and government offices. The building was a study in the contrasting cultures of Santa Fe. Built by Spanish conquerors in the early seventeenth century, its plain adobe facade had been updated by a porch that boasted turned posts and a balustrade very much in the Victorian style.

"Keep your shoes on this time," Christopher warned her as they stopped at the Plaza and descended from the carriage that he'd purchased only the day before.

Remembering the Tabor banquet in Denver, Maggie dreaded another evening of society matrons fawning over Christopher and looking at her as though she'd crawled from beneath a rock. "Don't worry, Your Most Proper Lordship, the night's too cool for me to be walking barefoot."

"Or rolling around on the grass, I trust."

His voice carried an edge, and Maggie wondered if he, like she, was thinking uncomfortably of the kiss that he had given her while she was barefoot on the grass.

"And by the way, since we're to be married in two days, you should start addressing me by my name."

"Yes, Your Mighty Lordship."

"Maggie!"

"Yes—Christopher." She did enjoy keeping him a bit off balance. He was less intimidating when he was off balance. "But all the ladies fawn over your title. I thought that I should too."

"Behave, Maggie cat."

Christopher wasn't actually worried that Maggie would misbehave. Notwithstanding her remark about the Americans fawning over his title, almost everyone at the reception had come to see not the duke's son so much as the claimant to one of the largest land grants in New Mexico. This reception was important to her claim being approved, and Maggie knew it. She would behave.

Besides, Christopher didn't intend to let her out of his sight.

Governor Lionel Sheldon himself greeted them. A man with a hearty handshake, the governor didn't stand on formality. "Christopher. Glad you could join us. So many people wanted to meet you." He regarded Maggie with a curious gleam in his eye. "And this must be the prize you've kept under wraps for such a long time. Miss Montoya, it is truly a pleasure. What a shame that such a lovely lady is introduced into our midst, only to be snatched away by this foreigner."

Maggie dimpled in a smile. "You flatter me, Your Excellency."

"Not at all. Maggie, isn't it? May I call you Maggie?"

"The name is actually Magdalena. But I would be delighted if you called me Maggie."

Christopher detected the slightest roll of her eyes and tightened his grip on her arm.

"Let me steal her away for a little while, Christopher. There's a gentleman here who knew Maggie's grandfather, and I'd like to introduce her. And"—his eyes twinkled—"there are at least a dozen ladies here anxious to make the acquaintance of a real English lord."

"Of course you may take her. I'll be able to monopolize her soon enough."

"That's the spirit. I'll take care of her, I promise."

The governor took Maggie's hand. "This way, my dear. What a shame you've been living in Denver all these years without knowing about your family holdings. If you'd lived in Santa Fe . . ."

The governor's voice faded as he led Maggie away. Christopher watched Maggie nod her head and smile politely at his conversation, then do the same as she was introduced to a couple who looked as though they had been part of the first Spanish conquest.

"Lord Christopher, how glad we are to see you back in New Mexico."

Christopher looked around. Mrs. Manuel Coriegas, a prominent Santa Fe hostess whom he had met during his earlier visit, stood beside him. She smiled beatifically. A spare, middle-aged lady with black upswept hair was at her elbow.

"Let me introduce Miss Consuelo Chavez, Your Lordship. The Chavez family has lived in Santa Fe since before the Pueblo Revolt of 1680."

Christopher bowed over the lady's hand. "I'm pleased to make your acquaintance, Miss Chavez. If I ever get my bride back from the governor, I'm sure she would like to meet you as well. Magdalena also has a family history that stretches far back into this country's history."

Out of the corner of his eye Christopher followed Maggie's progress through the guests while he conversed politely with Mrs. Coriegas, Miss Chavez, and others who crowded around to have a look at the English lord. Maggie was at her most charming, he was glad to note. Luisa had tamed the girl's black, curly mane into a creation that smoothly twisted the hair, fastened it at the crown, and then let it fall gracefully down her back in a mass of thick black curls. The style was young, and along with a modest, elbow-sleeved dress with lace insets at the neck and cuffs, it gave Maggie an innocent air she scarcely deserved. The ladies of the crowd looked ready to take the minx to their bosoms as if she were their own daughter, and the men—well, there was nothing fatherly about the smiles they gave her. Christopher acknowledged that he felt a prick of jealousy. The scamp truly appeared to be a lady that a man might well be jealous about. If the Talbot family could see Maggie now, Christopher mused, they would think he had not only regained Stephen's land but found an ideal wife as well. Little did they know what a little mongrel lay beneath that purebred exterior.

On the other side of the room Maggie surprised herself by enjoying the reception. Santa Fe society, despite its ancient heritage, was less exclusive than that of the self-appointed aristocrats of Denver. She met men and women descended from the first Spaniards to colonize the territory, great-great grandchildren of Spanish dons. In the same gathering were German merchants, bankers from the East, cattlemen lately moved from Texas, and one charming entrepreneur who proudly announced he was Jewish. Even though the Spanish families conversed more often among themselves than with others, they didn't once employ the down-the-nose look that Maggie had met in Denver. They didn't gaze at her through lorngettes with disapproving eyes because she wasn't one of their exclusive clan. The ladies were kind and welcoming. The gentlemen treated her with a gallantry that did little to disguise their admiration. They made her feel attractive and feminine in a way that the leering customers of the Lady Luck had never done. Of course, these people thought she was an aristocratic offshoot of their own exclusive clan. They didn't know she was a saloon dancer and daughter of a saloon dancer, and she wasn't about to tell them.

"Are you enjoying yourself, my dear?" Christopher's voice intruded into a pause in her conversation with a young man who was an assistant in the governor's office.

Maggie sent Christopher a triumphant smile. She hoped he noticed that these people thought she was worth some regard. "I'm enjoying myself tremendously, thank you." If she didn't know better, she'd have thought the flash in his dark eyes came from jealousy.

"Excellent."

"Have you met Mr. McCoskey from the governor's office?"

"I haven't had the pleasure."

As the two men shook hands, Maggie noticed that Mr. McCoskey's smile waned a bit. Christopher's stony gaze might have had something to do with the young man's discomfiture—that and the possessive arm the Englishman put around her. It was all Maggie could do not to jump when she felt his hand land at her waist. Perhaps

Christopher was not quite as indifferent to her as he pretended.

"Ah!" McCoskey exclaimed, seeming glad of a diversion. "Here comes Anderson. He's with the surveyor general's office."

"There you are, Your Lordship," Anderson greeted Christopher. "And is this Miss Montoya?"

"This is my fiancée, Magdalena Teresa Maria Montoya."

"A pleasure, Miss Montoya. It's good to see that the fine old Montoya family is represented by such a fine lady."

Maggie was hard-pressed to restrain herself from sending Christopher a triumphant smirk.

"Your Lordship . . . uh . . . I wonder if you might comment upon something that came to my attention only this last week."

"If I can."

"As you and I discussed several months ago, the only people currently working any part of the land covered by the Montoya grant are the Harleys—Theodore and his son, Todd. But are you aware that a fellow countryman of yours formerly owned, in fact, settled, the ranchland now owned by Harley?"

"Yes. I am."

Maggie's heart constricted. The scheme was discovered. She and Christopher were going to be tossed out of New Mexico on their behinds.

"Coincidentally, the former owner's name was Stephen Talbot. He transferred the title to Harley just over a year ago, then disappeared."

The planes and angles of Christopher's face settled into a harsh mask. Maggie felt his hand tighten around her waist. "Stephen Talbot killed himself after losing that land in a poker game to Theodore Harley. He was my younger brother."

Anderson nodded, as if Christopher's admission confirmed something he'd long suspected. "My sympathies, Your Lordship. I couldn't help but wonder why an Englishman, a foreigner, would expend such time and effort to locate the heir to this grant."

"The Talbots do not let such an injury to our family go unanswered. However, the motivation behind my search has nothing to do with the legitimacy of Miss Montoya's claim."

"Oh, I find no reason to dispute that Miss Montoya is exactly who you—and your considerable documentation —claim she is."

Maggie expelled a slow, relieved breath. She could hardly believe that Christopher was being so honest about his duplicity.

"In fact, I must congratulate you, sir, on finding a very clever way to regain what your brother lost. Few in the territory will spare any sympathy for the Harleys. Todd is all right, I suppose, but Theodore is not well thought of. Too many remember him as a slick cardsharp. The Montoya grant is some of the best grazing land in the territory. It doesn't set well with the other cattlemen to see it wasted on a man who'd rather fill his house with luxuries than tend his cattle."

Maggie listened to the conversation with increasing amazement. The two men had begun by discussing her, but somewhere in the exchange Magdalena Montoya had become a walking land grant. Anderson had immediately concluded that Christopher's only reason for marrying her was to regain his precious land, and Christopher hadn't even the decency to deny it. What's worse, Anderson seemed to admire the Englishman for his devious scheming.

To her chagrin Maggie noticed the number of people listening in on the discussion. It seemed to her that women who had earlier cast her glances of envy now regarded her with undisguised sympathy. And the men— damn their mercenary hides!—nodded in admiration as Christopher admitted without reservation that his marriage was nothing more than a land acquisition. Where earlier Maggie had basked in the esteem of people she was coming to respect, and had enjoyed a budding hope that Christopher Talbot might actually value her for something other than her inheritance, now she was catapulted back to the reality that she was worth precisely five hundred thousand acres of grassland. As a woman, as a person, she was nothing, at least in the eyes of the man who would be her husband. It was one thing for him to be honest with her about his motives, but how dare he display her worth—or lack thereof—to anyone and everyone who might otherwise think she might merit some respect for her own sake. The low-down skunk!

"Christopher." She put all the contempt she could in her voice. He'd wanted her to call him by name; let him hear in that name just what she thought of him. "I have a terrible headache. I'd like to leave."

He raised one brow, spearing her with a silent reprimand.

Her eyes narrowed. "If we don't leave, I think I just may become violently ill."

"Then by all means," he said stiffly, "we'll say our goodbyes. Excuse us, please." He took her arm in a grip like a vise. As they went in search of the governor and his wife, Maggie imagined the eyes of the whole room upon her, all pitying the poor twit of a girl who was the human equivalent of a piece of New Mexico dirt.

* * *

The night was as black as the devil's heart. It matched Maggie's mood. More than twenty-four hours had passed since His Cold Heartless Lordship had revealed to most of Santa Fe society that his bride was the price he had to pay to gain a piece of land. Her anger and humiliation hadn't diminished one whit. She'd spent the day in a huff, refusing to come out of her room. Allowing herself to be used in such a manner was bad enough; the whole of New Mexico knowing about it was mortifying.

What was worse, His Arrogant Lordship didn't even know what he'd done to make her mad. When they'd arrived home from the reception, he'd demanded the reason for her behavior. She'd simply turned up her nose and sniffed. If the witless fool didn't know, Maggie wasn't going to tell him. Maggie was surprised and disappointed when Luisa didn't understand, either, even when Maggie filled her in on the details of what had happened at the reception. Few marriages were made for love, the older woman had explained. No one would think less of Maggie because she brought more than just herself to her wedding. Luisa had concluded that Maggie was suffering from wedding jitters. The day before a girl's wedding is always beset with strange humors and jumps of temper.

Did no one but herself think that Maggie Montoya was worth something in herself? Maggie wondered as she stared at the black, moonless sky. All her life she'd clung to the fantasy that she was somebody. A special guardian angel shielded her steps, extricating her from situations that should have been the end of her: like the time when she was seven. Her mother was between jobs. They had both been hungry, so Maggie had stolen a beef roast from the kitchen of the Carousel Restaurant. The furious cook had given chase with a meat cleaver in his hand. He was faster than a little girl with short legs, but she'd found a secure hiding place—with special help, Maggie had always thought. Or the night when she had escaped Tony Alvarez's ranch. Her mother not buried for even a full day, Maggie had escaped on a stolen horse at the very hour that Alvarez had threateningly ordered her to be in his bed. For two cold February days she'd ridden without food to get back to Denver. She hadn't frozen, hadn't been caught, and she hadn't gotten lost—with special help. Surely a person worth all that special help was worth more than a patch of grassy dirt.

Maggie turned and looked at herself in the oval mirror that stood by the wardrobe. She'd never thought much about her looks. Now she wondered if something about her was so particularly unattractive that Lord Christopher Talbot—and seemingly everyone else she met—thought her most pleasing quality was her land. She saw dark, luminous eyes that she'd always believed were rather pretty. Her mouth was too wide, it was true. The tilt of her nose gave her face an impish look. Her wild, curly hair was hopeless except when Luisa set her mind to taming it. But taken altogether, from the neck up she wasn't entirely unattractive. Maggie had seen a lot worse.

From the neck down—Maggie surveyed her figure in the mirror, turned and looked around to evaluate her backside, then turned front again. She'd filled out since she started eating three meals a day; her figure wasn't half bad. The gathered skirt she wore—one of those that Christopher so despised—emphasized her slender waist and the flare of her hips. The loose cotton blouse draped gracefully over the swell of her breasts. Maggie threw her shoulders back and surveyed the result with a frown. She wasn't top heavy like some of the more popular whores on Market Street, but any man would notice immediately that she was female.

So what did it take for a woman to be appreciated for being a woman? Maggie wondered. The thought brought with it a swift and surprising pang of longing. Was there a reason other than pride that she wanted Christopher Talbot to want her for herself?

"I'm not putting up with this!" she flung toward the ceiling and her guardian angel. "This was a bad idea. I should have stayed in Denver and taken my chances."

She pulled a woven valise from under the bed, opened the dresser drawers, and started to throw chemises, pantalets, stockings, and corsets onto the bed.

What about Luisa? a voice echoed in her head.

Maggie snapped the valise shut, opened the wardrobe, and started pulling out dresses.

What about Luisa? the voice insisted.

An image of Luisa with the fireplace poker in her hand appeared in Maggie's mind. Luisa would be in much more danger in Denver than Maggie would.

"Oh, all right! Damn!" Guardian angels could sometimes be a real bother. She opened the valise, spilled the underwear onto the bed, and hung the dresses back in the wardrobe. The night darkness seemed to peer at her through the open window, mocking her. *Look out here*, it called. *Your future is just as black and just as empty.*

As if answering the call, she went to the window and leaned her hands on the sill. The maw of night had swallowed the hills, the trees, and the river. She looked out at nothing but gloom.

"Luisa can stay here," she told the sky. "She'll be fine."

Luisa wasn't the one who had to marry a man who couldn't see past a piece of dirt, a man who threatened to take her heart and give back nothing but emptiness. That was the crux of the matter, Maggie admitted, ashamed. Christopher Talbot, with his broad shoulders, his opaque eyes that every once in a while lit with hunger, his cynical smiles that occasionally softened to real smiles, his caustic wit that sometimes warmed to humor—Christopher Talbot had captured an unwary part of her foolish heart. If she married him, she wouldn't possibly be able to resist the spell he cast. She would surrender her love to a man who didn't even want her.

"I'm going," Maggie vowed to the dark heavens. "I'm not going to live my life tied to a man who thinks I'm a land grant. I'm a woman!" She turned and looked in the mirror, just to be sure. "Yes! I'm a woman. I'm young. I'm smart. I've got talents Christopher Talbot never even imagined, and I'll do just fine without him. Luisa will understand."

She stuffed her underthings back in the valise. Pulling another bag from beneath the bed, she filled it with three carefully chosen dresses. When she got a job, she would send Christopher payment for the clothes.

You're running away, the voice in her head accused.

She fastened her cloak, grabbed the valises, and doused the lamp before heading for the door. "I'm cutting my losses," she explained. "I'm not running away."

The stairs were dark. She tiptoed her way down. The whole downstairs was dark. The last chime of the clock that Luisa and she had bought for the fireplace mantel had been twelve strokes. Everyone was in bed, resting for tomorrow's big wedding. But when Luisa came to wake Maggie, Maggie would be on the train out of town, wherever that train was going. Not back to Denver. Maybe San Francisco, or a city back East. She'd find a job dancing, maybe become rich. Luisa was wrong to say that her dreams were childish fantasies.

Maggie set her valises beside the front door and stole into the library. Very quietly she opened the top desk drawer where the household money was kept. She took out twenty dollars, telling herself she would repay Christopher when she reached her destination and found a job.

Coward, the darkness accused.

"I'm not a coward!" she whispered furiously. "I'm not afraid of Christopher Talbot. I just don't want to marry the jackass."

Coward.

Guardian angels weren't supposed to argue with a person, were they? "Go step in a snakehole," Maggie invited.

You've never run from anything in your life, the voice insisted.

"That's because I hadn't met Christopher Talbot."

Chicken.

That did it! No one called Maggie Montoya chicken. Not even her guardian angel.

"I am not chicken!" she growled, heading for her valises and the door. "I'm just . . ." She looked at her packed bags. Tomorrow was her wedding day. She'd promised to marry Christopher Talbot, and everyone who was anyone in Santa Fe was coming to the Episcopal church tomorrow morning to see a duke's son wed to an heiress of five hundred thousand New Mexico acres. She had promised. Given her word. Struck a bargain with her eyes wide open. Now she was running out. "I'm chicken," she admitted.

Never in her life had she run from a challenge. She'd always believed that once a person started to run, he ran for the rest of his life. It was a bad habit to get into.

She sat down on her bags and rested her chin dejectedly in her cupped hands.

You can beat him at his own game, the darkness suggested. *A man who won't admit that he has a heart often leaves it unguarded.*

Her guardian angel must be a female, Maggie decided. A clever female, at that. The suggestion intrigued her. Christopher was so certain that he wanted her only for the land grant. He was so arrogantly sure of himself. What a triumph it would be to have the man falling all over himself to gain Maggie's favor.

That's the idea, the voice encouraged.

What sweet revenge for the humiliation he'd caused her. His heart would be hopelessly entangled by her charm, and she would let it be known far and wide that she'd married him only to get her land. She smiled. Or perhaps she wouldn't publicly humiliate him. She might let herself love him in return. It depended on how nicely he apologized for having embarrassed her.

You can make him love you, Maggie heard in her head. *You'll be doing him a favor*.

Her guardian angel was definitely a woman—probably one who'd had man problems when she was alive, Maggie surmised.

She picked up the valises and tiptoed back up the stairs. Tomorrow was her wedding day, the beginning of a challenge. Christopher Talbot didn't know what he was up against.

Six

The morning was not ideal for a wedding. In fact, it was downright ominous. Cold air had moved into the valley during the night, bringing with it clouds that shrouded the mountains and hung like a cold, moist blanket over the town.

"I fear it will snow before the day's done." Peter looked out the window at the threatening sky.

"Snow in April." Christopher shook his head. "This country is as unpredictable as the people it breeds. Come check my necktie, will you, Peter? This office doesn't have a mirror."

They'd come to the church early to check on the wedding arrangements, and the priest had suggested they use his office to change into their wedding finery.

"Speaking of unpredictable, I hope you're right that Mrs. Gutierrez has Maggie well in hand. The wedding won't be of much use without the bride."

"She assured me that Magdalena is suffering from nothing more serious than a case of the bridal jitters."

Christopher grunted a doubtful reply. Maggie was a mystery—one moment all charm, girlish smiles, and eager, inquisitive enthusiasm, the next moment icy glares, snapping eyes, and a stubborn, angry silence. Like the fickle mountains and plains where she'd spent her life, she could change from warm to cold, calm to blustery, in the blink of an eye. After her sudden change of mood at the reception, she'd scarcely spared him a word. Like a sullen child she'd taken to her room, and when he'd demanded to know what was troubling her, she had roasted him with her eyes as if he had just doubled whatever had been his first offense. Women! Who could understand them?

"You're quite sure you are doing the right thing?" Peter stepped back from straightening Christopher's tie. "You don't look at all like a happy groom."

Christopher smoothed the scowl from his face. "I suppose I don't feel much like a groom. This is more a business transaction than a wedding. Of course, most weddings are."

"Where do you get such cynicism?"

"I'm not cynical, old friend. Merely realistic."

"Then why don't you wait until after the land title is confirmed to wed Magdalena?" Peter smiled. "Is there a chink in your realistic armor?"

Christopher chuckled. "When one has a fighting trout on one's hook, it is best to land the fish before it slips off the hook and swims away."

"How very romantic."

"You insist on looking for romance where there is none, Peter. I wouldn't expect that of a confirmed bachelor like you."

"And what if the land title isn't confirmed?"

"The Office of the Surveyor General assures me all is in order."

"Yes, my boy. But what if by chance some officious government lackey decides differently?"

Christopher shrugged. "Then there will be no help for it, will there?"

A knock on the door announced the entrance of the Reverend Daniel Wickham. "Excuse me, gentlemen, but the bride has arrived. Your guests are all seated. We can begin the ceremony any time you're ready."

Peter grinned. Christopher raised a brow. Judging from Maggie's mood this last day, he'd half expected her to not show up, or at least to put on some show of rebellion.

"We're ready to proceed," Christopher told the priest.

He was about to gain five hundred thousand acres of prime ranchland, a solid base for a small financial empire, and what might very well be his family's salvation over the next few years. As he headed out the door toward the sanctuary, Christopher wondered why—despite what he'd told Peter—this felt more like a wedding than a business transaction.

"Omigod! Look at all the people!"

"Steady on, my girl. They're not going to bite."

Maggie flashed Peter an exasperated look. "I didn't think they were going to bite. But, Lordy! Are we going to feed all these people after the wedding? I thought Christopher said he and his family were strapped. After all," she said sourly, "he shouted to the whole world that he was marrying me to get my land."

"Try to forgive him, lass. Christopher would never be deliberately boorish, but he has very little understanding of feminine sensibilities."

"He has little understanding of a lot things, as far as I can tell."

Peter's sigh was half sympathy, half frustration.

"If he's so hard up, why don't we just go stand in front of a judge to get hitched instead of feeding half the town?"

"I suspect that the Talbot family's idea of strapped and your idea of it may be a bit different, Maggie."

"More than likely." She peered again through the anteroom doors into the packed church sanctuary. Faces blurred into a sea of flesh tones, but Christopher seemed etched in bold relief as he stood in front of the altar with the priest at his side. In the pit of Maggie's stomach something started to shiver. She tried to ignore it. "Looks as if he wants the whole town of Santa Fe to know we're good and married."

"I think that's the idea."

Maggie felt Peter's sympathy as he took her hand and gently squeezed it. She didn't need the barrister's sympathy, she told herself with an attempt at confidence. Christopher might, though.

"I believe they're all waiting for the bride," Peter hinted.

"Well, then, let's not disappoint them."

Peter took her arm. Suddenly she felt a rush of warmth toward the man who had so patiently put up with her over the last months. She gave him a warm smile. "I would have liked for my father to be like you, Peter."

Peter patted her hand. "Thank you, my dear. If I had a daughter as bright and lovely as you, I would be a very proud man."

They started down the aisle. The guests rose. They all

knew that it wasn't the bride that Christopher Talbot was interested in, Maggie thought. It didn't matter, though. Maggie knew who she was and what she was worth, and someday Christopher would also.

The walk was interminable. The high lace collar of her dress itched, her corset pinched, and the bustle and train of the peach silk dress dragged like a lead weight. Maggie could feel the probe of every eye. The measuring scrutinies, envious gazes, and curious stares weighed her down. Heaviest of all was Christopher's. He stood tall and straight, dressed in formal black. The elegant tailoring of his cutaway tailcoat emphasized the broad shoulders and lean waist. The slim cut of his trousers underscored his long masculine legs. But his face was the focus of Maggie's attention. He watched her advance with a flinty concentration she couldn't interpret. He looked unassailable, invulnerable, and daunting.

For a moment Maggie was tempted to turn tail—until her pride surged to the surface. Devil take them all, Christopher Talbot included. She lifted her chin and smiled a wide, gaudy smile that told everyone she was queen of the day.

They arrived at the altar. Peter placed her hand in Christopher's, which was warm and dry. His hand enveloped hers completely. For a moment she felt ridiculously helpless before she could once again whip up her courage. Christopher smiled down at her, but the smile didn't quite reach his eyes.

"Thought I was going to back out, didn't you?" she whispered softly.

His lips twitched in surprise, and suddenly the smile warmed his eyes. "I never doubted that you're a woman of your word."

"You bet I am." She thought of her promise to herself.

Christopher Talbot would someday eat his words about wanting her only for the land.

"Dearly beloved," the priest began, "we are gathered together . . ."

Christopher gently squeezed her hand. Maggie didn't know if it was meant as comfort or a warning. The priest's words tumbled together in her mind. Love and cherish. Christopher didn't love her; she didn't love him. What was the punishment for standing before God and declaring your love when you had none?

Sickness and health. Poorer or richer. That was a joke. Right now she was poor as dirt, but soon she would be rich—from dirt. Christopher was taking her for richer and no other way. It was the only reason he was taking her. The priest knew it; the guests knew it. God must know it too. What did He think of this charade?

"If any person knows a reason why this man and this woman should not be joined in holy matrimony . . ."

Maggie knew plenty of reasons. She felt the squeeze of Christopher's hand—definitely a warning this time. Could he read her mind?

"Do you, Christopher Barrows Talbot, take this woman . . ."

Through a growing numbness she heard Christopher answer in a firm, steady voice.

"Do you, Magdalena Teresa Maria Montoya, take this man . . ."

Maggie opened her mouth. Nothing came out. The priest gave her an encouraging smile. Christopher's mouth tightened almost imperceptibly.

Let His Land-Grabbing Lordship wait, Maggie thought. *Let him sweat for a few moments.*

"Miss Montoya?" the priest asked. His voice sounded a bit strained.

"What?"

"Do you?" he prompted.

Maggie sighed. "I do."

Christopher flicked her a stern glance. She smiled innocently.

"By the authority granted me . . ." The priest made the solemn pronouncement that bound her to Christopher Talbot for as long as they both lived, but Maggie didn't feel like a wife. She felt like a fool.

Suddenly Christopher's long fingers gently touched her chin and tipped it upward. His face hovered inches above hers, and then warm, dry lips touched her mouth. For just a moment the kiss was a chaste peck, then, briefly, his mouth opened and moved against hers, urging her lips apart. She tasted brandy, male impatience, and a swift, reluctant passion. Then she was free. He regarded her with cautious speculation, and cool air swept into the distance between them—at least it seemed cool to Maggie. She knew with sudden certainty that she'd bargained herself from one precarious world into another just as perilous.

Night fulfilled the day's threat. Big, heavy flakes of snow swirled through the darkness and plastered the trees of the plaza, the buildings, and the lampposts on the street in white. Looking out the window of Christopher's hotel room, Maggie shivered as though the cold wind were swirling in her heart. Though a cast-iron stove kept the room warm, her hands were icy, and in the pit of her stomach a lump like cold lead made breathing a chore.

Finally she turned away from the winterlike scene and pulled the draperies over the window. She wished with all her heart that Luisa were here to tell her what was the acceptable and approved manner for a bride to greet her husband on their wedding night. But Luisa was several miles away—as good as a world away—in the house on the Santa Fe River. She couldn't answer the questions that a girl only thinks about after the wedding is accomplished, the dinner and reception over, and she is deposited by her groom in a hotel room and left alone to make ready for the night.

Should she be in bed when Christopher returned? Or should she wait demurely, sitting in a chair in her wedding finery? Was she expected to undress herself, or would Christopher want that pleasure? Should she don her fragile nightdress—a ridiculous frippery that Luisa had insisted on purchasing for the wedding night—or perhaps put on nothing at all and wait for her husband covered over by the bedsheets? How was she supposed to know what a gentleman expected his wife to do? And why had Christopher sounded so gruff when he'd told her he would leave her in privacy to prepare? He'd been cheerful enough at the dinner and reception, accepting congratulations from one and all.

Maggie sighed and began to unbutton the tightly fitted bodice of her gown. To hell with all the uncertainties of the situation. Her dress itched, and she'd been in the thing all day. She reached behind her to fumble with the buttons at her neck—and that was as far as she got. The tight armholes only allowed her to stretch so far.

"Damn!" As soon the imprecation escaped, she bit her lip. If she was to win over her husband, she would need to be more careful about such things. Ladies did not curse, Peter had told her time and time again. What ladies did when they were frustrated or angry Peter had never said. Perhaps ladies did not get frustrated or angry. If they did, they certainly never let their feelings exit by way of their mouth.

Cursing was not the only thing ladies didn't do, Maggie knew. The whores of her acquaintance on Market Street had been very explicit in telling her what ladies didn't do in bed with their husbands, and why those husbands sought out tarts for a woman who wasn't afraid to be a female. To hear the crib girls and parlor-house fancies tell it, men chased a girl, married her, bedded her, then very shortly got tired of her. Wives didn't know how to please a man and even less how to please themselves. The way to a man's heart was not through his stomach, as the conventional wisdom would have it, but through a portion of his anatomy a bit lower down.

Maggie paced back and forth in front of the stove, mulling over a newborn idea. Christopher certainly hadn't chased her—except in the sense that he was hunting down the heir to his precious land. There was no pretense of affection between them, and he didn't seem particularly anxious to bed her, if his dumping her in his hotel room and absenting himself for over an hour was evidence. More than likely a mongrel saloon girl was beneath his taste when he was accustomed to pedigreed ladies. But suppose she showed him that mongrels had some advantages over delicate-minded thoroughbreds? Might the sporting women be right? The way to a man's affections was not with ladylike manner or wifely domestic skills, but through a good roll between the sheets?

This was something Maggie hadn't thought on before. Since she first grew breasts she'd been diligent in avoiding just such an activity. Having scrubbed floors and cleaned rooms in whorehouses for several years, her education about mating was quite complete. If she lacked in experience, she certainly considered herself an expert in theory. Could she use this to her advantage on an unsuspecting husband? What could she lose by trying, since she was expected to lie in his bed in any case?

Not that she wasn't a touch nervous about the prospect. Not afraid, mind you. Magdalena Montoya—no, now it was Magdalena Talbot—wasn't afraid of something that women had been enduring since the beginning of time. But any girl was permitted to feel a bit uncertain about her first time lying with a man, especially if that man regarded you as someone about as important as a door-stop.

A knock on the door interrupted her reflections. "Maggie? Are you ready?"

As ready as she was ever going to be, Maggie told herself. "Come in."

Christopher entered and closed the door softly behind him. He gave her a look of surprise. "I . . . uh . . . expected you would want to get dressed for bed."

"I couldn't get to my buttons." She gave him a rueful smile. "The arms of the dress are too tight."

He cleared his throat. Maggie thought that her new husband looked as uneasy as she felt. "Yes, of course. I should have sent someone to help you."

For a moment they stood looking at each other in awkward silence. Then Christopher sighed. "Turn around."

Maggie felt his fingers unfasten the buttons, one by one —quite efficiently. This certainly wasn't the first time he'd dealt with a woman's garments, Maggie noted. The cool air caressed her skin as the back of her bodice parted and the front sagged partway down her shoulders and chest. On the nape of her neck his breath was warm in contrast. Maggie shivered.

"Would you like me to leave while you undress?"

If he left for another hour, she would surely lose all her courage. "No. We *are* married, after all."

"Yes, we are."

"Do—do you want me to put the nightdress on?"

"That won't be necessary—unless you want to, of course." His voice was flat, as though he were discussing the price of English wool with Peter. But then he was, after all, discussing the price of New Mexico land.

She turned around. Christopher had taken off his coat and was matter-of-factly unbuttoning his shirt. "Do you want the light off?"

"No." If she was the price of his land, then he was the price of her safety. She might as well see what she'd gotten herself into. Tobacco Nell, a girl who worked at the Gold Flower, had once told her that men liked to be undressed by their women. In fact, one of Nell's customers had offered her twice her going rate if she would unbutton his trousers with her mouth. Nell had said she'd had a time doing the chore, but in the end it was worth the trouble.

"Do you want me to help?" Maggie didn't wait for his answer, but pushed his hands away from the shirt buttons and took over the task herself. She felt him start as her fingers brushed his skin, but one sardonically arched eyebrow was the only other reaction she got. After one quick glance at his face, she couldn't meet his eyes. Instead, she stared straight ahead into the mat of black, curly hair that the opened shirt revealed. Who would have thought that a prissy gentleman would have such a masculine pelt?

Next she attended to his cuff fastenings, then eased the expensive silk shirt down over his shoulders. His skin was almost hot to her touch—and soft, like satin. His arms were powerfully muscled, his chest a broad expanse of taut sinew that narrowed downward to the hard-muscled ridges of his abdomen. The tightly curled black fur narrowed also, an arrow pointing downward past the waistband of his trousers.

Maggie didn't look up, but she could feel the heat of Christopher's eyes. She was getting rather warm herself. Christopher caught her hands in his as she reached for the fastenings of his trousers.

"You'd end the game too quickly." His voice sounded

hoarse. His bare chest rose and fell as if he had run a good distance. "I think it's time for me to assist you, wife."

Wife. The title sounded strange to Maggie's ears, perhaps because of his inflection as he'd said the word— more of a taunt than an endearment. A taunt to her, or to himself?

With tantalizing slowness he eased the unbuttoned bodice from Maggie's shoulders. Her camisole and corset seemed a fragile thing against his intense scrutiny. Her breasts ached for no reason and seemed to swell and strain against the thin material. He discarded the bodice, dropped his hands to his sides, and pinned her with his eyes. His fists doubled at his sides, fingers twitching.

Her turn now, Maggie decided. She reached for the buttons of his trousers, then hesitated as she noticed how tightly the material stretched over his groin. Something akin to triumph mixed with the apprehension that shivered down her spine. Men certainly did rouse easily.

Christopher caught her hands. "Not yet," he chided. "You have more layers than I. I get another turn."

She smiled up at him in a way that she hoped was seductive and was rewarded with an instant leap of fire in those dark, shadowed eyes. He reached around her to untie the ribbons of her skirt. The movement brought her face only inches from his chest. Fascinated, she stared at the hard, puckered male nipple in front of her eyes.

"You women wear too many petticoats by half," he complained. Her skirt and one layer of petticoats pooled around her ankles. She felt his fingers work at the ribbons of the second layer. Tentatively, she raised a hand and circled a finger through the whorls of hair that covered his chest. He jumped, then grabbed her hand.

"You do make it hard on a man, don't you?"

"I certainly intend to," she confided.

"You're used to getting it fast. It can be better when you enjoy yourself along the way."

She didn't have a notion of his meaning.

Still, he made short work of the rest of her petticoats, and moments later she stood with only her camisole, corset, pantalets, and stockings. If the heat of his eyes could have reached out, those fragile garments would have burned away in seconds. Maggie's face flushed.

"My turn!" she insisted loudly to hide her embarrassment.

He made no objection this time as she reached for the fastenings of his trousers. Her fingers shook. The muscle of his stomach was hard and warm against her hand as she accidentally brushed against him. He twitched. His breathing grew faster as she worked. When his trousers finally came loose, they slithered down to his knees. He casually stepped out of them and kicked them to one side.

"Is that all?" he asked.

He didn't wear the usual male long underwear, but cotton drawers that reached only to midthigh. From the bottom of his drawers to the tops of his stockings were revealed straight, firmly muscled legs darkened by hair that was almost as abundant as the covering on his chest.

Maggie's hands seemed paralyzed. Her plan of brazen seduction seemed suddenly like diving into a deep pool without knowing how to swim. But Christopher was caught up in her game. With a wicked lift of one brow he took her hands and placed them at his waist, at the drawstring of his drawers.

"Did you forget something?" The question was husky with his arousal.

There was no going back. Maggie pulled at the drawstring, then hooked her thumbs under the drawers and slid her hands down his lean flanks. The last piece of his clothing fell down around his ankles, and he discarded the drawers with a flick of his foot. He stood before her in naked male glory, unembarrassed as if he paraded his manly attributes before ogling women every day. And Maggie couldn't help but ogle. She'd pulled enough reluctant-to-leave whorehouse customers out of bed to have a more than passing familiarity with male anatomy, aroused and otherwise. Her husband was a bit more of a man than she'd expected.

"Well?" His mouth lifted into a crooked smile.

"Uh . . ."

"You seem to need some help getting the rest of your clothes off."

Maggie's instinct was to back away as he advanced, the shaft of his sex outthrust toward her like a thick spear. Tobacco Nell wouldn't back away, Maggie scolded herself. French Marie and Pearl the Knife wouldn't back away. Maggie knew what they would do. They would take steps to guarantee a man wouldn't be bored.

Maggie's heart raced as she reached out to touch Christopher's chest. Her fingers traced a sinuous path through the mat of hair, following the arrow as it pointed downward. When she reached her destination, Christopher inhaled sharply.

"Uh-uh, little alleycat." He gently disengaged her trembling fingers. "My turn now."

Slowly he unlaced the fastenings of her corset and threw the stiff garment aside. His hands returned to cup her breasts through the thin fabric of her camisole, thumbs tracing the undersides of the soft mounds, and then rubbing lightly back and forth over the taut, puckered nipples.

Maggie sighed and closed her eyes as an unfamiliar, delicious warmth flowed from her breasts to the secret, untried softness between her thighs.

"You like that?" Christopher asked in a soft voice.

She smiled. If she had truly been the cat he often called her, she would have purred.

"There's a certain advantage to taking a bride who is neither a frightened, mewling virgin nor a high-minded lady." His voice was thick with passion. "Touch me, Maggie."

She opened her eyes to see his face harsh with desire.

"Touch me," he commanded.

Her scheme of seduction seemed ridiculous now. A growing desire ruled her body and wiped all plans and ambitions from her mind. As if he were a magnet and she raw iron, she reached for him. Her hands explored the lush growth on his chest, the hard ridges of his stomach, the muscled smoothness of his buttocks.

"Maggie," he whispered. In a sudden motion he ripped the camisole from top to bottom, exposing her breasts. "I'll buy you a dozen more," he promised at her startled squeak.

For a moment he stood as if frozen, his eyes fastened on her breasts. They tingled and heated as his eyes traced their firm contours. When his gaze moved upward to her face, the look in his eyes made her whole body heat to the point of flashing into flame.

"Come here."

She didn't hesitate to step closer to him. Her puckered nipples brushed his chest. The hard swelling of his sex prodded her stomach. She didn't have time to question what she should do next, for suddenly she was in his arms. He bent to cover her mouth with his. Driven to get closer still, she clutched at his shoulders and neck.

"Open your mouth, Maggie. I like a kiss hot and deep."

She obeyed. His tongue thrust deep in an action that should have been repulsive and ridiculous, but was neither. It was possession, demanding and arrogantly male, and Maggie wanted to be possessed. She wanted to merge

with him, to be absorbed, to unite male and female as one
and never withdraw to the cold isolation of once again just
being female.

Never breaking the kiss, Christopher lifted her off the
ground as he straightened. Instinctively she wrapped her
slim legs around his waist. His hands slid under her buttocks to support her. Fingers strayed between her legs to
run gently along the moist cotton of her pantalets. Maggie
gasped as a desire so sharp it was painful speared through
her body. She twisted her pelvis against the hard bulge at
his groin like a wild creature seeking relief from an instinct it cannot control.

"Touching you is like setting a match to tinder," came a
moist, warm whisper against her ear.

He laid her on the bed, still keeping his position between her legs. "No," he said as she drew up her legs to
remove her pantalets. One brow curved in a devilish arch.
"Hidden treasures are sometimes even more tantalizing if
they remain hidden for a time." He leaned down to kiss
the breasts that were flattened against her chest, and the
weight of his body against her feminine core made her
squirm in frustration and need. Pinning her to the bed, he
moved his mouth leisurely from one breast to the other,
then her throat, then her lips.

"You are a hot and impatient one, aren't you?" he said
against her mouth. His hand slipped smoothly under the
material of her pantalets and found the moist, aching core
of her. One finger, then two, slid inside her. She breathed
out a gusty sigh of sweet relief, then moaned when he
withdrew.

"Hold still," he commanded. There was a new note in
his voice, an urgency that sent a thrill of anticipation rip-
pling along her every nerve. In one efficient motion he
removed her pantalets and stockings. Then he hunkered
back on his heels and looked at her, his eyes dark and hot.

Feeling suddenly vulnerable, Maggie started to draw her thighs together, but he leaned forward with a wicked smile, his body a barrier between her knees.

"I like the view just the way it is," he teased. "It seems like a long time I've imagined you lying naked on a bed, your thighs spread, with that look in your eyes—the look you have right now. You're more beautiful than I could have imagined, Maggie cat."

He bent forward and placed a kiss in the concave valley of her stomach, then lower in the nest of soft black curls that guarded her woman's mound.

"Open wider," he commanded. "Oh, yes. You are beautiful."

Maggie jerked with surprise as his tongue delved deeply between the moist, swollen lips of her most private flesh. Lightning shot from his caress. Again he traced the path, and again, lingering at the very center of her craving.

"Oh, Maggie!" His husky voice strummed along her flaming nerves as he settled his hips between her legs. "I think we've played long enough."

Desire made her want to beg him to take her and end the agonizing wait. But that was what he expected her to do—lie supine beneath him like an obedient wife. Perhaps she could provide a little more interest. He lowered his mouth to kiss her. His tongue tasted of her own desire and raw male lust. His sex tantalizingly rubbed over the path his tongue had opened.

"Not yet," she whispered against his mouth. She smiled at the surprise on his face and took advantage of his momentary imbalance to push him off of her and onto his back on the mattress. "You are a hot and impatient one, aren't you?" she mimicked.

She kissed him, and he responded by taking her head

in both hands and sealing her mouth to his. When he released her he smiled with rigid control.

"You are a little witch, Maggie Montoya."

"Magdalena Talbot," she corrected. Tantalized by a sense of power, she watched his face as her fingers traced swirling patterns through the mat of chest hair, circled his taut navel, then traveled toward his thighs, brushing by the organ that stood at such rapt attention. A low growl came from Christopher's throat as she bent over him and let her breasts caress his straining sex.

"Maggie!" he warned.

She gave him a smile of seductive mischief, then lowered her mouth to the nest of coarse hair at the base of his shaft—the dark forest from which the tower rose.

"God!" His voice broke.

Like a curious cat she flicked her tongue along the tower, surprised by its velvet hard texture. The sharp intake of his breath encouraged further investigation. Then suddenly she was pulled from her explorations and tossed none too gently onto her back.

"Enough, woman! You'll have me spilling onto the sheets or into your greedy little mouth."

Maggie smiled. He certainly wasn't bored.

"Now you'll reap the rewards of your little tricks."

Without preamble he parted her legs and thrust. Maggie gasped and cried out, feeling as though he'd impaled her on a knife. Forgetting her vow to be a temptress, she tried to push him away. The whores hadn't said anything about it hurting!

Christopher halted halfway to heaven, every fiber of his being driving him to bury himself in his wife's slick, hot core. But a fragile barrier and a cry of pain stopped him. He didn't believe it. He couldn't believe it, but it was true. The saloon dancer who teased men with her seductive dancing, the hot little temptress who had just driven him close to losing control, was a virgin. He was taking her like a whore, but she was an innocent.

"Damn!" His anger with himself spilled over onto her. "You little witch! Why didn't you tell me!"

"I did."

She had, but he hadn't listened, so sure was he that any woman who danced in a saloon was a tart.

"I'm sorry." He held her hips still and drove into her with a clean, quick thrust. She gasped, but his body was beyond his control.

"That's the worst of it. I promise." Desperately he tried to hold himself still within her until she accustomed herself to his invasion. She was tight, so tight. Hot, silky, every man's dream of a woman.

"It's all right. Really." Her voice sounded small, and he didn't believe her for one moment, but he accepted her reassurance because he so badly needed what she offered.

Slowly he withdrew and slowly he pressed into her again. She wriggled against him impatiently.

"More," she demanded.

He wanted to give her pleasure. God, how he wanted to see her face alight with the same fire that scorched him. He thrust again, harder. Her slim legs twisted around him and pressed him deeper. He groaned in bliss.

"Oh, Maggie!" He could contain himself no longer. Again and again he pumped into her. Her hands found his buttocks and drove him wild as she tried to urge him faster and harder. The bed danced with their lusty rhythm. She cried out, this time not from pain, and her muscles squeezed him in a frenzy of ecstasy as her body found its peak of satisfaction. Seconds later he spewed into her with such fervor that she climaxed again, her hot sheath contracting in rhythm with his pulsed offering.

"Omigod!" She sighed against his neck.

He collapsed on her, more spent than he'd been in his life. She didn't object to his weight.

"Maggie?"

She didn't answer. He raised himself on his arms and looked down at her, amazed to find her already asleep with him still inside her.

"Magdalena?"

With a satisfied smile she breathed a gentle sigh.

Gently he disentangled her legs from around his waist and allowed himself to slip out of her. Careful not to wake her, he washed the blood and semen from her skin with a cloth from the washbasin. Lying sprawled on the bed, her wild mane of hair spread in riotous curls over the pillow, she looked innocent as a child.

A virgin, of all things. She'd been a virgin, and he'd treated her like a whore. He'd indulged his lust in ways that no gentleman would ever ask of his wife.

Not that she'd behaved like a virgin. Christopher resisted a renewed stirring of passion that mixed strangely with affection. He had no call to indulge either desire or affection. His arrangement with this woman was a business contract. A consummation had been necessary to legally seal their relationship, but involving her in his life more than necessary was a cruelty he couldn't condone. Within a half year he would be leaving for home, and she would stay here. Burdening her with his passion, with the possibility of children, would be the height of irresponsibility.

He'd had this one night with her, but there would be no more.

Quietly Christopher got into bed and covered them both with the sheet. Maggie shifted, sighing contentedly as she snuggled into him spoon-fashion and pressed her firm little buttocks against his groin. Christopher released a strained breath. The next few months loomed before him, days upon days of temptation. He wondered if he wasn't asking too much of his gentlemanly honor.

Seven

The morning sunlight speared through the space between the curtains and moved in a bright line over the rug on the hotel-room floor. Slowly it crept onto the bed, inched its way across the pillow, and struck Maggie's closed eyes. Her eyes opened.

"Hmmmm." She pulled the sheet over her head and burrowed down into the pillow. A smile curved her lips as she thought about the night before. For another moment she savored the incredible memory, refusing the new day entrance to her thoughts.

"Mmmmm?" As she rolled over, her arm encountered the cold, empty bed beside her.

Christopher was gone. Maggie opened her eyes and frowned.

"Christopher?" She looked around the room. He was nowhere to be seen.

A knock sounded on the door. "Mrs. Talbot?"

"Come in."

One of the chambermaids entered. "Mr. Talbot asked me to see if you were awake, ma'am."

"Where is Mr. Talbot?" Maggie asked.

"In the dining room, ma'am. He said to tell you he's ordered breakfast. Should I help you dress?"

"No, thank you." These Englishmen had strange ideas of what a person could and could not do for herself. Then she remembered trying to unbutton her bodice the night before. "Wait. Yes. I'll probably need help with the buttons."

"Yes, ma'am."

Maggie hastened to don petticoats, camisole, and corset, then chose a lightweight gabardine gown from clothing of hers that had been delivered to the room the day before. She wanted to be alone for a few minutes at least so she could remember with pure and crystal clarity the experience of the night before. While the maid was in the room, Maggie felt self-conscious about allowing her memory free rein. Surely such lewd thoughts would be revealed somehow in her eyes, and they were for private consumption only.

"Thank you," she said to the woman when the last button was secure. "I'd appreciate it if you would tell Mr. Talbot that I'll be right down."

"Yes, ma'am."

Maggie chuckled as the woman left. She'd never been "ma'amed" in her life. If the chambermaid knew who she really was and what she had been doing five months ago, the poor woman wouldn't have been caught dead in the same room with her.

She brushed her hair vigorously, tugging at the snarls caused by all her tossing on the pillow the night before. A slow smile spread across her face as she tied the sides back and pulled forward a few wispy curls. She didn't appear any different in the mirror today than she had yesterday, but she felt different. She felt like a woman, like she was female personified, one with nature's grand scheme. She loved making love to Christopher Talbot. Never in her wildest dreams had she imagined such desire, such aching ecstasy, and such grand fulfillment. Marriage was certainly better than she had anticipated. And Christopher—for all that he was an attractive fellow, and he could fight like the devil himself when he was riled—up until last night she'd still thought him a bit prissy with his fancy way of talking and his manners and airs. But there was nothing prissy about Christopher at all. He was all the man any woman could crave.

Maggie hugged herself and whirled in a pirouette. She loved being married, and she was going to love living with His Sublime Lordship. Perhaps she even loved the man himself.

The direction of her thoughts stilled Maggie's happy whirling. Was she in love with Christopher? She'd seen plenty of lust in her young life, but little love. She wasn't sure she believed in love or even knew exactly how it felt. All in all, Christopher had been a part of her life for such a short while. She knew Peter Scarborough much better.

But she knew Christopher Talbot much, much more intimately than she'd known any man. Maggie purred like a cat remembering a bowl of rich cream. She didn't care whether this was love or something else, but whatever it was, she liked it.

Maggie entered the dining room with her heart racing

in excitement. She was anxious to see the warmth in Christopher's eyes, the silent communication of their intimacy. After their night together he would surely think of her as more than the price of a piece of land.

He was sitting at a corner table. The white tablecloth combined with his snowy starched shirt to make his skin look very bronze and his eyes darker than ever. As she came across the room he stood, all politeness. His face was like stone, lacking even the amused condescension that had marked it before the wedding. His eyes were flat black and unreadable. Maggie felt her heart deflate like a pricked balloon.

"Good morning, Maggie." He pulled out her chair.

She sat. "Good morning."

"Did you sleep well?"

Did she imagine a quick flash of humor in his eyes? She must have only imagined it, because his words were stone-cold respectful courtesy.

"Yes, thank you." As if they had not tumbled together in ripe passion on their bed the night before. As if she had not dared to use every part of her body to please him. As if he had not possessed her in the most intimate way a man could possess a woman. "I slept fine."

"Good. I ordered you a beefsteak and some eggs."

"Fine."

A heavy silence descended upon them both. Her eyes questioned, but his didn't answer. How could a man be a wild creature of passion during the night and a still pillar of reserve during the day? High society gents were not only a mystery, they went against nature.

When the meal was served Maggie sighed in relief. Eating at least gave her something to do with her mouth. She certainly wasn't using it in conversation.

"How is your beefsteak?" Christopher asked.

"Excellent." She stabbed the meat viciously with her

fork. She could be just as prissy as he. Just watch her!
"And how is yours?"

"A bit rare."

"Too bad." Her knife grated across the pewter plate.
The night before she would have guessed he ate his meat
raw.

Mercifully, the meal was soon over. Christopher collected his valises and her small overnight satchel and
hired a cab to drive them to the house through the wet
spring snow—already melting in the morning sun. Maggie had never been so glad to see anyone in her life as she
was to see Luisa. She had several pertinent questions to
ask the older woman about marriage and husbands.

Christopher stayed at the house only long enough to
drop off Maggie and the valises. He would be out most of
the day, he explained without giving a reason. He refused
Peter's offer to keep him company. Maggie was glad to
see him go.

"Be glad you didn't go with him," Maggie told Peter as
he, she, and Luisa walked into the house. "He's about as
friendly as a bear this morning."

Peter and Luisa exchanged a worried glance.

"Did . . . uh . . . is something wrong?" Peter asked
delicately.

"You tell me," Maggie shot back in a huff. "You're a
man." She pronounced the gender as if it were a curse.

Luisa took Maggie's arm and urged her toward the
master suite that was now her and Christopher's bedroom. Maggie looked at the big four-poster bed, the marriage bed where she would sleep from now on with
Christopher beside her. Would tonight be as delicious as
the last night had been? Would Christopher's cold manner melt and then boil over in passion, as she now knew it
could? She compressed her lips in a confused frown.

"Magdalena, tell me what the problem is. Did Christopher hurt you last night? Was he too rough? I thought you of all girls didn't need a warning about a man's passions, but perhaps I should have had a talk with you before you left the reception for the hotel. What happened?"

"He didn't hurt me," Maggie said impatiently. "Well, that's a lie." She raised her brows in a meaningful appreciation. "He's big enough to hurt a cow."

"Magdalena!"

"Well, these Englishmen—at least this Englishman—isn't as prissy as I thought."

"My dear, a man almost always hurts a woman when it's her first time."

"I'm not complaining." A bit of delicious memory lightened her mood. "Bedding a man is"—she grinned impishly—"it's like eating cherry pie, only better. Much better."

Luisa gave her a wry smile. "Yes, dear. I'm not so long widowed that I don't remember."

Maggie's face fell. "Then you can tell me why Christopher's acting like a January icicle this morning."

"He did seem rather starched," Luisa agreed thoughtfully.

"After last night, I thought—I thought . . . Well, bedding a man takes you so close. I thought we'd have some of that closeness left when the sun came up."

Luisa clucked sympathetically. "Magdalena, child, for all you've seen of men at their worst, you still have illusions. To a man sex is no more than scratching an itch. Who scratches it for him doesn't matter."

Maggie thought of Christopher's eyes burning through to her very soul. She remembered his wicked grin, his gentle teasing, the sound of his words telling her she was beautiful. "I don't know if I believe that," she told Luisa.

"Believe it, child. You married an honorable man who probably won't stoop to beating you. You have a grand piece of property waiting for you and a smart husband to manage it for you. You've been given more than most women on this earth would dare hope for. Don't expect miracles."

Don't expect love, Maggie interpreted Luisa's warning. When had she started to think about Christopher in terms of love? Only yesterday she'd vowed to make the Englishman eat his cruel words and salve the pride he'd wounded in telling the world that he was marrying her for her land. Now she wanted more than her pride back. She wanted more than his recognition that she was a desirable woman. She wanted him to love her.

A miracle, Luisa had said. Maybe so. But miracles had happened before.

Christopher had the cab take him as far as the Plaza. He had nothing particular to do in the town that day, and plenty of work waiting for him at the house. Over the past week letters from his solicitor, his accountant, and his business partner in the Pitney and Talbot Overseas Freight Line had clamored for his agreement or disagreement on a number of decisions—to repair or scrap one of their oldest, least seaworthy ships; to sell the property he'd inherited from his uncle or hold out for a better offer; and how best to settle the complaint of a certain formerly virginal young woman against his younger brother Rodney.

Amelia Hawthorne had also written. Her letter was chatty and filled with the latest gossip and social news—inconsequential morsels that the ladies thought so important. As always she was sweetly concerned about his having been gone so long. If Amelia was so concerned about him, Christopher wondered, why had she refused him when he'd proposed a year ago? Her refusal didn't sting quite as much now as it had when he'd first left

London, but reading her letter still brought a certain heaviness to his heart.

Also disconcerting was a letter from his mother, who complained of his father's deteriorating health. She asked Christopher's opinion of a young physician with whom he had a slight acquaintance. Should she engage the man's services for the ailing duke? Christopher knew that his mother wasn't so much soliciting his opinion of Dr. Holloway's competence as reminding him of his father's precarious health. She and the whole family had agreed that his mission to America was necessary, but at the same time his mother wanted him back in London where he could take the burden of the family off her shoulders. Christopher's older brother James, heir to the title, was much too concerned with attending to his amusements and mistresses to attend to family matters, and his younger brother Rodney was too busy gambling and drinking away his allowance. Elizabeth, his sister, was the most levelheaded of his siblings, but being a woman, there wasn't much she could do to influence the others.

Christopher remembered the last line of his mother's letter. *Do wrap up this affair in Mexico* (she had never quite grasped the difference between Mexico and New Mexico) *and come home to us. Your father and I need all of our children around us during this most difficult time in our lives.* Christopher didn't know which made the times most difficult for his mother—the family's failing finances or the duke's failing health. But whichever, she wanted him home where she and everyone else could lean on him.

Christopher wandered aimlessly into the Plaza along one of the snow-covered walkways that radiated from the central obelisk monument. He should be at the house, sitting at his desk in the library, paying attention to family and business problems and answering his correspondence. But Maggie was at the house, and he needed time away from that tempting and deceitful female. No, in all fairness, he couldn't really label her deceitful. She'd told him that she "didn't go with the customers," and he'd chosen not to believe her. But what sensible, sophisticated man would believe that a saloon dancer could be a virgin?

Last night he'd been perfectly justified in thinking her an experienced little tart, Christopher consoled himself. She certainly hadn't behaved like a virgin on her wedding night. She'd been enthusiastic, downright bawdy in fact. No frightened modesty, no maidenly shyness, no reluctance at all until he'd actually hurt her. Even after he'd brutalized (he could think of no kinder word) her maidenhead, she'd recovered in a mere moment and had enticed him into the most uncontrolled, fierce fulfillment he'd ever known.

Christopher flinched at the thought. If he'd known she was virgin he might have kept himself under tighter rein. He shook his head, admitting to himself that he had exerted the limit of his control and had found it woefully inadequate. Maggie had deliberately tantalized and seduced him in ways no gentle lady would dare contemplate. With her pert breasts, her round little backside, her satin skin, and that wealth of wild, silky hair, she was the devil's own temptress. He'd sensed even before they were married that she was an enticement to his less-than-gentlemanly instincts, of which he had many. The only way he could avoid further complicating this affair was to keep her at a distance. Even at that he was going to need a saint's own willpower to keep his hands off of her.

If only this project hadn't become so bloody complicated. He'd thought the hard part would be finding the Montoya heir. Peter and he had constructed a dozen alternative plans for every possibility—not finding her, finding her dead, finding her married, finding her unsuitable for marriage under any circumstances; but they hadn't planned on finding her stubborn, mischievous, intelligent, seductive, and capable of rendering a man helpless from a carnal firestorm. Maggie was a creature that Christopher had never before encountered: a woman who was neither a lady nor a tart, ignorant and intelligent at the same time, virtuous yet bawdy, a common little sparrow with the blood of eagles running through her veins. Confusing, appealing—dangerous.

Dangerous, Christopher acknowledged to himself. Strange to think that a ignorant mongrel of a female could be dangerous. But unless he exercised a bit of self-discipline, she could turn an erstwhile straightforward piece of business into a disaster of unimaginable proportions.

He finished a second circuit of the Plaza. The benches were still covered with wet snow, in spite of the warm morning sun. Sitting and taking his leisure was out of the question, and quite against his nature in any case. He had no business to attend to in town. He did not dare go to the Office of the Surveyor General to check on the Montoya claim; he'd been there only two days ago. The sensible course was to go home. Yet he didn't feel quite ready to face his wife. It had been all he could do to sit through breakfast without reaching for her hand or relaxing into a casual, fond intimacy that seemed natural after a night spent in passion. The confused hurt in her eyes had pricked his conscience, but the sooner Maggie remembered that theirs was a business arrangement, not a personal entanglement, the happier she would be.

He finally disposed of the morning by perusing the shops that bordered the Plaza and lined the streets around it. He had no intention of buying anything until he spied a necklace of black onyx set in silver. The onyx reminded him of Maggie's eyes, and the polished silver was made to set off her dark ivory skin. Almost against his will he bought the piece, slipped the box into his pocket, and told himself that it was a belated wedding gift, nothing more. Even in a marriage of convenience one should observe the amenities.

The afternoon and evening he whiled away in a gambling parlor. Christopher normally didn't frequent such places, but today he was in need of the comfort of liquor. He found an establishment that was quite refined for this part of the world. Still, with its gaming tables and bar, it reminded him of the Lady Luck—and Maggie. Every damn thing reminded him of Maggie. Even when the girl wasn't in front of his eyes she tagged along on his thoughts. What would it take to put her back where she belonged, as a minor player on a stage that was only a small part of his life?

For an hour Christopher sat alone at his table and nursed a glass of fine whiskey. Then a man he recognized only slightly sat down across from him just as if he'd been invited.

"Lord . . . uh . . . Talbot, isn't it?"

Christopher smiled tolerantly. "Mr. Talbot will do."

"Sorry. Don't quite have the hang of these titles."

"That's all right. I wouldn't expect an American to know the ins and outs of such a thing. The fact is, the younger son of a duke is called 'lord' only when his first name is used, never with the surname alone."

"You don't say. Complicated."

"Actually, the whole thing's bloody ridiculous. I'm beginning to prefer your American system where everybody is either Mr., Mrs., or Miss."

"Yes, there's a lot to be said for that, I suppose. By the way, I'm Thomas Kilgore. We met at the governor's reception a few days ago and again at your wedding dinner yesterday."

"Your face is familiar. I apologize. Usually I'm good at remembering names and people, but my mind is a bit distracted today."

Kilgore chuckled. "Marriage does that to a man. You'll get used to it."

Christopher hoped he wouldn't have to. Before too many months had passed he would be able to put an ocean between himself and his distracting bride.

"A couple of friends of mine were wondering if you'd like to join us in a friendly game of poker."

Christopher's mouth twitched in a smile. "Thought you spotted a sucker, did you?"

Kilgore laughed. "Nothing like that. Bets are limited to five dollars, tops. This is just a social game, not a professional one."

"Can't say I've ever tried my hand at poker."

"Glad to teach you."

"I'll bet."

Kilgore grinned. "That's part of it."

Thomas Kilgore's friends were Silas Colby, a local merchant, and Derek Slater, the owner of the Rocking R Ranch, a piece of property a day's ride northwest of town. The game was a friendly one. The men stripped Christopher of only fifty dollars before they filled him in on some of the nuances and strategies that weren't written in the rule book. In an amazingly short time he began to win instead of lose.

"Damndest poker face I've ever seen," Colby complained after a hand in which Christopher successfully bluffed on a pair of queens to Colby's three fives.

"Gotta give the man credit," Slater admitted. "He's a natural at the game."

"You'd think the day after his own wedding, a man

wouldn't have that kind of concentration," Kilgore commented with a chuckle.

The truth was that Christopher's concentration was sorely tattered. At frequent intervals during the game, "entertainers" performed on the gambling parlor's stage. There were two acts that alternated. A willowy young woman sang both French and English in a clear soprano, and a quintet of buxom girls cavorted in a dance that consisted mostly of high kicks that showed a good deal more than their garters. Neither of the acts was as enticing as Maggie's Spanish dance. Fully clothed from her neck to her ankles, Maggie, with her slow, sinuous movements, had far more sensuality than the quintet with all their high-stepping, panty-revealing kicks. As for the willowy singer—she was ladylike, proper, sweetly feminine, and compared to his wife, deadly dull. The entertainment only brought Maggie's attractions more sharply to his mind. Christopher was grateful that poker was a relatively simple game once one got the knack. Otherwise, he'd have lost every dollar he had on him.

At the end of the evening Christopher was ahead by seventy-five dollars. Fortunately, his fellow players were still friendly.

"You sure you've never played this game before?" Kilgore asked amiably when they had agreed to call it a night.

"Cardplaying is a common entertainment in England, but this is a game I've not played until tonight."

Kilgore shook his head. "Good thing you don't have a hankering to turn professional gambler."

"There are more interesting ways to make money," Christopher said with a smile.

"Glad you think so."

"Say, Mr. Talbot," Derek Slater joined in, "Thomas

here tells me that you're the fellow who's going to be ranching the Montoya Grant out on the Pecos River."

"If the grant is confirmed. My wife is the heir."

"That's so? Married her just yesterday?"

"Yes." Even to Christopher the implication was unpleasantly mercenary.

As they walked toward the door, Slater fell in beside Christopher. "Ever ranched before out in these parts?"

"I'll admit I haven't ranched in any parts," Christopher answered.

Slater shook his head pityingly. "I wonder if you realize what you're getting into. The winters on the Llano Estacado—Lordy, those blue northers sweep through the plains and the snow will fly so thick, a man can't see his hand in front of his face. The cattle can freeze right where they stand. And the summers get hot enough to fry an egg on a flat rock. In some of that country a man can ride for days without seeing a tree—nothing but grass and damned yucca stakes for as far as you can see. And when you do come across a tree, it's nothing but a scrub cedar or scraggly juniper. It takes a special breed to live out there."

The cold spring night greeted them outside the door. Overhead, a milky sweep of stars girdled the sky, so much brighter in the clear, dry mountain air than Christopher had ever seen in England. Kilgore and Colby took their leave, jokingly vowing revenge on Christopher's winning streak. Slater walked beside Christopher as he crossed the street and headed toward the Plaza.

"I expect you're right." Christopher picked up their conversation where Slater had left off. He didn't bother to tell the man that he had no intention of living on the Llano Estacado. "I've been in many different parts of the world," he said, "and I've learned that each has its own dangers. A man who barges into a place without knowing the land and the people is asking for trouble."

Slater nodded. "That's the truth."

"I plan to hire a competent ranch manager to oversee my wife's property—assuming her title is confirmed. I'd be a fool to waste good ranchland under my own incompetent management."

"You English fellows are more sensible than I thought." Slater's voice hinted at a grudging respect.

"And you Americans are more interesting than I thought," Christopher returned. One American in particular. Curse the woman for sticking to his mind like a burr.

"Damned if I don't think a fellow like you just might make it out here, Talbot. I tell you what. Why don't you and that pretty bride of yours come out to the Rocking R for a visit for a week or so? We're not out on the plains, but in some ways, a cattle ranch is a cattle ranch. I'd be glad to show you some of the basics." He chuckled. "Following the ass end of a cow is the same one place as another. We could get out and do some hard riding together, and my wife, Jenny, is always anxious for female company. We're only a day's wagon ride from town."

An automatic negative response sprang to Christopher's lips, but he didn't speak the words. Though he'd never pictured himself "following the ass end of a cow," as Slater so colorfully described it, learning some of the basics of cattle ranching wasn't a bad idea. It was a much better idea than waiting for the disposition of the Montoya claim with nothing to do but think about his new wife. What's more, Maggie might enjoy herself. Slater's wife might be a good example of the proper behavior of married women. Slater himself seemed to be a stable sort.

The trees of the Plaza loomed ahead of them, skeletal branches starkly outlined by streetlights that dotted the darkness with isolated pools of yellow light.

"That's a very kind offer, Mr. Slater. I'll certainly consider it."

"We'd be glad to have you. Company out in the cattle country gets scarce at times, as you'll soon find out. I'll be in town another two days—staying at the Exchange Hotel on the corner over there. I'm taking a wagonload of supplies back with me, and there'd be plenty of room for you two to come along. Let me know."

"I will." Christopher stood for a moment after Slater left, inhaling the cold, clear air. He wondered if doing some "hard riding" with Slater might weary him enough so that he could ignore the temptation of his wife.

Maggie spent the day fretting. Conversation with Luisa was useless. Whatever the subject of their discourse, Maggie always ended up complaining about having been unceremoniously dumped at the house by a husband who had promptly taken a powder for who knew where. Maggie hated complainers. Stoicism and hope for the future had always been the code she lived by. She was surprised and distressed to hear her own voice complaining of Christopher's neglect, but somehow she couldn't make it stop.

Neither did Luisa seem in much sympathy with Maggie's complaints. The older woman had somehow gotten it in her mind that, now Maggie was married, there was no more need for a "companion." Alarmed at the idea that Luisa might return to Denver, Maggie begged her friend not to go. Denver still meant danger to both of them, and Maggie had no wish to have Luisa on her conscience. Besides, she argued, once the land claim was settled, Maggie would need someone to teach her about running a household.

When Luisa still looked unconvinced, Maggie warned that Peter would miss her. Luisa flushed and looked more uneasy than ever. Sensing she'd taken the wrong tack, Maggie begged her friend not to send her into this new life alone. After a long pause Luisa agreed. Looking thoughtful and somewhat troubled, she left Maggie to keep herself company for the rest of the day.

Maggie tried to pass the time by reading. Jules Verne's *Around the World in Eighty Days* was engrossing, but not so engrossing that she didn't look at the library clock every five minutes and wonder where her husband was. Halfway through the adventure's second chapter Maggie gave up trying to read. She paced and worried, not able even to distract herself with work. It seemed that the wife of a high-and-mighty lordship didn't bother herself with useful work. Juan was king of the kitchen and shooed her out each time she ventured within. Isabel, a formidable woman despite her small stature, reigned in the rest of the house; and Pedro dominated the grounds outside. It was a sin for the mistress of the house to lift a water pail or wield a feather duster, according to Isabel, and she made her opinion known to Maggie without hesitation.

Therefore the new mistress of the house had plenty of time to brood. What had she expected from Christopher? Maggie asked herself as she wore a path in the library rug. Had she thought that one single night of passion was going to make a difference in his attitude? Had she believed that the heat of desire she'd seen in his eyes would translate into warmth of regard during the day? If she had, then she was a stupid fool. She wasn't some naive miss who could fool herself into thinking that sex had anything to do with the way a man actually felt about a woman.

Neither was she a quitter who gave up a plan because it proved to be a challenge. After all, she was Mrs. Christopher Talbot now—or maybe since he was an English lord, she had some fancy title. In any case, she was married to the man, tight and legal as a marriage could get. He was stuck with her, and she was determined to win the jackass even if she had to stand upside down on her head and stick an English flag between her toes to get his attention. He couldn't stay away from her forever.

Maggie began to doubt just how long Christopher could stay away, however, as she readied herself for bed and her husband still had not come home. The hour was late—past midnight. Not wanting to reveal to Luisa or Peter just how discouraged she was, Maggie had retired when the clock chimed ten. She'd sat at the window of the master suite, looking out at the bright stripe the moon painted on the little Santa Fe River. The moon set. The silvery-bright stripe faded. The rustlings and snatches of conversation from Peter and Luisa stopped as they found their separate beds. After an hour of silence Maggie gave up and donned the lacy nightdress she'd not worn the night before. Tonight it appeared that she would not only get to wear it, she would keep it on all night.

As she climbed into the big four-poster bed, Maggie spitefully pounded the pillow with her fists. She'd thought for sure that Christopher would come home in time to retire. In the bedroom, at least, she might have found a way to reclaim his attention.

Still wide awake, Maggie heard the clock chime three before Christopher came home. His footstep beside the bed started her heart beating in anticipation. For a few moments no sound or movement disturbed the stillness, as if he were simply standing frozen beside the bed. Then she heard the rustle of clothing being discarded, his soft footfalls as he hung his garments neatly on the valet by the dresser. She knew he was hanging them neatly, because everything His Prim Lordship did was according to his damned gentlemanly rules; gentlemen and ladies did not throw their clothing about in untidy heaps. Though last night he'd been untidy enough about their clothing, that was for certain.

The bed sagged under his weight. Immediately Maggie felt the heat of him lying next to her—so close. The bed was wide, but Christopher was broad. Broad and tall. Maggie smiled to herself, wondering if his feet hung over the bottom of the bed. She wanted to look for herself, and then touch him. Lordy, how she wanted to touch him.

Why not? she asked herself. They were married. Husbands and wives touched each other, especially late at night in bed. Husbands were bored with wives who simply lay like a log waiting for sweet invitations and pretty-pleases.

She rolled over and touched his shoulder. He jerked as though her fingers were burning hot.

"Christopher?"

"Good night, Maggie."

His voice was tense enough to concern her. He sounded almost as though he was in pain.

"Are you all right?"

"I'm fine. Good night."

He said it with a finality that chilled her heart. After only one night with her he was bored already, if he'd ever been interested.

"Good night," she said softly.

After a moment of silence he spoke again. "In a few days we're going to visit a ranch north of here."

"Why?"

"Because I have a lot to learn about ranching. There's a woman there anxious for female company. You might learn a few things as well."

What she'd like to learn was how to breathe some life into the living lump of ice that lay next to her. If Maggie was to make a human being out of Christopher Talbot, she certainly had her work cut out for her.

Eight

The Rocking R Ranch headquarters spread out over a broad, scrubby valley floor a day's ride northwest of Santa Fe. A sprawling one-story log cabin housed the Slater family—Derek, Jenny, and three children who greeted Christopher and Maggie in a stairstep from youngest to oldest in front of the cabin's wide covered porch.

Martha, the youngest, was three. When introduced, she executed a one-handed curtsy (the other hand was in her mouth), and giggled at Christopher's accent when he gave her a grave hello. Red Roy was seven. He sported scrapes on both elbows, freckles, and a thatch of red hair that all but hid his eyes. He also giggled at Christopher's greeting.

"You talk funny," the little boy said with childish candor.

"Roy!" his mother warned.

"I sound like this because I come from another country."

"Oh." Roy didn't look convinced. "Okay."

Christopher went up a notch in Maggie's regard when he unhesitatingly shook the grubby little hand that Roy offered and resisted the need to wipe his own hand after the unhygienic handshake.

The tallest in the stairstep of children was Buck, who was almost six feet tall at fourteen. His name, Buck explained gravely, was really Cornelius. The nickname came from his teeth, which he displayed with no self-consciousness at all.

After the children had stumbled through their manners, their mother sent them off about their chores with an admonition to keep little Martha out of trouble.

"What wonderful children," Maggie said wistfully.

"Our pride and joy." Jenny Slater clasped Maggie's hand as if she were a long lost friend. "It's wonderful to have you here. I so seldom have a chance to visit with another woman. This is a genuine treat. Sometimes out here a body gets to wondering if the rest of the world has up and disappeared."

Maggie took to the woman at once. She had a tall, long-boned frame and was slender to the point of being downright skinny. Her hair was as red as Roy's and her freckles just as abundant. The wide smile with which she greeted her guests stretched every freckle on her face.

"You're very kind to let us impose on you like this, Mrs. Slater," Christopher said.

Christopher's polished manners and accent made

Jenny's grin grow wider. "Just call me Jenny. Everybody does. In fact, that's the most respectful thing they call me."

Christopher's surprise was perceptible only to Maggie —a infinitesimal increase in the arch of his brows. He and Peter had both drilled her in the etiquette of never calling anyone by a first name unless you were intimate friends or close relatives. Here was Jenny Slater, whose example Christopher had urged her to emulate, every bit as friendly and casual as a puppy dog with its tail wagging up a storm. She immediately decided she liked Jenny Slater very much, but she doubted that the lady would teach her what Christopher had in mind.

If Christopher was disheartened by the Spartan nature of the Slater household, he gave no hint of it. The cabin was spacious and clean, with a large common room, one bedroom and a "guest room" downstairs, and a loft above the kitchen that served as the children's bedroom. Most of the furniture was homemade out of pine, oak, and rawhide. The only hint of gentility was an upright piano that Jenny had had shipped from her grandmother's house in St. Louis.

Jenny showed off the kitchen with pride. Above the wood-burning stove hung a beautiful set of copper pots ordered from Sears and Roebuck, while on open shelves sat the usual cast iron Dutch ovens and skillets. A hand pump brought water from the well directly to the twin sinks that stood below a bank of windows. The room was dominated by a big, gleamingly clean pine table with attached benches, where the family took their meals.

For a man who was accustomed to servants, feather beds, china dishes, and Turkish carpets beneath his feet, Maggie thought Christopher was quite a good sport about being led to a guest room that was little more than a storeroom with a narrow, rope-sprung bed and a raw pinewood dresser. A tin pitcher and washbasin were the only amenities, but Jenny assured them she would put a chamber pot under the bed before they retired.

When their hostess had left, Maggie plopped herself onto the bed with a smile. "This reminds me of home." At the inquiry of Christopher's raised brow she explained: "My room at the Lady Luck, not where I've stayed since I met you."

Christopher looked around. "I've slept in worse places."

"You have?"

"Indeed I have. Right out of Oxford I obtained a commission in the Royal Army, in a regiment of horse. For a while I was in Africa, then India for a number of years. I've slept in tents and outdoors, knee deep in mud, in rain, sometimes with a flying army of insects that was more thirsty for my blood than the bandits we hunted." He smiled. "Once I even slept in a tree in the middle of the jungle."

He moved up still another notch in Maggie's regard. She remembered the sleek, lean muscles in his chest and legs and the power of his grip. She should have known that a man didn't develop such strength sipping from china cups in an English parlor.

"I've slept in rain and mud—even snow, a time or two. But I've never slept in a tree in the jungle."

"I wouldn't recommend it." He looked more relaxed than she'd seen him since the Tabor banquet, the harshly chiseled planes of his face softened with memories. Then his eyes met hers. The stiffening of his spine and expression was almost imperceptible, but it made all the difference. Once again he was the formal gentleman. Maggie wondered if he could really dislike her that much. Perhaps his passion on their wedding night had simply been the reaction of a man to any woman, no matter who she was. Perhaps she was a fool for having imagined that something special and private had passed between them.

As Christopher removed his coat, he hesitated, then took a small box from an inside pocket. "I forgot to give you this before we left this morning."

Maggie took the proffered box. Inside was the most beautiful necklace she had ever seen—black onyx and silver.

"When we return to Santa Fe, I'll buy you a dress to go with it. You need something special to wear when we celebrate the return of your land."

Suddenly the gift lost its glow. It was the land Christopher had thought of when he bought the necklace. Always the land.

Derek Slater wasted no time in initiating his guests into the rigors of ranch life. The first morning they awoke well before dawn to the raucous clanging of an iron pipe beating against the triangle hanging on the front porch. Christopher sprang up as if a snake had bitten him, then groaned and sank wearily down onto the narrow bed.

"Good morning," Maggie chimed, deliberately goading him with her fresh cheerfulness. If he'd spent a sleepless night, it was his own stubborn fault. The narrow bed accommodated two people only if one slept practically on top of the other. Maggie had certainly been willing to cozy up, and for a few moments Christopher had seemed to like the arrangement well enough. When she'd slid up against him, back to front so they fitted together like soup sliding into a spoon, she'd felt his reaction. She couldn't miss it, in fact. His aroused sex had lodged against her bare buttocks like a prod of hot, velvet-covered iron (her nightgown had conveniently ridden up above her hips, with a little help from Maggie). Almost roughly, as if controlled by a leash about to snap, his hand had touched her.

He hadn't been truly rough, though—hadn't hurt her with that big, long-fingered hand as it cupped her breast, traveled over her ribs, slid across her stomach and down her thighs. When he brushed the sensitized curls that guarded her most private flesh, Maggie had moaned with anticipation. That most unladylike sound had broken the spell. His hand gripped her thigh, trembling as if he were afraid. He inched backward on the bed, removing his body from any contact with hers.

"Good night, Maggie." The finality in his voice was punctuated by his rolling over so that his back was to her.

She snorted in disgust—another unladylike sound. His new position on the bed had her clinging to the edge of the mattress to keep from landing on the floor. Miffed, she ignored his obvious aversion to touching her and turned over herself, fitting herself tightly against him, her breasts against the hard muscles of his back and her knees drawn up to rest against the back of his thighs. It was the only position that gave her a secure purchase on the narrow mattress, and if Christopher was offended by the forced intimacy, to hell with him—or Hades, whichever was more genteel. His whole body had gone rigid at her touch, and he'd remained tense even as she drifted off to sleep, comfortable in the warmth of his closeness.

So when the triangle clanged its greeting to the morning, Maggie had little sympathy to spare for her husband. If he hadn't been able to sleep, maybe it would be a lesson to him not to treat her like poison. With an energy in deliberate contrast to his inertia, Maggie bounded from the bed and pranced across the floor as the cold planks chilled her feet.

"Aren't you going to get up?" she asked cheerily. "You were the one who wanted to learn more about ranching."

"Just give me a minute," Christopher growled.

"I smell hot coffee."

"Mmmph."

Maggie scrambled into her clothes and left him alone to wrestle himself out of bed. In the kitchen Jenny Slater greeted her with a cup of steaming coffee. She looked dubiously at Maggie's fashionable costume—a tightly fitted long-sleeved bodice and skirt of fine, lightweight wool.

Maggie grimaced in agreement. "I know; it's awful. I can't even fasten all the buttons by myself." She turned around. "Would you mind?"

Jenny obliged.

"Christopher insists on selecting all my clothes. Englishmen really have no idea of practical."

"I was thinking you might want to ride along with the men today. In fact, I thought we both would go." She fastened the last button.

"I'd like that." Having spent several years on Tony Alvarez's ranch Maggie wasn't surprised at the thought of Slater's wife riding out with the cowboys as though she were a man. She'd done a man's work for Alvarez, and no one had blinked an eye at a half-grown girl hauling supplies and working the herd at roundup—that is, until Alvarez decided it was time for her to take a woman's place in his bed. "I haven't been on the back of a horse since I was fourteen, though."

"Oh, once you learn to ride, you never forget." Jenny regarded Maggie's dress through the steam that rose from her cup of coffee. "Not in that dress, though. I have a heavy cotton shirt and a divided wool skirt you can wear. The skirt comes only midcalf on me—probably to the ankles on you. But that's all right. When I first married Derek, I tried working the herd riding sidesaddle. It wasn't impossible." She grinned, stretching one set of freckles and bunching others. "I didn't want to work that hard to stay on a horse, though. So I gave up and sewed myself a whole set of divided skirts."

"What did your husband say?"

Jenny's eyes sparkled. "He said he likes the way they fit my rear end."

Maggie laughed. She wished that Christopher might be as appreciative of his wife in a divided skirt, but she doubted that he would.

The sun was still just a promise in the east when the Rocking R hands rode away from the headquarters corrals in groups of two and three to begin the morning's work. Christopher and Maggie rode with Derek, Jenny, seven-year-old Red Roy, and a stocky, grizzle-chinned cowboy named Curly Sims.

As they walked out to the corrals after a breakfast of sourdough flapjacks and eggs, Christopher's first unobstructed glimpse of Maggie in Jenny's divided wool skirt (it fit Maggie's rear end quite as enticingly as it fit Jenny's) probably got his eyes fully opened for the first time that morning. As their hostess wore the same type of garment, though, he could scarcely lecture Maggie on the impropriety of such unladylike dress. Maggie acknowledged his momentary glare with an impish smile and a pirouette that let him admire the fit more completely. When she swung her leg over her saddle to sit astride, one of his brows arched into a sharp curve of silent disapproval. She smiled again, until her conscience pricked her with a reminder that flaunting His Proper Lordship's values was hardly the way to win his affection. Maggie silently told her conscience to take a hike; she was having a grand time and intended to continue.

Most of the hands would spend the day pulling bog, Derek told Christopher. Three pairs would be ranging over the high valleys and timbered hills to look for mavericks and sleepers. A maverick, Slater explained, was a calf that weaned itself before it could be branded at the spring roundup. On the open range a maverick without a branded mother cow to establish ownership was fair game for any rancher to claim and brand. A sleeper was a nursing calf that was old enough to survive if forcibly weaned. Rustlers made a practice of notching the ears of such calves so that during roundup, the animal would look as though it had already been branded. When opportunity arose after the calf was weaned, the rustler would change the notch to his own earmark and brand the calf with his own brand.

"You can lose a fair amount of stock like that," Slater warned. "We'll be branding the spring calves in another three weeks or so, but even after roundup we have to be alert for any we missed. With the herd milling about it's easy to leave a sleeper in the herd unbranded. We assume that an animal with a notch also has a brand, but that isn't always true."

Maggie listened silently to the men's conversation, but her mind wasn't on mavericks and sleepers. She was too busy admiring the way Christopher sat his saddle—like he was born to a horse. When they had first headed out, he'd asked a few questions about the purpose of the saddle horn and the rear saddle cinch, proving his unfamiliarity with the stock saddle, but he rode as if he'd been raised on a cow pony. For just a moment she felt a certain pride in being married to him, greenhorn or not.

They rode steadily for more than an hour, climbing from the juniper- and scrub-covered hills of the high desert to the higher, timbered ground to the northeast.

"It's amazing to me how you keep any of your stock in this wild open land," Christopher commented. "No fences or walls. Amazing."

Derek grimaced at the mention of fences. "There's some who fence in their range, but generally fencing's more expensive than the land itself. Open range is still the best way to go. Course, over on the Staked Plains, where you'll be, you don't have problems with cattle getting lost in the brush or wandering into the hills. Get a bit east of the Pecos and there's hardly a tree or bush to be seen. Nothing to block your view. Far as I'm concerned, in that flat country you can't tell one spot from another a hundred miles away. Don't know how a man knows his range from his neighbor's. Give me the hills any day."

"Is the range on the Llano Estacado still open range?" Maggie asked.

"Most of it is," Derek answered. "Like over here, there's a few who'll try to fence it, but it's not real popular when they do. They're likely to find their fences torn down." He paused and squinted into the distance, then pointed. "Look over there."

Maggie followed the direction indicated by his arm. Two brown dots were all she could see.

"There's our first customers of the day." Waving his guests forward Slater kicked his horse into a canter.

The two brown dots were a cow and her calf. The cow struggled in a deep mudhole created by the recently melting snow. The calf, a youngster with spindly legs and a winsome face, stood at the edge of the mud on dry land and bawled plaintively.

"You're lucky," Slater said as he uncoiled his rope. "You're about to get a firsthand lesson on how to pull bog. When the ground is wet like it is now, these stupid cows don't know any better than to wander into a mire and get stuck. Most often they don't take too kindly to being pulled out, either, which goes to show how much brainpower these animals have." He swung his lasso twice, then sailed it out to land squarely over the cow's horns. "Jenny, love, why don't you drop a rope over that calf so it doesn't get the stupid idea of running into the mud after its ma?"

Jenny untied her rope and handed it to Maggie with a grin. "Didn't you tell me you'd done this a time or two some years back? Want to try?"

"Oh, yes!"

Christopher gave them both an incredulous look, which tempted Maggie to rope her husband rather than the calf.

"Just put it over his head gently," Jenny instructed. "Then wrap the end of the rope around your saddle horn."

Maggie smiled as she headed for the calf, thinking of how startled Christopher would be if she headed for him instead. The loop of rope felt familiar in her hand. It freshened memories of the ranch where she'd spent four years of her life. She hadn't liked Alvarez or the manner in which her mother served the man, but the work, though hard, had been the best part of her life. She'd pulled bog, searched out sleepers and mavericks, hauled mail and supplies in a wagon. She hadn't been the only child, or the only female, to work alongside the men. On a frontier cattle ranch everyone pulled his or her own weight.

She flipped the loop in a circle over her head, took careful aim, then let fly. The rope hooked over one ear. The calf shook its head, and the loop dropped securely around its neck.

"That was good," Red Roy complimented her.

Slater agreed. "Good job."

Maggie thought she detected a twinkle in the rancher's eye. The look of amazement on her husband's face was all that she could have hoped for. She allowed herself a small, satisfied smirk.

"Pull the calf away from the edge," Slater directed. "Roy, you help."

Little Roy effortlessly threw his own loop over the calf's head, and together he and Maggie pulled the reluctant baby away from danger as Slater started his battle with the mother, and a battle it was. The cow bellowed and bucked as Slater's well-trained horse put steady pressure on the rope. Instead of emerging from the mire, she worked herself deeper into it.

"Curly, throw another rope out here. This may take two of us. She's really stuck."

"What'll you do if you can't get her out?" Christopher asked.

"Shoot her," Slater answered impassively. "No sense in letting her die slow. But we'll get her out, one way or another."

With two horses pulling, the cow fought even harder. Then, just as her chest cleared the sticky mud, all the fight went out of her. She went limp as a deflated balloon and lay over on her side.

Slater cursed, then looked at Christopher with a speculative gleam in his eye. "She's given up and decided to die. Christopher, wade in there and get behind that ol' cow. Give her a push at the same time we pull. That might work."

Maggie stifled a grin. Christopher's brow inched upward. "This is revenge for that forty dollars I won off of you at poker, isn't it?"

Slater grinned.

Maggie expected Christopher to make an excuse. A proper English lord didn't slog through mud to push on a cow's caboose. To her surprise he dismounted and marched into the muck.

Slater's grin grew wider. "Twist her tail a time or two. That'll get the old gal's attention."

The cow bawled and heaved up as Christopher followed directions.

"Now give her a good push." Slater was almost laughing aloud as he and Curly spurred their horses forward. The ropes grew taut. "Push," he urged Christopher.

Christopher pushed. The cow bawled and bucked. Her tail slapped back and forth, painting Christopher's face and shoulders with mud and other assorted unsavory muck.

"Omigod." Maggie bit her lip to keep from laughing.

"He's doing swell," Roy told her with a seven-year-old's condescension.

The cow slowly struggled from the mire with the two horses practically pulling her head from her body and Christopher's shoulder lodged firmly in her posterior. When she was free, Christopher grabbed her tail and let the cow pull him out of the mud behind her.

"Not bad for a greenhorn," Slater said with a chuckle as he and Curly flipped their ropes free of the cow's horns. "Let go the calf."

Maggie dismounted to loose her rope. When her loop was free, she watched as Roy, with a flick of his wrist, flipped his own rope free.

"Not bad for a kid," she teased. Roy grinned.

"Maggie! Watch out!"

Maggie spun around at Christopher's shout. The cow was rushing toward her, head down, horns foremost. She sprinted for her horse.

Christopher flung himself after the charging cow. He caught at the muddy tail, the only thing within his reach, hauled back, and set his feet.

Miraculously, the beast stumbled and flipped over on its side. Christopher was flung into the air and landed backside first, ten feet away. The cow got up, but Curly's and Derek's ropes settled over her head and held her in place.

Slater laughed out loud. "Lordy, what a tale this is going to be!"

Maggie ran to Christopher, who groaned and collapsed backward onto the ground. She knelt beside him and felt for broken bones. "Are you all right?"

He grunted and closed his eyes in misery. He was covered from head to boots with mud, dung, and grass. Blood seeped through the mask of mud from a cut at the corner of his left eyebrow.

"Oh, Christopher! Are you hurt badly? Talk to me!"

Slater seemed less concerned. "I don't believe you tried to stop that cow by grabbing her tail! I've never seen such a sight."

Maggie's heart crowded her throat. Christopher had tried to save her. No matter how ridiculous the attempt had looked, he'd tried to save her. Perhaps he cared just a smidgen after all.

"You all right?" Christopher croaked.

"Oh, sure. I'm fine." Suddenly she was embarrassed by the way his eyes seemed to devour her from out of the mask of goo. "Thank you for attacking the cow."

Christopher's eyes moved from her face to the ring of faces. Slater, Curly, Jenny, and Red Roy had gathered around to grin down at him. For a moment Maggie feared what his bruised English dignity would move him to do.

"I attacked a cow." He sounded surprised. "I attacked a cow's tail."

To Maggie's surprise he laughed out loud. The drying mud crinkled around his eyes and on his cheeks.

Slater offered him a hand up. Christopher winced as the rancher pulled him off the ground. He shook his head and looked at the angry cow that was immobilized by the two well-trained cow ponies. Riderless, the horses still kept the ropes so taut that the cow couldn't charge.

Slater chuckled. "Like I said, these stupid cows just plumb don't appreciate getting a helping hand."

"Or a lift from the rear. I think you got your forty dollars' worth." Christopher grimaced and spit mud.

"Now, I wouldn't do anything low down and sneaky like that."

"And if I believe that statement, undoubtedly you have some snake oil to sell me as well," Christopher replied amiably.

Roy untied his neckerchief and handed it to Christopher. "You know, Mr. Talbot, you ain't half as sissy as you sound."

Christopher glanced at Maggie from under slightly raised brows as he wiped some of the mud from his face. His eyes were warm with a sparkle of humor that made her heart expand.

The rest of the week was somewhat less traumatic. Christopher rode out every day with Slater or a team of cowhands. He came back each night tired and dirty. The calving season was not yet over, and in addition to the usual work, the entire range had to be checked for cows and newborns in distress. The melting snow made the valleys muddy and hard-going, the timbered hills wet and cold. The range cows and steers were irritable, the bulls downright dangerous. The cowboys had their hands full dealing with bogs, predators, heavy brush, and the ever-present rustlers.

Christopher rode with them and never complained. In fact, it seemed to Maggie that he reveled in the work. Who would have thought that His Well-Groomed Lordship would take so readily to dressing in borrowed denims and a flannel shirt and grubbing around dirty, smelly, ill-tempered cattle? And who would have thought he would look so good with dirt on his face and under his well-trimmed nails, a sunburn reddening his neck and a hat line crimping his straight black hair? Maggie began to think there were several sides to Christopher Talbot that she hadn't before seen.

Some days Maggie and Jenny rode out with the men. Other days they worked at the house. Jenny could not only rope and ride with the best of the cowhands, she also was better with figures than anyone else on the ranch, so she kept the account books. She was an excellent cook, and though a German woman by the name of Gertrude helped in the kitchen and with other house chores, Jenny cooked much of the two daily meals—breakfast and midafternoon dinner—that were served alike to the family and ranch hands. Her housekeeping skills were as sharp as her cowboying skills, but she wasn't as enthusiastic about sewing, churning, canning, and cleaning as she was about working the herd alongside her husband. Gertrude willingly handled most of those chores, and much of the family's clothing, linen, towels, blankets, and other items that many ranch wives made by hand came from the pages of Sears and Roebuck catalogs.

"My Jenny's the most valuable hand on this ranch," Slater commented one afternoon at dinner. "Why, if I didn't have her, I'd never know whether we were making money or losing it, I'd never know what supplies to order, and I'd have to hire and feed another hand to boot. I've known some city fellas to treat their women like lilies that'll wilt at a touch of real life, but they for sure didn't live on a ranch. My Jenny's smarter than most men, and stronger than some." His eyes crinkled in a weather-beaten smile. "Not me, of course."

Jenny gave her husband a wide, challenging smile. "That hasn't been quite proven yet."

Christopher chuckled. "Mrs. Slater, you're an extraordinary woman. My mother considers herself a tower of strength, but if she saw what was expected of you, she'd faint dead away. I'm afraid our Englishwomen are a bit more delicate than you Americans."

"Perhaps because they're expected to be," Jenny replied with some asperity. "Men and women alike generally grow up to fit into the mold that's set for them."

Christopher smiled. "You may have a point."

Maggie thought he didn't sound convinced. She was suddenly very curious to meet one of these delicate English flowers that he seemed to think were the pinnacle of feminine perfection. Certainly she had never met anyone who possessed the qualities of meekness, delicacy, amiability, and sensitivity that both Christopher and Peter regarded as desirable, and Maggie was sure such a female would be the dullest person imaginable. Perhaps now that he was away from such English delicacies, Christopher's taste would improve—maybe improve so much that he would see that Maggie herself wasn't such a bad match after all.

For his part Christopher was rather surprised at how much he was enjoying the Rocking R Ranch. The Slaters were a charming family. His mother would have called them common, and the fashionable set of London wouldn't have been caught dead socializing with them. Christopher liked them, however—something he hadn't really expected. They were honest, hardworking, intelligent, resourceful people with a courage and strength that amazed him. The children especially won his heart. Buck, who rode out with the crews every day and thought nothing of a fourteen-year-old doing a man's work; Red Roy and his impish mischief; Martha, who toddled after him as if he were some strange and wonderful phenomenon that she had just discovered. His first night here he had told her a nursery tale that the Talbot nurse had often told to Christopher and his brother James when they were small.

Ever since then Martha had regarded him as her personal property.

Christopher hadn't been aware that he even liked children. In upper-class English households children did not impose on their elders; they were raised mostly by nurses and governesses. Families that didn't have the money to maintain a private staff for their children commonly sent them away to boarding school for much of the year. At the Slater ranch Christopher began to understand why some parents were reluctant to relegate their offspring to being raised by others.

Maggie, also, seemed taken with the children, and they with her. Red Roy, especially, developed an infatuation. At the end of each day when Roy was allowed to ride out with the men, he would regale Maggie with his exploits. She always listened attentively and showed the proper degree of astonishment at the boy's prowess. Watching them together Christopher felt a prick of conscience in depriving Maggie of the chance to have children of her own. He rationalized the guilt by telling himself that he was giving her a life that was far better than what she would have had if he'd not interfered. As the week wore on, however, he got tired of hearing his own excuses.

His marriage to Magdalena Montoya daily became more complicated than what he had bargained for. At night he could scarcely sleep for the thought of her lying warm and soft on the bed next to him. Using the chivalrous excuse of giving his wife more room, he had finally taken to sleeping on the floor, which was a good deal less comfortable and only fractionally less frustrating. If Maggie weren't so brazenly willing to participate in what most women of breeding considered an onerous duty, abstention would be a hell of a lot easier.

What upset Christopher the most, however, was that he could not hold Maggie at bay by telling himself that she was merely a means to an end, a simple, uneducated strumpet whom he could mold for both his and her own good. In the first place, she wasn't and apparently never had been a strumpet. Furthermore, she was anything but simple. She had intelligence, courage, strength, and humor—and a sense of adventure amply demonstrated as she and Jenny trekked with the ranch hands and never complained about the cold, the work, the heat, or the long days. Maggie always found something to laugh at; frequently that something was Christopher. Christopher began to wish that he had left his wife in Santa Fe with Peter and Luisa. It was bad enough that he was sexually attracted to the little scamp, but he was starting to like her as well. The situation really was bloody hell.

This wasn't the real world, Christopher reminded himself sternly. At least it wasn't *his* world. Maggie would never fit into London life, even if she had the desire. And no matter how invigorating Christopher found this frontier, he couldn't live as a simple rancher. His life was in England, and his duty was to his family—and also to Maggie, to protect her from the possibility that their marriage might produce unexpected complications that would make life harder for both of them. He was letting sentiment run away with him as though he were a scarcely breeched boy.

At the end of the week, when Christopher announced that he and his wife would be returning to Santa Fe the next day with the supply wagon, he wasn't surprised to see Maggie's face fall in disappointment.

"You'll be on your own ranch soon enough, Maggie," he told her gently. "And perhaps you could convince Mrs. Slater and the children to come for a visit."

Maggie immediately brightened. "Would you?" she asked.

"Wouldn't miss it," Jenny said with a smile. "I've never

been in those parts. Hear tell you can see a hundred miles horizon to horizon. That's something I'd like to see."

"Well," Derek said, "since this is your last day, why don't we all ride up to the east meadows? It's the prettiest spot for miles around, and besides, Curly told me a couple of days ago that he thought some of those blamed heifers had wandered into the timber up there, but he couldn't find 'em. I'd like to have a look. We'll pack a lunch and make a party out of it."

A three-hour ride from the ranch headquarters, the east meadows was truly one of the prettiest pieces of country that Christopher had ever seen. Meadows lush with new spring growth alternated with dense stands of dark-green pine in a jigsaw-puzzle pattern.

"Did someone clear these meadows for grazing?" Christopher asked Slater.

"Nope. The trees just don't grow in these meadows, even though they grow everywhere in between. Nobody knows why, leastways far as I know. The Mexicans call the meadows *ciénagas*. Great grazing country. Trouble is, these stupid cows like to wander out of the *ciénagas* into the woods, and sometimes they get into trouble there, 'specially with a new calf taggin' along. Let's split up and have a look. Christopher, you've gotten to be a fair hand with a rope. Why don't you and Maggie look through the trees on that little rise over there. Me and Jenny'll take that stand there on the other side of the creek. Buck, you take Red and go up the creek. Meet back here in, say, an hour."

The group scattered, and Christopher and Maggie rode toward the timber-covered swell of land that rose gently from the creek. Christopher inhaled the aroma of new grass and the sharp scent of pine. Maggie was not the only one sorry to be leaving the next day.

As they rode into the trees, Maggie echoed his thoughts. "I suppose we have to leave tomorrow?"

"We need to check on the progress of your claim. Besides, don't you think Luisa misses you? She's stuck alone in the house with no one but the servants and Peter to talk to."

Maggie's quick smile reflected the gleam in her eye. "I don't think Luisa minds talking to Peter. She'd probably rather we stay another week at least."

Before Christopher could figure out her meaning, an unsavory smell diverted his attention. Thirty feet away flies buzzed around a small mound of mottled brown and white. Christopher reined his horse closer. The animal snorted and crowhopped. Maggie's mount tested the wind with dilated nostrils, then tried to back away.

"They don't want to go anywhere near it." Christopher dismounted, handed his reins to Maggie, and walked over to the mound, swatting at the flies to keep them away from him. "It's a calf. A young one. Very dead. Looks like it's been gnawed on by some sort of animal." He backed away and looked around. "Wonder where the mother cow is."

"We should try to find her."

Suddenly, Maggie's horse shied violently and reared. Christopher's mount jerked the reins from Maggie's hand and galloped away.

"What?" Maggie had her hands full trying to calm her horse. She didn't see the nightmare beast that crashed through the brush, spotted the two people near its kill, and rose up on its hind legs. But Christopher saw. He froze. The grizzly's head, its snout wrinkled back from daggerlike teeth, was fully ten feet tall. The massive forelegs spread wide and ended in paws that boasted six-inch claws.

"Maggie, get out of here! Let the horse have its head!"

At Maggie's horrified cry the bear turned its massive head toward her and roared.

"No!" Christopher roared in a voice almost as loud. "Maggie! Go!"

The rifle Derek had given him was in a boot on his saddle—by now a mile away. Maggie carried no weapon. They were barehanded against the beast.

"Get on behind the saddle!" Maggie screamed as she fought her plunging horse.

Greenhorn though he was, Christopher knew that a bear could outrun almost any horse that lived. With two people on its back the horse had even less chance of winning the race.

"Go, goddammit! Do as I say!"

"No!"

Time ran out. The bear dropped to all fours and charged Christopher. Christopher ran for the nearest tree, even though he suspected the bear could climb a tree even faster than he could. An exposed root caught his foot. The ground came up to meet him; his head struck something hard, and stars burst before his eyes just as he smelled the bear's rancid breath on his face. Time seemed to stretch, giving him the leisure to regret that he never again would see Maggie Montoya, or touch her, or make love to her. Then the world went mercifully black.

Maggie's blood chilled to ice when she saw the huge grizzly charge Christopher. Her husband didn't have a breath of a chance against a monster who could kill a full-grown bull with one swipe of its paw. She would never get to know the man who'd married her, bedded her, then frustratingly rejected her. She would be a widow before she was truly married, and the warmth, the humor, the loving tenderness of which she'd had only glimpses would be forever beyond her reach.

Red flooded Maggie's vision. Her head swam with rage. She jumped to the ground and let her panicky horse go, then picked up a stone and flung it at the grizzly.

"Get off him, you mangy bear!"

The bear swung its massive head toward her.

"Go! Git!" She let loose another stone.

The bear stretched its mouth into a yawning cavern of teeth and roared. Maggie grabbed a jagged-ended stick and charged in a whirlwind of fury. The bear grunted, blinking in surprise.

"Get away from him, you flea-bitten fur-bag!"

Swiping at the stick with a dinner-plate-sized paw, the bear backed away. Maggie wielded the stick like a sword while she waved her other hand in the air. "Get away! Go on!"

With a final disgusted grunt and a look that conveyed the clear opinion that its attacker was insane, the bear lumbered off. Maggie turned and looked at Christopher, who was out cold. His chest was a crimson disaster, and blood smeared his throat and face as well.

"Omigod!" Her strength spent, Maggie collapsed in a heap and cried.

Nine

Theodore Harley flicked a speck of dust from his coat and then resumed his angry pacing of the floor. "How long am I going to have to wait?" he asked the little man who sat at an equally little desk in the painfully small anteroom.

"I can't say, sir." The man didn't lift his eyes from the document he was reading. "Perhaps you should have written for an appointment. The governor's a busy man."

"So am I, goddammit!"

The little man looked up contemptuously. Harley cleared his throat and tried to regain his composure. Losing his temper with an underling was going to accomplish nothing.

"I'm an important man in this territory. The governor will want to see me."

"As I said before, the governor is in a meeting."

"When will he get out of his meeting?"

"Hard to say."

Harley held on to his fraying temper. Why did the little people of the world always enjoy harassing those who had surpassed them in the race for power and riches? The little twit of a "private secretary," as the black-clad, beak-nosed little man had titled himself, relished giving Harley those veiled looks of contempt. Harley considered saying something to the governor to get the presumptuous fool booted out of his job. If he couldn't tell the difference between a nuisance petitioner and a person who deserved a bit of deference, then he didn't deserve to be working in the governor's office.

"You might want to take a seat, Mr. Harley." The secretary's eyes were once again fastened on his reading. "The governor may be some time."

An hour and a half later Governor Sheldon walked into the anteroom. "McNealy, get me the file on . . ." The governor trailed off when Harley caught his eye. His Excellency scowled, then rearranged his features into a polite smile. "Hello, Mr. Harley. Are you waiting to see me?"

"He doesn't have an appointment," McNealy said ominously.

"That's too bad. When's my next opening?"

"Tomorrow."

"Tomorrow?" Harley cried. "Governor Sheldon, I must talk to you about this letter! I know you're a very busy man, but this is extremely important."

"Well, I'm about to leave for an appointment. Are you sure this can't wait until tomorrow?"

"This will only take a moment of your time, sir. I assure you."

The governor sighed. "Very well. Come in."

Harley speared McNealy with a venomous glare as he followed the governor through the door.

"I suppose the letter you've got in your hand is from the Office of the Surveyor General," the governor said.

"Then you know about it."

"Of course I know about it. I'm the governor." Sheldon dropped heavily into the chair behind a large polished oak desk. On his right was the flag of the United States, and on his left the flag of the Territory of New Mexico. Behind him was a wall of bookcases laden with treatises on the law, the American West, and published diaries of Indian campaigns as well as a few volumes of American poetry. A rich red carpet softened the plank floor, and heavy draperies of a matching color blocked the bright New Mexico sun. Harley admitted that it was an impressive office, even though it was in a centuries-old adobe building that looked rather like a run-of-the-mill army barracks.

"Have a seat, Harley. Tell me what I can do for you."

"You can tell me about this business of someone claiming a damned Mexican land grant that includes my ranch!"

The governor sighed as Harley started to pace back and forth in front of his desk.

"The Montoya claim has been on the records a long time, Harley. Dammit, man, would you please sit down!"

Harley sat.

"No one paid much attention to it. The Montoyas never did anything with it even when this was Spanish and Mexican land. But now a Montoya has shown up and wants what's owed her."

"Her? A woman? God!"

"Her claim seems to be legitimate."

"Legitimate?" Harley snorted. "Governor, you know as well as I do that every Mexican in New Mexico and Arizona has fantasies about grabbing some land on the pretext that their great-great-granddaddy had a grant from somewhere or another. Hundreds of these claims have been frauds. Now you're telling me some Mexican thinks—"

"Actually, she's from Denver."

"What does it matter where she's from? You can't just hand over a hundred thousand"—he checked the letter—"no, five hundred thousand acres of the best grazing land in the West to some woman who suddenly pops up out of nowhere."

The governor looked at his pocket watch. "I've been informed that this lady's claim is entirely in order, and according to our treaties with Mexico, a legitimate landgrant title awarded under Spanish or Mexican rule has to be honored by the United States government."

Harley felt as though he were talking to a brick wall. Why couldn't the government appoint a governor who knew what the hell he was doing? "This letter says the matter hasn't been settled yet."

"A decision was made a couple of days ago—after you got the letter, no doubt. It looks like you're going to have to move, Mr. Harley."

Harley detected the slight smirk on the governor's face, and it drove him close to losing control. "Damn it all! Don't United States citizens have any rights?"

"I suppose you could apply to the government for compensation."

Harley put his head in his hands. He had to think. There was some way around this problem. There was some way around every problem in the world. He had no intention of returning to professional gambling to make a living; he'd grown too used to the luxury of having an unlimited wealth of rich land.

"What do you suppose this woman wants?"

"I would imagine she wants her family's land."

"A woman can't manage a ranch that big. Hell! No one could! How much do you think she'd take for the part that I'm working?"

"You'd have to talk to her husband about that, I'm sure."

"Her husband?"

"The Montoya girl married an English fellow—a genuine blue-blooded lord—a few days ago. They're visiting Derek Slater's place up north for a few days. Actually, I expected them back two days ago, but they must have extended their stay. When they return, no doubt they'll want to get the wheels rolling to take possession of the land. This fellow seems quite anxious to become an American rancher."

Another Englishman. Harley had a bad feeling about that coincidence.

"What's this English fellow's name?"

"Christopher Talbot."

Harley tried to remember the name of the sucker who had lost the land to him. Talbot sounded familiar, but surely it couldn't be the same. "He married the girl for her land, eh?"

The governor looked once again at his pocket watch. "I wouldn't know." He stood and brushed the wrinkles from his coat. "Talbot's a decent enough fellow, and a smart one if I don't miss my guess, even if he is a foreigner. I wouldn't mess with him, Mr. Harley."

"If he's smart he'll take a fair price for the land and go back to England. This country isn't a place for greenhorns."

"Could be that's what he intends to do. I don't know."

"Would you be kind enough to set up a meeting between me and Mr. Talbot when he returns to Santa Fe? I'd think it would be to the territory's advantage to have the ownership of such a large tract of land remain in the hands of an American rather than going to a foreigner."

Sheldon sighed impatiently. "I'll see what I can do."

The governor showed Harley out with very little ceremony.

"Thank you for seeing me on such short notice, Governor Sheldon. I appreciate your help." Harley smiled ingratiatingly. It wouldn't do to get the governor angry with him. This thing was by no means settled. Harley had been a gambler long enough to know that losing a hand didn't mean the whole game was lost.

Maggie sat in the rocking chair that Jenny had brought into the guest room for her. One oval fingernail tapped thoughtfully on the envelope that lay in her lap while her eyes watched the man who lay sleeping on the rope-springed bed.

For the past day Christopher had done nothing but sleep—sleep as though he were dead. Maggie still could hardly believe he wasn't dead. Sometimes, just to be sure, she rose and held her hand in front of his face to check his breathing. What a miracle that they had both survived such an adventure. Her guardian angel had come through yet again.

Maggie could still taste the sick horror and rage that had prompted her to insanely attack the bear and her stunned amazement when the bear retreated. With the bear gone, all strength had left her. She had collapsed on Christopher's still form and wept hysterically—until she noticed that Christopher was still breathing. Frantically she had examined him to discover the extent of his injuries. He'd been clawed from his left shoulder to his ribs, his upper right arm bore punctures from the bear's fangs, and his head sported a bloody knot where it had slammed against a rock. She'd used strips torn from the bottom of her skirt to bind the wounds, then folded her wool jacket and placed it under his head as a pillow. As she had knelt by his side on the damp ground, Maggie had promised him anything if he would live: she would be the best wife in the world, she would make him glad that he'd married her; she would be anything and everything he wanted in a woman.

Christopher Talbot was practically a stranger to Maggie, yet she desperately wanted him to stay in her life. For so much of her life she'd been alone. She was dismayed at the prospect of losing Christopher just as she was discovering how very special he could be.

Before thirty minutes had passed, Derek Slater found them, leading their horses behind him as he rode up. After he'd taken a quick look under Maggie's makeshift bandages, some of the grimness left his face. He surveyed the surrounding woods cautiously. "What happened to the bear?"

Maggie didn't question how Derek knew that a bear had caused the mayhem. "I chased him off," she croaked, her throat rough from crying.

"You what?"

"I chased him off. I was angry."

"I guess you were. Lord, woman! I hope you never get mad at me!" Slater chuckled. "That bear's gonna be embarrassed for the rest of his days for being chased away from a good lunch by a little mite like you."

Derek had unceremoniously draped Christopher over a horse and taken him back to the house, where Jenny had sewn him up. For three days the patient drifted in and out of consciousness, obediently eating when Maggie fed him,

enduring Jenny's poultices with a stoicism that moved
Slater to comment that Englishmen had more grit than
one would think, and allowing Maggie to tend to his personal needs with a grim embarrassment that made Maggie
want to laugh, even though she didn't dare. Once Maggie
realized that her husband was neither going to die nor be
crippled, she found herself enjoying the situation. His All-
Powerful Lordship was helpless as a baby, and Maggie
was in charge. She pampered him, fed him, washed him,
read to him from her Jules Verne novel and Jenny's Sears
and Roebuck catalogs, and once even sang him to sleep.

However, Maggie's enjoyment of the situation had
ceased when she'd found the letter that now lay in her
lap. In search of a clean shirt for her patient, she'd come
across several pieces of correspondence that her husband
had packed along with his shirts and underwear. All the
letters were from London: one bore a wax seal of the
duchess of Torrington; another was from a fellow named
John Pitney; another from an attorney. But the letter that
had caught Maggie's eye, the one she had dared to read,
the one that her fingernail tapped in such contemplative
rhythm, was a missive from one Amelia Hawthorne.

Amelia Hawthorne was apparently a very good friend of
Christopher Talbot. A very good friend. Phrases like *my
darling Christopher* made that quite clear. Amelia missed
the "wonderful times" they had shared. She worried for
his welfare in such a savage land as America and wished
he would finish his mission and return—return to
Amelia's sweet arms, no doubt, Maggie speculated wasp-
ishly. She imagined how the fair Amelia might appear:
blond hair, china-blue eyes, porcelain skin, a little rose-
bud mouth, a plump, feminine form bedecked in silk,
lace, and ribbons. No doubt the little English flower
never let an uncouth word escape her pretty lips, and she
would downright faint if a gentleman was less than polite

in her presence. Probably the most strenuous part of her life was making her round of daily social calls—as Peter had told her all genteel ladies did.

Did Christopher love this woman? Did she love him? Was Christopher such a cold bastard that he would sacrifice poor Amelia's tender heart, and his as well, for his mercenary plot to regain the land his brother had lost?

Maggie's finger continued to tap the letter as she gazed at her sleeping husband. She wondered if he was recovered enough for her to beat him up. Jenny had said he would be off his feet for a few days and painfully sore for a few weeks at least, but unless the wounds putrified, which so far they hadn't, he would recover with only scars to show for the encounter. He would probably be the only English lord who could boast of grizzly-bear scars. Maggie's brow puckered into an irritated frown. She wouldn't mind giving His Two-Timing Lordship a few more scars to add to those he already had.

The envelope felt cold in Maggie's hand, or perhaps it was her hand that was ice cold when she thought about the without-a-doubt lovely, amiable, meek, well-bred, dull-as-a-rock lady who had written the letter. Did Miss Amelia Hawthorne know that her beloved Christopher had married? Would she be heartbroken when she found out? Was Christopher heartbroken? Was that why he had been only distantly polite since their marriage? Was sacrificing Amelia too much to bear?

She was tempted to confront Christopher with the letter when he woke, but with uncharacteristic caution she admitted that such a confrontation would do little good. If he harbored a secret affection for this English girl, Maggie's shouting at him about it would do little more than let some of her frustration out. With a grimace of regret she gave the envelope a last tap with her finger, then silently tiptoed to the raw pine dresser and put it under his folded shirts with his other correspondence. It was really too bad she had to yield to common sense. A good yelling match might have made her feel better.

"Maggie."

Maggie turned to meet Christopher's waking scowl. His voice was hoarse from disuse.

"What are you looking for?"

"Nothing." She hastily closed the drawer. "I was . . . just straightening your shirts."

"What day is it?" he rasped.

"Still today . . . Tuesday." She went to the side of the bed and adjusted his pillows. "No, don't try to get up, Christopher. Jenny says you need to be still and rest."

Christopher's color was better, Maggie noted as he reluctantly sank back into the pillows. The dark onyx sparkle had returned to his eyes.

"We've got to get back to Santa Fe soon."

"Right. I'll ask Derek to bring around the wagon."

Christopher smiled at her sarcastic tone. "Not now, but maybe in two or three days. Soon, anyway. Perhaps I should write Peter to tell him why we're delayed."

"I'll write him. Since Peter took all that time teaching me to write, I might as well put it to some use."

"Tell him we'll be back inside a week."

"We're not leaving until Jenny says you can go. You wouldn't want to spoil all that fancy stitching she put in you." He was itching to check on the Montoya claim, damn him—the land that had made him sacrifice his boring little Amelia and marry an ignorant, unladylike saloon dancer.

She walked over to the side of the bed and laid her hand on his forehead. "The fever hasn't returned. Good."

Before she could take her hand away Christopher managed to grasp her wrist in his fingers, no mean feat for a man who could scarcely lift either arm. "Maggie, sit down."

She glanced at the rocker, which was five feet away. "You're going to have to let go."

"Not there. On the bed."

She sat, careful not to jar his abused body.

"I don't think I've thanked you properly for saving my life."

"It wasn't anything."

"To my way of thinking it was quite something. I only wish I'd had my senses about me so I could have witnessed you scolding that bear until he fled. Anyone who doesn't know you will never believe that tale."

"Well, you and Peter have always warned me that when I'm angry my language is enough to make a muleskinner faint. I guess the bear didn't like it much either."

"I guess I should be glad you were angry."

"You should be glad that damned bear wasn't very hungry." She grimaced at the realization of what she'd said. "Sorry."

Christopher chuckled. "Maggie, you are truly an extraordinary woman."

His fingers slipped from her wrist to enfold her hand. Maggie felt a warm tingle spread from where he touched her straight up through her arms and into her heart.

"I want you to know that I'm very much aware of my debt to you—for more than your extraordinary bravery in saving my life. I vow that you'll never regret trusting me with your affairs and your land."

What about her heart? Maggie was tempted to ask. Land and money were nothing, but a heart was a very special part of a person.

"If it's in my power, you'll never want for anything again."

She smiled. "You don't really know what I want, do you?"

"Tell me what it is. If I can get it, it's yours."

He would probably laugh if she told him she wanted his heart. A heart wasn't something that could be bought or obtained by stratagems and intrigue. Perhaps Christopher Talbot's heart wasn't even his to give; it might already belong to an English miss by the name of Amelia.

"When I know what it is myself, I'll let you know."

There was still hope, Maggie told herself. Christopher held her hand as though he were reluctant to let go.

"I'll go to the kitchen and find you something to eat."

Maggie felt her husband's eyes on her as she left the room. What a shame that hearts could not be ordered about as a person wished. She never would have given hers to Christopher Talbot. Or having given it, she might have demanded his in return for saving his life.

Why did life have to be so damned complicated?

When Christopher and Maggie returned to Santa Fe, a message awaited them from the Office of the Surveyor General. Magdalena Talbot, née Montoya, was confirmed as the heir to a Mexican land grant comprising five hundred thousand acres on the Pecos River in eastern New Mexico Territory. Word also awaited Christopher from the governor, asking if he would consent to meet with Theodore Harley.

Sitting with Maggie, Peter, and Luisa in the *placita* the morning after their late-night arrival, Christopher crumpled the governor's note in his hand and smiled.

Maggie slanted him a knowing look. "You look like a cat that just swallowed a bird. Is your precious family honor now mended?"

Christopher enjoyed a grim satisfaction. "Whoever said revenge is sweet knew what he was talking about." He took Maggie's hand and raised her fingers to his lips. "Because of you, Mrs. Talbot."

Maggie colored. Christopher made a mental note: scoldings didn't faze his wife's composure, but kissing certainly did. He tried not to show his amusement as she pulled herself back together.

"There's other sayings about revenge, husband."

Christopher grinned. "What is that?"

" 'Revenge is mine, sayeth the Lord.' "

He lifted one brow. "Quoting the Bible, Maggie?"

She shrugged. "After I finished *Around the World in Eighty Days*, I couldn't find anything to read at the Slater's other than the Sears and Roebuck catalog and the Bible."

"Revenge may be the Lord's, but God helps those who help themselves," Christopher rebutted.

"Does the Bible say that?"

"My mother says that," Christopher admitted. "But it didn't originate with her."

"If the Bible doesn't say it, how do you know it's true?"

"My mother is always right," Christopher told her with a chuckle.

"Indeed she is," Peter agreed with a wry grimace. Maggie, not included in the private joke, gave both men a vexed frown.

Christopher wasted no time in replying to the governor's message. He sent a note to the Palace of Governors that very morning and received a reply in the afternoon. At supper he announced that he would meet with Theodore Harley in the governor's quarters that evening.

"Do you think you should be going out in your condition?" Luisa asked.

"I'm fine. I may still move like an old man, but I don't expect sitting in the governor's parlor is going to require much strenuous activity."

"You see, my dear Luisa?" Peter said. "You Americans aren't the only ones with 'grit.' Isn't that the word I keep hearing in this country—*grit*? Christopher can tangle with a grizzly bear and then eight days later take on a low-down skunk of a cheating gambler."

Christopher smiled at Peter's picturesque vernacular. "Peter, I think you've been in the American West too long. We need to get you back to London for a dose of civilization."

"To tell the truth, my boy, I'm beginning to like it here. It's . . . colorful."

"It was certainly colorful when that grizzly decided to have Maggie and me for lunch."

"Speaking of grizzlies," Peter said, "what do you expect Mr. Harley to have to say?"

"I expect he'll propose some sort of a deal."

"A deal?" Maggie asked. "What would he have to deal with? It's my land, isn't it?"

"Indeed it is. But if American gamblers are anything like English ones, I expect he'll try to bluff when he's backed into a corner. I'd be glad to give him the same sort of a deal he gave Stephen, but I'm afraid inviting the man to go shoot himself might be considered poor sportsmanship."

"Maybe he has an ace up his sleeve," Maggie said with a frown.

"It'll take more than an ace to save him."

"I guess we'll find out tonight, one way or another."

Christopher caught a whiff of impending trouble. "I'll find out, Maggie. I'm going to the meeting. You're staying here."

Maggie blinked in surprise. "What do you mean, I'm staying here? This is my land you're going to discuss."

"And I am your husband. It's my duty and my right to administer your land as I see fit."

"Oh, bosh! That can't be true!" She looked to Luisa for support.

"He's right, Magdalena. Everything a woman owns is in the charge of her husband."

"That's ridiculous!"

"A woman has more appropriate things to attend to than the tawdry plots and schemes of business," Christopher said.

"Like what?"

Christopher opened his mouth to recite the standard lines about child rearing and creating a smooth-running, comfortable home, but before he said the words he realized how pointless they would be. He certainly had no intention of giving Maggie children, and as yet they'd established no place she could really call home. "Women have no place in business meetings, Maggie."

"I didn't hear a reason," she said with a taunting little smile.

"Such a thing is inappropriate."

"It's my land," she reminded him.

"And I'm your husband."

She sniffed to show her opinion of how significant that fact was.

"You're staying here," he told her in his best husbandly tone. "That's final."

"Is that so?"

Christopher didn't care for the tilt of her smile, but she said nothing more. Neither did she sulk. When the meal was finished she excused herself and went upstairs. Luisa followed, a suspicious pucker drawing her brows together.

An hour later Christopher donned coat and hat in preparation to leaving for the Palace of the Governors. Pedro was waiting in front of the house with the carriage.

"Are you sure you don't want to come, Peter? You worked a long time to make this night happen."

"And you paid me very well for it," Peter said with a chuckle. "No, I'll let you have the satisfaction of watching Mr. Harley lose what he got so corruptly. I only wish we could get Stephen back along with his land."

Christopher felt the familiar pang of loss. "If I could trade the bloody land for Stephen's life, I would."

"Are we ready to go?"

Both men looked up as Maggie descended the staircase. Dressed in a dark-blue, long-sleeved, high-necked gown, a pert hat tilted forward on the front of her head, a cloak over her arm, she looked every bit a genteel lady. And every bit a determined little hellcat.

"Maggie!" Christopher tried to sound ominous. "I thought we'd discussed this."

She didn't look impressed. "We didn't discuss it to my satisfaction."

"We discussed it to *my* satisfaction!"

"It's my land, and I'm going with you to hear how Mr. Harley thinks he can keep it."

"It's inappropriate for a wife to attend such a meeting."

She smiled sweetly, obviously enjoying her ornery little self. "Inappropriate, hm? You really do overuse that word, Christopher."

Christopher glared at her.

Peter smiled and shook his head. "Well, my boy, it seems that this part of your strategem, at least, is doomed. As I have a passing acquaintance with your wife's tenacity once she makes up her mind, I would suggest that you surrender gracefully. Short of locking her in a closet or tying her to a chair, I don't see how you can make her stay."

Christopher found the twinkle in Peter's eyes to be extremely vexing. Unfortunately, though, the barrister was right.

"All right," Christopher conceded reluctantly, "you may go."

"Thank you."

"But you may *not* say anything."

"I wouldn't dream of embarrassing you."

Maggie twitched a brow upward, and Christopher knew he was in for trouble.

Governor Sheldon gave them both a hearty greeting when he walked into the parlor, where Christopher and Maggie had been escorted by the housekeeper. If he was surprised or shocked by Maggie's presence, he had the diplomacy not to show it.

"Maggie, my dear!" His huge hand engulfed hers. "I heard of your exploit on the Rocking R. When the news gets about town you'll be a genuine heroine. And Christopher! You look a bit stiff, my friend. I think we're going to have to make you an honorary American now that you've tangled with a grizzly and lived. Very few can make that boast."

"I'd just as soon the bear had kept his distance, sir."

"If he'd known your wife had such a temper, he probably would have," Sheldon said with a laugh.

How true, Christopher thought. That bear was smarter than it knew.

"Sit down, sit down." Sheldon gestured to a plush Victorian sofa. "Mr. Harley will be here in a few moments, I'm sure. Marta will bring us some coffee—unless you'd rather have tea, my dear."

"Coffee will be fine."

"I'm so pleased that your case was processed swiftly by the surveyor general. Some of these cases take years, you know. It's nice to know that such a fine old Spanish family still has roots here in New Mexico. The Spanish and Mexican heritage is what makes this territory so unique, don't you think?"

Before the governor could launch into a speech, Christopher managed to change the subject. "Have you talked with Mr. Harley?"

"Well . . . yes. He came to see me while you were at the Rocking R. It was then that he requested that I set up this meeting. The man's upset to be put off the land—naturally; but then, it isn't as though he invested a great deal of money in purchasing it." He gave Christopher a shrewd look.

"You know the story, Your Excellency. I've been forthright about my motivations."

Out of the corner of his eye he saw Maggie's brow pucker in irritation. What was vexing the girl now?

"I can't say that anyone's sorry to see Harley go. He's a better gambler than he is a rancher, and the amount of land that he won from your brother carries a certain influence in the territory. I think that influence might be better administered by you. Fortunately, though Harley's land does not cover the entire Montoya acreage, he is the only person who is living within the boundaries of the grant. No one else will have to be moved."

Marta came into the room with a tray of coffee and tea cakes. "A horseman just rode up front, sir. Probably the gentleman you're expecting."

"You can bring him right in, Marta."

Christopher stood when Theodore Harley entered the room. The man was not quite what he had expected, but then, he didn't know quite what he did expect. Tall, lean, with graying hair and a pleasant face, Harley was dressed in a conservative, well-tailored brown suit and the high-heeled leather boots favored by most cowhands.

"Lord Christopher Talbot, may I introduce Mr. Theodore Harley. Mr. Harley, this lady is Magdalena Montoya Talbot, Lord Christopher's wife."

"Lord Talbot. Lady Talbot."

"Mr. and Mrs. Talbot will do," Christopher said, correcting the man's error.

"So this lovely lady is the last of the Montoyas. One can hardly resent losing land to such an enchanting creature."

Christopher didn't like the way Harley looked at Maggie. The gaze he swept from her head to her feet was frankly admiring. And Maggie smiled at him with all the charm of a gently bred lady, the little fraud. But then, wasn't that why Peter and he had labored to polish her rough edges?

Christopher sat down. "Governor Sheldon tells me that you requested this meeting, Mr. Harley. I'm sure you know that the Montoya grant has been confirmed and even now the surveyor general is drawing up a title."

Harley couldn't seem to take his eyes off Maggie. Christopher put a possessive hand at her waist. Maggie gave him a quick glance of surprise.

"So I've been informed." Harley sat and smiled condescendingly at Maggie. "It's a mighty big piece of land for a little lady."

"The little lady has people who can manage it wisely for her."

Harley's eyes swung to meet Christopher's. The gambler had what Derek Slater would have called a poker face. It revealed nothing of what he was thinking.

"So I see," Harley said. "It's apparent, Talbot, that you're a man who gets right down to business. I like that. I'm not one for shilly-shallying around myself. That's why I asked Governor Sheldon to set up this meeting. I have a proposition for you."

"I'm listening."

"The Office of the Surveyor General has informed me that the legitimacy of the Montoya Grant is not going to be disputed by the United States government. Five hundred thousand acres is a mighty big piece of range. Right now I'm only grazing cattle on a little under one hundred thousand acres, and I'm one of the biggest ranches in the territory. I'm prepared to make you a good offer on those hundred thousand acres. You'd still have four hundred thousand left, which is more than any rancher in his right mind would want to manage, and for an Englishman who doesn't know cattle or land . . ." He left the obvious unstated.

"The Maxwell Grant is over a million acres," Maggie said in a concise, confident voice.

Both men looked at her in surprise.

"I'm prepared to offer fifty thousand dollars."

"Not nearly what the land is worth," Maggie told him.

Christopher's respect for his wife's business acumen climbed a reluctant notch. All the same, he sent her a warning glare to keep her comments to herself. "I'm afraid the land is not for sale, Mr. Harley. None of it. When the title is drawn up, we'll want to take possession. Naturally we'll give you a reasonable time to move off."

Harley's scowl lasted a mere moment before he smoothed it from his face. "Can I assume that your reluctance to sell has something to do with your brother Stephen?"

Christopher's face hardened into implacable planes. "It definitely does."

"It's common knowledge here that you've come to . . . shall we say . . . even the score?"

"In the Talbot family we don't consider the loss of such valuable land over the gambling table to be a transaction that we can live with."

"Are you accusing me of cheating?"

The room was suddenly tense. Christopher could sense that everyone had stopped breathing.

"I can scarcely accuse you of cheating when I wasn't present at the game. Nor can I accuse you of aiding my brother in getting drunk, as everything I've heard is secondhand. But I do want you off my brother's land. My land."

Harley looked merely thoughtful. He glanced at Maggie, then back to Christopher. "I heard that Stephen shot himself. I had no idea he would take the loss so hard. In America a man who gambles with such stakes generally is prepared for the consequences of losing."

"If he's sober and thinking right." Christopher's eyes bored into Harley with all the bitterness he felt in his heart.

The room was still. The governor looked uneasy, and Maggie was about to bite through her lower lip. Finally, Harley sighed. "Well, I can see that I've lost this game. But I've been a gambling man all my life; I've learned to take the bad with the good. Sincerely, Mr. Talbot, I hope that you don't believe I cheated your brother or contributed to his loss—or his death—in any unethical way. Just because a man makes his living at the gambling tables doesn't mean he's not law abiding and honest."

Christopher was silent.

"I'll tell you what. Just to show that there's no hard feelings, why don't you and your lovely wife come on out to Rancho del Rio—that's the name your brother gave the place, by the way. It'll take my son and me a bit of time to arrange the details of moving out, and while we're still there we can show you the ins and outs of what you're getting yourself into." He smiled. "You may change your mind yet."

Christopher was cautious, and he saw the doubt on Maggie's face. But the sooner he got on the land, the sooner he could go home. No doubt Harley was a determined and creative scoundrel, but Christopher suspected he was a cheat and a liar rather than someone from whom he needed to fear direct action. No doubt the man would spend the whole time trying to convince him of his innocence and persuade him to sell the hundred thousand acres that he now worked. Watching Harley squirm might be a diverting entertainment.

Besides, if his wife could chase off a grizzly bear, he was anxious to see what she could do to Theodore Harley if the man stepped out of line.

"That sounds like a reasonable idea," Christopher told Harley.

On his way back to his hotel Theodore Harley reflected with satisfaction on the subtle tension he had sensed between the Englishman and his heiress bride. There hadn't been anything specific, but a gambler becomes an expert at reading faces and discerning the hidden meaning behind simple gestures and expressions; it was part of the trade. All was not well on the honeymoon, he speculated.

Harley had gone to the meeting with only a slight hope that Talbot would accept his offer for the land. A man pursuing honor and vengeance would seldom take money as a substitute. The effort had been worth a try, however. And it had yielded something he might be able to use, given the opportunity.

When one couldn't win with the cards that were dealt, a smart player could usually find an ace up someone's sleeve, even if it wasn't his own.

Ten

Rancho del Rio on the Pecos River was nothing like Maggie had expected. The river valley was shaded by cottonwoods and bordered by rough, flat-topped bluffs that were covered with scraggly juniper. East of the river the land smoothed out to a flat plain broken only by an occasional gully or limestone mesa. Vegetation included prickly pear, needle grass, cat's-claw, and yucca as well as the lush grama grass that made the land such a paradise for cattle. Wildflowers added a touch of color, and the yucca plants were putting on their springtime show. Long, slender stems—sometimes six feet high—shot out from between daggerlike leaves. Each stem sported a bright blossom. Moss Riley, the ranch hand who picked up Maggie and Christopher at the rail station at Santa Rosa, explained that the blossoms would die as summer advanced. The long yucca stems would wither down to a single "stake" that would stand several feet high—thus the land was known as the Staked Plains, or Llano Estacado. In places the yucca stakes were so thick that a horse could scarcely maneuver between them.

Rancho del Rio headquarters were situated on a little rise overlooking the Pecos, which was murky with the springtime runoff of distant mountains. The sprawling, one-story house was made of caliche rock held together with mud mortar. The roof was earth-colored tile and extended beyond the walls to shelter a stone porch that wrapped around three sides of the house. The outbuildings and corrals were also stone. Just east of the stone corrals a little stream of water known as Cibola Creek tumbled down to the Pecos. Along both watercourses weeping willow and cottonwoods struggled for survival. During late summer, Moss Riley told them, Cibola Creek dried up, and sometimes even the Pecos got mighty small, but enough water ran underground to keep the trees alive.

The ranch house was not at all what it appeared to be on the outside. Caliche stone and earthen tile made it seem a part of the landscape, but the inside of the house rivaled the most elaborate Victorian mansion. Furniture had been imported from eastern states and Europe—sofas, love seats, wing-backed chairs with ottomans, and ornately carved occasional tables. An elaborate marble mantel framed the parlor fireplace. The floors were polished oak covered with expensive Turkistan rugs. A beautiful oak table and buffet with cut-glass doors reigned in the dining room. The library was done in cherrywood—the desk, the tiers of bookshelves, even the mantel.

Everything in the house gleamed, from the chimneys on the oil lamps to the waxed and polished floor. Not a speck of dust marred the perfection. Three housemaids dressed in starched uniforms kept the house that way. Also on the house staff were a cook and assistant cook, a scullery maid, and a stern-looking, gray-haired housekeeper to supervise the lot of them.

The guest room where the housekeeper escorted Christopher and Maggie was immaculate. A large feather bed with brass bedstead was covered with linen sheets and a down quilt. A fine china pitcher and washbasin rested on the marble top of an oak dressing table. A wardrobe with a beveled mirror stood along one wall next to a tall chest of drawers with carved legs.

"I hope this is satisfactory," the housekeeper said stiffly.

"It's very nice," Christopher said.

"Mr. Talbot, you are in the next room down the hall. As these rooms are quite small, Mr. Harley believed you would be more comfortable each having your own."

"How thoughtful," Maggie said sourly as she noted the quick flash of relief on Christopher's face.

"Mr. Harley and his son are at Fort Sumner on business," the housekeeper told them, "but they will join you for supper. The meal is served at seven. Mr. Talbot, you will find your room down the hall to the right."

"A far cry from the Rocking R," Christopher said when the housekeeper left them.

"I've never seen anything like it," Maggie said. "It's—it's ridiculous is what it is." She giggled. "Imagine coming in from a hard day on the range, your clothes full of dust and sweat and your boots covered with mud, sitting down on that velveteen love seat to wait for your dinner to be served on expensive china and crystal."

Christopher smiled. "From the looks of things Mr. Harley leaves the dust and sweat to his hired hands."

"You can't run a ranch by sitting in a parlor admiring your fancy furniture."

"Most English and European landowners do just that, and they've been quite successful at it over the centuries." Rancho del Rio, however, was a frontier ranch, not a well-oiled working estate with tenants to till the land. Christopher wondered how well the ranch could be run from England, a concern that had not bothered him before.

"I'm glad Luisa will be here in a couple of weeks," Maggie said. "Once the Harleys are gone, this house is going back to a place that can be lived in. Right now it looks like—like . . ."

"Almost exactly like a very small English country house."

Maggie grimaced. "Is this what those mansions in England are like?"

"They're considerably more ornate," Christopher said.

She wrinkled her nose. "Who would want to live with all this fuss and clutter?"

Christopher speculated how Maggie would react to the duke of Torrington's town house, the huge, castlelike seat in Essex, the duke's three country houses, and Christopher's more modest but still elaborate town house and his "farm"—more of a mansion, really—in Devon. Fortunately, she would never have to see such "unlivable" residences. The thought gave him a twinge of regret. He was beginning to think all the stately fuss and clutter would be considerably enlivened by her presence.

Unlike most working ranches in the West, Rancho del Rio served the conventional three meals a day, at least to the Harleys and the house staff. Dinner was promptly at seven, and Maggie guessed that in this house one dressed for dinner much as one might in the starchy upper-crust homes in Denver. She was right. Theodore Harley and his son, Todd, met them in the dining room dressed in white linen shirts, silk-fronted vests, carefully tailored coats, and dress trousers. Maggie was glad she'd brought along one dressy gown—a wine-colored silk that emphasized the red highlights in her hair and the ivory smoothness of her skin. And Christopher—well, no one could top an English lord when it came to looking fine, Maggie decided. His coat fit his broad shoulders to perfection. His white linen shirt was startling against the dark hues of his skin and hair. The crease in his trousers had magically suffered not at all from being packed in his valise. Maggie was very proud that he was her husband. She wished that he were equally proud that she was his wife.

"Sorry we weren't here to greet you," Theodore said as they sat down to a first course of duck soup. "But I'm sure you understand that under the circumstances I have quite a few loose ends to wrap up before we leave. Mrs. Talbot, Mr. Talbot, this is my son, Todd."

Todd sat on one side of the large dining table with Maggie, while Theodore and Christopher faced them from the other side.

Todd flashed a charming smile that was aimed primarily at Maggie. "I can't say that I'm happy about losing the ranch, but if a Montoya had to claim it, surely there could be no other quite as beautiful as you, Mrs. Talbot. Your loveliness takes the sting from a bad situation."

Maggie sensed Christopher's subtle stiffening, and her eyes brightened. "Why, thank you, Mr. Harley. May I call you Todd? It would be confusing addressing both you and your father as Mr. Harley."

"Please call me Todd. Actually"—he laughed amiably—"call me anything you want, pretty lady, and I'll come running."

"How flattering." Maggie met Christopher's dark look

with an innocent smile. It wouldn't do her husband any harm to see that some men found her attractive.

The duck soup was followed by a plate of braised beef surrounded by potatoes, carrots, and onions, served with marked obsequiousness by the girl who was the assistant cook. The food was excellent, but it didn't appear to improve Christopher's humor. He talked with stiff civility to Theodore, but his face had a granite hardness that Maggie had never before seen. Sitting down to dinner with the man who had swindled his brother put him in a sour mood, Maggie speculated. Any red-blooded American in a similar situation would have punched Harley in the nose long before this—that is if he didn't gun him down. The English were so civilized about their revenge. Maggie didn't understand it, but then, she couldn't claim to understand Christopher either.

One thing she did understand was that Todd's chivalrous attention to her was making Christopher's mood even darker. The black looks her husband shot her way had more to do with Todd than with Theodore. Feeling contrary, Maggie loved every minute of the jealousy and happily carried on a conversation with the handsome and engaging Todd while her husband heated to a slow simmer on the other side of the table.

Todd was devilishly attractive, with blue eyes, wavy brown hair, and features of classic comeliness. His rapt attention to her was balm to Maggie's tattered pride. Ever since she'd left the Lady Luck she'd been picked at and criticized: her speech was coarse, her taste nonexistent, her manners atrocious, her ignorance appalling, and her ambitions childish. Even Luisa at times had joined the chorus of disapproval. At least Peter and Luisa had been kind in their criticism. Christopher had been downright cruel at times. He'd thought her a whore, a worthless slut. He'd broadcast to all of Santa Fe that she was worthy to be his wife only because of her land. And worst of all, after introducing her to desire, he'd rejected her in the most humiliating way a man could reject a woman. He didn't even find her worthy of his animal passion.

So let the His Cold-Hearted Lordship suffer when another man found her attractive, Maggie thought. She enjoyed the dinner more than she'd enjoyed anything else during the last few weeks. Well . . . almost anything.

"What do you think of them?" Theodore Harley lounged in the leather upholstered chair behind the library desk. The hour was late and their guests had retired for the night to their separate rooms. He looked around him in possessive pride, not at all like a man preparing to move out.

Todd answered carefully. "She's not quite what I expected. Neither is he."

Theodore snickered. "The little Montoya's a pretty piece, isn't she?"

"And intelligent, I'd say."

"And her husband's a greenhorn and an asshole into the bargain. You never met his brother. When he was on this land you were back East at that fancy school I paid to educate you. That Stephen Talbot had a real lack of sense. Looks to me like it runs in the family. This English dimwit thinks he can just walk in here and take this land because of some obscure clause in a treaty that no one gives a damn about. Hell, you think Mexico's gonna object to the United States keeping its land for loyal United States citizens? If they did object, we'd cross the border and beat their butts, that's what we'd do!"

"Tell the law that," Todd said with a sigh.

Theodore snorted in contempt. "The law doesn't have anything to do with it. This country's always been ruled by men who are smart enough and tough enough to take what they want. That's how I got this land, and that's how I'm going to keep it."

"So what are you going to do? Polish them both off and hope that the governor doesn't catch on?"

"Don't get sarcastic with me, boy!"

"Then what?"

"There's a couple of possibilities playing through my mind. The only thing you have to do is keep cosying up to the woman. She seems to like you all right."

"I suppose you want me to seduce her right from under her husband's nose."

"Why not? Getting under women's skirts is about the only goddamned thing you ever learned to do with any style. It's about time you made yourself useful around here."

Todd flinched. "I'll think about it."

"You think damned hard about it! That girl's the real owner of the grant. The Englishman's only involved because he married her. I'd think a lily-livered English prick wouldn't prove too much competition for you, and if he is, I'll just have to think of a way to make him less competition."

Not meeting his father's eyes Todd got up from his chair. "I'm going to bed."

"You better dream about the fair Magdalena, you hear? Just to make it easy for you I gave her and her husband separate rooms."

Todd shut the library door behind him, cutting off his father's voice. The fair Magdalena. She was fair. Fair, intelligent, witty. She laughed at his jokes, listened when he talked about his ambitions. Her skin was the smoothest ivory, her hair a fall of black fire. He imagined how the hair between her thighs would look—so dark against the white satin of her belly, wet and hot as she begged him to satisfy her.

Todd shook himself out of the fantasy. He was hard just thinking about her. He couldn't imagine that cold Englishman being able to satisfy a woman with hot Spanish blood. Perhaps his father was right. Everybody might be better off if Magdalena Montoya decided that she would rather be married to Todd Harley than Christopher Talbot. Everybody would be better off but Talbot, that is.

Christopher stared out the window of his room, the scowl on his face as dark as the New Mexico night. Hours had passed since they had left the dinner table. Maggie was asleep in her room. He should be asleep also. God knows he had tried to sleep, but the anger boiling in his blood had kept him awake. Damn the woman anyway! Married women did not make cow eyes at strange men. Nor did they flirt, laugh at the man's lame jokes, or sigh raptly at his tales of boring exploits. Her behavior toward Todd Harley had been outrageous.

He pushed himself away from the window, paced the length of the room and back, then stared again into the blackness that matched his mood. Damned if he wasn't trying to be civilized about this. After all, what did Christopher care if Maggie made a fool of herself flaunting her saloon-girl ways? Her title to the land was confirmed. His purpose with her was almost finished. Soon they would be going their separate ways and all she would bear of his would be his name. It wasn't, after all, as if a bond of deep affection existed between them.

But damn it to bloody hell! She was his wife! Some standard of decorum had to be enforced if the Talbot name was not to be disgraced. Decorum! That was what he cared about! As long as the woman was discreet about it, she could have a dozen men at her beck and call. After all, he couldn't very well expect her to shut herself up like a nun after he left. But the little witch might at least wait until he left!

Christopher's fist slammed painfully against the windowsill. The little wanton's behavior was simply not tolerable, and he was going to tell her so before he slept. If he woke her out of pleasant dreams of Todd Harley, then so much the better.

Maggie's door was shut and the room dark. Christopher didn't bother to knock. She was his wife, after all; he had a right to walk into her room. At first he'd been glad that Harley had given them separate rooms, glad that he would get a few days of relief from the endless nights of temptation. The moment he walked into Maggie's room, though, he realized that one of the reasons he'd been unable to sleep—besides his vexation—was that he missed the scent of her, the small sounds she made in her sleep, the sense of warmth in the room when she was present.

In the darkness he missed a step and stumbled into the bed. Maggie woke with a start. He stifled her incipient scream with a hand over her mouth.

"It's me, your husband." He gave ominous emphasis to the last word.

Maggie's teeth bit into the fleshy part of Christopher's palm.

"Ouch. What the . . . ?"

"Oh. It is you."

"Of course it's me. I just told you it was." He lit the oil lamp. "There. Satisfied?"

Maggie blinked, looking half asleep. "Sorry. Where I come from, when some man sneaks up on you in the middle of the night, you defend yourself first and ask who it is later." She tossed her mane of tousled hair out of her face. "What are you doing here, anyway?"

Christopher could scarcely help being distracted by her

appealing disarray. He remembered too well the fragrance of the silky hair that cascaded over her shoulders. The buttons down the front of her nightdress were unfastened. The disordered garment hung off one shoulder and revealed the upper swell of a pert breast. Her lips were sultry with sleep, her eyes dark and heavy.

"I . . ." He was hard pressed to remember his anger, but what he'd had to say had seemed extremely important just minutes ago. "I was not at all pleased with your behavior at the dinner table."

She smiled sweetly, as if she didn't know exactly to what he was referring.

His anger began to build once again. "What did you think you were doing?"

"Being friendly?"

The imp actually sounded satisfied with herself.

"You acted like a saloon girl."

She had the nerve to look indignant. He got even madder.

"Married ladies do not flirt with men who are not their husbands. They do not bat their eyelashes and laugh at some man's stupid jokes; they do not hang on his every word as though he were a prophet, and they bloody damn well do not act as though they would get on their backs at the twitch of his little finger!"

"Tch, tch. And you accuse *me* of vulgar language!"

"Damn it, Maggie!"

"I was just being friendly. Just because Theodore Harley is a villain doesn't mean his son is also."

"That's not the point! You behaved like a whore!"

Maggie's eyes flashed like the glint of hot sun on a knife blade. "You of all people ought to know I'm not and never was a whore."

"Then why are you behaving like one?"

"I don't think your blood is warm enough for you to

know how a whore behaves! I was being friendly. People in the West have a habit of being friendly to each other. We're warm, we're alive, we value companionship—unlike some cold-fish foreigners I could name."

"What do you mean by that?"

She swung herself out of bed and confronted him from the height of her imposing sixty-two inches.

"I mean that if wives are supposed to behave a certain way, then surely some very basic standards apply to husbands as well."

Unfortunately for Christopher, she was standing directly in front of the lamp. The soft light shone through her thin nightdress and silhouetted her curves like a halo. Another kind of heat began to boil through the cauldron of his anger.

"For instance," she continued tartly, "a proper husband doesn't treat his wife like she has the French pox. He also doesn't embarrass her in front of half of the population of Santa Fe by announcing that she's worth no more to him than a piece of New Mexico dirt. Proper husbands at least pretend to the world that they have some affection for their wives, even if they don't. And I've heard that most living, breathing men are not adverse to a bit of a cuddle with a girl even if she's not quite the refined, quality lady that their well-bred taste prefers."

"I am trying to hold my temper and be civilized!"

"Bosh! Do you have enough real blood in your veins to have a temper?"

"I am not cold-blooded! Anything but! Civilized men do not sacrifice reason to their animal lusts. I am trying to be unselfish and considerate of your future."

"Unselfish? Considerate? Is that what you think you are? Lordy! I don't understand you at all. You English are hardly human, as far as I'm concerned. Don't talk to me about how a wife behaves until you've learned a few lessons about being a husband!"

She propped a hand on one slender hip and tilted her head with saucy indignation. She was truly angry, Christopher realized. The seductiveness of her pose and her voice were simply a side effect. The madder she got, the hotter became his loins, his desire growing hand in hand with his vexation. Damn the little tart, anyway. She wanted a cuddle? Maybe he should give her one. She didn't understand his gentlemanly sacrifice? Perhaps he should throw good intentions to the wind and indulge his instincts while he could. His groin caught fire at the very thought.

"You think I don't have real blood running through my veins?" he asked ominously. "You think I'm made of stone? Of ice?"

The heat of his desire reflected in Maggie's eyes as a sudden flash of surprise.

"Don't look so amazed, wife. I thought you wanted me to act more the husband."

Maggie's surprise melted quickly into a smile of seductive challenge. He tried to imagine a well-bred lady smiling such a primitive invitation and found that right now he didn't want a well-bred lady. He wanted Maggie. His arms went around her. She melted against him, sweet as warm honey. No longer thinking, he lowered his mouth to take hers. She opened to admit him, her tongue touching his in tiny darting attacks that made him groan with need.

They fell together on the bed. Her nightdress conveniently bunched above her hips. Satiny warm skin met his seeking hands. In an instant her strong legs wrapped around him and she arched against his aching groin. Through the soft material of his dressing robe he could feel her hot, enticing wetness. He had only to part the robe and they would be flesh on flesh, and seconds later joined in a furnace of passion.

"Oh, Christopher, I do love—"

His mouth swooped down on hers to cut off her declaration. Cold rationality intruded on his passion, cooling the heat just enough to let him realize what she had wanted to say. He didn't want a declaration of love. He didn't want her love. He didn't want the silken web she would spin if he let her.

Carefully, painfully, he separated himself from her warmth. Shaking his head like a man awakening from a trance, he climbed off the bed.

"Christopher?" Maggie's face was transparent with hurt. He didn't want to hurt her, but Lord, he didn't want to love her either.

"Maggie." Her name came out of his throat in a hoarse whisper. "Maggie, you don't understand."

She folded in on herself like an injured blossom. "You're right. I don't understand."

Christopher turned away, unable to meet her eyes. "Maggie," he said to the impartial wall, "what we have is a business arrangement more than a marriage. Treating it like something it isn't will only bring grief to both of us." *Coward*, he thought, hating his own lack of courage to face her. He could feel her eyes on his back like a lead weight.

"You asked me to marry you and I said yes. The reasons don't matter."

Were there tears in her voice? Damnation. Why wasn't she the mercenary, hardened saloon girl he'd first thought her? The situation would be so much easier for both of them if she were.

"We took vows in a church," she reminded him. "You didn't hire me to play a part. You didn't buy my services with an indenture. You married me. That should mean something."

"It means something; it means I'm responsible for your welfare, and I intend to live up to that responsibility. Maggie, I'm not a lovesick swain and you're not a girl who should be given to romantic fantasies. Be practical. I know what's best for both of us. Don't fight me like this."

"I didn't think what we were doing was fighting," she said tartly.

He sighed and turned around. Her cheeks were wet. He didn't want to notice, but he did. "You're a truly extraordinary woman, Maggie. I don't think I've ever met anyone like you. I'm very fond of you; and I'm indebted to you. That's why I don't want to see you hurt."

Her silence was an accusation.

"I promise that someday I'll turn you loose to live life the way you see fit, and you'll have everything you need to make you happy. Just bear with me for a little while longer."

"I really don't understand Englishmen," she whispered as he turned toward the door.

Christopher closed the door behind him and leaned back against its solid support, feeling as though he'd just left a battle zone. He'd commanded his horse regiment through easier battles than the one he'd just been through. Knowing well that he wouldn't sleep, he headed back to his own bed.

Maggie stuck out her tongue at the door as it closed behind her husband. Englishmen were not normal, sane men; she was convinced of that now. They looked and sounded like normal people, but they were a breed apart.

Christopher did want her. She'd learned that much tonight. His heart, if he had one, might belong to the perfect Miss Amelia Hawthorne, but he wanted Maggie with a man's desire. That was something, she supposed.

She wasn't about to give up. Magdalena Montoya was not a quitter, and she wasn't easily beaten. If she could just get His Gentlemanly Lordship to act on his passion, she might eventually capture his heart as well. After all, she was his wife. Who was in a better position to win his love? Miss Perfect was thousands of miles away.

Maggie got back into bed and pulled the quilt up under her chin. She had accomplished something tonight. Jealousy over Todd Harley had almost driven Christopher into her arms. If a small dose had almost worked, then surely a larger dose of the same medicine would do the trick.

She smiled to herself as she fell asleep.

The next morning, when Theodore and Todd conducted the new owners on a tour of the nearer reaches of Rancho del Rio, Maggie felt intensely alive. She enjoyed the morning birdsong, the fresh, cool air, the wide sky, and the warm scent of the horses. Most of all she enjoyed the dark circles that cast Christopher's eyes into even deeper shadow than usual. He looked as though he hadn't slept a wink. That was a good sign. She, on the other hand, had slept like a log, confident in her eventual victory.

Maggie rode comfortably astride a little bay mare with a smooth gait and an obliging nature. When Todd had chivalrously helped her mount (almost elbowing Christopher out of the way for the honor), he had expressed admiration for her costume. Maggie and Luisa had sewn up five sturdy divided skirts, copying Jenny Slater's pattern.

"How very sensible," Todd had exclaimed. "And extremely becoming."

Christopher gave the pair of them a black look, but if Todd noticed he gave no clue. Maggie simply smiled at her husband in what she considered a very ladylike manner.

Theodore Harley and his son showed a surprising lack of animosity about losing the land. With possessive pride they showed the Talbots a windmill about an hour's ride from the ranch headquarters. Creeks were few and far between, and away from the Pecos River much of the water for the cattle came from wells. The water was lifted from the well by the windmill and spilled into a large watering tank for the cattle.

"There's windmills all over this range," the older Harley told them. "Highest things for miles around."

"Did you build them?" Christopher asked coldly.

"Actually, your brother did."

Maggie wasn't surprised. Theodore Harley reminded her of a parasite. He lived off the land without improving it. For all the luxury of the house and its efficient staff, the ranch hands whom she had seen so far that morning seemed a sullen, shoddy lot. She had noticed also that the barn and one of the corrals needed repairs.

Todd himself commented on his father's lack of enthusiasm for ranching as he rode knee to knee with Maggie. The younger Harley had made it a point to stay by her side since they'd started on the morning's ride.

"Father's a city man at heart," he told Maggie. "He loves fine wine, fancy clothes, servants bowing and scraping. He doesn't much like to get his hands dirty."

"What about you?" Maggie asked.

"Me? I love it out here. I'm out riding with the hands all the time. In fact, there's a number of improvements I would have made if Father had given me the authority." He didn't specify just exactly what those improvements were, but his eyes roved over the flat grassland with a fervent glow. "If I'd just had the money and the authority, I could have made this into a right dandy working ranch, not just a two-bit cattle operation that just barely supports my father's taste in luxuries." His fervent gaze came to rest on her, and for the first time Maggie felt slightly uneasy.

Still, she was glad to notice that Christopher's face was stony, and whenever he glanced at the two of them his face was black with jealousy—at least Maggie hoped that sour look was jealousy.

They rode for most of the day looking at windmills and wells, scattered bunches of cattle, and endless, flat grassland. In places antelope shared the range with the cattle. More than once Maggie spotted the tawny flash of a coyote running through the grass, and cottontails abounded. Todd warned her about the nasties to watch out for: rattlers, tarantulas, scorpions (there were some living in the walls of the stone ranch house, he said), poisonous Gila monsters, and sidewinders. Just as dangerous were bobcats and pumas. Skunks were also a nuisance if one had to sleep outside. Wolves as well, though he assured her that wolves almost never attacked a human being. They preferred to feed on the weak and old cattle that fell behind the herd.

At midmorning they spotted a swift flash of tawny brown darting through the grass a long stone's throw away—a small pack of coyotes. Todd indulged himself in a bit of target practice without managing to hit one of the creatures. He flushed, and Maggie tried not to smile at his ineptitude. She'd been rooting for the coyotes.

"Those varmints are harder to hit than anything I know. Look at the devils! They're circling back to give me another round. You'd think they were human, the way they goad a man." A slow smile crept over his face. "Mr. Talbot, why don't you try your hand?" He nodded to the holstered Navy Colt that rested against Christopher's thigh. Theodore had insisted that he take it that morning, telling him that no man went unarmed in this country. The ex-gambler had found great amusement in explaining the basic principles of aiming and firing the pistol. "Think you can hit one of the beasts?" Todd asked condescendingly.

"I don't see why I should try," Christopher said. "Are they a serious threat to the herd?"

"Nah. Mostly they're just good target practice."

"I think I'd prefer to practice on targets that don't bleed when you hit them."

Todd snorted his contempt. "You need to be less squeamish if you plan to survive in this country," he warned. "Around here a man survives on his wits and his gun hand. A man who can't handle a gun isn't considered a man in these parts."

Todd glanced at Maggie to see if he had scored a point, but the effectiveness of his statement was suddenly diminished by a quiet laugh from Christopher.

"I wondered why every fellow in this part of the world swaggered about with a pistol hugging his leg. It's proof of manhood, is it? In England we don't feel the need to display our manhood quite so blatantly."

Maggie almost laughed at the look of confusion on Todd's face. The younger Harley suspected that he'd just been insulted, but he wasn't quite sure how.

They ate lunch at a line camp. No one was there, but the little sod hut was stocked with jerky, salt pork, beans, and flour for the hands that rode line and might need to spend the night there. The size of Rancho del Rio's range often precluded the cowboys from returning to ranch headquarters for days at a time, so a series of camps dotted the borders of the Rancho del Rio range.

Maggie noted that the flour was weevily, the beans had been invaded by centipedes, and the jerky and salt pork had been gnawed on by some four-footed passerby who had left tracks in the dust on the floor. She wondered how long it had been since the camp had been restocked. Had this been one of the improvements that Todd had wanted to make?

After lunch they were overtaken by a bank of gray clouds that had spent the morning sitting on the eastern horizon. The afternoon turned cool and drizzly. Cattle turned their tails to the wind and stood in stoic groups. There was no shelter from the rain for either cattle or humans. Maggie was happy when they rode back into the ranch yard and a half-grown Mexican boy dashed out of the barn to take their horses. She was ready for a hot bath and dinner.

"You haven't even seen a fraction of the ranch," Todd told Maggie, as they walked toward the house, "and your land extends far beyond where we've been ranging the cattle. Your grant almost rivals 'Jingle-Bob' Chisum's outfit for size, I'd think. I've heard his range stretches from the Pecos River all the way west to the mountains." He added with a smile, "I hope your husband can do this place justice when he takes over the management. One wouldn't expect an Englishman to know very much about ranching, though, would one?"

It wasn't until she was comfortably soaking in a brass tub in her room that Maggie realized she'd scarcely spoken to her husband all day long. Todd had monopolized her attention, and she had allowed it. Being the object of male admiration was a pleasant change from Christopher's coldness.

She had kept an ear closely tuned to the conversation between Christopher and the older Harley, though. They'd negotiated a fair price to be paid Harley for improvements on the land and the cattle, which of course were not included in the grant. Harley wanted entirely too much money, Maggie had thought, especially considering that the improvements had been made mostly by Christopher's brother and the cattle had belonged to him as well. But, as spoils in a poker game, they were legally Harley's. Christopher had managed to whittle the gambler down to a reasonable price, and Harley consented to think it over. Her husband had learned much about the business end of ranching from Derek and Jenny Slater. Christopher might be a jackass, but he was a smart jackass. Maggie couldn't help but be proud of his acumen. He would do better as a rancher than Todd gave him credit for.

If only Maggie could get him to do better as a husband!

Eleven

By the time dinner was served—at precisely seven o'clock—Maggie was more tired than she'd been in a long time. She'd forgotten how much a full day in the saddle took out of a person, even though one would think that the horse was doing all the work.

Todd greeted Maggie warmly when she appeared in the dining room. He immediately tried to take her arm but was neatly cut off by Christopher.

"If you don't mind," Christopher said to him with cold civility. He took Maggie's arm and led her to the table.

"Of course not." Looking rather miffed, Todd

sat across from them as Christopher seated Maggie next to himself.

Maggie was glad that neither Todd nor Christopher expected her to carry on a conversation during dinner. She was too tired, and the two men were occupied in their own silent hostility. Theodore had a smile of satisfaction on his face as he observed the tensions. Maggie suspected that he'd like nothing better than for her to fall madly in love with his son and kick Christopher out of her life on his stiff English behind, but that wasn't going to happen. Todd was all right. Handsome, attentive, smooth talking, he would be a balm for any woman's pride. But that was all. For all his faults Christopher struck a chord deep within her that no other man had ever managed. Todd was all surface polish. Shallow. Christopher was a cold block of steel, but he had depth and heart when he cared to reveal them.

Right after the main course of broiled game hens was served, Maggie began to notice a buzz in the room—despite the lack of conversation. She looked at her wineglass. Had she emptied it twice? Or was it three times? She couldn't remember. It was a good thing no one expected her to stay on a horse after dinner, as tipsy as she felt.

As apple pie was served, Theodore made an attempt at conversation. "Mrs. Talbot, where did you live in Denver before you met your husband? I'm quite familiar with the town, myself. Quite fond of it, also."

"Fourteenth Street," Maggie lied without hesitation. "I lived there with friends after my mother died."

"You must have been terribly distressed to lose the last of your family. I understand your father died when you were very young."

"When I was a year old. My mother died of pneumonia when I was fourteen."

"Had she remarried?"

"No. She was . . . a professional dancer."

Christopher gave her a sharp look.

"Your mother was a dancer on the stage?" Todd asked.

"Yes. She was very famous." A few embellishments didn't do any harm, Maggie decided.

"How exciting! You must have been very proud of her. Did you ever get to see her dance?"

"All the time. Sometimes I danced with her. She taught me to dance before I could walk, almost—the traditional Spanish dance that has been danced in Andalusia for a long time."

"Flamenco?" Todd asked.

"Yes, that's it." The wine brought Maggie's memories into a focus that was larger than life. She forgot the dingy saloons and rowdy audiences, the beer-stained stages— when they'd had a stage at all. She only remembered dancing with her beautiful mother while the onlookers applauded raucous approval. "The audiences liked to see us dance together."

"I'm entranced," Todd declared.

Christopher did not look entranced, however. Maggie saw the warning in his eyes.

"I'm quite good with a guitar," Todd said. "If I played, would you dance for us? Father and I would be extremely flattered."

"Magdalena, that would not be appropriate," Christopher chided.

There was that word again. *Appropriate*. Everything in Christopher's world had to be appropriate.

"Don't be silly, Christopher. Dancing is always appropriate."

Maggie ignored her husband's warning glare. The wine had overtaken her reason. Once dancing had been her life. The world had been harsher then, but not nearly as complex. The urge to dance again seized her irresistibly. "Of course I'll dance for you. I'd love to."

Maggie danced her heart out. Todd was better with the guitar than she could have believed, and he knew all the pieces that she used to dance to in the Lady Luck, some even that her mother had once danced to. After the first tentative five minutes of the performance she kicked her shoes off and got serious about the dancing. The spell took her as it had so often before, making her forget where she was and who she was. Her weariness melted away; her troubles dissolved in the music. She didn't feel the weight of Christopher's eyes, or remember that when she'd gone to her room to change into a loose cotton bodice and skirt (one couldn't dance properly in tight-fitting silk!) he'd emphatically forbidden her to make an exhibition of herself. Christopher hadn't learned yet that forbidding Maggie to do something only ensured that she would do it. Neither did she note the speculative gaze of Theodore Harley or the rapt attention of his son as he plucked and strummed the strings of the guitar. Maggie danced into another world and was glad to be there.

The flagstones of the patio were rough against the soles of her bare feet. The cool night air kissed the skin of her bare legs. Maggie swayed and strutted, pirouetted, wove a graceful pattern with her arms. How she had missed the dance! She hadn't realized how much. As she gave her body over to the music she felt herself become whole once again. And when the music ended, for a brief moment she remained perfectly still, as if all her animation had come from the music. When it stopped, she became a statue, a carving of ivory with hair of black curling silk.

The three men applauded, catapulting her back into the real world. Todd's face was rapt, his eyes bright. Christopher clapped politely, but Maggie detected the angry twitch of a muscle in his jaw. His gaze was full of fury and shadowed by passion. She had moved him with her dance, she realized, and he hated her for doing it. A sudden revelation hit her with the force of a hammer blow. Christopher not only did not love her, he didn't want to love her. She was below him, dirt beneath his boots. He didn't touch her because he didn't want to become entangled with trash, and when his own passions threatened to betray him, he cut them off just as he would have cut off a foul, gangrenous hand. The more she made him want her, the more he would hate her.

Abruptly she turned away from his gaze. This blaze of awful truth made her want to cry, but she couldn't allow herself to be so weak. She lifted her chin and smiled. "That's how my mother taught me to dance. I'm not half as good as she was."

"Then your mother must have been a wonder," Todd said.

"Yes, indeed," Theodore agreed heartily. "My dear, you could have been on the stage in San Francisco or New York."

Maggie was in no mood to be cheered by Harley's vindication of her childish fantasies. She just wanted to be alone, someplace where she could cry in private, where Christopher could no longer fix her with his furious, contemptuous eyes. She struggled to remain dry eyed and calm.

"Thank you for playing, Todd. Now, if you gentlemen will excuse me, it's been a long day, and I'm danced out. I believe I'll retire."

Maggie expected Christopher to follow her to her room. She had no hopes now as she'd had earlier that he would fall into her arms. No. He would want to scold her, to tell her that her flirting with Todd today had been contemptible behavior, that her dance had been coarse, unladylike, and something he would have expected of a saloon dancer. Her spirits hit bottom as she waited for him to come, then sank even lower when he didn't. She donned her nightdress, brushed her hair, washed her face with the clean water in the basin, and still he didn't come. He hated her so that right now he didn't trust himself even to yell at her. After all, she thought miserably, if he killed her, his right to his precious land might be in doubt.

Maggie blew out the lamp and crawled into bed. How long she lay there she didn't know. The minutes labored by. Maybe hours. Sleep didn't come. How was she going to solve the problem of a husband who despised her, who with every flash of natural desire despised her even more? How could she deal with loving a man who would never love her, didn't want to love her, thought she was eminently unworthy of his affection? And why had she been stupid enough to love him in the first place?

Her guardian angel had really slipped this time.

Finally Maggie gave up on sleep. Restless and unhappy, she donned a wool robe and went out to the patio where she had so happily danced only a few hours before. Stone benches squatted beside a rather lame garden of shrubs and a few flowers that were just beginning to bloom. Maggie chose the bench farthest from the house and sat. She blew out the lamp that had guided her way through the house. A cool little breeze smelled damp from the afternoon's rain, though the clouds had long since gone. The moon was bright and bathed the outbuildings and corrals in a milky light. From horizon to horizon the sky was swathed in stars.

Maggie swung her feet back and forth, only now noticing that she had forgotten her shoes. Never in a million years would she learn to be a lady. Christopher was right.

She was born trash, the daughter of trash, and trash she would remain. No wonder he didn't want to dirty his hands with her.

"Maggie?"

She started at Todd's voice. Couldn't a girl be left alone to feel sorry for herself?

"I was on my way to the kitchen for a drink and saw you come this way. Are you unwell?"

"I'm fine." *Just leave me alone*, she thought.

"We obviously worked you too hard today. It was selfish of me to ask you to dance. Have we tired you past the point where you can sleep?"

"I'm fine," she insisted. *Go away*.

Uninvited, he sat down beside her. He still wore his dinner clothes and smelled faintly of shaving lather. Why would a man shave in the middle of the night? Maggie wondered.

"What's this?" His finger touched her cheek. Surprised, she flinched away. "You've been crying."

She hadn't been aware of it, but she might have been.

"That bastard has been abusing you!"

"Todd!"

"Pardon me, Maggie. I didn't mean to use such language in the hearing of a lady. But it just makes me so angry to think of that foreigner abusing you."

"He doesn't abuse me!"

"Then why are you crying? I saw his anger tonight. He's jealous, isn't he? What did he say that distresses you so?"

"He didn't say a thing." At least tonight he hadn't. On other occasions he had said plenty. Only tonight had she realized the meaning of the words. She got up to leave.

"Don't go, Maggie. I didn't mean to scare you away."

"Don't be silly. You don't scare me."

"Then sit down."

Maggie sat. She really didn't want to face another attempt to sleep. This time when she sat it seemed that Todd had moved closer than before.

"Maggie, it's painful for me to say this. Probably even more painful for you to hear it. But has it ever occurred to you that Christopher Talbot might have married you only to get this land?"

Maggie chuckled, and even to her own ears it was a humorless, bitter sound.

"He would be a fool, I know. Any man in his right mind would fall in love with you. The land wouldn't matter. But this Englishman is a cold fish, it seems."

"Todd, it's not really any of your concern why Christopher and I married."

"It's beginning to be my concern. I've only known you a day, but I feel—I feel uncommonly attached to you."

She almost laughed again, but decided it would be cruel. Was Todd that young? That romantic? Or was this just another land fraud?

"Todd, really—"

"No. You listen to me, Maggie. Any man who leaves his wife to cry is abusing her. You deserve so much better."

"What makes you think I'm crying because of Christopher?"

"Because I see the way he treats you. Oh, Maggie! You deserve warmth, and passion, and tenderness."

He took her chin in his hand and turned her face toward his. Maggie saw the kiss coming but didn't try to stop it. She was curious what another man's kiss would feel like. Perhaps she was one of those women whose temperature soared for just any man. Perhaps Christopher wasn't the only one.

Todd's mouth covered hers. At first he was gentle and persuasive. When she didn't resist, the kiss grew more demanding. His arms pulled her close to him while his tongue pushed past her lips and filled her mouth. Maggie endured. She wanted to choke, but she endured.

When he finally released her, Maggie had an almost irresistible urge to scrub his touch from her mouth. But that also would be cruel. There had been nothing foul or repugnant about the kiss, except that Todd was not Christopher. With Todd a kiss was slobbery and awkward. With Christopher a kiss was heaven.

"Todd . . . You're a very attractive man. I like you. But I'm married. I've been wrong to be so—so friendly with you since we got here. If I led you to believe that— that I was looking for a man . . . Well, I'm not."

"You're going to let Christopher Talbot make you miserable for the rest of your life?"

"Yes . . . no. Of course not. *No* man makes *my* life miserable!" she said with a touch of her old fire. "I'm not some weak-willed parlor pansy who can't live unless some man is hanging on everything she says and does."

"Then you don't love your husband."

Todd's face was gentle with sympathy. Why couldn't she have fallen for someone like him? Someone who knew how to make a woman feel soft and feminine and needed.

"Yes, I love him . . . I—I don't know. I do love him," she said with more assurance.

Todd didn't look convinced. He leaned forward for another kiss. When Maggie flinched away, he planted a peck on her cheek instead of her mouth. "I don't think you know your own heart, my beautiful, sad Maggie. I'm here, if you should ever need me. If you were married to me, you wouldn't have any doubts about who you loved."

"Good night, Todd."

Todd watched as she disappeared into the dark house. With his looks and charm he'd never had to work very hard to get any woman he wanted. Seduction was one of the few things he did very, very well. But Maggie Montoya might be tougher to snare than he'd first thought. She was worth having, though. A woman like Maggie was worth a lot of effort. She was worth more than just keeping this rich New Mexico land. She was worth more than his father's schemes.

It might just be that Maggie was worth killing a man for.

Next morning Christopher was awakened by a soft knocking at his bedroom door.

"Who is it?" he grumbled.

"Mrs. Johnson, the housekeeper. Breakfast is ready, Mr. Talbot. Mr. Harley wants to be on the range early today. He thought you'd like to go with him."

"Fine, fine. I'm up."

The room was still dark; beyond the open window, the sky was unrelieved black. Christopher's eyelids were heavy from a restless night with too little sleep. Somehow, early mornings at Rancho del Rio were not as invigorating as early mornings at the Slater ranch.

He faced himself in the mirror and flinched. He looked as bad as he felt. His shoulder and side were still stiff with red and puckered scars. A heavy stubble of black covered his face and chin.

"Bloody coward," he accused the face in the mirror. "Bloody stupid coward."

As he lathered his face with shaving soap, he sternly forced his mind back to the night before. What was he doing wrong with Maggie? It had never in his life occurred to him that he might have difficulty controlling a wife. He had always regarded with contempt men who were so weak and ineffectual that the wife held the reins and the husband wore the bit in his mouth. And now here he was with his wife not only yanking at his bit but spurring his flanks as well.

He scraped away a strip of beard, rinsed the lather from his razor, and sighed. He should have confronted Maggie the night before, but he truly was a coward about facing her. How many times had he found the courage to face battle and possible death, only to find when facing something as harmless as a woman that he didn't have the guts of a timid rabbit?

Or perhaps he was simply putting wisdom before anger. All yesterday he'd watched Maggie with Todd Harley. The little wretch had been deliberately provoking with her flagrant "friendliness" toward the man. Then had come her dancing. Lord! Her dancing!

Maggie's dancing was not in any way lewd. She was talented, graceful, music made flesh. But the dance was subtle seduction—especially to one whose blood already ran hot for her. Christopher hadn't missed Todd's reaction. Maggie might think she was playing an innocent game with the younger Harley, but Christopher had seen no innocence in his lustful gaze. The man wanted Maggie, and he would take her if he could.

Christopher had watched the dance and teetered on the edge of losing control, his passion, his anger, his jealousy combining in one tidal wave of emotion. If he'd confronted her last night, God only knew what might have happened. His gentlemanly restraint was fast becoming tattered beyond repair. He felt like a stick of dynamite whose fuse had burned down to the last fraction of an inch.

Why the hell had the good Lord ever created women, anyway? Couldn't he have come up with a more manageable design?

Despite Christopher's state of mind he managed to nick himself only twice while shaving. He doubted that the rest of the day would pass with so little damage.

Breakfast was a silent affair. Even Maggie was subdued. Theodore seemed put out with his son about something, and Todd retreated into a silent sulk. When the meal ended, Theodore wiped his mouth, gave his son a last disgusted look, and spoke for the first time since he'd given Christopher and Maggie a curt good morning.

"Spring branding's starting this morning. We're starting a bit early this year, since it needs to be done before you take over the place."

"Have you decided to accept my price?" Christopher asked.

"Might as well. I could probably get more on the market, but the buyers don't come out until fall. I expect you'll want to take a look at the branding operation. Some of these hands are wanting to stay after you take possession. You'll want to see what kind of work they do. Mrs. Talbot will want to stay here, though. A branding isn't a pleasant place for a lady to spend the day."

"I've been to brandings before. I'll come."

"You sure you don't want to stay here?" Todd asked in a concerned tone. "I'm sure Mrs. Johnson is eager to show you the workings of the house. In fact, if you like, I could stay and keep you company."

Christopher held his breath. To his surprise Maggie didn't throw him her usual taunting glance and take Todd up on his proposition.

"I'd rather ride," she said.

Christopher thought he detected a bit of uneasiness in her answer. Perhaps she was tiring of her little game. He also noted that the Harleys didn't seem at all happy to have her riding along.

Once they arrived at the "work," as the cowboys called the roundup and branding, Christopher understood at least one reason why the Harleys were uneasy about Maggie's presence. The branding was full of disagreeable sounds, smells, and sights. He'd learned about such operations from Derek Slater. Twice a year, Slater had told him, the scattered cattle were gathered into a single large herd and "worked." In the spring new calves were branded and ear-notched, and the entire herd was inspected for disease, injuries, or other problems. In the fall of the year mavericks that had been missed in the spring roundup were branded and marked, and the market cattle were separated from the rest of the herd to be shipped to markets both east and west. The roundups, or works, were the time of hardest labor on any ranch. Cowboys always earned their pay, but in spring and fall they earned it twice over.

The site where the cattle were gathered was dense with wood smoke that hung in the still morning air. Dust roiled from beneath the hooves of the cutting horses that worked the herd. Cows whose calves had been taken from them bawled piteously, and the calves bawled even louder.

He would complain just as loudly, Christopher thought, if he'd been roped, hog-tied, sat on, branded with a white-hot iron, then had his ear mutilated into a bloody ear-notch. Yet seconds after they'd been so manhandled, the calves scrambled to their feet, shook themselves, then trotted happily toward their mothers, the traumatic experience seemingly forgotten. In fact, the calves didn't seem as upset as Maggie did.

Christopher kneed his horse to pull up beside his wife's. "You look green as a pea," he said. "Are you not feeling well?"

"I feel fine!" she snapped.

He raised a brow, and she grimaced rather sheepishly. "I always feel sorry for the cows and the calves."

"Didn't you say that you lived on a ranch for a few years?"

"From the time I was ten until I was fourteen. I worked the herd just like those boys are doing."

"They let a young girl do that?" He nodded to where the cutters were dodging between horned cows and steers to separate the unbranded calves.

"I didn't do the cutting, but I chased strays and held the cut. Anyone who can ride works during roundup. I didn't like the branding then either. Though I know it's silly to feel that way."

"I don't think it's silly to dislike seeing a creature in pain." He thought such sentiment was rather sweet, in fact. His scrappy wife had a soft side after all.

"It doesn't hurt them all that much if the man with the branding iron knows what he's doing, and this fellow seems pretty good. He leaves the iron on just long enough so that the hair won't grow back, but not so long that the skin is really seriously burned. We should keep that man on once the Harleys are gone."

Christopher smiled. The ranch manager he hired would have to be a man who didn't mind taking advice from a female, because he could see that Maggie was going to take an unwomanly interest in running the place. That was no surprise, of course. She'd never been shy about making herself heard. He was almost going to miss her outspokenness when he was back in England. A man never knew what an English lady was thinking. They generally said what they thought a gentleman wanted to hear. Their own thoughts were a mystery. Up until recently he had taken for granted that such was the way he liked women to be. Now . . . well, he was going to miss mouthy little Maggie, reluctant as he was to admit it.

"You know more about this business than I do," he admitted. "See anyone else you think is worth keeping on?"

She glanced at him in surprise, obviously not having expected his solicitation of her opinion. "Well . . . Harley's crew is a pretty scruffy lot. That old fellow who drove us from the train seemed to know his stuff, though. I think his name was Moss Riley. In fact, he might make a good foreman. He doesn't seem to think much of the Harleys."

This morning she was all business, Christopher noted. Not once had she tried to provoke him, tease him, or vex him. She had scarcely spoken to Todd all morning. In fact, all her rebellious fire appeared to have been expended in last night's taunting dance. On the other hand, neither had she been particularly cordial. Her subdued manner gave Christopher the impression that for the moment she had retreated. A strange word to come into his mind. Retreat meant withdrawal in battle, and the two of them were not at war. Or were they?

Theodore rode up and interrupted the train of Christopher's thoughts. "Ready to leave?" he asked. "Mrs. Talbot looks a bit pale. I told you this wasn't a place for a lady."

"No one said I was a lady, Mr. Harley."

The bitterness in Maggie's tone brought a slight smile to Harley's face, but his words were apologetic. "I didn't mean to imply any insult, ma'am."

She didn't look at Harley or at Christopher, simply continued to look sadly at the milling cattle. Christopher suspected that something more than the cattle was causing her melancholy, but he couldn't guess exactly what. What man could fathom a woman, especially a complex little creature like his Maggie? Certainly not he.

They didn't ride directly back to the ranch, but instead headed north, where Theodore wanted to inspect another of the many windmills that dotted the plain.

"Of course, the windmill's more your worry than mine at this point," he said to Christopher.

Christopher lifted a brow at the man's cheerful tone. Either Harley was the best loser he'd ever met, or the cards were not yet all on the table, in spite of appearances. From Maggie's slight frown he suspected that she was speculating along the same lines. Even Todd cast his father a worried glance or two.

They inspected the windmill. To Christopher it looked the same as any other windmill. It seemed to be in perfect working order, or at least, the blades were turning slowly in the slight wind and a trickle of water was emptying into the tank.

"Do you smell smoke?" Theodore asked, his face turned into the wind.

"The branding fires," Maggie suggested.

"Too far away, and in the wrong direction. The wind's from the west."

The breeze did carry a faint whiff of wood smoke. Theodore frowned in obvious—almost theatrical, Christopher thought—concern. Todd shifted uneasily in his saddle.

"Could be a drifter's campfire," Todd suggested.

"More likely a rustler's branding fire," his father snapped.

Maggie looked dubious. "A rustler in broad daylight?"

"They know my crew is busy with the work. Rustlers are a mighty bold breed at times. We'll just see about this!" He spurred his horse forward.

Christopher brought his horse even with Maggie's as they followed the Harleys. "Keep behind me," he told her. "I don't like the sound of this."

"Don't worry, Christopher. Rustlers almost always fade away before they're caught. They don't stay to fight."

"Stay behind me," he insisted.

She dropped behind slightly, but not without a glance that told him she was only humoring his ignorance. But Christopher had ridden into skirmishes enough times to know that when something didn't feel right about a situation, usually something wasn't right. In battle a man learned to trust his intuition.

They followed the smell of smoke until a wispy gray column rising into the air served as a more reliable guide. In a bend of Cibola Creek, in a gully that hid them from casual observation, three men were indeed carrying on their own private branding operation. When they looked up and saw four riders appear on the grassy bluff above them, they threw the branding iron aside and went for their shooting irons. Bullets flew.

Christopher heard Todd curse, but he paid no mind to the Harleys. His only concern was Maggie.

"Get down! Get off!" he shouted to her. The plain provided no cover except the tall grass itself. As she vaulted from her horse, he pushed her down into the dirt. "Stay here!"

"No, I—"

"Stay, dammit!"

Christopher peeked above the grass while holding Maggie down. Bullets flew everywhere as the air echoed with the thunder of gunshots, but none was hitting anything or anyone. Everyone involved seemed to be firing off his pistol more for effect than for murder. However, the three rustlers weren't running for their horses to attempt a retreat. So much for Maggie's theory about villains running before they could be caught.

"Get down, man! Get down!" Theodore waved at Christopher as he shouted. Actually, Christopher noted, he was pointing more than waving, which brought the rustlers' attention swinging around to him. One fired point blank. His pistol was aimed for more than just effect; a bullet whined past just inches from Christopher's left ear. Christopher hit the ground and drew his own pistol. The Navy Colt double-action six-shooter was a gun he'd never had occasion to use, but having a weapon in his hand was a familiar feeling.

He popped above the grass to take a quick look at the

situation. Immediately the man who had fired before spotted him and fired again with disturbing accuracy. Christopher stood, took calm and careful aim while the man fired once again—another miss, fortunately—and pulled the trigger. The man fell without a sound. His fellow rustlers ran to him.

"Goddamn!" one cursed. "The Limey drilled Jess right between the eyes."

The other bent to look at the body. "Shit! Let's ride!"

Father and son Harley both stared at Christopher with wide eyes. Maggie, who had popped up from the grass at the rustlers' shouting, seemed equally surprised. All three seemed content to let the surviving rustlers get away, but Christopher had no such charitable intentions. His suspicion that something was peculiar had just been confirmed by the rustler calling him a "Limey," and he intended to get to the bottom of this game.

"Let's go," he ordered, instinctively taking charge. One didn't boss around a horse regiment for three years without getting in the habit of command.

"We'll never catch them." Theodore remained where he was. He seemed to have lost his taste for chasing rustlers.

The outlaws reached their horses and mounted. Christopher mounted also, ready to pursue.

"No, Christopher!" Maggie shouted. "Not alone!"

"Stay here!"

His horse had scarcely hit its stride before Christopher realized that Theodore was right. He would never catch them. Out of frustration more than anything else he slid his mount to a stop, aimed his pistol, and fired at the fleeing figures. By a stroke of luck one fell. The other rode on. Christopher spurred his mount forward, hoping his victim wasn't dead.

The man lay on his back, groaning. His left arm and

side were crimson with blood. Christopher got to him only moments before the Harleys and Maggie rode up. He laid the muzzle of his pistol against the man's temple.

"You're not a rustler, are you, fellow?"

The man gagged. Blood dribbled from his mouth.

"Tell me, or you'll die right now."

"Trap. It was a trap. Harley"—his eyes slewed fearfully to where Theodore had ridden up and dismounted his horse—"Harley set it up. Thought . . ." He labored to breathe. "Don't let him . . . !"

Christopher looked around to see Theodore Harley draw his gun. The gambler fired a single shot into the fallen man's chest. The man jerked. His eyes rolled back into his head.

Chistopher straightened slowly. "Rather unsporting of you, Harley."

Harley's face settled into deep lines of contempt as he raised his pistol once again. "Drop your gun, Talbot. If I'd known you could actually hit what you shoot at, I never would have given it to you. Fortunately for me, aside from being able to handle a gun, you really are a stupid ass. Todd, get the girl and put her over by her husband."

Christopher let his pistol drop into the dirt. He had no choice. Maggie looked confused as Todd pointed a gun in her direction. The younger Harley gave his father a worried look. "You're not going to kill her too?"

"We have to. If she'd stayed home, we could have told her that her husband was killed by rustlers. Or if Jess had been a better shot, she might have believed we had nothing to do with this. But now . . ."

"She's not dumb. Once the Englishman's dead and she doesn't have anywhere else to turn, she'll marry me. Tell him, Maggie."

"You're as much of an ass as Talbot. She'll turn to the

sheriff or the governor, that's who she'll turn to the minute you turn your back on her. Put her over by him."

Todd moved slowly toward Maggie, his gun wavering. "If you'd just seen reason last night! God, Maggie!"

Theodore smiled at Christopher. His smile was no longer charming. "Did you think I'd just let this ranch go? That's not the way things are done out here, Englishman. Out here men live by their wits, not by some stupid law."

"You'll never get away with this, Harley. Your motive for killing us is too obvious."

"What with two dead rustlers and no witnesses, nobody will say a damned thing. Todd, quit yammering to that girl and bring her over here."

If he'd had the time, Christopher would have kicked himself. He had underestimated his enemy, a grave and often fatal mistake. Worse, he had put Maggie in danger as well. He saw her in desperate, quiet conversation with Todd. Trying to save her own life? He didn't blame her.

"Todd! The girl, dammit! Let's get this over with. You had your chance to screw the slut and missed it. If you were half as good with women as you thought you were, this would've been a lot simpler."

Maggie tossed Harley an indignant look. "I am not a slut!"

"Todd!" Harley warned.

Maggie's booted foot made connection with Todd's shin, and as he hopped about on one leg, her knee found a target in his groin.

Todd screamed. Harley whirled around. Christopher took his chance and leapt forward, but Harley turned back before Christopher reached him.

"You sonofa—ooof!" Harley doubled over as Christopher put all his weight behind the power of a right undercut to the stomach. A follow-up punch to Harley's jaw sent the pistol flying.

"You're better at plotting than at fighting," Christopher noted coolly. As Harley attempted to recover, Christopher retrieved the gun. Out of the corner of his eye he saw a grim-looking Maggie holding Todd's gun pointed at the young man's stomach. Todd himself was still trying to comfort his wounded parts. "And fortunately for me, my wife has some rather unladylike skills in dealing with fools like your son."

Maggie looked at him and smiled. Christopher noted that the twinkle had returned to her eyes. "Sometimes," she said, "it pays to be not quite a lady."

Twelve

 Christopher sighed and massaged his forehead with his fingers. He'd been playing accountant since early morning and the figures in the ledgers were beginning to blur before his eyes. He leaned back in his chair and looked out the library window to temptation. A beautiful July day beckoned. The sky was a hot azure blue dotted with the usual midday buildup of white puffy clouds. The breeze that blew through the open window smelled of sunlight, grass, and wildflowers. Today wasn't a day to be sitting in a musty office squinting at accounts.

Christopher scanned the set of figures he had just finished. The accounts were in good order.

He, Peter, and Luisa, who had a remarkable gift for figures, had made excellent progress over the last six weeks. From the chaos left to them by Theodore Harley, who had taken little interest in the business end of ranching, they had corrected and cleaned up and organized the records so that now they were an accurate register of expenses and projection of income. Orders from cattle buyers had already been received for the fall market. The Army was a big customer, and markets on the West Coast and in the East were doing well also. This year the ranch was going to turn a reasonable profit that would help bail out his family in England from their current financial difficulties and allow for a modest plan of expansion for the ranch.

All in all, Christopher thought with satisfaction, he owed himself a few hours of relaxation. He shut the ledger with a snap.

Luisa met him in the entrance hall just as he was about to make his escape. "I'm going out for a while," he told her.

"If you come across Maggie, remind her to be back for dinner at four, please. That girl loses all sense of time when she's out romping around with those kids. She's not much better than a kid herself."

"Um," Christopher grunted noncommittally.

Christopher saddled his horse—a long-legged gray gelding that he'd bought in Santa Rosa—and headed north along the river. The water level had dropped since June. Then it had been a muddy torrent; now it flowed quietly between its banks. The few afternoon showers of the last few weeks had not affected it. It dropped lower and lower every day. Christopher was glad that the stock wells were more dependable than the river.

Over the past six weeks he'd learned more about ranching than he had ever wanted to know. Following Maggie's suggestion, he had given Moss Riley the job of ranch

manager, and the man had proved as valuable as gold.
Moss had appointed Gray Smithers foreman, indicated a
few other hands he recommended Christopher keep, and
suggested that the rest be let go. The men whom they'd
lost had been relatively easy to replace. Christopher offered good wages and a decent place to live. Men who
were married were welcome to have their families live on
the ranch, and a row of small stone houses for married
cowboys with wives and children now stood behind the
bunkhouse. Bachelor cowboys still lived in the bunkhouse, but their lot was improved by the attention of the
womenfolk, who seemed to think it their duty to bake,
mend, and wash for the entire complement of hands, not
just their own men.

Now the ranch was tended by a crew that was as reliable as any in this country, Christopher thought with satisfaction. He'd learned to appreciate the qualities of the
rough men who had peopled the American West. They
were for the most part uncouth and uneducated. Their
manners were atrocious, their language foul—at least
when no women were present—their personal cleanliness
the equal of a pig's, and their pasts questionable. Or perhaps it would be better to say that their pasts were un-
questionable, for Christopher had discovered that in the
West one of the gravest breaches of etiquette was to question a man—or a woman, for that matter—about his or
her past.

Maggie had been as busy as he over the last weeks. She
and Luisa had redecorated the house so that it had more
the atmosphere of a comfortable Mexican ranchero than
an English country home. She had dismissed the housekeeper, the assistant cook, and two of the three starched
maids, rearranged the meal schedule to fit in better with
the cowboys' workday, and instructed the cook to serve
the family the same food that was given to the hands.

Christopher was relieved that Maggie had taken to life on Rancho del Rio with such great enthusiasm. Lately he had suffered a twinge of conscience on Maggie's behalf, and her apparent happiness with her new life relieved that burden somewhat. Why he should feel guilty about Maggie he couldn't fathom. He had lifted her from a life of squalid desperation to become a lady of property and very comfortable circumstances. He had assured her future, provided her with clothes, books, and servants. Why on earth should he feel guilty?

Christopher admitted that he had used the girl ruthlessly for his own purposes. There was no denying that. But he'd been honest with her about his motives, and he'd taken care that she benefited as much as he. How many other men would have denied their physical needs to insure that she wouldn't be left with additional burdens from their marriage? They had occupied separate bedrooms since since moving permanently to Rancho del Rio, and not once had he given in to the raging temptation to visit Maggie in the middle of the night. He was rather proud of himself for that, for the temptation was great.

Christopher had always picked his women with great care. Sexual appetite, like every other kind of appetite, was something to be indulged with prudence, and he'd never before had difficulty subduing his animal lusts when necessary. Maggie provoked him to irrational desire, however. Not just her body—tempting though it was —but her laughter, her insistence on enjoying life no matter what the circumstances, the emotional vulnerability that she was so embarrassed to admit, her courage, even her childish mischievous streak.

Christopher admitted he was suffering from infatuation. He wondered if Maggie would have held the same attraction for him if he'd met her in England, where more appropriate ladies abounded.

Probably she would have. Lady or not, Maggie was a unique woman. She was like the land she had sprung from—beautiful, open, honest, tough, and easy to rile. She would be happy at Rancho del Rio, a queen with a domain larger than some European countries. Already she was beginning to act like the mistress of the domain. She had been the one who'd suggested encouraging families to move to the ranch. The neat little stone houses behind the bunkhouse had been her idea, and now she was badgering Peter to help her start a school for the children who lived on the ranch. Luisa was teaching her about the ranch accounts and the basics of running a business, and Maggie was devouring these new skills the same way she had devoured the books Christopher had bought her.

Christopher's thoughts about his wife seemed to have drawn him right to her. He reined in the gray gelding and listened to the laughter coming from just ahead. Just around a bend in the river, cottonwood trees provided a shaded swimming hole that was popular with the ranch hands and their families. Today Maggie had taken the children of the ranch on a picnic. One of the buckboards was parked under a cottonwood tree, and the hobbled team grazed contentedly in the shade. Shade also dappled the sandy shallows of the river and the calm, deep pool that had formed where the current had cut the outside of the bend.

None of the picnickers noticed Christopher; they were having too much fun. Besides, he was partially hidden by the trees. The young wife of one of the hands was cheerfully setting out chicken pies, bread, honey, jam, cookies, and apples while Maggie supervised the children in the water. Actually, Maggie appeared to be more of a playmate than a overseer. Barefoot, she wore faded trousers with the legs rolled scandalously above her knees. She was as wet as the children. Even her shirt was wet and clinging to her in a most provoking fashion. As Christopher watched, a little boy of about eight years—a child Christopher recognized as belonging to the ranch-house cook—sent a fountain of water Maggie's way and got her even wetter. She squealed with delight, and the children laughed riotously.

"I'll teach you!" Maggie waded after the bold little culprit and gave him a dunking. He came up sputtering and laughing. The children swarmed around her like little water sprites around a scruffy Venus.

"Me next! Me next!" they clamored, and splashed her until she was soaked by the deluge. Christopher heard her laughter rise above the children's, clear and sweet as the sound of the bells. Smiling, he turned away and left the revelers to their picnic.

He rode east toward a line camp where a number of hands would probably stop for a midday meal. Not trusting himself to navigate by the position of the sun as so many men more experienced in this flat, featureless country did, once away from the river he followed the needle of a compass that he'd mail-ordered from Montgomery Ward. Since starting to use the compass, he'd felt much more comfortable leaving the security of the ranch compound and the river to ride out over the plains.

The sound of the picnickers faded, and the world became silent except for the faint sigh of the breeze through the grass and the occasional call of a bird. Christopher stopped and let the vastness of the plain engulf him. It was amazing how this wild land had grown on him. He'd come to love the muted browns and greens, the great blue vault of the sky, the distinct dust-and-grass smell of the breeze. How different it was from crowded London with its stuffy parlors and stuffier people.

Christopher reined his thoughts in short. Those were *his* people he was calling stuffy—his family, friends, and business associates. They were the people he loved, respected, and admired, and such judgments did them an injustice.

Maggie's image slipped into his mind. He saw her barefoot and bare legged, wet trousers hugging her bottom and wet shirt clinging to her breasts. Her laughter was the peal of a bell; her smile a pure draught of sunlight. Beside Maggie the proper English gentlewoman seemed quite pale. Such a thought was treasonous to his origins, but it was there just the same. It was a good thing he would soon be returning to England and civilization. He was becoming as much a barbarian as any American. What's worse, he was liking it.

The following night was Rancho del Rio's official inauguration of the new reign. The celebration was casual, as befitted the country. The just-completed barn that Christopher had had built to house the wagons and other heavy ranch equipment was the ideal size for a dance. The wagons and carriage had been relegated to the old stone barn while the new barn was cleaned spotless and decorated for a party. Outside, half a cow turned slowly over an open pit. Inside, kegs of beer and whiskey stood alongside bottles of expensive wine on the trestle tables set up as a bar. The plank floor had been swept clean and then covered liberally with straw. An orchestra consisting of the unlikely combination of two fiddle players, a piano that had just arrived from Santa Fe, a flute, and two guitars played music that made even the most sluggish feet twitch to dance.

Christopher stood near the bar with a glass of brandy in one hand and watched his guests. This wasn't exactly one of his mother's famous balls, but he'd never recalled seeing people having more fun. Some noted men were in attendance. The governor himself had come from Santa Fe. Maxwell, of the huge Maxwell Grant—a larger piece of land than even the Montoya grant—had come also, as well as executives from the Atchison, Topeka, and Santa Fe Railroad. Other ranchers from the Staked Plains— some prominent and others not so prominent—attended also, no doubt curious to see the foreigner who had moved into their territory. Maggie had written the Slaters to invite them, but little Martha was ill and they had been unable to attend.

"Quite a fête, Talbot." Governor Sheldon clapped him on the shoulder. "I haven't seen so many bigwigs in the same place since I was last in Washington, D.C."

"Not quite that big," Christopher answered with a polite smile. "I did want everyone in the territory very sure about the change of ownership here, though."

"Well, there shouldn't be any doubt after this hoopla. It was a shame that Harley was so vicious about the situation. I never much liked the man, to tell the truth, but I didn't think he was the type to resort to murder."

"Thousands of men have been killed over much smaller tracts of land."

"I guess that's true. We've got so much land out here, sometimes we forget just how valuable it really is. Harley got moved up to the territoral prison last week, but I suppose you know that. He won't be free for a long time. I'm not sure where Todd went. It was generous of you to not press charges against him."

"Maggie's the one who convinced me that he didn't have any real part in the plot. He's nothing without his father."

"Your wife is truly a remarkable woman, Talbot."

Christopher had to agree as he watched Maggie play the lady hostess. She was a striking picture in a green silk dress with her wild curls tamed into a becoming pile atop her head. He recalled how surprised she had been when he had ordered a dozen bolts of cloth from a delighted vendor who had been passing through Fort Sumner one day when he was there talking to Army suppliers. He had hired a seamstress to make Maggie a complete new wardrobe.

"In England," he had told her, "ladies often have new wardrobes twice a year."

"That's ridiculous, and this isn't England." Still, she had smiled when running her hands over the fine materials. The styles she had ordered were practical dresses, skirts, divided skirts, and shirts meant for daily wear on the ranch, but she had indulged feminine vanity with two ballgowns as well—the green silk and a red lacy creation that made her look like the devil's own seductress, at least in Christopher's eyes. He was glad she had chosen the green silk for tonight. It was a fetching dress but didn't make his blood run quite as hot as the red one. Only a few more days until he would no longer need to worry about giving in to his desire for her.

The governor continued his praise of Maggie. "You're a lucky man, Talbot. Land, wits, and a good disposition in one pretty package. A lucky man, indeed!"

Christopher doubted the governor would praise Maggie's disposition if he had to live with her. Just the same, he indulged himself in one intense moment of regret that he was not and never would be a simple New Mexican rancher who could live out the years of his life in this beautiful country with his charming, if somewhat difficult-to-handle, wife.

"I am indeed a lucky man, Your Excellency. If you'll excuse me, I think I'll claim a dance with that woman who makes me so lucky."

"By all means!" the governor said with a chuckle. "Be young while you can."

Christopher couldn't resist just one dance. Maggie drew him as the flame draws the moth. She looked every

inch a lady, but her eyes sparkled with the lively impish-
ness that made it impossible for her to act the lady very
long. He touched Maggie's arm just as she was excusing
herself from a matronly, kind-faced lady who was the wife
of Santa Rosa's one physician.

"I believe this dance is mine," he said.

"Is it?" Some of the liveliness fled from her eyes. So
often when she looked at him these days her face grew
still and cheerless. He didn't know exactly what he'd done
to make her so unhappy; he had tried his best, given the
circumstances, not to hurt her. Yet she would undoubtedly rejoice when he told her, as he must within the next
few hours, that he would be leaving within a week for
England. There was no reason for him to stay longer; he
had accomplished what he had set out to do.

"I'd like to make it my dance," he said softly.

Without a word she slipped into his arms to dance the
waltz that tinkled off the keys of the piano. Immediately
Christopher realized that touching her was a grave mistake on his part. She was warm and supple beneath the
green silk. She smelled ever so faintly of lilac, a tantalizing hint of scent combined with the tanginess of fresh
air and a dash of the wine she had drunk. The dance had
scarcely begun and already he wanted her so badly that
he hurt. He should end the dance and let her go, but
couldn't. He was a man, after all, not a saint.

Maggie allowed hope to rekindle as Christopher guided
her around the dance floor. The barn was crowded. Other
couples jostled them. Conversations buzzed above the
music, but all Maggie could feel, hear, or see was Christopher.

It had been so long since he had so much as touched
her. When they had made the move to Rancho del Rio, he
had moved his things into the bedroom Todd had occupied across from the big master suite. Too proud to show

her hurt, she hadn't objected. Neither Luisa nor Peter had commented, and though Luisa had given her sympathetic looks, Maggie hadn't confided even to the woman who was her best friend how wounded she felt. She missed Christopher's presence in their bed and in their room. Even though he disdained making love to her, just lying beside him was pleasurable. Frustrating, but pleasurable. At Rancho del Rio she didn't even have that.

Day by day it seemed Christopher withdrew a little more from her. He occupied himself with making the ranch into a well-oiled, profitable business, spending time with Peter and Luisa on the books, Moss Riley on the range, but never with her. Even mealtimes he sometimes didn't show his face.

Christopher Talbot didn't want to love her. She wasn't good enough for his love. Maggie wished she could hate him for the insult. Hate would make life easier than love. But hating Christopher Talbot was beyond her.

"You look lovely tonight." He looked down at her and smiled. She hadn't seen such warmth in his eyes for weeks. He'd hardly been close enough for her to look into his eyes. "You have a gift for being a perfect lady when you want to."

Resentment stirred. "You don't need to compliment me on manners—like giving a treat to a dog. By now I know what manners are and when they have to be used."

"I didn't mean any insult, Maggie."

His tone was sincere, and she was being a witch. "I'm sorry. My corset itches," she said in explanation of her mood. It was true. He was the main reason she was snappish, but an itchy corset certainly didn't help.

He merely chuckled. "Maggie, you are unique. One of a kind."

"Lucky for you," she said with a hint of bitterness.

He didn't question her comment. His arms tightened

round her, and her pulse leapt to the feel of his hard body moving in concert with hers. Maggie let herself be taken by the rare moment, let herself imagine that she could see herself reflected in his eyes, beautiful, desirable, beloved. For a moment she pretended that she and Christopher Talbot had a real marriage, not just a business arrangement. This night when the party was over and the guests were asleep, he would take her into his arms and they would create their own little universe of joined bodies and merged souls and aching love. For the few minutes left of the dance she would pretend. Perhaps if she pretended hard enough, the fantasy would come true.

Luisa stood with Peter at the sidelines of the dancing. Christopher danced by with Maggie in his arms, an oddity worthy of attention for someone who knew the both of them. Christopher's face was set in stone, a mask Luisa had learned that Englishmen—at least both Englishmen of her acquaintance—used when trying to hide what they considered inappropriate emotions. Maggie looked like a child with her eyes on a jar of candy just out of reach.

"Christopher is a fool," Luisa said in a low voice to Peter. "Strange. I've warned Magdalena time and time again that men are jackasses and not to expect much from them, but even I believed that he couldn't resist her for long. He truly is a jackass."

Peter drew himself up with English pride. "Lord Christopher is a gentleman. He has Maggie's best interest at heart."

Luisa sniffed. "Maybe he should ask Magdalena what she thinks is her best interest."

"Walk with me outside, Luisa."

She hesitated.

"I would like to talk to you without a crowd listening in." He offered his arm, and she took it.

The sun had set long ago, but the day's heat lingered. The house, corrals, and outbuildings were bathed in milky moonlight. "This truly is a beautiful land." Peter sighed. "I will be sorry to leave it. I think Christopher will be sorry also, for many reasons."

"He is still planning to leave, then? I had thought he might decide to stay. He seems to like it here. I'm sure Maggie hopes he will stay."

"Christopher can't stay, Luisa, any more than I can stay. Our lives are in London. Lord Christopher told Maggie at the outset of this project that once things were settled here he would return home."

Luisa remembered faintly that Christopher had made such a statement. She suspected that, after all the changes in her life, Maggie didn't remember at all. "It's rather cold-blooded of him simply to leave her here, don't you think?"

Peter sighed. "Luisa, do you really think Maggie would be happy in London? Do you think she would enjoy life in a society where a single inappropriate word or social misstep can make a person an outcast?"

"I can't imagine a place like that."

"Because you've never been to Europe or England and hobnobbed with the ton. Under the polish of manners and gentility they can be more vicious than wolves."

Privately, Luisa thought Magdalena could hold her own against anyone, even a pack of wolves. "I do hope Christopher plans to tell Maggie before he starts packing his bags," she said sharply.

"Luisa, let Christopher handle Maggie. Whatever is between the two of them is . . . well, is between them. I wanted to talk to you about—about me. I'm leaving tomorrow, you know."

"Of course I know," she said stiffly.

"I have some business associates in New York that I

want to see before sailing back to England, and I'll arrange passage for Christopher and myself while I'm there."

Luisa was silent. Against all reason she had dreaded the moment when Peter Scarborough would leave her life. There was certainly nothing between them, nothing but a few looks, a dance or two, a friendship of like minds that had not grown into something deeper because both of them knew there was no possibility for such a relationship to last.

"Luisa, I want to say—I've wanted to say for some time how much I have enjoyed your company. I helped Christopher on this project partly out of affection for him and his family, and partly because I've made a habit of charging into any adventure that would make my life less a bore. I have no family of my own, you see, and I've never married. I've never been much of a man for the ladies. Never cultivated the charm, I suppose."

"You underestimate your charm, I think."

Peter cleared his throat. "You're very kind, my dear. But the point I am trying to make is, I will miss you, dear lady. I want you to know that this old bachelor will remember our brief association as one of the high points of his life."

"*I* would not fit into London life either," Luisa said flatly.

"One must be born to the peculiarities of genteel society to survive them. I wish it were otherwise."

Luisa gave him a long look, knowing that in a very short time he would be gone from her life forever. Gray hair, gentle blue eyes, laugh lines around his mouth and eyes, quixotic smile. He was one of the most attractive men she had ever met in spite of his claim that he lacked charm. What, she wondered, did these London ladies call charm if they thought that Peter didn't have it?

A current passed between them. Peter leaned slightly forward, as if to take a kiss. Luisa was more than willing, but he stopped before their lips touched and reluctantly pulled away.

"You are the sweetest and most generous lady I have ever met," he said softly. "But I cannot offer you a future, so I will refrain from taking such liberty with your honor."

Luisa tried to squelch her sharp disappointment. Romantic fantasies were just that—fantasies—and she was old enough know better. "Christopher should be as honorable as you," she said softly.

"And Maggie should be as wise as you are, dear Luisa."

Luisa didn't feel wise. She felt old, sad, and foolish.

The party was over. Guests were stacked like firewood in every room of the dark house. In the master suite three women snored loudly in the big four-poster bed, and two more tossed and turned on the floor. Maggie alone was not asleep. Her blankets were crumpled in one corner of the room while she sat at the window and looked at the moon. She relived her dance with Christopher, the feel of his strong arms, the rock-hardness of his chest against her breasts, the fleeting warmth in his smile and his eyes. How long was she going to let His Almighty Lordship make her life miserable? Maggie wondered. All her life she had bounced back from hardship like a rubber ball, always finding some reason for enjoyment no matter how hard the circumstances. Now she was better off than she'd ever been in her life—a comfortable home, plenty to eat, clothes that were neither threadbare nor mended ten times over—and yet she was letting an insignificant detail like love make her miserable. Love had never figured in her life before. Perhaps that was why she didn't know how to deal with this particular misery.

A railroad executive's wife snorted mightily and rolled

over. Her two bedmates snored as if in concert. Maggie sighed. Tonight she really did want to be alone. Self-pity was more enjoyable in solitude than in company. She remembered suddenly that the blacksmith's cot in the horse barn was temporarily empty. The blacksmith had left a week ago and the new man whom Moss had hired would not be at the ranch for another ten days.

She donned a robe over her cotton nightgown and tiptoed out of the room. In the entrance hall she pulled a pair of boots onto her bare feet. They were Christopher's, and much too big, but she wasn't about to go rustling around her closet in the dark looking for her own shoes. As she quietly opened the front door and slipped out, she didn't look through the door of the library to see the dark figure seated at the desk watching her.

Christopher sat for a moment after Maggie left. Sleep had eluded him in a room with six other men, and he had come into the library to be alone with his thoughts. He should have been thinking about England and how nice it was going to be to go home. Unfortunately, his mind insisted on dwelling upon Maggie. She had looked like a lady tonight, beautiful and poised. Usually she looked like a hoyden, but to his eyes she was beautiful even then. A beauty inside her shone through even when she was drenched, dirty, sweaty, in trousers, those damn divided skirts, in nothing at all with her wild hair springing around her face in untamed corkscrews.

He was going to miss her. Lord, how he was going to miss her. She was frustration, laughter, vexation, courage, provocation, sweetness—a butterfly a man could neither capture nor pin down. One never knew from day to day or hour to hour to expect a lady, an urchin, an imp, a seductress, or a melancholy little girl.

Christopher sighed. Tonight Maggie had been a lady and seemed happy in that role. Perhaps now was the time to talk to her about how things should be managed after he left. Soon he had to get it over with; it might as well be now.

He followed her out, expecting her to be stargazing in the yard as he had observed her do several times before. She was nowhere in sight, though. Christopher was perplexed and a little alarmed until the lantern glow around the edges of the barn door revealed her hiding place. He found her spreading a blanket upon the blacksmith's cot in the little cubicle off the tack room.

"Maggie."

She gasped and jumped. "Oh! Christopher. You startled me."

"Sorry."

She looked at him as though he were an apparition that had suddenly appeared from a dream, or perhaps a nightmare.

"I saw that you couldn't sleep either. Perhaps this might be a good time for us to have a talk. It seems that during the day both of us are so busy . . ."

"Talk about what?"

He pulled up a wooden stool and sat. "Peter's leaving for New York tomorrow."

"I know."

"You realize that I will be leaving also in a week or thereabouts."

She looked stunned. "You are?"

"Things are settled here. Your land grant is confirmed. The ranch is in good order, and Moss Riley has things well in hand. I trust him. You've started a good life here, one that will keep you happy. There's no more reason for me to stay, and a number of things await my attention in London."

Her eyes widened. "I thought . . . well, I . . ."

"You knew I planned to leave once everything was settled, Maggie. I promised you I would be out of your hair after I was certain that everything was running well."

"Well, I . . . you did say something like that, didn't you? When we married, I supposed that everything had changed. But I should have known better."

"Maggie, I've always been honest with you."

"Oh, bosh!" In a flash she swung from confusion to anger. "You're not even honest with yourself!"

Christopher felt a twinge of vexation at her accusation. "What is that supposed to mean?"

"You come to poor, primitive America to get back at the cardshark who took advantage of your brother. You pull me out of a saloon and tell yourself that I'm just a pawn in your stupid private war. But I'm more than a pawn, and you can't accept that. Then you take over this ranch and discover that a cattle ranch in New Mexico is more than just an investment for your high-rolling aristocratic family, but you can't accept that either. London is the only thing that's worth a hoot. London is the whole world, and nothing else is worthy of your attention. So you're running away from a challenge just as you start to discover how much you like it, and you're running away from me because you're afraid you might come to like a mere scummy gutter slut too much. Isn't that what you're most afraid of, Christopher?"

He tried to be reasonable and civilized in the face of her ridiculous tantrum. "Maggie, you don't know anything about what you're saying."

"Oh, don't I, Your Gutless Lordship?"

"I certainly don't think of you as a—what colorful phrase did you use?—a scummy gutter—"

"Slut," she finished harshly.

"Don't ever refer to yourself by that term! You are certainly not a slut!" His ire rose faster from the names she had called herself than the ones she had thrown at him.

"But I'm certainly not good enough to be your wife! Isn't that what you've believed all along? You made sure that everyone within hearing knew that you married me for the land. You can't bring yourself to touch me past what you had to do to make the marriage binding, and now you're running off to your precious London to let the genteel ladies there help you forget that you ever had to lower yourself to play husband to a dirty saloon dancer."

"Maggie! I warn you. You'd be wise not to push me too far."

But he could tell from the flash of her eyes that her temper was boiling. She steamed in silence for a moment, seeming to struggle for the next words. Finally, she drew herself up with an appearance of iron determination.

"Suppose I want to go to London with you? After all, I am your wife. That's the terrible price you had to pay to get this land. I have a right to be where you are."

Christopher could see disaster rushing toward him like a giant, crushing wave. "You would be letting your stubbornness rob you of happiness." He tried to make his tone reasonable, but nothing inside him felt reasonable. Oddly enough, an undisciplined and foolish part of his heart leapt at her suggestion.

"I'm not afraid of London."

"You'd be much happier in New Mexico. Believe me."

"You Englishmen always think you know what's best for a person. Suppose I make my own decision."

"I do know what's best for you in this case. I won't take you to London."

She flashed him a grin. A dangerous light of mischief joined the anger in her eyes. "If you leave me here, I'll divorce you."

"What?"

"Divorce is not difficult in New Mexico, you know. You won't have this land anymore. It will be all mine. Magdalena Montoya, rich lady rancher. Maybe I'll end up marrying someone who isn't afraid to love an ex-saloon dancer."

He didn't know whether or not what she'd said about divorce in New Mexico was true, but it did seem he'd heard something about the territorial legislature being ridiculously willing to end marriages. With him being a foreigner and so much land involved, they might be more than willing to set Maggie and her land grant free.

He attempted to be logical. "Maggie, why would you want to go to London? Here you have everything you want."

Her eyes darkened.

"In London you'll be miserable."

"Maybe I have a hankering to hobnob with the aristocrats."

"You won't like them."

"I liked you well enough." She immediately looked chagrined, as if she had said something she'd rather not. "Besides, it doesn't matter. If you're going to London, I'm going with you. You wanted to have a business partner, but I've decided that I want a marriage. You married me to get your hands on this land. You're stuck with me."

She folded her arms across her chest with determined finality, and Christopher felt a flare of frustration ignite his temper. He was not accustomed to being bested, and it seemed this snip of a girl had been besting him one way or another since he'd first found her. She scoffed at his good intentions and disdained his efforts to arrange matters so that she would not suffer from his use of her. What was worst of all, many of her accusations had a painful nucleus of truth. The frustrations and trials of the last few months suddenly reached the flash point and exploded in his soul.

"You want a real marriage, Maggie? Then we'll have a

real marriage. If you want to be a wife, perhaps I should take advantage of being a husband."

She stood still as a statue as he advanced, like a doe facing a hunter, undecided whether to flee or stand her ground.

"I've taken great pains to spare you the complications of marriage, because I thought it unfair to leave you with the possibility of a child growing in your belly. But a real husband need have no such fear, does he?"

Christopher saw his own anger reflected in her face. She took a step back.

"You think to punish me by making love to me?" she demanded indignantly. "How many times have I offered myself willingly only to be rejected? Spare me the complications of marriage!" She made a rude noise.

"You think my attentions are punishment? Is that why you've been tempting me so artfully these past weeks? I've been too long without a woman, I think. Stop backing up and come here, Maggie."

"Been too long without a woman, have you? Well, I'm not a woman! I'm your damned wife!" A vindictive light glimmered in her eyes. "I think it might do you good to have a dose of your own medicine. Good night, Christopher."

He recognized the tone from all the nights he'd fended her off with the same words. "Wives don't have a choice about when and where they give themselves to their husbands," he taunted. The anger in her eyes only fed his own, and the heat of his ire made his passion grow all the faster.

"*I* always have a choice."

"You just made your choice, wife."

She swung at him, no ladylike feint but a solid roundhouse of feminine fury. All the frustration, confusion, and resentment of the past weeks were packed into one blow.

Christopher caught her fist before it exploded onto his face.

"Temper, temper!" he taunted with a grin. "Ladies do not try to beat on their husbands."

"Your blasted ladies can go to hell! Pardon me!" she mocked. "They can go to Hades. Is that more ladylike?"

She jerked her hand from his hold and glared at him balefully for a few moments. Then her mouth twitched. Her face contorted as if fighting for control, and finally she gave in and laughed—as if a thunderstorm had quickly passed and left a rainbow in its place.

The energy of Christopher's anger turned instantly to passion. Maggie wanted to be his wife. The little witch demanded to be his wife. There was truly nothing to stop him from being a husband. He stood silently and drank in her laughter, the flush of passion staining her cheeks, the reflection of himself in her eyes. He advanced. Her laughter faded, but she didn't retreat. Her lips parted. She waited, watching him, and he was flooded with a desire so intense that he almost groaned with the pain.

As if a tightly coiled spring released suddenly to set them both free, they moved at the same time into each other's arms. What followed was swift and fervent. Christopher took only seconds to free her from her clothing as she worked frantically at his. They fell together on the cot, their mouths joined and devouring.

Christopher tried to wait, but Maggie wouldn't let him. He tried to be gentle in spite of the urgent demand of his arousal, but Maggie was too impatient to wait upon tenderness.

"Now!" she urged. "Christopher, please now."

Her plea broke the last vestige of his control. He thrust into her wet, welcoming warmth and let his body take command. The cot shuddered and bucked with the violence of their passion. The world ceased to exist. What existed was his own driving, straining body and the woman who writhed and arched beneath him. Their path to paradise was brief but fierce. They soared and climaxed together, fused in a fleeting but intense ecstasy.

Together they settled back to earth. Unable to speak, scarcely able to breathe, Christopher shifted his weight off of his wife and pulled her sweat-slicked body tightly into his arms. He knew he was dancing with disaster. His careful plans were destroyed. The future was precarious. But at that moment he didn't care. He had never felt so good in his entire life.

Hours later Maggie awoke, cold and stiff. The warmth of the night had fled from the chill of predawn. Christopher slept beside her. The tip of her nose rested against his bare chest. His muscle-knotted thigh pressed against her woman's mound that still ached from his enthusiastic invasion.

Reluctant to wake her husband, she didn't move. The conclusion of the night had been like a dream. She sorted through her memories to make sure they were real. If it hadn't been for the masculine body still interlocked with hers and the ache from unaccustomed intimacy, she wouldn't have believed her recollection of how she had come to be here.

Christopher was going to England, and she was going with him. She had demanded the right to go with him. Maggie remembered making a tortured decision in the fraction of a second—to stay in New Mexico as a prosperous propertied lady, or to follow Christopher to a foreign land where he assured her she wouldn't fit in.

Perhaps she was a fool, but she loved this man, and couldn't give up. Giving up was not in her nature.

Still, she wondered fearfully what kind of strange land and strange life she had committed herself to.

II

England

Thirteen

Maggie considered herself quite well traveled.
After all, before she was eight she had been
from one end of Denver to the other running
errands for her mother. When she was ten she
had traveled a whole fifty miles southwest to the
Alvarez ranch, and four years later she had successfully negotiated alone the same long trail
back to Denver. If that were not enough to
qualify her as an experienced traveler, then certainly the trip to Santa Fe, the visit to the Slater
Ranch, and then finally the move to Rancho del
Rio, would. She had traveled more than any
person of her acquaintance with the exception
of Christopher and Peter, who didn't really

qualify as ordinary people because they were Englishmen. Luisa also might outdo her as traveled. She had come to America from Mexico City, and Maggie wasn't quite sure how far Mexico City was.

In any case, Maggie considered that she had seen a fair part of the world, or at least that was her belief until she traveled with Christopher and Peter to England. The trip was like nothing she had ever before experienced—emotional peaks and abysses following one after the other. Leaving Rancho del Rio had been difficult, and saying farewell to Luisa had been even harder. However, Maggie felt better about leaving her friend at the ranch than she would have if Luisa had returned to Denver. Much to Maggie's delight Christopher had convinced Luisa to stay at the ranch to oversee the household and the accounts.

The road Maggie followed from New Mexico to London was full of surprises, shocks, and revelations. New York was farther away than she had believed anything could be. Bigger, also. The city was a chaos of people, carriages, noise, and giant buildings as far as one could see. Maggie was glad to leave, even though the steamer they boarded in New York Harbor seemed to her much too flimsy to challenge the vast sea, and the ship seemed smaller and ever more fragile as they left land behind and all Maggie saw before them was water, water, and more heaving, endless water.

Once on their way Christopher assured Maggie that compared to many crossings, the vast Atlantic was on its best behavior. Maggie's stomach didn't agree, and during the sea trip nothing went down that didn't come up again in very short order. By the time the steamer put into the harbor at London, Maggie was almost miserable enough that the bustling wharves didn't make an impression. Once she set foot on land, however, the sights, sounds, and smells of London battered her awareness with an intensity impossible to ignore. The dingy buildings that crowded one upon the other, the smoke- and stench-laden air that filled her lungs and stung her eyes, and the noise —hawkers shouting their wares, people yelling at each other across the street from the upper stories of buildings, coachmen hollering at their teams, carriages rumbling over uneven cobblestones. Maggie wanted to shut her mind and her ears. Even New York hadn't been so bad. And what made it worse—all the shouting, yelling, and conversing was accomplished in accents even stranger than Christopher's, some completely incomprehensible to Maggie's ears.

By the time a hired coach deposited them at the duke of Torrington's town house in Kensington, Maggie felt like Alice in Wonderland. She hadn't yet decided if her particular Wonderland was a nightmare or a dream.

They were greeted at the door of the town house by a tall gentleman whom Maggie assumed was the duke, Christopher's father. The fellow was exceedingly courteous for a highbrow duke, Maggie thought as he took Christopher's hat and Maggie's traveling cloak. Her experience with the genteel society in Denver had taught her that in the upper strata of society people often thought too highly of themselves to be polite to others.

Christopher set her straight. "Maggie, this is Grays. Grays is the butler here at Torrington House. He runs the place. If you have need of anything, all you need do is ask him. He's very efficient."

"Thank you, Lord Christopher. Torrington House is honored by your presence, Lady Christopher."

Maggie looked around for Lady Christopher, then realized the butler was talking to her. "Uh . . . thank you, Mr. Grays."

Grays's brow twitched, and out of the corner of her eye Maggie caught Christopher's smile. She'd made a mistake already, and she didn't even know what it was. The house had a name, the butler looked like a duke, she was supposed to be some sort of a high-flown lady, and she could scarcely understand a word of what came out of these oh-so-English mouths.

"Her Grace is paying calls with Lady Stephen, my lord. Your brothers are at their club. Lady Elizabeth is home, however. I will inform her of your arrival."

As the butler left, Christopher said quietly, "Call him Grays, not Mr. Grays."

"But that's rude."

"He's used to it."

"And you're always lecturing *me* on manners!"

Christopher led her to a room that he explained was the family drawing room. "It's much less formal than the formal drawing room," he told her.

How the family drawing room could be less formal than anything was beyond Maggie. The decor made the overblown fussiness of the Harley ranch house look plain by comparison. The walls were pale rose-pink. Draperies and furniture upholstery contrasted in bright apple-green, and a huge fireplace boasted a pink marble mantel. The statuary that graced the room was also marble in shades of white, pink, and light gray. Ornately carved tables, chairs, and settees cluttered every corner of the room and the middle as well. Statues crowded between the furniture, and one corner sported a tiny fountain with water dribbling from a marble cherub's mouth and trickling into a pool at its feet. In the pool swam a school of tiny, glistening fish.

"This is . . . amazing," Maggie commented.

"I thought you might find it so," Christopher replied with a wry smile.

Maggie felt she could scarcely breathe in the clutter. The apple-green draperies were drawn to keep out the weak midday sun. Heavy oak doors isolated the room from the rest of the house, which no doubt was equally closed in. Perhaps with England being such a small island (Christopher had pointed it out on a map), the English people felt obligated to live in such small spaces between chairs and couches and statues and tables.

Suddenly the oak doors opened and a girl wafted into the room like a fresh, gentle breeze. She was blond and very fair skinned. Her eyes sparkled a pale blue to match her elegant silk gown.

"Christopher! Oh, Christopher! I thought you'd never come home!"

The girl flew into Christopher's embrace with an enthusiasm that made Maggie immediately think that this must be the flawless Miss Hawthorne—just as perfect as Maggie had imagined.

Christopher gave the impeccable little miss a hug then set her on her feet. "Maggie, this is Elizabeth, my sister."

Maggie let out her breath in relief. Christopher could hug a sister all he wanted.

"Elizabeth, meet Magdalena Montoya Talbot, my wife."

Elizabeth looked stunned. Then she smiled. The girl's smile immediately made Maggie like her. It was bright and genuine, flowing straight from the heart and glowing in her pale eyes.

"Magdalena. What a beautiful name." Elizabeth took both Maggie's hands in hers. The English girl's skin was as soft as a horse's velvet nose. "Welcome to London, sister. You must be absolutely exhausted from your journey. Christopher, you knave, why didn't you tell us that your wife was coming to London with you?"

Christopher raised a brow, and before he could say something cutting, Maggie spoke up. "I decided to come at the last minute, and Christopher just couldn't talk me out of it."

"Good for you! I'm delighted to meet another female who can get the best of my surly brother. There aren't very many of us, you know. You can have the French room. I'll have Mrs. Scrubbs make sure everything in the room is fresh and then you can take a nap. Knowing Christopher, he's probably had very little consideration of your comfort on this trip. Men simply do not understand feminine frailties."

Christopher interrupted. "Maggie will occupy my rooms. With me," he added to be sure he got the point across.

Elizabeth's brows twitched upward. She colored faintly. "Christopher, a lady should have her own suite of rooms; the French room is connected to yours, if you'll remember."

"I prefer that my wife share my rooms, Elizabeth. Don't look so shocked. In America it's done all the time."

"Mother will have a fit, Christopher."

"Mother will have a fit over more than Maggie sharing my rooms, as well you know. Are my rooms ready?"

"Of course. We've been expecting you for the last week."

"Good. I, also, feel in need of a nap. Maggie, let me show you the way." He gave his sister a peck on the cheek. "No doubt we'll see you at dinner."

Maggie had no idea what Elizabeth found so shocking. After all, they were married.

Christopher's rooms appeared Spartan in comparison to the rest of the house. A bedroom, sitting room, dressing room, and bathing room were decorated in tones of brown and blue. The furniture was simple and rather sparse. Two chairs upholstered in light blue chintz occupied the sitting room along with a daybed and reading table. A canopied oak four-poster bed dominated the bedroom. The only other furniture was necessary, not ornamental—a matching oak wardrobe, dressing table, and tall chest of drawers. The bathing room was a novelty to Maggie. A polished brass tub sat on a platform of tile. Nearby stood buckets for water. An oak washstand occupied the rest of the small room along with a fine china pitcher and basin and a small mirror.

"If you want to redecorate and add some feminine frills, you may," Christopher offered. "We won't be here long, though. I have a house of my own in Lincoln's Inn Fields, but I had it remodeled in my absence, and it will be several weeks before the house is livable."

Maggie turned slowly around to examine the bedroom. It was a masculine room ungarnished by clutter. She liked it much better than the drawing room or what she had seen of the rest of the house. "This is a far cry from a muddy alley or a cold storeroom, and I've slept in both." She stopped turning and found herself pinned by Christopher's dark eyes.

"Are you feeling better now that you're on dry land?"

"I feel as though the house is rocking beneath my feet, just like on the ship. But I am better. I could eat a whole cow," she hinted. "What time is dinner?"

"Not until eight."

"I'll starve by then."

"No, you won't. I'll ring for tea in a couple of hours."

Maggie missed having free rein in her own kitchen. "Why don't we just go downstairs and raid the pantry? Would your sister be too shocked?"

"She would." Christopher smiled slightly. "But she would be even more shocked by what I mean to do instead."

He took a step toward her before Maggie comprehended his intentions. She had been green with seasickness so long that she had almost forgotten any physical feeling except nausea. Now the look in Christopher's eyes flooded her with a warm heaviness that flowed from her breasts in a tightening, intensifying spiral to the female core of her. His gaze seemed to follow the path of that sweet warmth, then rose again to capture her eyes.

"It's the middle of the day!" she protested halfheartedly.

"The better to appreciate the sight of your loveliness."

Maggie fought the urge to giggle. Men didn't like to be laughed at when they were hot with passion, she'd been told. And Christopher was looking very hot. "Shouldn't we be taking a nap? Isn't that what you told your sister?"

"To hell with my sister. It's you I'm interested in right now. Don't play coy, wife. I've slept next to you for too long without touching you."

Maggie retreated until her back was to the wall, but her teasing eyes lured him forward. "That never bothered you before."

"It bothered me. Now be quiet."

He cupped her face in his hands and kissed her. Maggie melted. She had forgotten that kissing was such a delicious sport, that the caress of Christopher's mouth tingled clear down to her toes and struck every nerve in the pit of her belly.

"Mmmm," she murmured when he released her mouth. "I'm not tired any longer."

"Neither am I. Nevertheless, I feel an urgent need to be in bed." His fingers worked efficiently at the buttons of her bodice. The fastenings yielded. The material peeled easily down her shoulders, and his hands found her breasts. "A very urgent need," he whispered in her ear.

Maggie was feeling a bit urgent herself. She helped him dispose of the rest of their clothing and willingly fell with him on the bed. The temperature of her blood seemed to rise as he nibbled at her breasts, her ribs, her stomach. He devoured her, and she wanted to be devoured. She arched up to meet his caresses.

"Impatient as always," he murmured against her mouth. "Don't you know ladies are simply supposed to endure while gentlemen indulge their beastly appetites?"

"I'm enduring quite well," she replied breathlessly. "Be as beastly as you please." Every nerve was on delighted edge. His lips burned with sweet fire, his hands worked magic on her flesh.

He wedged himself between her legs and spread her thighs wide. A kiss caressed her navel, then slid smoothly down into the warm tangle of curls that guarded her sex. Hot as flame, his tongue touched her nether lips, parted her slick flesh, prodded, licked, and invaded. A jolt like lightning made Maggie convulse. She threw back her head and closed her eyes as pleasure sharp as pain flooded over her.

"Still enduring?" asked his silken voice.

She couldn't answer. She could scarcely breathe.

"So I see," he continued to himself with a quiet chuckle. In one swift action he rolled to his back and lifted Maggie from the bed. Startled and dizzy with passion, she let him position her astride his thighs. "This is another game, one that ladies seldom play."

His finger found the center of her desire and very gently stroked. She gasped in surprised bliss.

"Maggie cat, you are so easily pleasured. And you are so willing to please. Come here and please me even more."

He lifted her above the tower of his arousal. When she saw what he wanted, she was both astonished and intrigued. Willingly she lowered herself onto him. An imp of mischief made her stop just as his flesh parted the warm gate to her passageway.

"Does this please you?" she teased.

"Oh, Lord, yes!"

She moved, and he groaned with the pleasure of it. Fascinated by a new feeling of power, she moved and dipped in sinuous seduction, allowing him to penetrate her body a little deeper with each movement, torturing both him and herself with the promise of paradise.

Christopher grasped her teasing hips with both hands. "Witch," he accused in a strained voice. "I'm going to have to teach you some manners—afterwards."

He arched upward and pulled her down at the same time. Maggie allowed herself to be impaled. The sharp rapture of him driving inside her made spots swim before her eyes. He drove again, then again. Maggie caught the rhythm of his thrusts and moved in sensuous counterpoint. Climax overtook them in only moments. The pulses of his explosion combined with sharp contractions of ecstasy that rolled through her body. All strength seemed to leave her. Christopher caught her as she fell forward and rolled her beneath him. Still firmly inside her, he nestled comfortably between her legs and covered her like a blanket with his body.

Several deep breaths later Maggie's vision cleared to focus on the dark face above hers. The face looked thoughtfully solemn.

"I know." She sighed. "Ladies don't do that sort of thing."

Christopher's smile was warm as the embers that still burned inside her. "As you've said to me before, wife, it pays at times to be not quite a lady. You can do that sort of thing as often as you like."

When Maggie woke, the pale pink light of dusk was spilling into the room through the window. She was covered with a light quilt that had lain at the foot of the bed, and the sheets where Christopher had slept beside her were cold. She sat up and tossed the wild mane of her hair out of her eyes. Hugging her knees, she smiled.

She liked being a wife. If she was not beloved, at least she felt well loved—if only in a physical sense. Passion could and would lead to love, Maggie assured herself. She knew of a few whores on Market Street in Denver who had tried the same tactics and failed. But Maggie would not fail. She had become discouraged when she realized that Christopher disdained the idea of loving her, but now that she had committed herself fully to be his wife, surely his attitude would change.

As no one was about to help her into a proper gown, she donned a simple skirt and bodice and found her way to the staircase. She understood now why Peter Scarborough had thought of the house on Fourteenth Street in Denver as a cottage. The duke's town house was huge. From where she stood on the landing, the staircase led both up and down. Hallways branched in two directions —the main one more a gallery than a simple hallway. Maggie guessed that a person might get lost in the mansion and starve before he could find his way out. Her stomach rumbled at the thought. Christopher and she had been so preoccupied that they had completely forgotten about ringing for tea.

Looking around her curiously, she descended the staircase. The house seemed deserted. Not even a servant was in sight. Only the faint sound of voices coming from behind a closed door near the entrance hall bore witness that someone was indeed at home. Maggie recognized one of the voices as Christopher's. The other was feminine and a bit shrill.

Maggie banished a twinge of conscience and moved closer to eavesdrop, curiosity getting the best of her. As she pressed her ear against the door, a woman spoke impatiently.

"This is really quite unacceptable, Christopher. What will everyone say? How ever will the members of this family hold up our heads in public once Society has a look at this . . . what did you say her name is?"

"Magdalena Teresa Maria Montoya Talbot. Maggie for short. If it makes you feel better, she's a descendant of a very old Spanish family."

The woman sniffed loudly. "Maggie." She pronounced the name as if it soiled her tongue. "A bumpkin from America. I doubt there's any real aristocratic blood in her veins. What did you say she was when you found her? An entertainer of some sort?"

"A saloon dancer. She's really quite talented. You should see her dance someday."

"I doubt I would appreciate it. A saloon dancer. Lud, Christopher! I can't think of anything worse. This is a social disaster. What could have possessed you to bring her here?"

"Mother, you knew that marriage with the Montoya heir might prove necessary to regain Stephen's land. Peter Scarborough and I discussed the matter with you before we left for America. You raised no objection to the idea."

"My dear boy, you did what was necessary to aid the family finances and preserve the family honor. It was acceptable only because you are a younger son and therefore your marriage connections are not as important as your brother James's. But that doesn't mean that you should flaunt how we had to lower ourselves to achieve these assets. Some alliances are best kept out of the public eye. You should have learned that by now, Christopher."

Christopher voice grew hard. "Mother, I want to make one thing perfectly clear. Maggie is my wife. She is a woman of extraordinary courage and intelligence, no matter where I found her. She also happens to bring with her a sizable contribution to this family's welfare. If you intend to accept her land and the revenue it brings, then you must accept Maggie also. She's entitled to courtesy and kindness from every member of this family."

The woman's voice became peevish. "How can you ask such a thing of me or your sister? We are gently bred ladies with tender sensibilities. You've given this—this dancer your honorable name and a secure future. Must we all lower our standards by consorting with such a person?"

Maggie didn't hear Christopher's reply; her ears were burning too hotly from her anger. The word *dancer* coming from this woman's mouth sounded like a cuss word. *Person* also hid a wealth of contempt. Something "gentle ladies" found vulgar and offensive. And the old witch had the nerve to judge her before they'd even met!

Without a thought for the consequences Maggie opened the door and barged in. Bookcases lined the walls from floor to ceiling and a huge oak desk dominated almost half of the room. Over the fireplace mantel a painting of a stern-faced gentleman in the costume of two centuries past stared down at Maggie as if ready to shout her from the room. Wearing an equally stern expression was was a dark-haired lady dressed in mauve silk. She was draped on a love seat under the window like a queen on a dais. White wings at her temples were the only signs of her age. Her face was sharp featured and smooth as cold marble. Her eyes were a piercing, glacial green, and they widened at Maggie's sudden entrance.

"Madam, I am not a—a person." She loaded the word with a contempt equal to the lady's. "No one calls Magdalena Montoya names and gets away with it."

"Indeed!" The woman raised a lorgnette to one eye and scrutinized her as she might examine an insect who had crawled from under the plush rug. "I take it that this is the girl, Christopher."

Christopher closed his eyes briefly, then opened them with a sigh. "Mother, may I present Maggie, my wife. Maggie, this lady is my mother, the—"

"The duchess of Torrington," the woman interrupted. She paused, as if waiting to see the impression her title made on the intruder.

Maggie didn't greet the woman with a polite "Pleased to meet you." How could she be pleased to meet a person who had just talked about her as though she were dirt? Worse than dirt.

"Do you make a habit of listening in on other people's conversations, dear?"

Maggie refused to retreat before the duchess's cold stare. "When the conversation is about me, I figure I have a right to hear."

"Tch! Christopher, you could have at least taught the chit some manners before setting her loose on civilization."

"Seems to me you could use some manners yourself, Duchess."

Lady Torrington's mouth dropped open. A moment passed before she recovered. "I never heard such boldness! In England, miss, young people have respect for their elders and young women do not presume to speak their mind so brazenly."

"In the West people have respect for those who deserve it and anyone speaks his mind whenever he pleases."

"Impertinent girl! Have you no idea who I am?"

Christopher attempted to intervene. "Mother, please. Maggie, mind your manners. This isn't New Mexico."

Maggie glared at him. She'd been delighted at his earlier defense of her. Why didn't he stand up for her now?

He cocked one brow in sardonic reproach. "You wanted to come to London," he reminded her.

He had warned her that she wouldn't fit in, that she wouldn't know how to behave like a genteel English lady. She had scoffed, but perhaps he'd been right. The warm glow she'd carried from their lovemaking faded.

"Mother, Maggie is a stranger here and doesn't know our ways. She and I will be living at Torrington House for only a few weeks. During that time I expect you to be understanding. And, Maggie, I expect you to be respectful toward my mother."

Maggie felt like a chastened child. It was all she could do not to stick out her lower lip in a pout.

"Is that understood?" Christopher pinned first Maggie, then his mother, with flinty eyes. "Is it?" he demanded when neither woman answered.

"Of course I will be understanding," the duchess conceded in a sharp tone. "There is scarcely a lady in London with more understanding than I."

"Maggie?"

"I'll try. But she shouldn't be calling me names."

"She won't call you any more names now that she's met you."

Maggie wished she could have Lady Torrington for one day in New Mexico. She would let her pull bog for a few hours. A few minutes in a mudhole next to the rear end of a cow would do the woman good. "Then I'll give her all the respect she deserves."

From the look on Christopher's face he didn't much like her answer. The duchess's frown indicated the same. Well, Maggie thought, they would just have to be satisfied.

Maggie was spared meeting the remainder of the Talbot family until dinner, a formal affair presided over by the duke. The duchess was not present, having taken to her bed with a case of nerves.

"Mother is very sensitive," Elizabeth told Maggie apologetically. "The excitement of Christopher's arrival—and yours—quite did her in."

The young man who had been introduced as Christopher's younger brother Rodney snorted at Elizabeth's assessment of their mother's delicacy. "Mother's about as sensitive as a dragon. She's just putting on a show to make Christopher feel guilty about being gone so long."

"Rodney, you're being boorish," said James, the eldest of the three brothers. "What will our new sister-in-law think?"

Maggie thought that Rodney bordered on being sloshed. She could smell the whiskey on his breath from across the big oak dining table.

"Who? Our new who?" The duke peered at them all from the head of the table. He was elegant in black evening dress. Tall, lean, with steel-gray hair and a face that wore the lines of age well, he was obviously the source of Christopher's strong, striking features. Only the duke's slightly vacant expression and the uncomprehending haze of his muddy eyes betrayed the ravages of senility.

"Our new sister-in-law, Father." James sounded impatient. "Christopher married, you know."

"Of course I know! Melissa, Melinda, some such name. . . ."

"Magdalena, sir," Christopher provided.

"That's a Spanish name! You didn't marry a Papist, did you, boy?"

"No, Father. Maggie is from America."

"Oh, well, that's different. Your great-great-grandfather, the second duke of Torrington, fought the Americans in their little rebellion, you know. Got himself killed, he did. Lucky he had a son, or we wouldn't any of us be here."

For some reason Maggie felt guilty. "I'm sorry, Your Grace."

He focused on her face with obvious difficulty. "No need to be sorry, girl. I doubt you killed him."

"No, sir."

"Father!" Rodney interjected with a long-suffering roll of his eyes. "This is 1883. Of course she didn't kill him."

Across the table from Maggie the only member of the Talbot family who had not deigned to speak sat picking at her food with a stony face. She had been introduced as Lady Stephen Talbot, Catharine, the unfortunate Stephen's widow. Stony and expressionless as it was, her face was quite beautiful. Soft brown hair framed a perfect oval with pale skin and slightly heightened color on the cheeks. Fawn-colored eyes matched her hair. Full lips pressed into a tight line of disapproval.

"Adela!" the duke called. "Where is Adela?"

"Mother is in her room," James told the old man. "Her nerves again."

"Nerves, poppycock!" The duke stabbed at his beef-and-kidney pie. In a sudden change of subject he asked Maggie, "Where are you from, girl?"

"New Mexico, sir." If all family conversations were like this one, Maggie didn't blame Rodney for being drunk, James distant, Elizabeth timid, and Catharine silent. "In America."

"You don't say."

"Just how big is my husband's ranch?" Catharine spoke for the first time.

"It's not your husband's anymore," James told her in a cutting tone. "It's Christopher's. Actually, it's the family's."

"Actually, it's Maggie's and mine," Christopher clarified.

James gave him a sharp look.

"And to answer Catharine's question, Rancho del Rio is about one hundred thousand acres. The Montoya Grant, which is land given to Maggie's family by several different New Mexican governors, is five times that area. Eventually we'll be working all of the grant, I hope, but that will take some careful planning."

"How much planning does it take to set cattle to graze on grassland?" James said with a chuckle.

"There's a lot more to ranching than just turning cattle loose to graze," Maggie told James. All eyes turned her way, as if she'd said something odd. Then they looked away.

"How much is the total acreage worth?" James persisted. "We're a bit hard up, now, you know. Not that we're the only ones. Everyone's having difficulty collecting rents on the land since agriculture slipped so low. Perhaps it would be better to sell the land and invest elsewhere."

"You can't do that!" Maggie declared. "That land is the richest grazing in the West, and the cattle market's booming."

Again every eye at the table swung in her direction. Christopher was the only one who didn't look surprised at her outburst.

"Forgive us, Maggie," James said. "We should have better manners than to discuss business in the presence of ladies."

The conversation turned to a critique of an opera that James and Rodney had both attended two nights before. Elizabeth rattled on about a new artist who was taking the artistic set of London by storm, and Catharine brooded in silence. The duke regularly interjected comments that had nothing whatsoever to do with the conversation, but his family talked around him as if he weren't there. Soon he was silent.

For Maggie dinner seemed to go on interminably, but finally she and Christopher were allowed to retire to the privacy of their rooms. The first words out of Maggie's mouth once the door was securely closed behind them was a desperate question.

"You won't sell my land, will you? You can't. That ranch is—is . . ."

"Maggie, calm down. No one is going to sell Rancho del Rio."

"I should say not! Besides, even the sale of such a lot of land couldn't support *this*!" She raised her arms to indicate Torrington House and everything in it. Elizabeth had taken her on the tour before dinner, and Maggie had lost count of the rooms—from the servants' rooms in the attic, the family bedroom suites on the first floor, the public and private drawing rooms, morning room, writing room, library, and dining room, and upper servants' hall on the main floor, to the larder, scullery, kitchen, storerooms, butler's, housekeeper's, and footmen's rooms in the basement. "I can't imagine now why you wanted my land grant. You people must be rich as kings!"

Christopher chuckled as he took off his coat. "Once the dukes of Torrington were as rich as kings. But the family finances have eroded. We still have considerable sources of income: land, mostly. And I am a partner in a shipping business that has helped to support the family."

Maggie sat down upon the bed and tried to understand this strange land with its strange way of life. "Doesn't anyone work?"

"Well, no, actually. As you doubtless gathered from the dinner conversation, Rodney gambles, James spends most of his time flitting about with women, Father is in his dotage, and, of course, ladies of quality keep busy with social engagements and a certain amount of charity work."

"Hmmph! No wonder your family's running out of money!"

Christopher grinned engagingly. "You may have a point. It's not at all like New Mexico, is it?"

"I like New Mexico better."

"You could have stayed," he said, growing serious.

She lifted her chin a notch. "Just because I wanted to hobnob with the aristocrats doesn't mean I have to like them. It's a cinch your family doesn't like me."

"I didn't expect them to."

Because he didn't like her either? Maggie wondered. He liked her enough in some ways.

"Maggie, you came here of your own free will. Now that you're here, the situation would be much relieved if you tried to mold yourself a bit to English ideas of proper behavior."

There he went harping on propriety again. On the other hand, if she was ever to win the man, perhaps she should try harder to please him. "I'll think about it."

"And please limit your opinions on unfeminine subjects to the privacy of conversations between you and me."

"Unfeminine subjects?"

"Such as land and business."

"That was *my* land your brother was talking about selling to pay for his opera tickets and Rodney's gambling debts!"

"Maggie, one of the purposes of my regaining Stephen's ranch was to help my family. You can be sure I won't let James or anyone else make unwise decisions concerning the investment. I promised you once that you would never regret trusting me with your land and your welfare. I meant it."

She sniffed. "It looks to me like your family needs more help than any piece of land can give them."

Christopher dropped a boot in the process of removing

it from his foot. "That's enough. You're part of this family now and should learn something about family loyalty."

"Hmmmph!" After putting up with the Talbot family for just a few hours, Maggie had a better understanding of why the American colonies had rebelled against the English.

"Just smooth down those ruffled feathers and come here," Christopher said in a softer tone.

Maggie wasn't really in the mood for a cuddle.

"Come here, Maggie. I'll help you off with your gown."

When she didn't move he reached for her. At the touch of his fingers on her skin Maggie's pique began to melt. By the time he had removed the last of her clothing, she had thawed into a steaming puddle. It wasn't until after they had come together on the bed and merged in the common ground of passion that the painful uneasiness returned to her. England was more foreign than she had guessed: a strange land inhabited by a strange people. She ached for the familiar streets of Denver, the mountains and plains of New Mexico, the open, hardworking honesty of people like the Slaters, Moss Riley, and Luisa. How she missed Luisa and Rancho del Rio. How she missed home.

In front of the cold fireplace in the parlor, rocking in the rocking chair that Moss Riley had made her, Luisa Gutierrez sat with Peter Scarborough's letter in her lap. The last rays of the sun slanted through the window, and the coolness of dusk was already supplanting the heat of the day. Fall was on its way. Even now in late August one could feel the change of seasons in the air.

She scanned the letter for the tenth time. It had been written on shipboard in the Atlantic. Christopher regularly paced the deck, Peter reported. He didn't know if he was anxious to be reunited with his family, was fretting about his wife, or was worrying about leaving the ranch. Perhaps all three. Maggie was thoroughly seasick and therefore had behaved herself in an exemplary fashion by confining herself to the cabin she shared with Christopher. Otherwise, Peter speculated, she might have been pelting the sailors with questions about the ship. He'd never in his life known anyone with as much life or mischief as Maggie, but seasickness could bring down even the most energetic, he confided. He felt a touch of it himself.

Luisa smiled sadly. By now Peter was in England, going about his life as though he had never met Luisa Gutierrez. Christopher and Maggie were there also. She wondered how Maggie was faring. The English could not be so cold as not to love her. Luisa fancied herself quite as cold as anyone she'd met, and she loved Magdalena. Underneath her brash exterior the girl was as warm and giving as an angel.

The front door opened, then slammed shut. "Miz Luisa?" came Moss Riley's call.

"In the parlor, Moss."

He came through the door and hesitated, turning his sweat-stained hat in his hands. "Evenin', Miz Luisa. I learned somethin' in town that I thought you oughta know."

"Sit down, Moss. No need to stand. You look done in."

"Got rustlers over on the south bend of the river and a bunch of cows by Mescalero Springs that ate somethin' that's makin' 'em crazy. And the damned—'scuse me, ma'am—dagnabbed buckboard threw a wheel on the way back from town. That's why I'm so late."

"Let me get you some lemonade."

"I surely could use some."

Luisa fetched them both a glass of the sugary tart drink. She watched Moss Riley eye her over the rim of his glass.

He was a good man, a solid man, good looking in his way with his iron gray hair and deep blue eyes. She wished she could return his interest, but she couldn't.

"What was it you learned in town, Moss?"

"What? Oh, yeah. Guess who bought that big tract of land that borders the grant on the south?"

"Who?"

"Todd Harley, that's who. Heard he won a bit of money following his daddy's old profession up in Denver. Spent it all on that land."

"How interesting." And perhaps alarming. "Do you think he'll cause trouble?"

"Hard to say. Todd wasn't much more than a shadow to his daddy. Now the old man is locked up, hard to figure what Todd might grow up to be."

"Well, I don't think we should jump to the wrong conclusion. After all, as you pointed out, the son is not the father. And what trouble could he make, anyway?"

Moss shrugged and finished his lemonade. "Hard to say."

Fourteen

Maggie woke just as night was fading to gray morning. The sheets were cold where Christopher had slept. He was gone already. Maggie wondered if just once in her life she might be permitted to wake with her husband beside her. A sleepy cuddle before rising to face the day would be very nice.

She tried to go back to sleep, but couldn't. The rumbling of her stomach kept her awake. The food at dinner had been plentiful and good, but she hadn't eaten much. Dinner conversation at the Talbot table was not conducive to appetite. She wondered if she could find anything to eat in the kitchen.

Maggie rose, splashed her face with the cold water, and donned a rather simple lawn gown that Christopher had explained was a "morning gown"—he'd bought a dozen ready-made gowns for her the moment they'd docked at London, as if her clothes from New Mexico weren't good enough for the big city. What's more, he had promised to order more. Maggie swore that the English were so concerned about clothing that they must keep an army of seamstresses and tailors busy day and night. And to think for most of her life she had considered herself lucky to have one change of clothes.

At the foot of the stairs she was greeted solemnly by Grays. "Good morning, Lady Christopher."

"Uh . . . good morning, Grays." She wondered what the impeccable, owl-faced butler would say if she asked him to call her Maggie. She decided not to try it. He was more intimidating than the Talbots themselves. "Do you know where my husband is?"

"Lord Christopher went riding very early, I believe. Such is his habit whenever he resides at Torrington House."

"Oh." He probably needed the time away from his family to retain his sanity, Maggie thought.

"Lady Elizabeth is in the garden, my lady. I believe Miss Rachel is with her."

"Which way is the garden?"

"Follow me, my lady."

The garden was not a patch of dirt with rows of vegetables and flowers, as Maggie had imagined. It was a large walled enclosure where sculptured shrubbery and formal beds of carefully nurtured flowers were interwoven in intricate patterns. Double French doors led from the morning room onto a flagstone deck with stone benches and a tiny fountain that trickled water from a cherub's pouty mouth. Trees lined the wall and shaded the deck.

At the far end of the deck Elizabeth sat at an easel. Beside her stood a little girl with dark hair tortured into precise ringlets, each of which was tied in place by a short scrap of cloth. When the child turned to watch Maggie come into the garden, her long cotton nightdress belled out to reveal dirty bare feet.

"Look, Aunt Elizabeth! Someone's coming!"

Elizabeth looked up from her painting. "Maggie! Did you sleep well? You're up so early."

"So are you."

"I'm Rachel," the child piped up. "I escaped from Miss Fizzwater. Who are you?"

"I'm Maggie."

"Rachel," Elizabeth chided, "it's Miss Fitzwater, not Fizzwater, and you know better than to speak before you're spoken to." She turned to Maggie. "Rachel is Catharine and Stephen's daughter. Rachel, Maggie is your uncle Christopher's new wife."

Maggie sat on her heels to bring herself down to the child's level. "How did I miss meeting you yesterday, Rachel?"

"Miss Fizzwater said I wasn't to bother Mum and everybody."

"Miss Fizzwater—oh, pooh! Now you have me doing it! Miss Fitzwater is Rachel's nanny."

"Nanny?"

"She takes care of Rachel."

"Like a mother?"

"Well, yes."

"And Catharine lets her?"

Elizabeth's smile was tolerant. "Children are always raised by nurses and nannies, except in the lower classes, of course."

"I don't think I would want my children raised by someone else," Maggie said incredulously.

"One can't simply withdraw from the world to raise a child, not with all the social obligations that our class imposes."

Maggie's attention strayed to the painting that Elizabeth had been working on. Daybreak in the garden had been captured on canvas. The trees were silhouetted against the faint rose of dawn. On a stone bench was an open book and beside it two leaves that had fallen from the tree above. The painting was a mesh of colors in which the details were blurred but the spirit was clear. The scene was warm with the poignancy of late summer.

"Your painting is beautiful," Maggie said.

Elizabeth blushed and dithered. "Oh, it's just a casual avocation. Painting relaxes me. Mother says it's good for my nerves."

"Do you have nerves also?" Maggie asked, remembering the duchess's attack that kept her from dinner.

Elizabeth gave her a rather wry smile. "All ladies of any sensibility have a bit of nerves."

Maggie examined the painting more carefully. The sun had risen and the colors of dawn were now gone from the garden, but she could look at the painting and feel as well as see the garden at daybreak. "You really are good."

"Do you think so?"

"Oh, yes. You're an artist."

"You flatter me, Maggie. Mother and Catharine say I must remember to keep art in its place. It's only a pleasant pastime, really. It isn't as though I could be a real artist, one whose paintings adorn people's walls."

"Of course you could. I would love to have this painting on a wall. Every time I looked at it I would think of this garden with the first light of the day peeking through the trees and the summer almost gone."

"Then take the painting as a gift."

"Oh, I couldn't do that."

"Of course you can. It's my wedding gift to my new sister." She looked at Maggie wistfully. "Actually, landscapes are not my forte. I've always imagined myself as a portrait painter. Faces are so interesting, don't you think?"

"Faces must be very difficult to paint."

"To get one right requires patience." Suddenly, she smiled. "Maggie, would you let me paint your portrait? You could sit for me on early mornings when no one is about. The rest of the house seldom rises much before noon."

"Why would you want to paint me?"

"You have a most intriguing face. It has spirit and—and mischief, if you don't mind my saying so. And feminine mystery as well. I would like to see if I could capture it."

Maggie grinned. "Imagine it! My face on a painting! That's almost like being famous."

"I must warn you, I'm not the sort of painter who glorifies the subject."

"Being glorified would be nice," Maggie said a bit wistfully, remembering her old dreams of dancing in San Francisco and having posters of herself plastered all over the city. "But it's your paintbrush."

"Good. Let me set up a new canvas and we'll begin. The light is particularly good here this time of day."

Maggie spent the next hour trying to sit still on the stone bench that had been the subject for Elizabeth's first painting. Rachel watched critically as Elizabeth worked with her oils. Maggie tried hard not to squirm, but sitting perfectly still without talking was a near impossibility. She earned herself more than one scolding from the artist.

Between admonishments to be still Elizabeth chattered about the Talbot family. The duchess was known by her children as "the dragon," the girl confided. Since the duke's health had deteriorated, Lady Torrington had become accustomed to ordering her family as she saw fit. She had only good in mind for all of them, Elizabeth assured Maggie. Her mother really had the very best of hearts; she was simply strong willed.

As for the rest of the family—James, Elizabeth confided with a chuckle, was professionally bored with the world. Rodney indulged himself in drink and gambling until the duchess had been forced to limit his expenditures. Catharine was lonely and had little prospects of remarrying because Stephen had lost everything in New Mexico and, being the youngest son, had very little from the Talbot estates. With no fortune of her own poor Catharine might go to her grave still a widow.

Maggie felt as though she had been dropped into one of those weary English novels that Peter had forced her to read. "Where is everyone this morning? Have they already gone out?"

Elizabeth laughed. "Everyone is still abed, of course. Except Christopher, who I understand is riding."

"Isn't it late to be still sleeping?" The sun had been above the horizon for almost an hour.

"Sit still, Maggie. You just moved your head at least two inches. Move it back, please. Yes, that's much better." Elizabeth measured with her eyes and daubed at the canvas with her brush. "As to your question, my brothers and parents usually rise late. Many evenings they are out until the small hours of the morning. I'm the only one interested in seeing the sunrise, and when I've attended the opera or a soirée or late supper, I linger abed also."

"Oh."

"They'll be up especially late this morning, I suspect. The Lord Calamath is giving a ball tonight in honor of his daughter's debut. It's bound to be quite an affair, because Lord Calamath is shockingly rich, and he's determined to find a husband for poor Mary Victoria, even though the girl is half blind and sadly plain. I'd be surprised if the festivities don't last until dawn."

"Then why are you up so early this morning?"

"Oh, I shan't be going tonight. I still have a cough hanging on from a lung congestion I had a few weeks ago. Besides, my fiancé is in the country right now. It would hardly be proper for me to go to the ball and dance with other men while he is absent."

"You're going to be married? How exciting!"

"Don't bounce so, dear! My goodness, don't American ladies learn how to sit still?"

"Who is he?"

"Who is who?"

"The man you're going to marry."

"Oh. Viscount Standbridge."

"What is he like?" Maggie asked with typical female curiosity.

"He's quite amiable, and the family fortune is considerable. When his father dies, George will be earl of Woolford. Mother believes he's quite a catch. We're to be married next spring. Right now he and Mother and the family barristers are still negotiating dowry, dower, and monthly allowance after I'm married."

The matter-of-fact tone of Elizabeth's voice took Maggie by surprise. Did all the English regard marriage as a business enterprise?

"George sounds like a duck when he laughs," Rachel informed Maggie.

"Rachel! It's not polite to say such things."

"I don't like him."

"*You* don't have to marry him," Elizabeth said crisply. "Besides, he likes you very well. In fact, Rachel is the darling of us all, aren't you, dear?"

"Except Miss Fizzwater," Rachel said with five-year-old disdain.

"Fitzwater," Elizabeth corrected.

"Did you want me, Lady Elizabeth?" inquired a new voice. It belonged to a spare woman with mousy brown hair. She was dressed in a plain gray gown with starched white collar and cuffs.

"Miss Fitzwater!" Elizabeth sounded as if she were a child caught making mud pies by the nanny.

"I see Rachel is here. I apologize, Lady Elizabeth. She sneaked out of the nursery before I woke this morning. Rachel, you know you're not to bother your elders unless you're sent for. And look at you! Not even properly dressed. A young lady five years of age should know better than to run downstairs in her nightgown and—mercy! —are those feet bare? Young lady, come with me right now. There will be no breakfast for you this morning!"

"You needn't scold her, Miss Fitzwater. Rachel knows she's always welcome to watch me paint." She set down her brush and palette. "Maggie, dear, you may relax now. Allow me to present Miss Adelaide Fitzwater, Rachel's nanny. Miss Fitzwater, this is Lady Christopher Talbot, my brother's bride."

Miss Fitzwater gave her a brief curtsy. Maggie couldn't imagine such a woman raising a bright, lively child like Rachel. The woman looked to be stiff and dried up as a dead stick.

"I'm pleased to meet you, Miss Fitzwater. Did someone mention breakfast? All this sitting still has given me an appetite."

"Oh, dear," Elizabeth said. "I'm afraid breakfast won't be served until almost noon."

"Surely Rachel can't wait that long," Maggie winked at the little girl, who broke into a wide smile.

"Rachel takes her meals in the nursery," Elizabeth said.

"And she'll have no breakfast this morning as punishment for her misbehavior," the nanny reminded them.

"I haven't seen any misbehavior," Maggie said. She took Rachel's hand. "I'd bet that if I could find the kitchen in this place, I could rustle us up something to eat. What do you say? We could take it to your room and you could introduce me to your toys."

Rachel squealed in delight, drowning out Miss Fitzwater's objection.

Elizabeth looked uneasily from the nanny to Maggie. "I'm a bit hungry myself," she admitted. "Perhaps we could all have a morning picnic in the nursery."

The nanny opened her mouth to object, but an imperious look from Elizabeth silenced her. Maggie decided she would ask Elizabeth to teach her that look. It was probably something included in the education of every English lady.

"Come along, Maggie, Rachel. We shall find Cook. Miss Fitzwater, why don't you take the morning off?"

Miss Fitzwater looked as though a morning to herself was beyond her understanding.

"Really, Miss Fitzwater, Lady Christopher and I will watch after Rachel, and I will tell Her Grace and Lady Stephen that I insisted."

"If you truly insist, Lady Elizabeth."

When she was gone, the two women and one small child traded conspiratorial smiles.

Cook was more than happy to oblige them with a special breakfast served in the nursery when she heard that Miss Fitzwater was not to be present. (The cook and governess did not do well together, Elizabeth informed Maggie out of Rachel's hearing. Maggie wondered if there was any end to the twists and turns of this household.) Cook sent up to the nursery sugared rolls, a bowl of apples, oranges, and pears, a platter of bacon, a huge mound of eggs, and sweet tarts of pastry and marmalade. As they sat at a child-sized table in the schoolroom, Elizabeth and

Rachel both watched in wonder as Maggie satisfied a very unladylike appetite.

"You sure eat a lot," Rachel observed candidly.

"Habit," Maggie explained with a laugh. "On the ranch in New Mexico we eat breakfast before the sun rises— eggs, ham, potatoes, pancakes, bread and butter. That has to last all through the hard workday until a late-afternoon dinner." She didn't add that before Christopher had found her she'd had to eat hugely whenever opportunity arose, for too often opportunity didn't arise on a regular basis.

"What do you work at?" Rachel asked.

"Yes, do tell us about your ranch in New Mexico," Elizabeth urged as she took dainty bites of a marmalade tart.

Maggie filled the next two hours with stories of New Mexico and Colorado. Her audience was rapt. Rachel announced that she wanted to learn how to rope a cow. Elizabeth expressed shock that many of the women on American cattle ranches shared in the hard physical labor with their men, and that the owners of such ranches sweated and toiled along with their employees rather than running the operation from the comfort of a town house.

"Isn't that how it's done in England?" Maggie asked incredulously.

"Dear Maggie, if my father the duke had ever labored beside the men who worked his land, he would have lost their respect entirely."

Maggie wondered how a man could lose respect by honest hard work. But then, she understood little about this England and its people.

By noon the family was up and about, as Elizabeth had predicted. Breakfast was served in the "morning room," a sunny alcove surrounded by windows looking out over the garden with its late summer flowers. The room seemed to move the sun indoors. The table was adorned with a gleaming white tablecloth. Yellow chintz upholstered the chairs and draped the windows. Sunlight poured across the breakfast table and climbed the walls in bright squares and rectangles.

Despite the cheerfulness of the room, however, the family still gathered in solemn formality with the duchess ruling at the head of the bright white table. Christopher had returned from his ride and was elegantly handsome in morning coat and tailored trousers. Maggie admired the aristocratic figure he cut, but she thought he looked better in mud-splattered denims and cowboy boots. He gallantly held her chair while she was seated.

"Are you well this morning?" he inquired politely.

Maggie didn't point out that the morning had long since fled. Apparently the English had a different sense of time than Americans.

"Quite well, thank you. Did you have a pleasant ride?"

"Very pleasant."

Maggie noted that he didn't look entirely happy to be back at his old routine. Dared she hope that he had missed her on his morning's ride? Could last night's passion have spilled over into an intimate early-morning companionship if she had just awakened early enough to go with him? Next time, she vowed, she would offer to ride with him.

The conversation around the breakfast table was lackluster. Elizabeth sat at her place with proper primness. The sparkle that had brightened her face in the early morning was gone, though she did flash Maggie a brief, amused smile when Maggie stabbed a huge portion of bacon from the platter—it had been quite a while, after all, since their early-morning meal.

Rodney, the youngest brother, ate almost nothing at all. His face paled to a greenish tinge when the kidney pies were brought out, and he exited in haste. James was magnaminously polite with inquiries as to how Maggie had slept and an offer to hire her a personal maid.

"That won't be necessary, James," Christopher told his brother. "Maggie and I will be moving to my town house in a few weeks. I'll make arrangements then for a personal staff. While we're here, perhaps she could share Catharine's or Elizabeth's abigail."

Catharine was quick to respond. "My Joan is busy enough seeing to my needs without having to serve your wife as well."

"I'm sure that Nicole wouldn't mind splitting her time between Maggie and me," Elizabeth said.

"Oh, really! I don't need a maid," Maggie declared.

Catharine was aghast. "Of course you do!"

"No, I don't."

"You do," Catharine said with a contemptuous sniff for Maggie's plebeian ideas. "If word got out that you tended yourself people would think you are eccentric. Or worse, that we were so poor that we couldn't afford to hire an abigail for you. This is a duke's household, and you are the daughter-in-law of a duke. No matter what common habits and practices you had in your New Mexico, you must remember that now you are in England."

Maggie's ire began to rise, but before she could speak, Catharine continued her imperious lecture. "And as long as we are on the subject," the young widow said with a scowl, "I would appreciate your not filling Rachel's head with stories about that savage land you sprang from. I visited her in the nursery before I came downstairs, and she was spouting all sorts of nonsense about America. What's more, I understand you and Elizabeth had an early breakfast with Rachel in the nursery and sent Miss Fitzwater on a few hours of holiday. Adults do not have "picnics" in the nursery, and I'll thank you to let Miss Fitzwater tend to her duties. You're filling Rachel's head with lower-class ideas, and I will not have it. And you, Elizabeth! I was shocked to hear that you participated in this escapade."

Christopher stepped in calmly. "Catharine, telling Rachel stories about New Mexico is scarcely filling her head with lower-class ideas. The American West is a fascinating land. It won't do the child any harm to broaden her horizons and teach her that there are other countries besides England and other ways of living as well."

Catharine looked at Christopher as though he had uttered blasphemy. "She learns all she needs from Miss Fitzwater."

"Who I'm sure is a veritable fount of knowledge and the broadest-minded person imaginable."

Maggie smiled at Christopher's sardonic tone, but the rest of the family regarded him suspiciously. Finally, the duchess made a pronouncement. "Christopher, you're being contrary. Catharine knows best what her child should learn. And she's right. Even at Rachel's tender age a young girl should not be encouraged to show such curiosity about foreign places and foreign ways. Such interests make gentlemen suspect she is a bit of an adventuress and would not be content to stay home and be a proper wife."

"Mother, Rachel is only five years old."

"Bad habits start early," Lady Torrington proclaimed.

As the duchess raised her lorgnette and skewered Maggie with a sharp eye, Maggie got the feeling that the wife Christopher had brought back from "foreign places" was a bad habit all unto herself.

"Mother," Christopher said, "Maggie meant no harm."

Her Grace sniffed. "I'm sure she didn't know any better. Indeed, I'm sure she didn't."

From that point on in the conversation the duchess and Catharine ignored Maggie as though she were an embarrassing stain on the white tablecloth. They talked of the latest triumphs and blunders of London society. Lady So-and-So was cut dead by the countess of This-and-That. Lord High-and-Mighty was pursuing Miss Whoever, but only because of her money. And wasn't it a shame that Miss Whoever's family fortune had been made in trade? The admission of such commoners to Society as though they were true aristocrats made one question what the modern world was coming to.

Soon conversation turned to Lord Calamath's ball. Catharine was being escorted by James, and the duchess hoped the duke would be alert enough to attend, but she doubted that he would.

"I think that Christopher and Maggie should attend," Elizabeth said.

The table fell silent. Maggie felt her heartbeat increase a notch at the thought of attending such an elegant affair. It would be a chance to show Christopher that she could fit into English society if she really tried.

Finally, the duchess spoke in grave tones. "I doubt Maggie would be comfortable in such society, Elizabeth. It would be unfair to expect so much of her."

"I agree," Christopher said rather too quickly. "Let Maggie get accustomed to London before you throw her to those wolves."

Maggie gave him a black look, but Christopher shook his head almost imperceptibly. She sighed. The ball would probably be hot and noisy and too terribly proper to be much fun, she told herself.

"Yes, of course," Elizabeth said softly. She seemed to sense Maggie's disappointment. "I forgot that you've both just had a long journey. There will be other balls when Maggie is rested and more at home in London. How thoughtless of me to suggest that you should go."

The duchess raised an admonitory brow. "Do try to

think before you let your enthusiasms run away with you, Elizabeth."

Maggie suffered a pang of foreboding. She had vowed to make Christopher a good wife, to prove that she could fit in with his highbrow friends and family, to demonstrate that she could be as much a lady as anyone. And here she was, scarcely a day spent with Christopher's family, and already they thought her an ignorant bumpkin and a lout. She risked a sideways glance at Christopher. His eyes were on his food, and he seemed to be paying little heed to the conversation that flowed around him. The set of his features indicated that his mind was elsewhere.

Now that Maggie thought about it, Christopher had seemed distracted even the night before when he'd made love to her, an activity that usually engrossed his entire attention. She'd thought that following him to his home would make her a real wife to him, but here he seemed more distant from her than he'd ever been. England was somehow taking him away from her, perhaps by reminding him of how different she was from fine ladies like his mother and his sister.

The sunlight in the morning room and the cheerfulness of the yellow chintz chairs and draperies became suddenly less bright, or so it seemed to Maggie.

In the midafternoon the duchess invited Maggie to join the other ladies of the household in a carriage promenade. Maggie dared to hope that she had mistaken Lady Torrington's attitude toward her. As Elizabeth helped her to select an appropriate "afternoon gown" and told her of the prominent people they would most likely see on their outing, Maggie promised herself that she would play the lady so perfectly that the duchess and haughty Catharine would be astounded at her gentility.

Her hopes were dimmed by Lady Torrington's chilly

manner as the four of them set out from Torrington House. The duchess's greeting to her new daughter-in-law could have brought an early frost to the trees under which they passed. Her lorgnette came up time and time again, as if she couldn't quite believe what she saw sitting across from her in the carriage.

Their landau was driven by a groom and attended by two footmen who stood on a small platform at the rear. All three serving men were nattily decked out in identical livery—striped waistcoats with silver buttons embossed with the family crest, top hats, breeches, and white silk stockings. Maggie noted with amusement that the stockings were padded in the calves. She thought with pride that if Christopher were a footman, he certainly wouldn't have to pad his stockings to cut a fine figure. The thought of his long, muscular legs diverted her thinking to a path that was definitely not ladylike. Her husband might be the reserved English gentleman in the daylight, but at least at night he had learned how to be a barbarian.

"Maggie, you positively look like a cat with a bowl of cream," Elizabeth observed.

"But of course," the duchess noted, "she must love the out-of-doors, coming from a place that has so much of it."

"The air is nice today, isn't it?" Catharine said.

Maggie thought the air stank of smoke and manure, but she was willing to be amiable. "The air is nice," she agreed.

Elizabeth provided Maggie with a quiet commentary as they drove. The London Season was well over, but the ladies of Society still showed themselves in their splendid equipages on the drive traversing Ladies' Mile, the Serpentine, then back to Hyde Park Corner. The route was not as crowded as it was during the Season, Elizabeth informed her, when every lady with any pretensions to social standing displayed herself along the drive. Still,

Maggie thought the roads quite congested. She had never seen so many styles of horse-drawn vehicles. Landaus, town coaches, barouches, phaetons, coupes, Victorias, and broughams were a few pointed out by Elizabeth. All were attended by footmen and grooms who seemed to compete with each other for the most elaborate liveries. The teams of horses were bedecked grandly with silver-laden harnesses.

Catharine condescended to point out the different breeds in the carefully color-matched teams: Cleveland bays, Yorkshires, and hackneys were the most popular. The team of four pulling their own landau were gray Yorkshires that pranced with great spirit, necks arched, heads high, their long tails flowing in the breeze like proud banners. Maggie thought it a fine show until Elizabeth whispered to her that the groom forced the horses' heads into the unnatural arch by means of a cruel bit attached to the bearing reins, and two of the four horses had false tails. Maggie's indignation at such abuse grew each time the groom twitched his reins and the team threw their beautiful heads about in a showy and false exhibition of spirit.

The participants in the afternoon carriage promenade seemed to be very well acquainted with each other. Greetings were called from carriage to carriage, and frequently two vehicles would stop so the ladies could chat, uncaring that they blocked the road.

"Oh, do look!" Catharine exclaimed several minutes along the Ladies' Mile. "There's Lady Jane Trevour. I hear her father had to sell the family paintings. Poor dear. It's such a shame that she couldn't bring Lord Henley up to scratch. Everyone thought that the wedding was nearly set."

Catharine didn't sound in the least sympathy with the poor lady, Maggie noted.

"That Victoria she's in is hired from a jobmaster," the

duchess said. "They can't afford to maintain their own stables any longer. Such a shame. The Trevour family is old and honorable. They won their title in the fourteenth century. But the present earl is a wastrel, if I do say so myself."

The duchess didn't greet Lady Jane as they passed, despite the Trevour family's fourteenth-century title. Maggie understood enough to know that a duchess far outranked the mere daughter of an earl, and according to the brief lesson Elizabeth had given her in the higher forms of etiquette, the higher-ranking lady must initiate a greeting or conversation if there is to be one. Poor Lady Jane had just been "cut" by the duchess because the lady's father was a wastrel. Maggie thought the whole thing rude, ridiculous, and rather cruel.

Catharine's voice rose to an excited pitch. "Oh, my goodness! Coming toward us! Is that—? Yes, it is. I thought she was in the country—Amelia Hawthorne."

Maggie noticed Elizabeth looked uneasy. Her own heart jumped a beat. Amelia Hawthorne? The same Amelia Hawthorne who had written Christopher letters about how much she'd missed him?

Perfect Miss Amelia was driving her own phaeton with a liveried groom riding on horseback at a discreet distance behind her. As the carriages met, the duchess signaled the groom to stop. "Amelia, dear! How nice to see you. I thought you were with your brother in Cornwall for the fall and winter."

"Good afternoon, Your Grace. Lady Elizabeth, Lady Stephen. I just returned with my uncle. We are opening Shielding House. I decided Cornwall in the winter would be simply too dull."

"I am in total agreement. We're simply delighted that you've returned. The winter would have been twice as tedious without your presence."

Amelia glanced with polite curiosity at Maggie. The duchess gave them both a sly look. "Amelia, dear. Allow me to present Magdalena Teresa . . . uh . . ." She turned to Maggie. "What is the rest of your charming Spanish name, dear?"

"Magdalena Teresa Maria Montoya—Talbot." Maggie emphasized the last. The duchess scowled. The Perfect Amelia's brows puckered only slightly.

"Little Maggie is heiress to a large estate in the wilds of New Mexico—quite an uncivilized country, you know. She is Christopher's wife."

The dismay that flashed across Amelia's face was quickly banished. "How nice to meet you, Lady Christopher."

"Please call me Maggie. Everyone does."

"Then you must call me Amelia." The lady's smile hinted at nothing but genteel courtesy.

"Of course you are attending Lord Calamath's ball this evening," said Lady Torrington to the favored miss.

"Yes, of course. I will be there with my uncle and aunt. We were very honored to receive an invitation."

"Of course you received an invitation, dear. Even though your family is in trade, you are not at all crass like some of those who have earned their fortunes through common commerce. You are a sweet girl, and would be entirely acceptable to any social gathering."

The meek Amelia didn't seem at all offended by what Maggie considered an insult. In fact, the little twit seemed grateful as she thanked the duchess.

"We will see you this evening, then." Lady Torrington signaled the groom to move on. Maggie resisted the temptation to glance over her shoulder for a last look at Miss Impeccable. She was even more perfect than Maggie had imagined: rose-tinted cheeks, soft Cupid's-bow lips, skin that glowed like firelit satin, golden hair piled stylishly under a fetching little hat, and a driving costume that accentuated her generous curves without being at all crass. Maggie had hated her at first sight.

She looked up into Lady Torrington's knowing gaze. The dragon was going to make sure she knew all about Christopher and Amelia, Maggie realized. She braced herself.

"Amelia is such an accomplished lady," the duchess informed Maggie. "You would do well to watch and emulate her, my dear. Not, of course, that you could hope to bring yourself to her level. She is an excellent horsewoman and drives her own phaeton, as you saw. Her musical talent and dancing are exceptionally fine, and she speaks four languages fluently." She looked at Maggie from beneath arched brows. "Perhaps Christopher mentioned her to you?"

"In a way," Maggie admitted.

"They are such good friends. Season before last everyone thought they would be married, but of course, when the trouble with Stephen arose, Christopher realized he had obligations elsewhere. Family duty has always come first with my son."

"So I've learned."

Maggie refused to show the turmoil she felt. She wasn't about to give the old dragon the pleasure of seeing her cowed before Amelia's perfection. After all, she doubted that the talented Amelia could rope a cow, pull bog, chase away a grizzly bear, or dance the flamenco in a way that could have an audience of hardened miners and cowboys drooling in their boots. She wasn't so accomplished, that pale flower of genteel English maidenhood.

Lady Torrington's face settled into a decided smirk. Maggie felt her face grow warm. She decided that she'd been trod beneath these ladies' slippers long enough. She would show them that Magdalena Montoya wasn't so easily bested, and she would do it at Lord Calamath's stupid ball.

Maggie turned to Elizabeth. "Do you think Christopher would take me to the ball tonight if I asked him?"

Elizabeth looked surprised. Slowly a smile spread across her face at the same time expressions of consternation paled the visages of Lady Torrington and Catharine.

"I'm sure he would be delighted," Elizabeth lied. "Simply delighted."

Fifteen

"Ouch! You stuck me again!"

"Well, stop moving!" Elizabeth admonished Maggie. "I have never met a person who had so much trouble standing or sitting still."

Maggie flinched as Elizabeth pinned the final tuck in the waist of the ball gown that was being altered for Maggie's social debut. She regarded herself doubtfully in the bedroom mirror. "I don't see why I can't wear the red lace dress I brought from New Mexico."

"Because you brought it from New Mexico," Elizabeth told her. "This is London, Maggie."

"As if I would forget."

"This will do very well for tonight."

Maggie felt a bit exposed as Elizabeth stood back and gave the dress her critical scrutiny. The tiny sleeves of the gown left her arms almost bare, and the neckline plunged so low that it revealed more than she really wanted revealed. The bodice was shaped sections of silk that hugged her body in an almost indecent manner, and the volumes of material gathered at her rear made her feel terribly off balance.

"How I envy that wasp waist of yours," Elizabeth said with a sigh. "Still, the fit of the gown isn't bad with the tucks I've pinned. I'll ask Nicole to take it in. I'm not much good with a needle myself."

"If Nicole alters the dress, you won't be able to wear it again."

"That's no loss, dear. The lilac color never suited me anyway. It looks much better on you."

"I would feel more comfortable in the red dress."

"Really, Maggie, I can see that I must educate you about selecting apparel for different occasions. And you must ask Christopher to buy you a new wardrobe."

"Christopher is always buying me clothes. He bought me at least a dozen things the minute we got off the ship. I haven't even worn them all yet."

"Well, he hasn't gotten it right yet. I can see I must educate him as well. After all, you're his wife, and a wealthy heiress unto yourself. You can't be seen in London in anything less than the very latest and best. We'll make an exception tonight—only because the notice is so short."

Lordy! Christopher was right. Englishwomen did think of nothing but clothes.

"Now, step out of the gown and I'll give it to Nicole." She moved to help. "Oops. I've pinned you in, it seems. Just let me unfasten this at the back. Careful now."

Maggie managed to wriggle out of the gown only a few

pin scratches the worse. Her heart warmed toward Elizabeth, who seemed to be the only friendly person she had met in all of London.

"You might want to rest for a few hours. I'll have Cook send up a light supper about six. Until then . . ."

"Oh, don't leave, Elizabeth. It—it feels good to have someone friendly to talk to."

Elizabeth turned down the bed and gestured for Maggie to get in. "Poor dear. Christopher should have warned you about Mother and Catharine."

"Well, he did, sort of."

Elizabeth sat on the foot of the bed and pulled her legs up beneath her. "I don't think I've ever seen anything quite like the surprise on Christopher's face when you announced that he was taking you to the ball. Goodness, Maggie, I do admire your boldness. You didn't ask him; you told him."

"I'm afraid that's a bad habit of mine. And I don't think that was surprise on Christopher's face; I think it was panic. No doubt he thinks I'll make a jackass of myself."

Elizabeth laughed. "A jackass? You do have the most colorful speech."

"That comes from having colorful thoughts. Undisciplined, Christopher and Peter used to say. My thoughts are undisciplined."

"You mustn't take those two so seriously. After all, they're only men."

Maggie laughed, then she sobered. "Elizabeth, you know that Christopher married me only to get the land that your brother Stephen lost?"

"Of course I know." Elizabeth's voice was gentle. "Dear Maggie, that is certainly no insult to you. Marriages are made more often for economic reasons than for reasons of the heart. Certainly no one would think less of you for the circumstances of your marriage."

"Well, I've always believed that if one must marry, the marriage should be built upon love. *If* one must marry. Myself, I never believed I would marry. I always made my own way in life. Being dependent on a man seemed . . . well, very risky."

"A person cannot go through life without being dependent at times. Especially if that person is a woman. Our world is designed for men to rule and women to influence, don't you think?"

Maggie sighed and leaned back against the pillows. "Anymore, I don't know what I think."

"Mother once told me that being a woman is a constant state of balancing idealism and practicality, dependence and strength, innocence and wisdom. That's quite a lot to expect." Elizabeth sighed. "My road has been much easier than yours, though. I always knew that I would marry, and that I would marry for practical reasons, not romantic ones. Viscount Standbridge is a pleasant enough fellow." She grinned. "Though Rachel is right, I fear. He does sound like a duck when he laughs. I admit that I have only the most superficial of feelings for him, and he for me also, I expect."

Maggie looked at her with wide eyes. "Then why are you two getting married? If he's rich, as you say, he couldn't be marrying you for money."

"Of course not. If he were interested in a fortune, he would certainly marry elsewhere. We Talbots are not so wealthy since the agricultural depression. He desires a connection with the Torrington title."

"Doesn't he have his own title?"

"He'll be earl of Woolford someday. But I am the daughter of a duke."

"A duke is much higher?"

"Most definitely. Father used to have quite a bit of influence in Parliament. Since his health deteriorated, he's mostly ignored, but when James inherits the title, I imagine the family power will grow once again. That is what George wants to marry."

"And that doesn't upset you?"

"Not in the least."

Maggie heard the words, but Elizabeth's eyes told a different story. The girl was better at lying to herself than to others, Maggie suspected. She shook her head. "It's not right. None of it."

Elizabeth laid a sympathetic hand on Maggie's arm. "Dear Maggie, do you fancy yourself in love with my brother?"

"I . . ." Maggie hesitated. She had admitted her feelings to herself, but they were more difficult to admit to someone else. But Elizabeth had a gentle look about her that invited confidences. "Yes. I love Christopher. I didn't at first, of course. I thought he was arrogant and muleheaded and useless as a pistol with no trigger. But I came to realize that he's a better man than any I've met. I vowed I would make that jackass love me, and I'll do it yet."

Elizabeth smiled compassionately. "Perhaps you will, Maggie. But don't hope for too much. Christopher guards his heart well. My brother tries to be the perfect gentleman. He's kind, considerate, protective of his family and friends, but he's always been very stingy with his emotions."

"He wants the perfect lady to match his perfect gentleman."

"Perhaps."

"And he found her in Amelia Hawthorne," Maggie said sourly. "I suppose she's about as perfect as can be."

Elizabeth made a face. "Men can be so stupid at times. Amelia's flaws are perfectly obvious to me. I don't know why every man in London thinks she's such a paragon."

"What are her flaws?" Maggie certainly wanted to know, because she hadn't seen any.

"If you get to know her better, you'll see them."

"I don't want to know her any better than I already do."

"Don't let her intimidate you," Elizabeth advised. "Christopher truly admired Amelia, but I doubt that his heart was much involved."

"Why do you say that?"

"Because I don't think my brother knows that he has a heart."

Lord Calamath's ball was beyond anything Maggie had ever imagined. She had thought the social affairs she had attended in Denver and Santa Fe were sumptuous, but the Calamath festivity was sophisticated refinement at its highest. The ballroom was a fantasy of candles and flowers. The men were elegant in their formal evening clothes, and the women shone in silk, lace, gauze, ribbons, and velvet. Jewels winked from throats, wrists, fingers, and hair, their sparkle rivaling the huge crystal chandelier that hung above the crowd. The parquet floor was so highly polished that not even the punishment of so many boots, shoes, and dancing slippers marred its luster.

Maggie had thought Elizabeth's altered ball gown was daring in the extreme. She also felt uncomfortably fancified in the coiffure Nicole had concocted—the abigail had wound her hair with ribbons and pinned it into place as an elaborate crown of silken curls. As they were announced into the ballroom, however, and Maggie's gaze swept the assembled elite of London, she realized that she was dressed and coiffed more conservatively than almost any lady in the room. As eyes turned toward them, she suddenly felt plain and awkward. Perhaps coming to the ball had been a mistake.

Christopher's mother led their party into the crowd,

followed by James and Catharine, and then Christopher, Maggie, and Rodney. The duke was not well enough to attend.

Christopher held firmly to Maggie's arm. "Smile, Maggie. You look as though you were walking up a scaffold. You wanted to come, my dear."

Maggie smiled, but it was an effort. Still, the crowd was not yet looking down their collective noses at her. Perhaps she didn't look as out of place as she felt.

The dancing had already started. Lady Torrington believed in arriving at these affairs late enough to make an impressive entrance. But the dance being performed on the floor was a formal, stilted thing with which Maggie was not familiar. Peter had taught her the waltz. He hadn't mentioned anything about the elaborate twists, turns, and postures that were being done here.

Christopher steered her away from both the duchess and the dance floor. "We should greet Mary Victoria. She's Calamath's daughter and hostess."

And the girl whom their host was attempting to marry off, Maggie remembered Elizabeth saying.

When they approached their hostess, Mary Victoria was surrounded by a group of admirers who were vying for the next dance. She greeted Christopher with a wide smile.

"Lord Christopher Talbot. You're back in London. How delightful. You survived the wilds of America."

"I found them quite invigorating, actually. Lady Mary Victoria, may I present my bride, Magdalena Teresa Maria Montoya Talbot."

Maggie silently congratulated Christopher on pronouncing the long string of names without a stumble. He actually made her sound like a woman of some note, a woman whom he was proud to call wife. Maggie's heart lifted. She gave Mary Victoria a warm smile, which their hostess returned in full measure. Lady Mary wasn't nearly as plain as Elizabeth had implied, Maggie thought, but an unattractive squint did bear witness to her poor eyesight.

"I'm very pleased to meet you, Lady Christopher. May I call you Magdalena?"

"Please do."

"Maggie is American," Christopher explained. "From Colorado and New Mexico."

"How exciting. You must be very brave. I've read accounts of Indian massacres and raids."

"Well . . ." Maggie wondered if it would dim the girl's enthusiasm if she told her that the closest Maggie had ever come to being massacred by an Indian was when Tony Alvarez's Pueblo foreman had caught her playing cards with the hands in the bunkhouse. She decided that it would. "Most of the Indians are peaceful and on reservations. There are still a few that make trouble—mostly Geronimo and his friends."

"You shouldn't be reading such things," Christopher told Mary. "They're mostly exaggerations."

"That's what Father tells me, but I would adore hearing a firsthand account from Magdalena."

"Then you must call on my wife. I'm sure Lady Torrington would welcome you."

"I will make a point of it."

All during their conversation Lady Mary's suitors hovered in the background like wolves circling for a kill. Maggie remembered Elizabeth's comment on the large dowry Lord Calamath planned to bestow upon his only daughter. Did Mary Victoria know her father was buying her a husband? Of course she knew, Maggie thought. Perhaps that was why the girl looked so reluctant to turn back to her admirers.

The next dance was a waltz. Christopher led Maggie onto the dance floor. As they whirled in time to the orchestra's music, Christopher smiled down at her. "Is the ball what you expected?"

"It's unbelievable. If those stuffy society matrons in Denver could see this, they'd drop their teeth. Even Horace Tabor couldn't afford a hoopla like this, and he's almost as rich as God Himself."

Christopher chuckled. "You do have a colorful way of expressing yourself."

"Lady Mary Victoria seems very nice."

"She is very nice. Maggie, not everyone in London is like my mother and Catharine. People will like you if you let them."

Maggie's heart warmed.

Christopher's arm tightened around her as he said quietly in her ear, "You're doing very well, you know. Just remember to be a lady." His breath was warm, and the familiar scent of him started her nerves to humming and her blood to moving. The waltz was anything but dull when she danced it with Christopher, but the flush of feeling he created inside her made her long to express herself in her own dance—to move to the sensuous rhythm he inspired in the deepest fibers of her being. But she restrained herself. She would behave and prove to her husband that she could be as proper and perfect as any English lady.

The warm current in her blood quickly froze, however, when the dragon herself emerged from the crowd with her arm linked cozily through that of Amelia Hawthorne. "Christopher, dear, look who is here. It's dear Amelia."

To his credit Christopher scarcely blinked an eye or gave an uneasy twitch. That in itself was a bit vexing. Christopher might not realize that Maggie knew all about him and Miss Perfect, but she would have gotten satisfaction out of at least a small show of guilt.

"Good evening, Amelia. You're looking lovely tonight."

She looked like a froth of spun sugar, Maggie thought sourly—all sweetness and no substance.

"Why, thank you, Christopher. I hoped you would be here tonight. I saw your mother in the park this afternoon and was delighted to learn that you'd returned."

I'll just bet you're delighted, Maggie sniped to herself.

"Allow me to present my wife, Magdalena Teresa Maria Montoya Talbot."

Amelia turned her radiant smile on Maggie. "We met this afternoon. How nice to see you again, Magdalena. Don't you look fetching! Isn't that the wonderful gown that Elizabeth wore to Tamara Hodges's debut last season? It looks lovely on you."

Maggie stiffened. She didn't have to be a social savant to know a cut when she heard one. Christopher, being a man, didn't seem to notice.

"How is your family?" Christopher inquired.

"Splendid, really. Uncle Dan made a fortune in shipping this year. In fact, Christopher, I'm afraid he may be cutting into Pitney and Talbot's business."

Christopher smiled equably. "Now that I've returned, perhaps I can change that."

"Of course you will. But let's talk of something else. Business is so boring, isn't it? Aunt Clarisse is planning a grand Christmas gathering at Oakley Fields. I do hope you'll be able to come." She gave Maggie a measuring glance. "Of course the whole family is invited."

"I've already accepted for all of us," Lady Torrington said.

Maggie wondered if the duchess would have considered attending a gathering at the house of a mere tradesman—however rich he was—if she hadn't been so set on rubbing Christopher's nose in Amelia's charm.

"We'll look forward to it," Christopher said graciously.

Maggie would look forward to it with the same enthusiasm she felt for having a tooth pulled.

"We'll have an absolutely wonderful time," Amelia gushed. "Skating, hot cider around the fire, long walks in the snowy woods . . ."

Amelia waxed poetic, but Maggie knew the cozy rendezvous she planned did not included an unwanted wife.

"We have so much catching up to do," Miss Perfect continued. "I must hear all about your adventures in America. You must dance with me and tell me of your brother's estate in New Mexico." She gave Maggie a thinly veiled look of triumph. "You don't mind, do you, dear?"

Amelia whisked Christopher away before Maggie could so much as open her mouth. She saw a subtle smile of satisfaction curve Lady Torrington's thin lips. Apparently, this was war, and these ladies had launched the first attack. Maggie was accustomed to meeting conflicts head on. Subtlety and veiled feints were not her style. But she had to give these gals credit. A grizzly bear's charge was nothing compared with what a London lady could do with a mere cutting glance.

She wondered how the grand high duchess would deal with honesty and aboveboard fighting. Perhaps the time had come to give straightforwardness a try. It might be a tactic that would knock the ladies off their guard, seeing that they never used it themselves.

"What do you want, Lady Torrington?" Maggie kept her voice matter-of-fact and businesslike. "Do you want Christopher to divorce me? Are you disappointed that he didn't marry Amelia?"

The duchess's scowl could have flattened a whole pine forest. "What nonsense! Magdalena, dear, you have no notion of what you're talking about."

"I have a notion that you're pushing my husband up Amelia Hawthorne's skirts."

Lady Torrington's eyes widened. "You are a crude little chit, aren't you?"

Maggie refused to lower her eyes.

"Of course you must not divorce. Such a thing would be ruinous. And as I said before, though Amelia would have been Christopher's first choice, she was not suitable. Though her uncle has a respectable fortune, she was not the key to Stephen's land, and honor demanded that we set that situation straight. No, my dear, I am merely doing you the kindness of pointing out how unlike you are to the women Christopher admires and respects. If I must be brutally frank, I'll tell you that if you stay in England you will be an embarrassment to this family. You and my son must both get on with the lives you were destined for. Christopher has given you a future much better than the one you provided for yourself. Go back to New Mexico and enjoy it."

"And let Christopher get on with his own life?"

"Yes. Both of you can have lives of your own, lives that you are suited for. My dear Magdalena, trying to climb above your station in life never brings happiness."

With that final pronouncement the duchess turned and marched away. Maggie felt like making a rude gesture at the woman's back, but that certainly was not a ladylike thing to do—even though the old witch deserved it.

With lips pressed tight to keep from trembling, she swept the room with her eyes until she found Christopher and Amelia. They danced beautifully together, flowing over the floor as though one. Amelia smiled up at Christopher, and he looked rapt with admiration. Maggie comforted herself by imagining Amelia as she might have looked slopping the pigs on Tony Alvarez's ranch. Alvarez had owned a purely vicious hog that would have punched a few holes in Amelia's high opinion of herself. And when Miss Perfect had done a few days' worth of ranch chores, even that horny toad Alvarez wouldn't think she was much of a woman. Tony wasn't real picky, but even he liked his women to have some use other than decorating a parlor and making other women's lives miserable.

"Why, Maggie! I didn't expect to see you here!"

Maggie turned gratefully toward Peter's familiar voice. The tall barrister had a lady on his arm—a slender, dark-haired woman with pleasant laugh lines radiating from brilliant blue eyes.

"Maggie, this is my sister, Mrs. Alice Dunbar, a widow lady. Alice, meet Magdalena Montoya Talbot, Lord Christopher's bride."

"I'm honored," Alice said, offering a friendly hand. She seemed to be sincere. "Peter has told me so much about you and your friend Luisa."

Peter jumped at the opening. "Speaking of Luisa, have you heard from her?"

Maggie smiled. "There was no letter waiting when we arrived at Torrington House, if that's what you mean. After all, there's hardly been time."

"Ah, well." He sighed. "I'm sure she's fine. I've never met a woman more competent at taking care of herself than Luisa. Unless it's you, Maggie."

Maggie's eyes darted to where Christopher and Amelia were still dancing like entranced lovers. Peter followed her gaze.

"I see you've met Miss Hawthorne."

"Yes."

"She doesn't hold a candle to you, my dear."

Maggie had to laugh. "Of course she doesn't. I'm the grandest lady in the room, and happy as a pig in mud." She felt Peter's gentle scrutiny, turned to meet his eyes, then looked at the floor. Back in Denver he would have reprimanded her for unladylike sarcasm, not to mention overly colorful language, but now he simply sighed.

"How do you like London? I remember numerous times during our literature lessons you told me that English customs seemed entirely nonsensical to you."

"They still do. You should have warned me about these upper-crust English ladies. I've never met anyone so busy doing nothing. No offense, Mrs. Dunbar."

Alice chuckled. "We are a peculiar race, Lady Christopher. But you're bound to get used to us in time."

The question was, Maggie countered silently, would England get used to her?

After a single dance with Amelia, Christopher was trapped by Lady Hethrington, a formidable matron who had once pursued him diligently on behalf of her daughter, who was now married to a minor baronet. The lady's company was impossible to escape without being crassly rude.

"Is that your lovely bride?" Lady Hethrington inquired. "The petite little thing talking to Peter Scarborough and his sister."

"Indeed it is, my lady." Christopher was glad to see that Maggie had escaped his mother's company and had found protection with Peter. He was a bit ashamed of having allowed himself to be pulled away by Amelia, especially while his mother was sharpening her claws on Maggie's feelings. But without snubbing Amelia, he'd had little choice. Maneuvering around an enemy in battle was sometimes easier than maneuvering around ladies at a ball.

"My goodness but she's a pretty little thing!" Lady Hethrington exclaimed. "I hear you found her in America. Who would think that wild land could yield such a lovely flower. Everyone in the room is admiring her. An heiress, no less. You must be very glad that you could so easily retrieve your brother's land."

The lady's blatant assumption that he'd married Maggie for her land sat ill with Christopher, even though it was true. He himself had openly declared it to a roomful of New Mexicans in Santa Fe and had thought nothing of it. "Actually, my wife's land is a negligible asset compared to her other virtues. She has enormous courage. Single-handedly she once saved me from being killed by a grizzly bear."

Lady Hethrington gasped. "What kind of bear?"

"A grizzly. Most ferocious beast you could ever imagine." Unless one considered his mother. Maggie didn't seem to be doing as well with the duchess as she had with the grizzly. Though a glance at his mother sitting—as though on a throne—with Catharine at her side, made him think that the dragon might have come away from the recent encounter with Maggie sporting some wounds of her own.

Lady Hethrington pursed her lips in satisfaction. "I think that is just so romantic, Lord Christopher. Yours must truly be a marriage decreed by fate."

By morning all of London society would admire Maggie's heroism, if he knew Lady Hethrington. She was a gossip of the first order. Perhaps his fellow Londoners would realize that quality didn't necessarily come with upbringing. Perhaps it was time he realized that himself.

"Hello, my boy." Peter materialized at Christopher's side. "Good evening, Lady Hethrington. I believe Miss Richardson was searching for you a few moments ago."

When Lady Hethrington had dithered away toward Miss Richardson, Peter turned to Christopher. "Throwing little Maggie to the wolves already, are you?"

"What do you mean by that?" Christopher asked sharply. His eyes found Maggie in conversation with a

covey of middle-aged matrons. Her chin was up, her
shoulders square, and her lips curved in a brilliant smile.
Once again she had hit her stride playing the lady. She
should have been on the stage. "If those ladies over there
are the wolves you're referring to, then Maggie seems to
be holding her own."

"You know what I mean, my boy. Do you think the
gossip-mongers didn't drink in the sight of you waltzing
with Amelia while Maggie looked on with that hurt look
on her face? They thrive on that sort of thing, you know.
By morning every society female in town will be clacking
about how you left your bride to pine while you danced
with your lost love."

"Oh, bloody hell, Peter. You know that's drivel. Amelia
is a friend, and she has nothing to do with Maggie and
me. I doubt Maggie thought a thing of my dancing with
Amelia."

Peter shook his head. "Christopher, sometimes I think
you have even less understanding of women than I do,
and someday it's going to get you in serious trouble."

"I have as good an understanding of women as most
men—which is no understanding at all," Christopher said
impatiently. "What I do understand is that Maggie should
have stayed in New Mexico. She knows how to deal with
a stubborn steer or an angry grizzly, but I doubt she can
deal with my mother and rest of London Society. She'll
never be happy in England."

"Are you so happy in England?"

Christopher didn't answer. The question was ridiculous. He had bloody well better be happy in England. It
was his home and his birthright.

"I must admit that I miss New Mexico." Peter's eyes
seemed to focus somewhere far away, beyond the room,
perhaps beyond the English isle itself.

Christopher scowled. "What are you thinking, Peter?"

Peter shrugged. "Nothing, nothing . . . Just giving in to an old man's fantasies."

Maggie no longer wondered why the Talbot household rose so late in the day. They got home from the Calamath ball in the small hours of the morning, and still they didn't go to bed. The men retired to the library for a brandy, while Lady Torrington and Catharine exchanged bits of gossip they had gathered at the dance. Maggie stayed with the ladies, but the twosome excluded her from their conversation. She was grateful when Elizabeth walked into the parlor with the old duke on her arm.

The duchess pursed her mouth at her husband. "Edward, you should be in bed."

"Oh, bother, Adela. You want me to sleep the rest of my life away. I'll be asleep for good soon enough."

"Then you should be in the library with your sons."

"Piddle! I'm too old for brandy. This is my house. I'm the duke. I'll go where I please."

"Yes, Edward."

Maggie was surprised to note the shine of affection in the duchess's eyes. The old dragon loved her husband. Maggie never would have credited her with it.

The duke turned to Maggie. "You, gel. How did you like your first night out on London town?"

Maggie smiled. The duke seemed amazingly lucid. "I enjoyed myself very much, sir. The ball was exciting."

"Did Adela introduce you around? I'm sure she did. She knows everybody in this bloody town."

"Edward, your language."

"I'm too old to mince my words. This gel's not one of your fainting fannies. I'll wager she's heard colorful language a time or two."

"Yes, sir. I've even used it a time or two."

"Good for you. I knew our Christopher would find a

woman with backbone. Not like these proper pansies who call themselves women in London."

"Edward," the duchess said in a dangerous tone, "you're straining yourself."

The duke seated himself on the love seat. "Now I'm not. Come here and sit beside me, gel."

Maggie obediently sat. She was beginning to like the crusty old man.

"Tell me about this ball you dragged my son to. He doesn't commonly go, y'know. You must have him wrapped up tight. Good for the boy. I always said what the stiff-neck needed was a good woman."

"Edward, Magdalena does not have Christopher wrapped up in any way. In fact, she is traveling back to her home in America as soon as passage can be arranged."

Maggie's head jerked up in surprise. "No, I'm not."

"Of course you are, dear. Don't you remember our little discussion?"

Catharine looked smug. Elizabeth and the duke both seemed surprised. Maggie longed to call the duchess a witch to her arrogant prune face, but she supposed that since other family members were present, she couldn't. It wouldn't be ladylike. She satisfied herself with a black glare.

"You were the one so anxious for me to cut and run. If you knew me better you'd know that Magdalena Montoya doesn't run from anyone or anything." She tilted her chin in an arrogance equal to that of the duchess.

"What's this about the gel leaving?" the duke quavered. "She just got here."

"The girl's *not* leaving."

All eyes turned to the parlor doorway. Christopher leaned against the door frame, his arms folded across his chest, his expression dark.

"Mother, may I speak with you privately?"

The duchess huffed. "This matter concerns the whole family. We will discuss it here."

"The matter concerns only me and my wife, but if you want me to speak my piece in front of the others, so be it."

James and Rodney pushed past Christopher into the room. "What's going on here?" James asked.

Christopher ignored him. "Mother, I've asked you once before to show my wife the courtesy due her."

"I am not being discourteous." The duchess sounded outraged that he could accuse her of such a breach. "I'm being realistic."

"Realistic about what?" James demanded. "I'm the eldest and heir. I've a right to be included in this discussion!"

The duke snorted. "James, shut up! Now, Adela, what's this about the gel leaving? She just got here, didn't she?"

"I'm not leaving!"

"Maggie, be quiet," Christopher ordered.

The duchess drew herself up imperiously. "Now, see here, Christopher. And you, too, husband. It seems I must do the thinking for all of us. Christopher, you have always been a dutiful son, and it is beyond me why you insist on bringing this inappropriate person into our midst to embarrass us. This is a family of some note. The eyes of Society are upon us. Magdalena may be a very sweet gel, I'm sure, but she has no knowledge of proper speech, manner, or dress. One cannot learn such things in a few weeks or months of instruction. If a female is not born a lady, she can never become one."

Maggie had to force herself not to lower her eyes as the full force of Lady Torrington's exacting gaze swung toward her. "Magdalena, I certainly wish you no ill, gel. I respect the fact that you are an heiress and the offshoot of a noted family from . . . well . . . somewhere. But you cannot be happy here. Why you wish to stay is beyond my understanding. You are an embarrassment to yourself, to Christopher, and to the entire family. As I told you earlier, gel, trying to climb above your true station will gain you only misery."

"And I'm sure that you'll do everything in your power to make sure that I *am* miserable." Throughout Lady Torrington's speech Maggie's anger had warred with shame. The insult didn't bother her so much; she was an old hand at dodging insults. What made the words sting was suspicion that the old dragon was right. She fought to push the unwelcome notion aside.

"Mother! Maggie! End this!" Christopher's command cut through the tension as the two women exchanged glares. Elizabeth sat with tears trickling down her face, and even Catharine looked uneasy. "Maggie and I will decide what Maggie does and where she lives. If she stays, you will treat her as an honored daughter or you will lose my company as well. Do you understand?"

"Hear, hear!" The duke's voice meandered into the silence after Christopher's declaration. "Put the old bird in her place. Time someone did!"

The duchess spared her husband a quick, hurt glance before gathering her voluminous skirts and marching out of the room. Catharine hurried after her.

"Elizabeth," Christopher directed, "take Father up to his rooms, please. I think he's getting a bit confused."

Alone with her husband, Maggie turned and looked out the window at the black London night. One could not see the stars here as in Colorado and New Mexico. The air was too hazy with dust and smoke. The thick darkness suddenly seemed to smother her.

"Maggie"—Christopher's voice was gentle—"I'm sorry."

What was he sorry about? He had stood up to the old dragon. Maggie couldn't fault him, though it would have salved her feelings had he denied that she was "inappropriate" and an "embarrassment to the family." But Maggie supposed he didn't want to lie. He was too damned honorable for that.

"Let's go to bed, Maggie."

She allowed him to escort her upstairs. When the door of their rooms shut behind him, she inquired, "Why does your mother hate me so? What have I ever done to her?"

"She doesn't hate you. Try to understand. Her whole life is the family and its social standing."

Maggie fought to keep the tears behind her eyes, but they defied her and overflowed.

"Don't cry." He brushed her cheek with a finger.

"I'm not crying. I never cry."

"All right, you're not crying. Come here, little Maggie cat."

She slipped out of his grasp. He would give her this, but nothing else. She had been a fool to believe that love and lust were linked. "Is this your solution to every problem?"

Christopher caught her by the waist and held her in a gentle but unbreakable grip. "There was a time when you complained that I had no passion to give you. Make up your mind, little Maggie."

She felt her anger began to melt as she was pulled into his dark, warm gaze. Her heartbeat seemed loud in the silence of the room. Slowly he bent to take a kiss, his hands sliding upward over her ribs, her breasts, her throat, to cup her face and hold her still for his caress. Maggie couldn't find the will to resist.

As Christopher's lips touched hers, the room suddenly shook with a loud pounding upon the door.

"Christopher! Christopher, help!" came Lady Torrington's plea. "It's your father. He's collapsed!"

Sixteen

The old duke had suffered three similar collapses in the last two years—an apoplexy of the brain, Dr. Thomas Holloway diagnosed the disorder, resulting from a heart irregularity depriving the superior organ of blood. Each episode had left him weaker and more confused. His present collapse was so calamitous as to leave his survival in doubt.

Dr. Holloway stayed in constant attendance for almost a week, leaving the duke only long enough to eat and occasionally sleep for a few hours in the room that was provided for him. The household was sober. No social calls were made or accepted and there were no more carriage rides along Ladies' Mile. The only visitor to Torrington House was a dressmaker commanded by the duchess to begin work on a wardrobe in black for the ladies of the house and the female servants. Maggie thought the duchess was jumping the gun a bit, but Elizabeth conceded that her mother was only being practical.

"Poor Father cannot last much longer, I fear. It is best to be prepared." She daubed at her canvas. "Do sit still, Maggie. I cannot paint something that jumps about like a cricket."

"I'm not jumping about."

The garden was bathed in a muted afternoon light that almost made Maggie admit that London could be beautiful at times.

"Be patient another few minutes and I'll be finished," Elizabeth promised.

Maggie had heard that promise before. For the past four days they had spent several hours each day in the garden, Elizabeth painting and Maggie attempting to sit still. "Truly finished this time?"

"Truly finished. I promise."

"And then can I look at it?"

"May I look," Elizabeth corrected. At Maggie's request Elizabeth had taken up where Peter had left off in the task of turning her into a lady of refinement. "And, yes, when I'm truly finished, you may look. I've warned you before, though, I don't glorify my subjects as most portrait painters do."

"I think you've captured her perfectly."

Both women looked around as Dr. Holloway came through the double French doors into the garden, but neither was surprised. The young physician had frequently visited with them during their sessions together. He was a pleasant-faced young man with the clearest gray eyes and one of the most elegant set of whiskers that Maggie had ever seen.

"Shame on you, Dr. Holloway," Elizabeth protested. "No one but the artist must look on a portrait before the work is finished."

"I couldn't resist a peek," he said with a smile.

Maggie had never had a high opinion of physicians. The few she had met in the West were quacks. But Dr. Holloway did seem to be a different breed. He didn't sell nerve tonics or vile-tasting omnipotent cures. He seemed to genuinely care about his patient and the patient's family. Maggie had noted that the young widower especially cared about Lady Elizabeth Talbot.

"Do I look like myself?" Maggie asked him.

"You look very much like yourself," he confirmed. "Lady Elizabeth has truly captured that spark in your eyes and the rather spirited tilt of your chin."

Christopher would call that spark in her eyes the light of trouble, but Maggie thought it very generous of the physician to compliment her.

"I want to see. If Dr. Holloway can see, it's only fair that—"

"Sit down, Maggie," Elizabeth ordered. "You can see the painting when it's finished. And you sit down also, Doctor. Behave yourself. Tell us how Father is doing."

For another hour they sat in amiable conversation, though Maggie found it almost impossible to talk without moving some part of her body, which brought a reprimand from Elizabeth. The duke was doing as well as could be expected, Dr. Holloway assured them. He believed the patient was out of immediate danger. He told them of the current thinking in treating such ailments, saying that he himself believed such a patient should be allowed to go back to his normal routine as soon as he was able rather than linger abed being waited on hand and foot. Maggie noted that this Englishman, at least, did not seem to share the common male conviction that women should not be included in serious conversations nor should their thoughts be solicited on anything more momentous than the day's menu. Dr. Holloway answered Elizabeth's questions thoughtfully and seemed to think her opinions had some worth. In fact he was so attentive to everything that Elizabeth said that he seemed to forget that Maggie was even in the garden.

"Is the portrait finished yet?" Maggie asked, interrupting a discussion between Elizabeth and the physician about the style of the last portrait of Queen Victoria.

"What? Oh." Elizabeth turned back to her canvas and regarded her work. "Yes. I'd say it's finished."

Gratefully, Maggie got up and stretched her stiff muscles. She walked around behind Elizabeth to look at the painting.

"You have considerable talent," Dr. Holloway commented to Elizabeth. "There's more than one well-known portrait painter who couldn't have captured Lady Christopher as you did."

Maggie had to agree. As she looked at the painting, she looked at herself. Not only were her features correct, but there on her face were her ambitions, doubts, joys—and love. Did others see it so plainly?

"Remarkable! Simply remarkable!"

Maggie wondered if Dr. Holloway was commenting on the painting or the lovely Lady Elizabeth. He was a genuinely nice man—gentle, educated, and handsome to boot. She remembered Elizabeth's remarks about her fiancé, and suddenly felt sad.

As the days dragged by, the duke grew a bit stronger. Dr. Holloway returned to his own home and contented himself with once-a-day visits to his patient. For the sake of household peace Maggie and Lady Torrington reached a truce. Maggie respected the duchess's grief, which seemed to be genuine. The dragon had other things on her mind besides protecting her family from the danger of an unsuitable daughter-in-law. Catharine spent her time with the duchess, setting herself up as guard to the grand lady's apartments and making it clear that Maggie was not a welcome visitor within. James and Christopher spent most of their time in conference with the family's men of law, one of whom was Peter Scarborough, ensuring that the duke's will and other papers relating to the passing on of the estates and title were in order. Maggie and Elizabeth talked, read, and had picnics with Rachel in the garden. For two days Elizabeth attempted to teach Maggie fine embroidery, but the attempt was short-lived. Elizabeth was patient, but not that patient.

Maggie saw little of Christopher except at night. Since the duke's collapse he had been silent and withdrawn, even in the privacy of their rooms. Twice he made love to her, but his lovemaking was brief and mechanical, as if Maggie were an itch he reluctantly scratched. She urged him to talk about his father, but he merely told her that the duke represented the Victorian Era at its pinnacle. The old man whose body and mind had both betrayed him was not the same man Christopher remembered from the time before he had left London for Oxford, and then for the army.

Maggie awakened every morning to a lonely bed, and every morning she was informed by a solemn Grays that Lord Christopher was riding. Ten days after the duke's collapse Maggie woke while the night was still graying to dawn. The bed beside her was empty, as usual. She scowled into the early-morning gloom and decided that Christopher had the right idea. A daybreak ride might do her state of mind some good as well.

The Torrington stables were almost as elaborate as the

house, and it seemed to Maggie that the duke's horses lived in at least as much luxury as the duke's family. She had doubts that she would be allowed to ride any of these fine animals, but the sleepy groom didn't blink an eye when she asked for a mount. He led out a sleek, long-legged bay mare whose polished hooves were almost as shiny as the groom's impeccable boots. On the mare's back was a sidesaddle. Of course Maggie had seen such a contraption before. Even in the American West proper women commonly rode sidesaddle. But Maggie never had. Maggie had never been that proper.

The groom helped her mount, then climbed aboard a chestnut gelding that looked as sleepy as he. At her questioning look he cleared his throat. "It'd be my job if I was to let ye go alone, m'lady. If ye wishes fer privacy, I'll keep a distance back."

He looked so apprehensive that Maggie felt sorry for him. No one should be required to be that humble. "Come on, then . . . what's your name?"

"Greaves, m'lady. Robbie Greaves."

"Come on, then, Mr. Greaves."

The city looked enchanted this time of day. Maggie understood why Christopher chose the early morning to ride. As the day progressed, the air would fill with dust made up in large part of manure. The streets would clatter with carriages and hooves and resound with the shouts of vendors, coachmen, shoppers, businessmen, and tradesmen. Now the air was sweet and cool, the city almost silent as it awaited sunrise. She had the road almost to herself as she rode to Ladies' Mile, and only a few early-rising equestrians trotted along the paths in Hyde Park.

Maggie hadn't felt so much herself since she'd left New Mexico. Even the sidesaddle didn't mar her enjoyment of the morning. It was awkward, true; she felt as though she might tumble over backward at any minute. But the mare was gentle and had an easy pace. By the time she had ridden a few minutes, Maggie felt as though she might get the hang of the peculiar saddle if she tried.

Robbie Greaves rode silently behind her, there but not there. His presence didn't stop Maggie from sorting out thoughts and feelings. She wasn't ready yet to admit coming to London had been a mistake. There was nothing here that she couldn't conquer, given enough time and a little luck. Plenty to challenge her, but nothing she couldn't surmount.

The greatest challenge was the duchess. The woman could be as sour as vinegar. Twice as sour. But she had her soft spots. Perhaps when she saw what a lady Maggie was determined to become she would become more accepting. Catharine was just as unpleasant as the duchess, but for all her hostile stares and sullenness she was a vixen with no teeth. If Lady Torrington ever relented in her feelings toward Maggie, Catharine would likely turn about as well. James and Rodney were not really a concern. Christopher had promised not to yield to James's halfhearted attempts to dictate how Rancho del Rio should be managed, and Maggie trusted him to keep that promise. And Rodney—Rodney was a problem only to himself. If Lady Torrington was so concerned about family embarrassments, maybe she ought to have a few words with her youngest son.

But then, Maggie had learned even in her short stay that boorish behavior such as drunkenness, excessive gambling, and womanizing was an acceptable form of aristocratic entertainment. A man born to the upper class could do anything he pleased. But someone like her—she could probably polish her manners to pristine perfection and still have the duchess looking down her long nose at her.

But Maggie would win. Damned if she wouldn't. She would become such a lady that the dragon duchess would be proud to call her daughter-in-law, and Christopher would wonder what he'd ever seen in that pasty-faced Amelia.

Almost as if thinking about Christopher had summoned him, her husband's voice drifted to her ears through the morning air. She stopped and peered closely at a pair of riders who had halted beneath a huge oak tree beside the path far ahead. She recognized Christopher's midnight-colored hair and Amelia's carefully curled blond ringlets. The two blended into the shrubbery so well that Maggie had almost missed them. They were a good distance away, but the breeze carried their voices to her ears.

Heart jumping painfully, Maggie reined her horse behind a concealing hedge and motioned Greaves to do the same. It occurred to her that eavesdropping was not a ladylike thing to do, but she didn't care.

"Christopher," Miss Perfect was saying in a pleading voice, "you must know that I have a great fondness for you. You mustn't think that I refused your marriage offer last year because I lacked in feeling. If I elaborated on my emotions where you are concerned, you would surely have thought me quite forward."

Maggie thought Amelia quite forward as it was. She glanced at Greaves, whose blank expression indicated that he chose not to hear what was being said.

"Amelia . . ." Christopher did not sound happy. "What's past is past. You've no obligation to justify yourself. My feelings for you are—"

"Oh, Christopher! Don't say it. My hopes are that you still have an attachment for me. Tell me I have not lost your affection by sacrificing my own heart to family duty."

A long, pregnant pause made Maggie want to scream. She willed with all her might for Christopher to tell

Amelia that he loved his wife and that she should take her dutiful little heart and roast it over a slow fire.

"Amelia," Christopher finally said in a heavy voice, "what can I say to you? More than a year has passed since I asked you to be my wife—and you refused me. Circumstances have changed. I'm married and have a duty to my wife."

Duty. That wasn't the word Maggie wanted to hear.

"And of course you'll cling to that duty," Amelia declared. "That's why you'll understand. You did your duty by marrying where you had to marry. Can I do less? You married to regain your brother's land and right a terrible wrong. I must marry to better my family's connections. I must marry into a title."

Maggie felt her blood heat. Christopher had proposed marriage to the perfect Amelia; and Amelia, the little fool, had refused him. But having refused him, the Little Miss Ladylike refused to let go.

"Christopher," Amelia continued in a voice so low that Maggie could scarcely hear it, "I—I confess that I rode out this morning hoping to meet you. I must ask your help. Please don't think me wicked, though I realize well that I'm stretching the bounds of propriety."

Stretching was hardly the word, Maggie thought. *Shattering* was more on target.

"I'm at your service, Amelia. You should know that."

"I—I need you to encourage James in my direction."

Christopher was silent for a moment. Maggie wondered if he was as stunned as she was.

"I know such a request sounds very bold of me. James has escorted me often enough that Society considers us a pair, I believe. We suit very well, but you know James. He's reluctant to tie himself down with a commitment. But really, your family needs money, and I have tons of it. I need a title, and James will be duke of Torrington soon."

She continued hesitantly. "It isn't as if I haven't thought of you in my ambitions, Christopher—or thought of us. A married woman has so much more freedom than an unmarried girl. . . ."

Maggie closed her eyes, afraid to hear Christopher's response. So this was the woman he idolized as the perfect lady. Was there really any difference, she wondered, between a lady and a whore? It didn't seem so.

Christopher took an excruciatingly long time to answer. "Amelia, I think you and James might suit very well. I would be more than happy to encourage my brother in your direction." His voice had a raw edge. "And as for freedom, I suppose we must all take freedom where we can find it. If we can find it."

"I knew you would understand! I knew I could count on you."

Amelia would have done very well on Market Street in Denver, Maggie thought bitterly. She certainly had the right instincts.

The voices continued briefly. Maggie was no longer listening. The only thing she could hear was the painful beating of her own heart. When she finally looked up, the two of them were gone. Other riders trotted along the paths taking their morning exercise. The sun had climbed halfway up the sky; the morning was well progressed and promised to be a beautiful one, but for Maggie the day had already gone sour.

The placid little mare neighed in protest as Maggie pulled back sharply on the reins. Greaves frowned in sharp disapproval. Suddenly Maggie hated Greaves, she hated Amelia, she hated Christopher, and she HATED England. She wanted to be back in New Mexico, to weep on Luisa's shoulder, to ride like the wind over the flat grassy plain until she was too exhausted to hurt any longer, and then to throw a fit so violent that heaven itself would heed her anger.

Damn England. Damn His Low-down Skunkish Lordship. And damn Miss Scheming Society Slut. If Amelia Hawthorne was an example of a genteel lady, then Maggie didn't want any part of ladyhood. She suddenly felt smothered in this park where every tree was in its proper place and every hedge and shrub was more man's handiwork that nature's.

"Mr. Greaves, go back to the stables." Maggie jumped out of her ridiculous excuse for a saddle and landed lightly on the ground. "Only ladies need grooms to attend them." She unfastened the sidesaddle's cinch and slid the saddle from the mare's back. "You can take this damned thing with you."

"M'lady?"

"Don't call me that. I'm nobody's lady."

"M'lady . . . uh . . ." Clearly Mr. Greaves was at a loss. Christopher and Amelia's tête-à-tête hadn't shocked him in the least, but Maggie's behavior did.

"Oh, that's right. Your job. Stick around then. Just stay out of my way."

Maggie hiked up her skirts and swung aboard the mare bareback. Her riding habit bunched up around her legs as she settled astride the sleek little mare, revealing silk-clad calves above her riding boots.

Maggie didn't hear Mr. Greaves's last quavering "m'lady?" as she dug her heels into the mare's sides, for the horse took off with a snort of complaint. Maggie wanted to ride, to burn off her anger in speed and daring, to let the morning air whip against her and wash away the pollution of Christopher, Amelia, the vicious duchess, bitter Catharine, sad Elizabeth, useless James and Rodney— all of England with its surface niceties and hidden hypocrisies.

She rode like a demon. The horse caught the spirit of its rider and galloped along the bridle paths like a mustang with a burr under its tail. They sent mud spattering into a carriage amid the squeals of three ladies bedecked in their morning best. They startled the mounts of better-mannered riders, scaring one into a hedge and sending another into a display of bucking that launched the rider into a puddle left from the night's drizzle. Over hedges they flew, between trees, through carefully pruned shrubbery. When they emerged onto a path that was straight and unobstructed, they raced along, hooves flashing, hair flying, as though the devil himself pursued. Behind them at a distance growing ever greater, Mr. Greaves cantered on his fat chestnut, holding Maggie's sidesaddle perched on his horse's withers.

Like a hurricane that has expended its fury, Maggie finally faltered to a halt. She reined the mare to a trot, then stopped. The horse's foam-flecked sides heaved and its head dropped. Maggie leaned forward and rested her face on the wind-tangled mane. She was as out of breath as the mare. She'd become soft since she'd married Christopher. Soft in the muscle and soft in the head as well.

Slowly she became aware that she wasn't alone. She sat up and raked her hair back from her face with her fingers. Everyone within sight in the park was sitting on carriage seat or horseback still as a statue. They stared at her as though she were the Apocalypse come to life. Mr. Greaves sat on his chestnut a discreet distance away, his face carefully blank.

Suddenly Maggie felt good. Her hair hung down her back and over her face in untamed corkscrew curls; her hat had flown away. The skirt of her riding habit rode up to her knees on both sides. Face and clothes spattered with mud and the mare's foamy sweat, cloak hanging askew on one shoulder, Maggie sat astride her mount bareback like a wild Indian and gave her audience a wide, gaudy smile.

James and Christopher took lunch at the Athenaeum, the men's club in which the Talbot men had held membership since its first founding. The food in the dining room was the best of any club in London, but today it didn't whet Christopher's appetite. The morning's encounter with Amelia had left a sour taste in his mouth.

"It's a bloody shame that Father should fall ill again just as you return, Christopher. Spoils the homecoming, doesn't it?" James took a bite of his meat pastry and nodded appreciatively. "Um. Try some of this. Harrelson's outdone himself today."

"This seizure seems worse than the last," Christopher said.

"It is." James took another bite. "Dr. Holloway confided to me today that he really doesn't expect Father to survive this one. The old man may dodder on awhile, but he doesn't give him past Christmas at the very most."

"Are you sure Holloway's an experienced enough physician? He is rather young."

"I'd say the fellow's quite good. Mother found him through the Countess Covedale. He treated her gout and her daughter's pneumonia. He's quite well thought of."

"Hmm."

"Don't be so glum. Father's old. We must all pass on the mantle someday."

Christopher gave his brother a sharp look.

"Not that I'm overly anxious to assume the title, brother. But one must be realistic. That is why I thought we should dine together today, just you and I. Since I'm soon to be head of the family, I thought we should talk in some detail about plans for our American holdings."

Christopher cocked a brow. "Rancho del Rio, you mean."

"Of course. I feel I should have some say in the management of this new family acquisition. You indicated in your letters that you thought this land could serve as the launching point for a number of investments."

"Yes, I did, and I mean to follow through on expansion in the American West. But I rather looked upon such an enterprise as a Christopher Talbot project, not a family undertaking."

James's next bite stopped halfway to his mouth. "Did you really? Stephen acquired that land with funds provided by the family, Christopher."

"And I retrieved it using funds from Pitney and Talbot, which is my own shipping company. This ranch is not an inexhaustible source of income, James. I will be glad to use a part of it to relieve the family finances somewhat, but Rancho del Rio is mine and Maggie's. I will make all decisions regarding it, and I will distribute the income as I see fit."

"I say! This is a new twist. It was my understanding that this American estate was to be a family acquisition."

"That was when Stephen first bought it. Circumstances have changed."

James scowled. "Does Mother know of this?"

"She does. But Mother really has nothing to say about it."

"Tch! You have developed an independent streak, haven't you? Must be all that time spent in the hinterlands."

Christopher ignored the insult. "My advice to you, James, is to sell off a few of the farms and invest the money in shipping, or perhaps the railroads. Agriculture is too risky right now, the return too small."

"Hm. Sounds very plebeian to me. It's all very well for

you to dabble in trade and such, Christopher. After all, you're a second son. But I'm the heir. I must be more careful about the family reputation. Income from land is the traditional support of the aristocracy. Sooner or later prices will climb."

"Then you'd better start curtailing family spending, James, since you're soon to inherit the title. I won't squander Maggie's inheritance to support Rodney's gambling and high living for the rest of the family. The stable staff could be cut, one or two of the carriages sold, and the ladies certainly do not need complete new wardrobes twice a year."

"Really, Christopher, you'd have us live like the middle class? America gave you ideas as common as your little bride. Though Maggie is a fetching little thing, I'll admit. I'd wager the marriage hasn't been an entirely unpleasant sacrifice when it comes to the bedroom, eh?"

James' lewd wink set a match to Christopher's temper. He had to restrain himself from grabbing his brother and dragging him across the table to pound some manners into him. In one way James was right. Christopher had associated too long with American barbarians who expressed their opinions with their fists. He clamped down on his anger.

"I won't tolerate talk of that sort about Maggie, James. From you or anyone else."

"Really, Christopher. I didn't insult her. It's not as though she's a lady of our class, after all. Where did you say you found her? In a public house?"

"A saloon." The words were not an admission; they were a challenge.

James looked up from his meal. His answer was cautious. "Yes, well, the best lineages fall on sorry circumstances now and again, don't they?"

The rest of the meal was eaten in silence, with James

glancing at Christopher curiously, as though his brother were a stranger.

A short time later, as James and Christopher passed through the reading room on the way out, a commotion blocked their way. A clot of gentlemen surrounded another whose voice was raised in displeasure.

"I tell you, I don't know what this city is coming to when hoydens and such persons as this are given free rein to disrupt others in public places. I've never seen anything like it. Unthinkable that such things should be tolerated."

One of the other gentlemen, a young one, dared to chuckle. "You do look a bit worse for wear, Danforth. I warned you that new hunter of yours would toss you."

The injured party glared. "Twasn't the hunter, Loudon, or a lack of horsemanship on my part. That *female* was the cause of it all."

"A lady?"

"A female. Most certainly not a lady." He glanced through the knot of listeners and caught sight of Christopher. "*His* wife! Sir! Lord Christopher Talbot! May I have a word with you, sir!"

An icy premonition gripped Christopher's stomach.

"You there! Lord Christopher!" Charles Danforth, hatless, damp, wrinkled, the seat of his trousers plastered with mud, pushed through the curious gentlemen and confronted Christopher. "Sir! Not two hours ago your wife ran rampant through Hyde Park, flinging mud in all directions to land on frightened ladies and outraged gentlemen. She took a hedge in front of my new green hunter and startled him into a tantrum which landed me—in truth would have landed the finest of horsemen—in the mud. It took me almost two hours to catch my mount. If I had lost a valuable animal, you can be sure that I would have demanded recompense!"

James came to Christopher's defense. "My brother's wife did this? You must be mistaken, Danforth."

"Oh, it was her, all right. If you remember, Talbot, you made the introductions at Lord Calamath's ball. Your wife has a very distinctive look about her, and I'm certain it was she galloping like some wild savage loosed from a zoo. What's more, she was riding astride, bareback. Most shocking thing I've ever seen. If you insist on marrying a wild woman, Talbot, do spare the rest of Society from her. Lock her up, if you must."

"I apologize, Danforth. My wife must have lost control of her mount. Please send me the bill for a new suit. I do hope your hunter wasn't injured."

Danforth glared. He didn't believe a word Christopher said, of course. But to continue complaining after an apology had been offered—especially by one who ranked higher in Society than he—would not have been the thing.

"Fortunately, Nero sustained no injury. I suggest you teach your wife to ride or keep her home from now on," Danforth said coldly.

Christopher made as graceful an escape as could be expected under the circumstances.

"That couldn't have been Maggie," James protested as they hailed a cab.

"Oh, yes it could have. You don't know her as I do."

Christopher entertained a horrible suspicion of what had happened. Maggie had decided to ride in the park early that morning. Somehow she had seen him meet with Amelia and had assumed the worst. A flood of regret washed over him that was partly anger with himself and partly exasperation with Maggie. He would never deliberately hurt her. She didn't deserve to be hurt. But bloody damn it all—she was the one who had insisted on coming to London. She had to learn that one couldn't erupt like a volcano whenever she was vexed.

Luisa closed the account ledger and momentarily pressed her fingers against her weary eyes. For the past week she had pored over the accounts and worked diligently to make reasonable predictions of expenses for the coming winter, spring, and summer. Against that she balanced income projections based on the number of cattle they had just delivered on their Army contracts and to other buyers. She had gone over the figures once already with Moss, and this evening she would confirm her projections with the ranch manager once again. Then tomorrow she would write Christopher with her report.

She rested her head against the back of the big leather chair and looked out the window as the wind played endless games in the grass. Tomorrow she would write Peter also. Perhaps it was unwise to answer the letter he had written her. She had hesitated a long while, wondering if they were prolonging something that should die a natural death, but she found that she couldn't let him go completely. Their feelings, silently held, unexpressed, and yet so obvious to each other, could never blossom into anything, but that didn't mean they couldn't be friends. With a sea and most of a continent separating them, he was no danger to her heart, and she was no danger to his.

A knock sounded at the library door. "Señora Gutierrez. Señor Riley rides in with a stranger. I thought you would want to know."

"Thank you, Anita."

Luisa got up and looked out the window. Moss and a paunchy stranger had just stepped onto the porch. The stranger walked stiffly. Saddlesore, she thought. Certainly not from around these parts, where children were bounced on the back of a horse more often than they were bounced on their fathers' knees. Curiosity aroused, she hurried to the parlor to meet them.

"Afternoon, Luisa," Moss greeted her. "Found this here fella in Santa Rosa this morning. He was askin' questions about you and Miz Talbot and the ranch."

Uneasiness fluttered in Luisa's stomach.

"I figgered if he was gonna ask questions about you, he might as well ask them to your face."

The stranger took off his hat. He had sandy hair, a red face, an impressive handlebar mustache, and pale blue eyes whose sharp gleam belied his soft-looking pudginess. "Mrs. Gutierrez, my name's Dan Schiefflin. I'm a private detective."

The flutter of uneasiness grew to near panic. "Moss, I can handle this. Thank you."

"Whatever you say." He gave the detective a meaningful glare. "I'll be within earshot."

After Moss left, Luisa directed the detective to a chair. "You look done in, Mr. Schiefflin. Can I get something for you?"

"Water would be a godsend, ma'am."

Luisa sent Anita for a pitcher of cold water, then sat in the chair opposite her guest. "What can I do for you, Mr. Schiefflin?"

"Would you mind answering a few questions?"

"About what?"

"Are you the same Luisa Gutierrez that ran the Lady Luck saloon in Denver?"

"I ran it and owned it. I still own it, but I have a man running it for me now."

Anita came in with a pitcher and two tall glasses on a tray.

"Thank you, Anita." Luisa's hands shook as she poured the water.

The detective accepted his glass gratefully, took a long

drink, and wiped his mouth on his sleeve. "Well, then, Miz' Gutierrez, maybe you can help me. Do you remember anything about a customer of yours who got himself murdered last November—a big fellow by the name of Arnold Stone?"

Seventeen

"Apologize? Me?" Maggie shot up from the drawing-room chair and faced Christopher with hands indignantly on her hips. "You're the one who should apologize. I'm not the one sneaking around in the bushes with a blond, blue-eyed tart."

"Maggie! I was not sneaking."

"I suppose Amelia cut you off at the pass!"

"I beg your pardon?"

"She launched herself at you from the bushes? Ambushed you from the trees? Or maybe you knew all along she was going to meet you."

"Actually, she did rather ambush me. It's no

secret that I ride most early mornings. She knew where to find me."

"It's a shame she wouldn't marry you. You two deserve each other. But she'll make a perfect duchess of Torrington, won't she? Your mother will love her. After all, Amelia's everything an English lady should be. And no doubt she'll make you the perfect mistress once she gets settled in with your brother. Isn't that what you call them in England—mistresses? In Denver we call them whores."

"You were eavesdropping."

"Of course I was eavesdropping. And don't tell me that eavesdropping isn't ladylike. If Amelia is a lady, then the standards couldn't be all that high."

Christopher cocked a sardonic brow and folded his arms across his chest. "Maggie, sit down. You look like a Valkyrie ready to swoop down and wreak vengeance, and there's no vengeance necessary, really."

"I look like a what?"

"A . . . never mind. I'll buy you a collection of the Norse legends. Sit down."

Maggie tilted her chin higher. "I don't want to sit."

"Sit anyway!"

She sat.

He stabbed an admonitory finger in her direction. "Now listen to me, and listen well, for I want this settled here and now. There is no attachment between Amelia Hawthorne and myself. And there will not be, ever. In the past I had the poor judgment to admire her, but now James is welcome to the chit. Do you understand?"

Maggie was glad he admitted his poor judgment. Still, love did not always depend upon judgment. Look whom she had fallen for. "If you weren't married, would you still love her?"

"I never loved her, Maggie. I admired her. I don't admire her now. She's not what I thought she was."

"Maybe I'm not what you think I am."

He gave her a bleak look. "What I think you are, Maggie, is a walking calamity."

Maggie was nonplussed. Here she thought she had him on the run, so to speak, because of Amelia, and he was trying to turn the whole thing back on her, the skunk.

"Whatever possessed you to tear through Hyde Park like a demon, riding astride, of all things, and making a spectacle of yourself? Do you realize the consequences of such behavior?"

"I was mad."

"That is no excuse!" His scowl was as black as Maggie had ever seen it.

"I didn't do any harm," she said lamely.

"You got Charles Danforth thrown from his horse and spattered mud over ladies and gentlemen who deserved no part of your anger."

Maggie set her jaw and stared stubbornly out the window. "If a man rides a skittish horse, he should expect to be thrown. And a little mud never hurt anybody."

Christopher paced back and forth with a few long strides, then sat on the divan across from his wife. He reached out to turn her face until she was forced to meet his eyes. "What am I to do with you, Maggie cat?"

Maggie was tempted to suggest that he try loving her, really loving her, but was wise enough to know that this was not the moment. She read the disappointment in his face, and began to feel uncomfortable stirrings of guilt. She had jumped to conclusions, behaved like a child, and made a jackass of herself. What's worse, she had disappointed Christopher. She had vowed to make him love her and be a good wife, and this is how she accomplished her goal?

"All right, Christopher. I apologize."

"I don't need an apology, Maggie. You should apologize to the family."

Maggie grimaced. That would be harder. "Why do I have to apologize to them?"

"Because they have to bear with the consequences of Lady Christopher Talbot's Wild Ride, as it will probably be called in the annals of Society."

She huffed out an exasperated breath. "I don't understand. Lordy! A little ride through the park! I don't see why everyone's making such a fuss!"

Christopher shook his head and sighed.

Shortly, however, Maggie learned firsthand the consequences of her tantrum. Lady Torrington, Catharine, and Elizabeth had left for a carriage promenade shortly before Christopher had returned home to confront his wife. As Maggie had succeeded in sneaking unnoticed into the house after spreading her terror, the ladies of Torrington House had no knowledge of the morning's debacle. On the Ladies' Miles and in Hyde Park, however, they were made unpleasantly aware that something was amiss. Though they didn't know the details, the duchess had a very good idea of who had set things awry.

The clatter of the ladies returning interrupted Christopher and Maggie's discussion. Christopher raised a speculative brow as the complaints of feminine voices preceded the women into the drawing room. "Perhaps now would be as good a time as any for that apology," he suggested.

The duchess marched into the drawing room with Catharine and Elizabeth behind her. Lines of fury were etched into the stone of Lady Torrington's face. Catharine's cheeks ran with tears, and even Elizabeth was a bit flushed. When the duchess caught sight of Maggie, she halted and raised an imperious arm to point accusingly.

"You! You—you hoyden! I know it's you who's at the bottom of this. I don't know how, but I know you did it."

"Did what?" Maggie asked, trying to sound innocent.

Catharine burst into tears. The duchess rounded on her in a fury. "Shut up, Catharine. Stop your whining. They'll not get away with this. I'll see them crawling to us to apologize, and I'll refuse to receive them. They'll be banned from the parlor of every hostess in the city."

Lady Torrington's mood didn't bode well for Maggie's apology.

"Mother, what happened?" Christopher asked.

"Disaster! We were cut dead by both Lady Hethrington and Countess Westlake. The nerve of those old hens! They are both my social inferiors, and I'll make sure they regret this day until they die." She pinned Maggie with a lethal stare. "Your wife had something to do with this. I knew from the moment I saw her that disaster would follow in her wake. She's a social catastrophe. Tell me what you did, girl, so I may know how to defend our family from your blunder."

Maggie looked at Christopher, who merely folded his arms across his chest and waited. "I didn't mean any harm," Maggie began tentatively. "At least, no serious harm. . . ."

The duchess listened aghast at Maggie's confession—a confession which was not quite accurate, for Maggie omitted Christopher's part in the little drama. For a moment the stern matriarch simply stared at Maggie as though her daughter-in-law were an insect that had crawled from beneath the rug. Then she sat down heavily in the huge wing chair that usually served as her throne when she held social court at Torrington House. "Elizabeth. Fetch me a sherry. Catharine, close the doors. I won't have the servants hear this discussion, though they'll learn of our disgrace soon enough from the belowstairs gossip." She turned a heavy stare on Maggie. "Whatever possessed you, girl? Even with your obvious limitations I wouldn't have expected such scandalous behavior from you."

Christopher explained before Maggie could answer. "She didn't tell you the whole tale, Mother. Maggie saw me have a conversation with Amelia in the park this morning. She assumed we were indulging ourselves in a clandestine meeting, and therefore had ample justification for her anger."

Lady Torrington twitched her brows in surprise. "Amelia Hawthorne? What nonsense to believe that Amelia would allow you to make improper advances. But then, with Magdalena's sorry background, I suppose she doesn't understand those of us whose behavior is more refined than one finds in a public house."

Maggie coughed. Christopher shook his head in an almost imperceptible warning.

The duchess took the sherry Elizabeth handed her and sipped delicately. "Well, I suppose we must deal with this as best we can. You should never have come here, gel, but now that you have come to Society's notice, we can't send you away without seeming to be in retreat. A Talbot never retreats, do you understand?"

"But you must send her away, Mother!" Catharine cried. "She'll ruin us! Absolutely ruin us! I will not have her living in the same house as my precious Rachel. The child already is emulating her coarse speech and hoydenish ways."

"Be quiet, Catharine. The gel stays for now. Sending her away is the worst thing we can do. We must brazen it out. After all, the Calamath affair and one carriage promenade with us have been her only appearances in Society. If we stand our ground and admit nothing but outrage that anyone should accuse a Talbot of such behavior, most will come to believe that her accusers made a mistake of identification. Eventually it will appear that we are the wronged party and I shall demand apology from anyone who mentions the incident. And you, Christopher. You must admit after this sorry affair that your wife is a misfit of the first order. You have an obligation to this family to keep us from further scandal. Do you understand?"

Christopher didn't answer. All through his mother's outline of her battle plan, he had been regarding Maggie thoughtfully. Maggie had felt the weight of his dark eyes but had refused to meet them.

"Christopher? Do you understand?"

"I will deal with my wife," he promised in an enigmatic tone.

"I shall depend upon that promise. Tomorrow night we will all attend the opera. Magdalena will go with us."

Catharine wailed. "We'll be snubbed. Oh, Mother, please reconsider!"

"Let them dare to snub us!" She stood, looking like a queen sending troops into battle. "We will triumph in the end. What you must learn, Catharine, and you, too, Elizabeth, is that the one who shows weakness in the face of attack is the one who loses. Truth has very little role in determining who must back down in such a situation as this. We will go to the opera and make it clear that the hoyden who wreaked such havoc in the park this morning has no connection to our family, and those who accuse Maggie are clearly in the wrong. I shall tell James and Rodney that they must find suitable ladies to escort. The more support is shown Magdalena the less ready Society will be to believe her scandalous behavior."

With a sweep of her arm the duchess directed her troops from the room. No matter how much she might support Maggie in public, she was making it clear that she didn't care to occupy the same room with such a person.

Catharine paused at the door and gave Maggie a baleful

look. "Stay away from Rachel, do you hear? I won't have you filling her head with your lower-class ideas and confusing her with your disgraceful lack of education and manners."

Elizabeth was the only one who lingered with Christopher and Maggie. She knelt beside Maggie's chair and took her hand. "I'm sorry, dear. They'll get over it. Truly they will." She gave Maggie's hand a final pat and glided gracefully after the other two women.

Maggie heaved a sigh. "Well, I guess now I understand."

The excursion to the opera the following night was not Maggie's idea of a success. Elizabeth begged off, claiming a headache, which ailment Maggie had learned was the feminine excuse for anything a lady wanted to avoid. Maggie suspected that Elizabeth wasn't so much reluctant to accompany them to the opera as she was eager to stay home with her father, for Dr. Holloway had expressed his intention of checking on the earl that evening.

Maggie worried about Elizabeth more than she worried about herself. In Denver and on the Alvarez ranch she was accustomed to being battered—by hunger, by the raw elements, by a rough town and the rough men who lived there. But Elizabeth, even though born to this strange England, seemed vulnerable somehow to its cruelties, cruelties of the spirit and heart that seemed harsher somehow than any physical hardship. If Elizabeth was truly falling for the good doctor, as Maggie suspected, what would it do to the girl to have to choose between her heart and her duty?

Catharine fretted the entire coach ride to the opera house. The duchess was silent, her concentration directed inward, like a general preparing for battle. Christopher, who had spent the night before at his club instead of in

Maggie's bed, was thoughtful and withdrawn. He held Maggie's hand firmly as they sat side by side in the family's brougham coach, his thumb caressing her palm in lazy circles, but Maggie had no clue to his thoughts. He'd said little to her since the family confrontation the day before.

James and Rodney met the family at the opera house. Maggie had anticipated a difficult evening, but she hadn't realized just how difficult it would be until she caught sight of the lady whom James had chosen to escort—none other than the Perfect Miss Amelia. As James and his lady greeted the duchess in the lobby, Maggie felt Christopher's hand tighten on hers. She wondered what was running through her husband's brain—embarrassment, anger, jealousy?

"Amelia works fast," she commented dryly to Christopher. "You can't fault her for lack of get-up-and-go."

Christopher looked down at her with a peculiar light gleaming in his dark eyes. "I recommended to James that he escort her."

Maggie felt a weight lift off her heart. Perhaps Christopher had meant it when he'd said that James was welcome to Amelia. Her mouth twitched upward in a smile. "What do you have against your brother?"

Her husband frowned at that bit of impertinence, but she could see that the frown was forced.

The private exchange between them was the last hint of brightness in a dim evening. To Maggie's ears the opera was incomprehensible. Few people in the audience, however, seemed to pay attention to the performance; everyone was too busy sneaking a look at the Torrington box. Maggie could see the whispers and smiles, the subtle glances, curious peeks, outright glares. The opera was not a comedy, but people laughed with each other while looking in her direction. Everyone else in the Torrington box ignored the attention they drew, but Maggie felt her face grow hot. Who would have thought that a simple gallop through the park could raise such an uproar?

Amelia, of course, had heard the gossip. Who in London Society hadn't? She was all understanding, with sympathy that curdled Maggie's stomach.

"People can be so cruel," she commented softly to Christopher, just loud enough for Maggie to overhear. "You'd think they would be more understanding of someone who lacks an upbringing. I'm sure your little Maggie is trying very hard."

James was visibly proud of his lady's generous kindness. Christopher's face remained unreadable, and Maggie itched to rearrange a few of Amelia's perfect features. In any sporting house on Denver's Market Street a witch like Miss Perfect would rate a faceful of knuckles from the more honest whores. But then, Amelia was English, and the English seemed to tolerate more from their ladies than Market Street tolerated from its tarts. Maggie contented herself for the rest of the evening with imagining how a certain Denver sporting woman by the name of Gorilla Gertie might have instructed Amelia in acceptable behavior.

The next morning late, the family gathered for breakfast in the morning room. On this rare day with the sun shining through the curtains and onto the yellow chintz chairs and white linen, the family were all present. Even the old duke had left his bed to attend the table. Elizabeth, who sat next to her father to cut his food and help him eat, seemed unusually lively. The duchess also was cheerful. Once the meal was served, she sent the servants from the room and gave an optimistic evaluation of the tactical situation in view of what she considered the family's success at the opera house. Maggie did not consider the night's ordeal a success, but by now she accepted that English ideas on such subjects were beyond her grasp.

"I have some wonderful news!" Elizabeth announced halfway through the meal.

For having wonderful news the girl seemed suddenly nervous, Maggie noted.

"Dr. Holloway has commissioned me to paint portraits of his little twin daughters, Adriane and Hester."

Lady Torrington's bite of eggs halted halfway to her mouth, which she pursed in disapproval.

"Holloway?" the duke dithered. "Fine young man, that. Didn't know he had daughters. Thought he wasn't married."

"He's a widower, Father."

"Oh. That's different, then. You're to paint his girls, are you? Always thought you could paint better by half than most of the fools who call themselves artists. Holloway's a fine young man. Smart too."

"Edward, please!" the duchess pleaded. "Elizabeth, I do hope your use of the word *commission* does not imply that Dr. Holloway has offered to pay you for the painting."

Elizabeth plucked at the tablecloth. "He said a person of my talent should be paid. He wouldn't feel right about it otherwise."

"Hmmph! He shouldn't have felt proper about asking you in the first place. If you wish to do some little paintings of his girls in consideration of the kindness he has shown your father, then you may. But naming your work official portraits and accepting money for the work is unthinkable. You should know better. Ladies might cultivate art as an accomplishment, but they never lower themselves to *work* at it. That sort of thing should be reserved for people of a lower class, dear."

Elizabeth stilled the nervous movements of her hands

and stole a glance at Maggie as if for courage. "I shall paint the portraits, Mother. Sometimes I think that the only time I'm truly happy is when I'm painting. Dr. Holloway is a very proper gentleman, and he sees nothing wrong with offering me the commission." Abruptly, she rose.

"Elizabeth, sit down!"

Leveling steady eyes on her mother, Elizabeth declared, "I shall paint the portraits. I shall." With that she swept from the room. Maggie could see the trembling of Elizabeth's hands and the stiffness of her shoulders, but she could also see the determination in the pale porcelain face. She silently cheered her friend's courage.

"You!"

Maggie looked up to meet Lady Torrington's glare.

"You've been filling my daughter's head with nonsense, haven't you? She painted that portrait of you, and now she believes herself a painter. And, Christopher, you are as much to blame. You made much over that portrait when Elizabeth gave it to you. You even hung it in your room as if it was something more than a lady's dabbing. Lord have mercy! Elizabeth has always been an obedient daughter, and now this!"

"Mother," Christopher interrupted, "Elizabeth has a talent that goes far beyond a lady's casual accomplishment. You should be proud of her. Being acknowledged as an artist is no disgrace."

"Elizabeth is a *lady*, not an artist. What's more, she is an engaged lady. What do you think Viscount Standbridge would think if he knew about this? He is due back from the country sometime this week. Lord help us, if Elizabeth offends him, I shall never forgive her. His family's fortune is prodigious. Such an advantageous marriage is not easily arranged even for our family. In fact we shall be extremely fortunate"—she shot Maggie another glare—"if he does not have second thoughts when he hears of the current scandal."

"Scandal?" the duke quavered. "What's this about a scandal?"

"Nothing that I can't handle, Edward."

The old man hit the table with his fork. "Tell me, you old bird! I'm still head of this family!"

The duchess flushed. Christopher attempted to hide a smile. Maggie cringed inside. She liked the duke, in spite of his confusion and doddering. No doubt his disapproval would now be added to that of everyone else.

"Very well, Edward, if you insist on knowing, yesterday morning Magdalena tore frantically through Hyde Park on a horse, bareback and riding astride like a wild savage. All of Society was looking on."

"I wasn't frantic. And there were really very few people who saw me." Maggie felt obliged to defend herself.

The duchess sniffed. "But those who saw you have of course spread the story throughout the city. Mere hours after the incident the ladies of this family were snubbed in Hyde Park. We cannot go out of the house without becoming objects of ridicule."

A great bark of a laugh bellowed forth from the duke. "Bareback? Riding astride like a wild Indian from that savage country of yours? How splendid! Christopher, my boy, I always knew when you got caught by a female she would have to be a ripper." He laughed, choked, then laughed again until his face was crimson and sweat beaded his brow.

"Edward! You're overtaxing yourself."

The duke couldn't answer. He was too busy laughing. Maggie began to be concerned.

Christopher rose and helped his father from the chair. "Come, Father. Let's go up to your rooms. Maggie, will you help, please?"

Maggie gladly added her support to the duke as Christopher guided him out of the room. She felt Lady Torrington's eyes burn holes of indignation in her back.

Two days later the duke died. The same day, only an hour after the old man had breathed his last, Viscount Standbridge called on Lady Elizabeth. When he left, Elizabeth explained to the family that the viscount was most reluctant to add to the family's burdens, but under the circumstances he could not afford his name to be associated with the Talbots. Within an hour of his return to London the day before, no fewer than three people had regaled him with the details of Lady Christopher Talbot's wild ride. With deepest apologies he had called off the engagement.

The fortunes of the Talbots had never been quite so low, and it seemed that Maggie was at the root of much of their trouble.

Lady Torrington secluded herself in her rooms. Catharine followed suit. Rachel was sent with her nanny to cousins in Surrey until the family could regain its equilibrium. Rodney indulged himself, as always, in a spree of drinking and gambling that he couldn't pay for. Christopher spent considerable time with James at the family barrister's offices, and when he was not thus occupied he rode two horses almost to exhaustion in his own private battle with whatever devils plagued him. Even before the duke's death he had been withdrawn and moody. Maggie had almost given up ever being able to see into his heart.

Maggie was left with no one to turn to. Not really a member of the family, and yet the focus of much of their trouble, for the first time in her life she began to lose her sense of who she was and what she could do. She wept without quite knowing the reason, paced the garden restlessly, not knowing what she sought.

Disapproval seemed to emanate from everyone Maggie

encountered. The portraits in the gallery, the walls of the house, the air itself, seemed to breathe hostility. At last she understood how Baby Doe Tabor had felt all those months ago with all of Denver regarding her as an unworthy interloper. She remembered thinking at the time that the lovely wife of a rich man had no right to be upset just because those around her showered her with disapproval. How wrong she had been, Maggie realized.

On the day of the duke's funeral she pleaded illness as an excuse to not attend the elaborate procession and ceremony, then retreated to her room. Elizabeth followed.

"Maggie! What is this? Are you truly ill?" Elizabeth sat down on the bed beside the weeping Maggie and put an arm around her shoulders. "Are you ill?" she asked again.

"No," Maggie choked out.

"Then what? Christopher is already at the head of the procession with James. Shall I send for him?"

"No!"

"I shall if you don't tell me what this is all about."

Maggie gestured helplessly, indicating the world and everything in it. "I—I just can't face them."

"Oh, Maggie, you haven't let my old dragon mother wear you down, have you?"

"Your father," Maggie wailed. "He—he laughed himself to death . . . because of what I did."

"That's ridiculous. Father may have strained himself a bit when he heard the story, but he enjoyed himself hugely. All of us knew that death was waiting for Father around the corner of every hour. The only thing you did to the duke, dear Maggie, was brighten his last days with a touch of laughter."

Maggie was not finished castigating herself, however. "You. Poor Elizabeth. Viscount Standbridge. Oh, Elizabeth! I never meant to hurt you with my temper tantrum."

"Hurt *me?* You did me a favor, really. Being jilted is not so bad. I wasn't overly fond of George as it is, and my reputation will recover eventually. What's more, you've shown me that a woman should have the courage to reach out for her own happiness. The many exciting things you've done, and the stories you've told me about women in your American West, have inspired me. Someday I'd like to travel there and paint what I can see with my heart."

A flood of homesickness gushed onto Maggie's cheeks as hot tears.

"Don't be unhappy, dear. Please. I vow I will give Christopher a firm talking-to when the funeral is over. He's neglected you abominably. He's always been reserved and stingy with his emotions, but he has no right to be cruel."

"Don't talk to him," Maggie pleaded. She knew Christopher was fighting something other than just her, and her instincts told her that he had to conquer whatever devils were pursuing him before he could give anything to her—if he ever could.

"Please come with me to the funeral, Maggie. We can support each other. Please."

Maggie nodded and allowed Elizabeth to wipe her face with a cold cloth. Hand in hand they left the room.

That evening, the funeral over, the family having dined quietly, James, now sixth duke of Torrington, stood in his place at the dining table and made an announcement. Miss Amelia Hawthorne had consented to become his wife.

The duchess nodded her head gravely. A sad smile curved her mouth.

"The announcement will not be made public until a decent period of mourning has passed," James told them. "Amelia hopes we can have the wedding during the

Christmas season. I realize, Mother, it may seem to you that we're rushing things a bit, what with Father just having passed away, but I must think of our family's future, of producing an heir to the title to follow after me. . . ."

He droned on about his noble motives, but Maggie suspected he was more interested in Amelia's satiny skin and seductive curves than her ability to produce an heir. That and her money. The new duke eagerly reminded his family that Miss Hawthorne not only had a fat dowry from her wealthy uncle but had a considerable fortune of her own inherited from her deceased parents. With one clever triumph in the marriage market James had, at least temporarily, solved the Talbots' financial problems, and Rancho del Rio's significance shrank accordingly.

Maggie was not interested in James's enumeration of Amelia's virtues and monetary worth. She was more interested in the sudden pallor of Christopher's face when James announced his triumph. In spite of everything, did Christopher still pine for the woman who had turned away his affection in favor of chasing a title?

When James had finished his proclamation, Christopher's congratulations were hearty enough to hide any hurt he felt inside, Maggie noted. But the smile he gave his brother held a slant of bitterness.

"Don't worry about Christopher," Elizabeth said softly to Maggie as the men adjourned to the library to drink their brandy. "He saw through Amelia long ago. Amelia and James deserve each other if ever two people did."

Later, in the bedroom she shared with Christopher, Maggie sat on the bed, her legs drawn up to her chest and arms wrapped protectively about her knees. Christopher had not yet come upstairs, though Maggie had heard the tread of James's boots along the hall, and later, Rodney's staggering steps. Perhaps he would not come tonight, she speculated. Perhaps he would sit alone in the library, or haunt the downstairs nursing his hurts. She had seen the look of pain on his face when James had announced his engagement to Amelia. Christopher had claimed that he had no feeling left for the girl, that James was welcome to her, but Maggie didn't really believe him. She wanted to believe him, but she couldn't. Amelia might not be the perfect lady that he had admired, she might have the heart of a whore, but at least on the outside she was refined. She dressed in the latest fashion; her hair was always coiffed without flaw; her diction was elegant, her speech articulate, and she never slipped up and let "colorful" words slip into her oh-so-proper vocabulary. Not at all like Christopher's inelegant, uneducated, and very unfashionable wife.

Maggie sighed and allowed her head to drop down upon her knees. The last weeks had given her much to consider. She wondered if the Talbot family was always in a state of crisis or if it had been her coming, as the duchess had declared, that had unleashed the cataclysm. She had tried hard to become a lady for Christopher's sake. The notion that she might not succeed had never occurred to her. All her life she had believed she could do whatever she tried hard enough to do and be whatever she tried to be. Up until now the belief had proved right. Now, she had not only failed, she had lost herself in the trying.

Perhaps, she mused bitterly, success came from being true to oneself. Until she met Christopher, Maggie had been proud to be just exactly who she was. She bowed her head to no one and shrugged off others' disapproval as a goose shed water. Not until Christopher came into her life did she get the idea that Maggie Montoya might be better off being someone else. That was where she had gone wrong, Maggie decided—trying to make herself over into something she wasn't, something she didn't even want to be except for one reason: to earn Christopher's love.

Wisdom had come too late. One couldn't earn love. It had to be given freely, as she had given hers to Christopher. But Christopher had given his elsewhere—perhaps. Or perhaps, as Elizabeth had implied, he had none to give.

Soft footfalls padded down the hall. The latch to the door lifted, the door slowly swung open, and Christopher stood bracing himself on the door frame. Even sitting on the bed Maggie could smell the sweet odor of brandy that came into the room with him.

Christopher's eyes glinted like shards of obsidian as they fastened on Maggie. His skin drew tight across the strong features of his face. She could feel the heat of him even over the distance that separated them.

Maggie had seen the same look about other men—the same taut desperation, the same air of a predator seeking prey. Her husband wasn't drunk, as Maggie had first thought. He needed a woman. And she was the only woman available.

She turned away from him as he came for her.

Eighteen

"Maggie." Christopher's hands landed on her shoulders and began a slow massage. The brandy odor about him was strong, but his hands were sure and gentle. The warmth of him crept insidiously into her flesh and threatened to thaw the anger that had surged through her when she had seen him at the door. Anger and hurt—that she had failed, that he would never return her love, that he might treat her with kindness and find pleasure in her body, but she would never occupy his heart as he did hers.

Maggie closed her eyes, trying to will away the first stirrings of passion. But she could feel Christopher's desire in the touch of his hands and the heat of his breath in her hair, and the knowledge that he wanted her inspired a sweet answering surge in her blood. Since his father's collapse Christopher's love-making had been brusque, but even such matter-of-fact attentions had tightened his grip on her heart. Now he gave her tenderness—now of all times when she had finally realized that she would never truly be a part of his life, when she needed anger to protect her from the hurt —now he came to her in passion and gentleness, wooing her to desire. He left her no defense against him.

"Maggie. Don't turn away." He turned her toward him while lowering her to the bed. Gentle hands brushed wild dark curls from her face and smoothed the pucker from her brow. "You grow more beautiful every day, do you know that?"

Maggie wondered if Christopher was seeing her or Amelia. He kissed her brow, her nose, the corners of her mouth, then brushed his lips across hers.

"Passionate little Maggie." His lips touched hers in tantalizing invitation. "Not-quite-a-lady Maggie. I don't think I care much for ladies anymore."

Maggie read the pain in his eyes and gave in to the need to soothe it away. She touched his cheek, smoothed the taut line of his brows, then threaded her fingers through his thick black hair to pull his mouth down upon hers. Their breath merged. His lips twisted savagely over hers, no longer gentle, and his tongue thrust in urgent possession. The heat of him surrounded her. The hard blade of his sex swelled against her thigh, and Maggie felt the world slip away, carrying anger and hurt with it. In a remote corner of her mind where reason persisted, Maggie knew this was an ending. She wanted it to be a good ending, something she could carry with her as comfort when the emptiness of her failure settled over her soul.

"Christopher," she whispered against his mouth,

"please love me. Now. Please." She needed him with an ache that was pain and pleasure combined.

"I will love you, sweet Maggie. I will love you until you don't know inside from out or up from down." Expertly he unfastened the front buttons on her gown and parted it, exposing her breasts to his view. They were hot and swollen, the peaks tingling for his touch. He traced the underside of one breast with a finger. Maggie gasped.

"My beautiful Maggie cat. You're a jewel with so many lovely facets. I wonder if I'll ever learn them all." He followed the path of his finger with his tongue, laving the lower contours of her breast with warm wetness, then moving up, a little at a time, until his mouth closed around the turgid nipple. He sucked, and Maggie arched against him, her eyes closed, her world centered on the warm darkness where his mouth joined her flesh and created bliss as sharp as a knife cutting her soul.

Giving in to an irresistible need to touch him, Maggie ran her hands along the hard muscles of his arms and glided over the taut sinews of his shoulders. The urgency of his desire coiled in the flesh beneath her hands. As her fingers brushed lovingly through his hair, he sighed, his warm breath tantalizing the damp skin of her breast. A sigh of passion or sadness—Maggie couldn't tell. She longed to love away the devils that plagued him, but if her love was not what he wanted, then she would be content to comfort him with their passion.

"Maggie. Sweet Maggie." His breath heated her skin, and the tender touch of his mouth on her breast made her rise toward him in longing. With firm hands he held her still, silently chiding her impatience while his mouth continued its avid exploration of her breasts, ribs, belly, and thighs. Delicious tendrils of fire flicked along the path of his caresses. Her blood turned to sweet honey, flowing warm and languid from a heart that beat only at the demand of his hands and mouth. Every nerve in her body waited tautly for the comfort of his touch, the feel of his flesh against hers.

Finally he covered her with himself and settled his lean hips between her thighs. She sighed in bliss and wrapped her legs around him. She saw his smile through the darkness. His voice, heavy and warm with desire, was a caress. "My passionate little Maggie. You turn desire into joy."

He kissed her, his tongue invading her mouth in a sweetly savage onslaught that prefaced the final possession. She surrendered her breath, her very soul, into his keeping. Between her thighs his flesh expertly tantalized hers. The rigid blade of his sex poised hungrily at her entrance. He pressed forward just enough to make her gasp with pleasure, then withdrew.

"I want you so much," he confessed against her lips. "You've been a fire in my blood since I first saw you."

He kissed her again, swift and hard, then uttered an almost inhuman growl as he plunged deeply into her.

Lightning ripped through Maggie. She tightened her legs around him, wanting to absorb him into herself, to make him a part of her that could never be torn away. He thrust again, lifting her hips to drive even more deeply into her body. Pleasure sharp enough to be pain rammed through her body with every plunge of his hard, devouring flesh. All thought dissolved into feeling as she matched the desperate cadence of his passion. The bed rocked with their furious climb toward a climax, then was still as he drove deeply in a final thrust and imprisoned her in his grip, sealing her tightly to him. For one moment of heaven they seemed totally merged, no more man and woman, but one flesh, breathing, sighing, pulsing with joy. The world spun away from them, leaving them to their own private universe.

* * *

When Maggie opened her eyes, she found her husband peacefully asleep, though he still gripped her firmly. She was wet with the warm flood of desire's offering, and the creature that had attacked her and gorged on her passion now lay sated and flaccid against her husband's thigh.

Looking at Christopher sleeping, replete with male pleasure, his features relaxed and looking far more innocent than they should, Maggie couldn't help the smile that twitched her mouth. She did love this man far beyond the lust that sparked between them whenever he permitted it. She loved him for his stupid idealism about the helplessness and purity of "ladies," for the humor that struggled to break through his serious soul, for his appreciation of the beauty of a strange land, and his friendships with people who must have seemed to him coarse and uncivilized; she loved him for his loyalty to his family, and for his dutiful loyalty to her, no matter how that loyalty split his soul in two; she loved him for his strange and incomprehensible notions of honor.

She loved Christopher Talbot, His High-and-Mighty Lordship. How she loved him. And he lusted after her, sometimes. Sometimes he might even like her a little. But that wasn't enough.

Careful not to wake Christopher, she climbed out of bed. A decision waited for her, and her soul would be leaden with its weight until she disposed of it. But she could not think clearly in a room still musky with shared passion, with Christopher's warm presence tempting her to snuggle down beside him and give in to sleep, hoping her pride and her needs would go away.

She padded through the dark, still house and out into the garden. The air was cold. There would be frost before morning. Maggie wrapped her dressing robe more tightly around her and let the sharp night breeze clear the mushiness from her mind. She sat on a stone bench and looked at the moon. A harvest moon, some called it. Full and radiant, drenching London with its milky light, the same moon shone down upon the Alvarez ranch where her mother was buried, on the Lady Luck in Denver, on the house with the bell chimes in Santa Fe, on Rancho del Rio and Luisa.

Suddenly Maggie longed to dance. The world and its complications were too much for her; she longed to lose herself in rhythm and movement as she had so often before. Ignoring the cold, she kicked off her soft slippers and took off the dressing robe that covered her thin nightgown. She strutted out onto the paving stones around the little fountain—just as she had so often strutted onto the stage at the Lady Luck. Her own voice provided the music that beat in her ears. Maggie stepped, turned, stepped, whirled, her arms and hands weaving a sensuous web of enchantment through the milky night. The corkscrew strands of her hair swayed and tangled with her arms, shimmering like a dark cloud alive with flashes of lightning. Her bare feet trod out a rhythm, her torso swayed, her eyes closed. Maggie willed herself to become the dance. Her heart was the rhythm, her soul the music, her body the song. She summoned the spirit of the dance to carry her away as it had so many times before.

The spirit did not come as summoned, however. Maggie's feet stepped, her arms moved, her body arched and postured and swayed, but she was still Maggie Montoya Talbot. A woman moving to music, but not part of the music, not the embodiment of the dance.

Her rhythmic steps stuttered to a halt. Her whirls and weavings lost life and died. For a moment she was still, her head thrown back, her arms outstretched as in pleading. Slowly she wilted and sank down upon the stone bench. For the first time in her life the dance hadn't come. She covered her face with her hands and closed her eyes.

She had lost the dance just as she had lost herself. For months she had corrupted her soul by trying to be something she wasn't, and this was the price she had paid.

She sat for a long time while the cold seeped into her bones and reached for her soul, then she straightened and clutched the dressing robe about her. She knew what she had to do, and the realization both frightened and saddened her. Maggie Montoya was still somewhere within her, but to get her back she had to return to her own world. The thought of leaving Christopher sent a spear of pure pain through her heart. It didn't matter that he didn't love her, that he had wanted to leave her in the first place. She loved him, and leaving would tear a bloody wound in her heart.

Maggie put on her slippers and stood, straightening her spine and squaring her shoulders. A wise decision was no good until it was acted upon. She could put off the parting, linger in Christopher's shadow, and gobble the few morsels of casual affection he might throw her way—her will growing weaker and weaker while her true self faded away. Or she could simply gather her courage and leave. The Maggie Montoya of old would not have hesitated. The agonies of slow good-byes were not for her.

Christopher stood on the little balcony that overlooked the formal garden. His blood surged through his veins in time to Maggie's dance. Her soft voice wove a song through the night air. Her hair caught the moonlight in a shimmer of black silk as it fanned out around her. Her bare arms and oval face flashed glowing ivory; her feet propelled her sinuous female body in rhythms that stirred his senses from drowsy appreciation to full life.

But before the dance was well begun, Maggie slowed and stuttered to a stop. She flung her head back and extended her arms as if offering herself to the moon. Christopher felt suddenly as if he were spying on someone's prayer. Silently he backed through the double French doors into their bedroom.

He felt a bit like praying himself. Over the last few weeks he'd suffered purgatory. His life had changed. He had changed, and he had fought the change with a sullen vengeance. All his life he had been the second son of the duke of Torrington. England was his home, genteel aristocracy his heritage. His place and his life were mapped out for him, a path bounded by expectations of family and Society. Rules and propriety governed his thoughts and actions. Duty limited his life.

Then came America—and Maggie. Perhaps he had begun to love her at the same time he realized that his soul was in tune to the vast spaces and lusty, brawling adventurousness of the West. She was the embodiment of unfettered spirit—mischievous, taunting, ever hopeful, ever believing in ridiculous things like love and happiness. In New Mexico Christopher had told himself that the attraction was fleeting, but Maggie had proved more determined than his skepticism. Innocent that she was, she had taken their wedding vows seriously, and put teeth in her seriousness by daring to follow him to England.

Had she known what she was doing? Had she thought Christopher would protect her? He hadn't, as it happened, and now he was heartily ashamed. He had been so concerned with his own painful battle that he had scarcely noticed hers.

The England to which he'd brought Maggie was not the England he remembered; but then, perhaps what he remembered had never really been England. All his life he had tried to escape, he realized now. He had escaped with the Army, and during lulls in military obligations he had escaped on trips in the interest of his shipping business. Then came America. Only since he'd returned to

London, with Maggie as a constant reminder of what he really longed for, had he begun to realize that he hated the superficiality, the rigid boundaries, the hypocrisy.

The realization had not come easily. What he thought he valued most in his life became a sham. Old ideals disintegrated, old goals suddenly became unimportant, and his future stretched ahead of him in uncharted chaos. His father's collapse seemed to personify the crumbling of the world he'd always thought was his. But finally he came to realize that the duke's death had set him free—as if his loyalty to his old life had been tied to his loyalty to a man he admired and respected.

Strange how he had always admired people instead of loved them. He'd admired his father—or at least the man his father had once been. He had admired Amelia.

Admired. What a pale word beside *love*, a tepid trickle compared to a boiling river of feeling. It had taken Maggie Montoya to teach him that love was worth the strain on the heart and the senses. Bless her stubbornness and determination. Bless her seductive body and innocent heart. He loved her. He didn't care who approved or disapproved; he didn't care about the purity of her pedigree or the quality of her manners and education. He loved her smile, her warmth, her strength, her courage, the spark of trouble in her eyes, and the hint of mischief in her spirit. And he especially loved the way she felt against him when she was naked and aroused and taunting him with a frank sensuality that no lady would dream of displaying.

Maggie wanted a real marriage? He would give her a real marriage. After his father's funeral and brother's wedding he would take his bride back to New Mexico. Somehow he would make up for the weeks he had left her to London's mercy; they would forget the miserable journey to a place where neither of them belonged and carve out a niche that both of them could call home.

As he settled back in the bed that had been so recently warmed by his wife's passion, Christopher's mind hummed with plans. Rancho del Rio would be just a start. He would sell out his partnership in Pitney and Talbot Overseas Freight and combine that capital with the income from the ranch to expand into other areas—timber, perhaps, or mining. With Maggie at his side, with only her heart to bind him, he felt as though he could conquer the world.

Christopher grinned and let his thoughts dwell on his wife, his little midnight dancer. When she returned to their bed he would tell her he loved her. He should have told her long ago. He would tell her, and then he would show her. His loins heated in anticipation as he relaxed into the softness of the bed.

He woke to the pale light of morning. The bed beside him was empty and cold. On Maggie's pillow lay a folded piece of paper. Christopher shook his head to drive away grogginess as he unfolded the paper and read the laboriously written but painfully correct script that drove a stake through all his hopes:

"Christopher—

I'm sorry for leaving without saying good-bye, but when something ends it should end. Now I know you were right about our marriage being business, not anything else. In England I have made everyone unhappy, even myself. Even you. I do not belong in London any more than you belong in New Mexico. We will both be happy living our own lives.

I'm sorry for acting like a child and causing you trouble. My infatuation with you is over. I am wiser now and know better. Oh, yes—I took some money from the desk in the library. I will repay you when I get to the ranch."

Christopher crumpled the note in his hand and hurled it at the wall. "Damn! Bloody damn!"

He vaulted from the bed and flung open the wardrobe. Maggie's clothes were still there—or were they? The wardrobe didn't seem as full as it had been. Her favorite shoes were missing, as was the heavy wool coat he'd bought her for the coming winter. He looked carefully. The rather plain green gown that she'd liked so well was gone, and at least one other.

Christopher cursed, long and loud, in most ungenteel phrases. From the mantel of the bedroom fireplace Maggie's portrait regarded him with dark, mocking eyes. Expressive lips curved in a smile that rivaled the Mona Lisa's, and sunlight glinted in sparks off a scarcely tamed mane of black corkscrew hair.

Elizabeth had truly captured Maggie's spirit—a child-woman sprite aglow with life and energy. Until Christopher Talbot had tried to put out her fire.

All the times Christopher had told himself that Maggie shouldn't have come to England, it had never occurred to him that she might leave it without him.

He looked at the portrait and cursed yet again.

III

Home Again

Nineteen

"The frost has already melted," Maggie told Luisa as they passed the stone corral, which only an hour ago had been covered with rime. "It's going to be a nice day."

"Likely," Luisa agreed.

They stopped just beyond the wagon shed and squinted into the December sun at the little square building that was growing out of the labors of five Rancho del Rio cowboys. The walls were constructed of sod bricks each a foot high, two feet wide, and eight inches thick. The roof would be canvas at first, but Maggie planned to replace the canvas with good shake shingles before the winter got too harsh. The oilcloth that now covered the window openings would also be replaced—with expensive real glass.

"Moss says they'll be putting down the floor in a couple of days," Luisa told Maggie.

"We should be ready for the pupils first thing after Christmas, then. I didn't realize the schoolhouse would go up so fast. I still have to order books and slates—you tell me which books to order, since you'll be the teacher this winter. And maybe Cleave can make us some benches and tables." She ticked the items off on her fingers. "We'll need a stove—I'll look through the Sears catalog—and a big desk for you—perhaps Cleave could make that also. Curtains for the windows would be nice, and a big cupboard to store supplies."

Moss Riley emerged from the sod schoolhouse and clumped across to where the women stood. He tipped his hat. "Miz' Talbot, Miz' Gutierrez, Stony thought I oughta ask you ladies if you want a porch."

"A porch?" Maggie envisioned the pupils sitting happily on a covered porch while eating their midday meals. "How long would it take to build a porch?"

"My guess is they could slap one on in a coupla days."

"Then let's have a porch."

"Yes, ma'am." He touched the stained brim of his hat and ambled off toward the schoolhouse.

"Isn't this exciting, Luisa? I'm so glad you said you'd teach this winter. It may be months before we can finally hire a teacher who's willing to come way out here. Thanks to you the children won't have to wait." She grinned. "I think I'll come to class when you talk about ciphering. I still don't understand the account books."

They walked together back toward the ranch house. "Don't you think you should slow down a bit and let yourself ease in to becoming lady of the ranch a little more gradually?" Luisa asked somewhat cautiously. "You've

been back a month, Magdalena, yet I don't think I've once
seen you sit down and simply drink a cup of coffee or read
one of those books you bought in New York City. You
haven't given yourself time to rest—or to think."

"I don't feel like resting or thinking."

"You don't feel like thinking about England and that
husband of yours, you mean."

Maggie was stonily silent.

"What happened in England that has you so busily not
thinking about it?"

"Nothing happened. I didn't like it there, so I came
back. Christopher was more than happy to see me go. He
didn't want me in England in the first place."

"So now you're both very happy leading your own
lives."

"That's right."

Luisa shook her head as they walked into the house. "I
think you're a liar, Magdalena Montoya Talbot."

Maggie ignored her.

The Rancho del Rio headquarters ranch house bore little resemblance to the opulent abode that Theodore and
Todd Harley had inhabited. Maggie and Luisa had redecorated before Maggie had left for England, and Maggie
had swept through the house once again when she had
returned. Everything that reminded her of England had
been given away or discarded. Now the house was filled
with furnishings made from the pine and oak native to
western New Mexico. Mexican and Navajo rugs and wall
hangings purchased in Santa Fe added color to the floors
and walls.

Purifying her home of English influence had occupied
only part of Maggie's time since her return. She had
struggled to learn the accounts from Luisa, with only par-
tial success. The painstaking task of working with rows
and columns of numbers without making mistakes still

eluded her. The actual work of the ranch was more satisfying, and she rode often to the line camps with Moss Riley to check on both the hands and the herd. She picked the ranch manager's brain about the utilization of the rest of her vast grant of land—how much to expand the herd and with what kind of cattle, the advantages of raising and marketing horses or sheep as well as cattle, the building of satellite ranches to better manage such a large tract of land. As long as the land was managed effectively, she figured, Christopher would not care how it was done. After all, his heart was in England. What did he care about Rancho del Rio as long as it produced a good income?

On top of everything else Maggie had now taken it into her head that the children who lived on Rancho del Rio needed an education. She had been ignorant of reading and writing until Christopher and Peter had taken her in hand; she saw no reason for other children to suffer the kind of ignorance that she had endured. And of course, she invited the children of neighboring homesteads and ranches to attend school as well. All in all she thought there might be as many as fifteen pupils starting school after the new year. Planning the schoolhouse and trying to find a teacher had occupied a good chunk of time—still was occupying her time, in fact. Luisa had consented to teach for a few months, but Maggie continued to write letters in hopes of finding someone willing to come to Rancho del Rio as a full-time teacher.

"Are you riding out today?" Luisa asked.

"Not today. I have too much to do here. Accounts and supplies." Maggie grimaced.

Luisa chuckled. "I'll be in the kitchen with Anita and Rosa if you need me."

"Thank you."

Glad to get away from Luisa's probing questions about

England, Maggie went straight to the library to make up a list of supplies to be bought in Santa Rosa at week's end. She had lists of foodstuffs from the cook; hardware from Cleave, the blacksmith; assorted items of rope, leather goods, and tools from Moss, household supplies from Luisa, and individual requests from the wives of the hands who lived in the cottages behind the bunkhouse. She struggled for an hour to put the lists in order and figure the necessary expenditures against the funds available.

At the end of an hour she sighed and rubbed at her brow. Luisa was right. She needed to take some time for herself. Since her return she had spurred herself into a gallop and kept the pace for every day of the week. She had scarcely allowed herself to appreciate being home.

Home. What a lovely idea. Maggie had thought returning home would salve her wounds and give her back the certainty of who she was and where she was going. For the first few days—maybe the first week—it had. She had reveled in the fresh air and clean wind, the treeless vistas bereft of people and buildings, the still nights, the quiet days undisturbed by the rattle of carriage wheels or the raucous voices of hawkers. But as the days had passed she realized that she would never again be the girl who had danced in the Lady Luck in Denver, or even the young woman who had first moved to Rancho del Rio.

Something was missing that made her feel empty inside. Christopher Talbot was missing. He wasn't there to scold her when she let her language become too colorful; he wasn't there to surprise her with an unexpected appearance of his crooked smile; he wasn't there at night to keep her warm with his strong masculine body, or to take her to paradise with his loving.

But she didn't want to think about Christopher. An ocean and most of a continent separated them, and that was the way it should be.

Anita knocked on the library door. "Señora Talbot, someone comes."

"Who is it, Anita?"

"I think it is Señora Collins from the Circle T."

"Thank you. I'll be right there."

Relieved to have her thoughts interrupted, Maggie set her lists aside and went to greet her guest.

Martha Collins was already sitting on the porch with Luisa when Maggie stepped out the door. Cleave's son, Jed, was helping the three teenage Collins boys unhitch the team and lead them to the corral.

"Maggie," Luisa said, "you remember Martha Collins from the Circle T?"

"We met once before I left for England. It's nice to see you, Mrs. Collins."

"Just call me Martha, honey. My! Don't you look fit! London must have agreed with you, girl. We're all anxious to hear about your trip."

"There's not much to tell, really."

"Oh, fiddle! Don't tell me that a body can travel to England and back and live in a duke's palace and not have a tale to tell. But I won't bother you about it now. I'm on my way to Santa Rosa with three of my boys and thought I'd stop by to say welcome home."

Maggie felt a spark of warmth in her heart. "That's very nice of you."

"We'll pick up everybody's mail in town, so I'll stop back in two or three days on my way home. I was telling Lu that Saturday week we're having a get-together for our girl Katy's birthday. Since the weather's been holding so good we figured people wouldn't mind driving out. We'll be expecting both you ladies—that husband of yours, too, and whatever hands you want to bring along to ride shotgun. Haven't had too much trouble up here, but you never can tell about them Apaches."

"My . . . uh . . . husband didn't return with me."

Mrs. Collins's brows twitched. "Well, then, when he comes back, we'll have another excuse for a social, won't we?"

"We'll look forward to the party," Luisa said quickly. "Maggie's near worked herself to death since she got back. It'll do her good to cut loose for a day or so."

Martha shook her head at Maggie. "Can't drive yourself too hard, girl. This land will kill you fast enough without you helping it along."

They sat on the porch talking for an hour while the Collins horses rested in the corral and the Collins sons—at thirteen, fifteen, and eighteen already counted men—lent a hand at the schoolhouse. Mrs. Collins tactfully avoided the subject of Maggie's husband, as there was plenty of other conversation available. Three months' worth of news was aired, for that was how much time had passed since Martha and Luisa had last talked. The weather, the price of cattle, the Indians, Geronimo—who had just this last summer made a pact with General Crook to return to the reservation but had not yet come in—the new school, children and how to raise them, men and how to tolerate them, and Luisa's new recipe for potato soup.

Finally Martha called for her boys to hitch their team. "I guess I'll see you on the way back, and again on Saturday a week." She smiled. "Aren't we becoming the social butterflies, though?"

"We'll have to visit more often," Luisa said. "I never realized how lonely a woman could get until I moved out here."

Martha chuckled as one of her sons helped her onto the seat of the wagon. "That's right. You two haven't spent a winter out here yet, have you? Once those blue northers start howling through, there won't be much visiting back and forth. We're lucky it's held off this long. Come spring, after roundup, we'll have another get-together, though."

"We'll host that one," Luisa offered.

"I'll hold you to that."

As the Collins wagon rattled away, Luisa turned to Maggie. "A party will do you good. You turned down two invitations while we were in Santa Fe—one from the governor, no less. You've had your head in a hole ever since you came back. It's time you started living again, my girl. Feeling sorry for yourself won't get you anywhere."

She wasn't indulging in self-pity, Maggie insisted to herself. But how did one live without a heart?

The good weather held for Katy Collins's birthday party, and families from the neighboring ranches and homesteads celebrated hard—their last chance before true winter set in. Christmas being only a little more than two weeks away, all the children received a gift. Tables set up in the barn were laden with cookies, mincemeat, apple and peach pies, baked beef, potato soup, thick gravy, and candied yams. Two cast-iron stoves provided warmth, for although the sun shone brightly, the air was crisp with December's chill. Wagons, animals, and tools had been moved out of the barn for a day and replaced with hay bales to sit on and fresh straw spread over the floor to dance on. Two fiddles provided music. The adults danced, talked, and ate while the children played ball, marbles, and pop-the-whip outside.

"Now, *this* is a party!" Maggie said breathlessly to Moss Riley after she'd endured two rounds of what he called dancing.

"Ain't no other kind!" He helped her limp to the nearest hay bale. "Sorry about that toe."

"It's nothing."

"Can I get you a plate?"

"You did help me work up an appetite."

Moss headed for the tables. Maggie sat on the hay and watched her neighbors cutting up like calves in spring. She'd been reluctant to come, but now she was glad that she'd given in to Luisa's insistence. A New Mexico barn dance had nothing at all in common with the social affairs she'd so hated in London. Here people came to have fun. Everyone was in their Sunday best, but no one came to show off their clothing and pick apart their neighbors'. Gossip flew around the room, but it was the chatter of friends who had not seen each other in weeks or months. No one's reputation would be shredded because he or she said a word out of place or wore clothes that had been seen once too often. These people were too busy surviving in a harsh world to worry about petty social maneuvering.

Moss returned with an offering of food to make up for nearly breaking Maggie's toes while dancing. The plate was piled high with beef, potatoes, and gravy. "There's pie when you've polished this off. Just give me the high sign when you're through and I'll bring you some."

"Moss, really, the toe is fine. I can walk."

He looked dubious. "Me and my big feet." His face brightened. "There's Luisa. Wonder if she'd like to dance."

Maggie felt a pang of sympathy for Luisa as Moss elbowed through the crowd in pursuit.

"This must not be what you're used to," came a voice from one side of her.

Maggie turned to find herself staring into Todd Harley's baby-blue eyes. For once in her life she was nonplussed. "Why . . . why . . . !"

"Todd Harley," he reminded her.

"Todd. Well, of—of course I remember you."

"How could you forget?" he asked with a wry grin. "In

case you're wondering what I'm doing here, I bought twenty-five thousand acres that border your grant on the south. I'm starting a cattle operation of my own."

Maggie felt like an idiot sitting there with her tongue tied in knots, but what did she say to a man who had held a gun on her last time she'd seen him? On the other hand, she'd been rather vicious in her reaction, yet that didn't seem to bother Todd. Most men wouldn't start an amiable conversation with a woman who had once put a knee into their private parts.

"I—I'm glad to hear you're doing well," she managed to say.

"I wouldn't go so far as to say that I'm doing well. Not yet. But I will be. At least I can run my ranch the way I want to without having to convince my father first. I'm afraid my father doesn't think much of me. He never listened to my ideas. But then, I don't think much of him either."

Maggie gave him a lame smile.

"Do you mind if I share your bale of hay?" he asked.

"No, of course not. Do you mind if I eat?"

"Go ahead. That beef looks good, as a matter of fact. I think I'll get some for myself."

He returned minutes later with a full plate. Maggie had hoped he would go away after proving that they could be civilized neighbors despite the awkward past, but it seemed he would be satisfied with nothing less than an avowal of friendship.

"Maggie," he continued after taking a few bites, "—may I still call you Maggie?"

"Go ahead. It's still my name."

"Maggie, since we're to be neighbors, and since you've got every right in the world to hate my guts, I . . . well, I wanted to see if I could somehow set things straight. I wouldn't like you thinking that I had any part in my father's plotting last spring."

Todd was as handsome as ever with his startling blue eyes and thick wavy hair. The sincerity of his face matched the regret in his voice.

"I'm not my father, Maggie, and I don't ever want to be like my father. I hope you'll forgive me for allowing myself to get sucked unintentionally into his plot. I'd like for us to start over, if that's possible."

The warmth in his voice made her uneasy. She was a married woman, after all, and he was looking at her as a dog might look at a juicy bone. Once she had flirted with him to make Christopher jealous. No doubt he'd gotten the wrong idea.

"Well, we're neighbors," she told him in what she hoped was an unencouraging voice. "I don't object to that."

He smiled a smile that had probably charmed the drawers off ladies from Denver to Santa Fe. "I guess that's all I can ask for right now. Unless, of course, you'd consent to this dance." He put down his plate and held out his hand.

Maggie regarded his hand as though it might bite. Todd would interpret a refusal as a sign that she held a grudge. She didn't, at least not against him. And they were neighbors, after all.

"Last time I danced Moss Riley stepped all over my toes," she said in excuse.

"I promise to not touch your toes," he persisted. His eyes challenged her, daring her to take his hand and dance with him.

"One dance. Then I'm going to attack one of those pies over there."

"I'll help you lead the charge."

The fiddlers were murdering a Strauss waltz. Maggie easily floated into the familiar rhythm of the dance. Todd kept his promise and didn't once step on her toes. Being held again in a man's arms felt good, and yet the dance didn't seem quite right. The wrong man held her. His smell, his feel, and his movement were not Christopher's. He was not Christopher. Todd might be handsome, charming, and devour her with his eyes as though she were the most desirable woman in the room, but his attention didn't draw an answering response from either her body or her mind.

After one dance Maggie managed a graceful escape, pleading a craving for pie. She sought out Luisa and found her separating two young boys who were fighting over a ball.

"Luisa! Did you know that Todd Harley bought land just to the south of us?"

Luisa sent the youngsters on their way and turned to Maggie with a touch of chagrin on her face. "Moss told me about that some time ago."

"Why didn't you tell me?"

"Because in the month you've been back, we've hardly gotten a chance to talk about anything besides accounts, cattle, and the school. You've been rather single minded about what you wanted to talk about.

"What else haven't you told me?" Maggie grumbled.

Luisa looked around to see who was within earshot. "Since this seems to be the night for revelations, perhaps I should tell you that a private detective dropped by a while back asking about Arnold Stone."

"What?" Maggie nearly screeched.

"Shhhh!"

"Omigod! What did you say?"

"I said that Arnold Stone was a frequent customer at the Lady Luck and a casual acquaintance. What could I say?"

"What did *he* say?"

"He didn't say anything, not even whom he was working for. The sheriff's men haven't come pounding on the door, so I suppose whoever was investigating reached a dead end."

Maggie let out her breath. "You should have told me."

Luisa looked at her reproachfully.

"Okay, I haven't been easy to talk to. I'm sorry. But that was important. You should have told me."

"So you could have spent your time worrying about it? Maggie, there isn't anything either of us can do. The past is gone and out of our hands. You can't let it ruin every day of your future. I don't intend to spend the rest of my life running from every mention of Arnold Stone's name. Life's too short as it is." She started toward the tables, then looked back. "I want some of that pie. Care to join me?"

Maggie followed her, wishing she could put the past—Arnold Stone, England, and Christopher Talbot—as firmly behind her as Luisa had.

Five days later Todd Harley rode out to Rancho del Rio for a neighborly visit. He brought a gift for both of the women—a volume of Byron's poems for Maggie and a lace handkerchief for Luisa.

"Merry Christmas!" he said as the women opened their tissue-wrapped packages.

"Todd, this is very generous, but it wasn't necessary," Maggie objected.

"Just trying to be neighborly."

Luisa eyed him with distrust, Maggie with exasperation. But it would have been terribly rude not to have shown at least a little courtesy.

Todd exclaimed over the changes to Rancho del Rio headquarters when Maggie gave a short tour—the new wagon shed, the family housing behind the bunkhouse, which had been enlarged, the new enclosed *placita* with its well and evergreen shrubs.

"You know, ladies," he told Maggie and Luisa, "I suggested to my father that we move families out here to the ranch. Women and children have a moderating influence on the cowboys' behavior, haven't you found? I plan to follow this example once I'm on my feet. Maybe next fall after roundup."

He also approved of the change in decor, complimenting Maggie on her use of native styles and simple furniture. Maggie figured he was angling for an invitation to dinner, and she didn't intend to accommodate him. She didn't need Todd Harley cluttering up her life.

Todd did talk his way into a glass of cider, however. Maggie was glad that Luisa refused to leave them alone, even though Todd hinted that he wouldn't mind having Maggie to himself for a few minutes. Luisa's chilly manner let their guest know that if it was courting he had come for, she, at least, didn't approve one bit.

"I was rather surprised to learn that you'd returned from England alone, Maggie." Todd gazed thoughtfully into his cider. "I expect your husband won't be far behind, though."

"My husband prefers England."

"Then you're just here for a visit."

"No, I'm here to stay. London is interesting, but I prefer New Mexico."

Todd feigned surprise. "If you don't mind my saying so, Maggie, if I were married to a woman like you, I certainly wouldn't let her live on one side of the world while I stayed on the other side."

"You're not married to me," Maggie said sternly. "Christopher and I are both very . . . independent people."

The sudden intensity of Todd's gaze was almost chilling.

Luisa broke the tension. "Did you notice the new building that's going up, Mr. Harley? Maggie is starting a school."

"How interesting." For a moment his eyes clung to Maggie with unwavering regard, then he visibly drew back. "A school. A very worthy idea."

Maggie tried to shake off the sudden feeling of being stalked. "Luisa will be teaching this winter, but we hope to find a teacher who will be willing to come out here permanently. The neighboring ranchers who plan to send children have all said they would chip in to pay a salary."

"Hm." Todd pulled at his chin thoughtfully. "I may be able to be of some help."

"But you don't have any children."

"I do have a friend in the publishing industry—a fellow I met when I attended school in New York. I might be able to get any books you need."

"That would be wonderful!"

Todd smiled at the light that came to Maggie's eyes. "Let me write a few letters."

"That's really very nice of you."

"It's nothing. The school's a much-needed addition in this remote area. I admire you for having the generosity to provide one. After all, you don't have any children either." He set his cider glass upon the side table. "I think I've kept you ladies long enough. The cider was delicious. Thank you."

Maggie walked him to the door. She wondered if she had judged the man too harshly. Even before the incident with his father Todd had seemed all charm and no substance. Now she wasn't sure. Perhaps she wasn't giving him enough credit.

"I'll let you know about the books. And if there's anything else I can do to help with the school, just let me know."

"You're very kind."

He gave her a wry smile. "Don't confuse me with my father, Maggie. I'd like to make up to you what he did, if ever I can."

"There's no need, Todd."

"I have the need." He paused, seeming to consider his next words. "I want you to remember that no one would blame you if you wanted to be free of that cold Englishman. A man who's not willing to stay by his wife's side doesn't deserve her, and a beautiful woman like you could have her pick of any man in New Mexico."

"I take my marriage vows seriously."

"I expect you do. He doesn't deserve you, Maggie."

As Maggie watched Todd ride away, Luisa came up behind her and placed a gentle hand on her shoulder. "In a way he's right. No one would blame you if you decided that a marriage stretched halfway across the world isn't going to work. If it makes you so unhappy—"

"No." Maggie shut the door and turned. "What makes you think I'm unhappy?"

"You do."

Maggie shook her head. "I'll stay married to Christopher, if for no other reason than because I'm going to have his child."

The December wedding of the sixth duke of Torrington to Miss Amelia Hawthorne was an event that outshone Christmas. No expense was spared. No expense needed to be spared, for the bride was wealthy as well as beautiful, and everyone agreed that her poise and gentility were remarkable for one whose family had made its fortune in trade. The ladies present at the wedding and reception agreed that the new duchess would be renowned for her beauty for years to come. Wasn't it fortunate that she was sweet and modest as well as beautiful? Quite plainly the bride was in love with her duke, and he fairly doted on her. Lady Hethrington remarked to her cousin Letitia— and her opinion spread quickly among the wedding guests—that such an obvious love match was refreshingly romantic in the mercenary London marriage market.

One of the few at the wedding festivities who seemed unimpressed with the nuptials was the duke's younger brother. Upon the old duke's death and with the new duke's consent, Lord Christopher became earl of Dunbar, a title involving remote northern estates that no one in the family had visited for at least a century. Those in the social know agreed that the duke had been very generous in granting this title to his younger brother, for the heir might have kept it—and its attendant revenues—for himself. Those same knowlegeable souls noted that the new earl showed a very forbidding face at the wedding, and they remembered that not too long ago Christopher had been the one courting the lovely Miss Hawthorne. Now the earl was married to an American heiress who had proved herself most scandalously unsuitable, and the heir to the dukedom was taking wedding vows with beautiful Amelia. Brows were raised. Heads shook. And the imagination of the gossipmongers started refining raw material that promised to make the duke of Torrington's wedding even more interesting.

In reality Christopher did not suffer the jealousy that his forbidding expression might indicate. The wedding and subsequent formal reception simply underscored for him how drastically his perceptions of his life had changed. He didn't mind in the least that James was taking Amelia Hawthorne to wife and to the marriage bed. Nor did he much care to be earl of Dunbar—or earl of Anything, for that matter. What he wanted was something he'd once had and then thrown away. He wanted Maggie Montoya Talbot as his wife in truth. He wanted to take her to his bed every night—and day, if she would let him —and watch her grow big with his children and grow old in the decades of years they would spend together. He wanted a sprawling New Mexico ranch, and he wanted to be a part of the burgeoning progress that was part of a raw land not yet tamed.

Maggie, however, had made her feelings very clear in her straightforward note of farewell. Ironically, they had switched positions. Now it was he who wanted a marriage, companionship, and love and Maggie who was content leading separate lives half a world apart. The situation was his own fault, of course. He'd had his chance and hadn't come to his senses until it was too late.

"Are you feeling sorry for yourself again?" Peter Scarborough asked, handing Christopher a glass of Scotch whiskey. "I convinced the footman to find us some of this. The punch they're serving is terrible."

Christopher lifted one brow in cynical inquiry. "Why should I feel sorry for myself?"

"I thought perhaps you'd just realized what a jackass you'd been and decided that Maggie was worth more than all this lot put together."

"Jackass? You did adopt some interesting vocabulary while we were in America."

"It's an appropriate word in this case."

"Um. Well, for your information, my friend, I didn't just now decide that I've been a jackass; I've known it for some time."

"Then why don't you go to New Mexico and let your wife know that you've come to your senses? Women usually appreciate that sort of humility."

Christopher made a rather ungentlemanly sound. "What do you know about women?"

"More than I once did. I expect you to congratulate me, my boy—on my courage, if nothing else. Two days ago I posted a letter to Luisa Gutierrez asking her to become my wife."

Christopher's brows shot up.

Peter grinned. "There's just something about those American women, isn't there?"

"My congratulations, Peter. Most sincerely. Luisa is a lovely woman, and a fortunate one, I might add." He lifted his glass in salute.

"Thank you, my boy. Now, tell me why you don't have the guts to go to New Mexico and win Maggie back."

Christopher's face grew dark.

"I've never known you to back down from a fight," Peter persisted.

"I'm simply respecting her wishes in the matter."

"Since when have women in love ever said what they meant in matters like this?"

"Unfortunately, Maggie always says what she means."

"Maybe she doesn't know what she wants."

"I've never known a female who is more sure of what she wants," Christopher countered.

Peter shook his head. "You two are a perfect pair, you know. One is as stubborn as the other." He pulled a letter from his formal coat. "Perhaps you should read this letter from Luisa. It came the day after I posted my proposal to her."

Christopher read. His black brows knitted together and looked even blacker than before. "Todd Harley. The bastard."

Peter smiled in satisfaction.

Twenty

The fine New Mexico weather lasted only until Christmas. On Christmas Eve Mother Nature decorated the grasslands with a foot of snow. The temperature plunged so low that Cibola Creek froze solid and the Pecos had a crust of ice thick enough for a full-grown man to walk across the river and not break through. Two weeks into the new year a blue norther howled through the plains. The wind was so fierce that snow falling in New Mexico didn't hit the ground until it reached Texas. Drifts piled high, blocking roads and practically burying two toolsheds on Rancho del Rio. Cattle turned their tails to the wind, hunched down, and endured. People did the same.

When the storms passed, the sun rose on a new world. The sky was a sweep of clean azure, the land blindingly bright with its cold blanket of white. As the Rancho del Rio cowboys mounted up to ride, their horses breathed out clouds that condensed and froze to tiny crystals of ice. Icicles dripped from the horses' nostrils and thick rime coated the beards and mustaches of the cowboys.

Moss Riley clapped his arms against his body to ward off the cold as he grinned at Maggie. "We'll warm up soon enough once we start riding. We got a job ahead of us checking on the cattle scattered by the storm. Those dumb beasts can wander miles with a wind like that pushin' 'em."

Maggie shivered. Even her thick sheepskin jacket and heavy gloves didn't soften the bite of the cold. "How can the sun be so bright and the air so cold?"

"This ain't hardly cold, ma'am. Why, by the time the sun gets a wee bit higher all these icicles are gonna start to drippin'." With a creak of saddle leather Moss mounted up and gave the high sign to the men. "I'll be at the line camp over by Cibola Springs tonight. I left Toby here to help Cleave and Jed fix those wagons. If need be you can send him for me."

Maggie waved as the hands trotted away, their horses' hooves ringing on the frozen ground. When they were gone the world seemed very still and silent. She inhaled deeply, letting the clean cold bite her lungs. There had been nights this cold when she had slept in the alleyways of Denver. Now she had a warm feather bed with goosedown quilts, a cast-iron stove that kept the chill from the air all night long, hot food and drink, good friends that she trusted. What more could a woman want?

She pressed a protective hand to her stomach, which

had just started to boast a slight curve of pregnancy. Indeed, what more could a woman want than the bounty Maggie possessed? Christopher's image rose in her mind, and she wondered if her husband would find such a cold, bright morning as invigorating as she did.

An hour later Moss's prediction came true. As the sun rose higher, the air lost its bite and the icicles that hung from every possible surface began to drip. The ranch came to life. Cleave, the smith, had his forge red hot and with the help of Jed and young Toby Ross was rimming the wheels of two wagons and repairing an axle on another. Children emerged from the cottages behind the bunkhouse to have snowball fights and try to build snowmen out of fine, powdery snow that slipped through their gloved fingers like sand.

Luisa looked out the window at the children's antics. "They'll be bored and up to mischief soon. If Todd brings those books over this week we can start school Monday. It's taken them a long time to get here."

Maggie peeked out the window at the bright sun, then put aside her broom. "I think I'll take the children on a picnic."

"You're crazy. It's cold as a miner's nose out there."

"The children don't mind the cold. We could take them to the swimming hole and they can skate."

"Don't include me in this. I have work to do. Take Cleave's wife with you. She's as crazy as you are, and for the same reason." Luisa shook her head sympathetically as Maggie donned jacket and boots and headed out the door. "It never fails. The minute a woman becomes pregnant she can't get enough of children. Must be Mother Nature's plot to keep the world in babies."

Maggie's outing was a huge success. The pool that served as a shady swimming hole in summer was hard frozen, and the older children skated, slid, and tumbled on the smooth ice that they had swept clean of the powdery snow. They glided by on hand-carved wooden skates and store-bought steel ones, and those with no skates at all improvised with the imagination unique to children. A line rider's boy had brought an old board that he used as a makeshift ice sled, and an eight-year-old curly-headed daughter of Clem, the horse wrangler, sat on an oilcloth rain slicker while ten-year-old Juan Ortega spun her in circles on the ice.

Maggie watched the antics while she minded three-year-old Jake and four-year-old Sarah on one edge of the icy pond. The little ones were having a time of it trying to keep their footing on the slippery surface. They clung to Maggie's hands, hung on her skirts, and hugged her legs while filling the cold air with high-pitched giggles. On the other side of the trees Sadie, the smith's wife, had started a bonfire, and Tamara, the wife of one of the line riders, was preparing a kettle of hot chocolate. In the wagon box, cold chicken, biscuits, and mincemeat and apple pies waited for the children to work up an appetite.

Little Sarah slipped and thumped her bottom on the ice. With a wail of protest she reached out for Maggie. Young Jake watched with manly disdain while she was comforted. But when Sarah was once again playing happily on the ice, he tugged at Maggie's skirt for a hug of his own.

Maggie willingly folded him in her arms. He smelled of little boy and wet wool. Suddenly she was very glad that the child growing inside of her would grow up in New Mexico instead of London. London was a beautiful city, and England was a very nice place—for the English. Maggie was the child of a more raucous, freer land, however, and she wanted her child to take the same joy in the land that she did.

The only thing Maggie missed about England was Christopher, and someday enough time would have passed that she wouldn't hurt every time she thought about him.

"Lunch!" Sadie called. "Come and get it."

The children were quick to respond. Little Jake latched on to his older brother, who slid him across the ice in front of him as he made for the opposite bank. Sarah, however, seemed uninterested in food. She had discovered the fun of running precariously across the ice and then sliding on the soles of her shoes. She squealed in delight and didn't even mind when she ended up on her well-padded little behind. Maggie joined in the game, giggling with as much glee as the little girl. Only when she landed on her backside for the third time did she admit that this activity was better left to children.

"Still a hoyden, I see."

Maggie thought at first that she'd dreamed Christopher's voice, but when she looked up, there he was, sitting atop a long-legged black gelding at the edge of the pond. Her heart did a somersault. Her voice stuck in her throat. For a moment she stared at him as though he were a mirage that might disappear at any second, and he returned her stare with a hungry intensity that was beyond the capabilities of any mirage.

"A hoyden?" she asked in a voice that seemed to startle the silence. "I've never been anything else, as well you should know." Maggie tried to sound composed and casual—as though his sudden appearance weren't making her heart flop about in her chest like a fish on dry land—but the words came out pugnacious and too loud. More quietly she asked, "What are you doing here, Christopher?"

One brow lifted. "I'm eating crow. Can't you tell?"

"What?"

He dismounted, walked out on the pond, and stretched out a hand to little Sarah, who sat on the ice watching him with suspicious eyes. "Could you use a hand up, young lady?"

"You talk funny," she accused.

"Yes, I do. I'll have to learn to speak . . . more colorfully."

Sarah puckered her face comically, but she took his hand and allowed him to set her on her feet. "We have a school. You could go there if you asked Maggie."

"Could I? Perhaps that would help."

The little girl turned to Maggie. "Can I go to lunch?"

"Run along. Be very careful as you cross the pond. I'll be right there."

"Yes'm." She peeped up at Christopher one more time, then with careful steps set off for dry land, where hot chocolate, chicken, and pie awaited.

Christopher offered his hand to help Maggie up. She took it gingerly, as if his touch might burn even through the heavy gloves they both wore, but he shifted to a firm grip on her wrist and pulled her to her feet. A familiar warmth enveloped Maggie at the sight of him standing there, tall, straight, with his broad shoulders and sardonic smile. She tried to ignore it. Just because he was at Rancho del Rio didn't mean anything had changed. She should have learned by now to quit hoping.

"I didn't expect to see you here." She avoided his eyes. Those wicked black eyes had always been trouble for her; they had the power to melt her reason and ignite feelings that were most unwise.

"You didn't expect to, or you didn't want to?"

She was silent.

"Maggie, I came a long way to hear from your own lips that you really think we're better off apart."

"Isn't that what you kept telling me all the time we were together?"

"I kept telling that to both of us." He hesitated. "It seems I convinced you more thoroughly than I convinced myself."

Maggie allowed herself a brief flare of hope.

Christopher leaned negligently against a bare-limbed cottonwood and gave her a crooked smile. "I can tell you're not going to make this easy."

"Make what easy?"

"Eating crow. Maggie cat, you're about to witness a rare phenomenon: an Englishman admitting that he was wrong. I behaved stupidly and shamefully towards you both here and in England. I crave your pardon for it, and I hope some spark of affection for me remains and will inspire you to forgive me."

Maggie couldn't believe what she was hearing. If this was a dream, it was certainly a jackpot of a dream. She was beginning to enjoy herself.

Christopher continued. "You made very clear in your letter that you no longer wished to live as man and wife. I believe you also said your infatuation with me was childish and that now you were wiser, or some such thing."

Maggie remembered the letter very well. She remembered crying over the lies she wrote, lies designed to relieve Christopher of the burden of responsibility for her. She had wanted to convince Christopher that she didn't need him, and perhaps convince herself as well.

"I'm hoping that the letter didn't say what was really in your heart."

"Why?" she demanded.

He looked uncomfortable. Maggie rather hoped he was. For all the grief he'd caused her, he deserved to be very uncomfortable. On the other hand, for all he'd given her —a whole new world, the very land she stood upon, a glimpse of love, nights of passion, and the child that was growing within her—Christopher deserved some mercy. Not much, but some.

"Christopher, why are you here?"

He took a deep breath. Maggie could almost see the patience bleed out of him. "I am here, sweet wife, because I'm bloody in love with you. That's why." He pushed himself away from the tree and threw his arms wide in surrender, no longer the casual, composed aristocrat. "I can't get through a day without you hounding my thoughts. I can't climb in bed without wanting you there beside me. You march through my dreams. Bloody hell, Maggie! You are my dreams."

"My goodness!" Maggie regarded him from beneath the thick lashes that veiled her eyes. "Cursing in front of a lady. Tch!"

"Dammit, Maggie! You're no lady, and I like it that way. I like you—no, I love you!—just the way you are."

"And I love you," Maggie admitted softly. "I've loved you so long—maybe from the first time I saw you sitting in the Lady Luck looking like a fish out of water."

He took her by the shoulders as if he would keep her from running from him. "And that damned letter you wrote?"

"I lied."

His eyes began to gleam dangerously. "You lied?"

She smiled brightly.

"Why did you lie to me? No! Don't tell me, you incorrigible little alley cat. I'll have it out of you later. Right now I have more pressing things to attend to."

Maggie's smile drooped a bit. Here they had just made declarations of mutual love, and Christopher was about to run off and attend to some business?

"You'd best introduce me to those two ladies at the fire.

They look as though they're about to pistol-whip me if I make another move toward you."

"Then you'd better behave yourself, Your High and Mighty Lordship. You know what barbarians we American women are." She slanted him an irreverent grin as she took his arm.

Sadie and Tamara gave Christopher looks both curious and suspicious as Maggie led him to the bonfire.

"Ladies, this fellow is my husband, Christopher Talbot. Christopher, the lady holding a spoon like it was a weapon is Sadie, our blacksmith's wife, and the lady with black hair is Tamara. She's married to one of our new line riders."

The women's suspicions instantly melted into smiles of welcome. They practically cooed as Christopher exerted his best English charm.

"He talks funny," came a reminder from little Sarah. "I told him he could go to school with us."

Sadie glared at the child, but Maggie laughed. "He's allowed to talk funny, Sarah. When I was in England, folks there thought I talked funny. In fact, they thought I was stranger than a cow with two tails."

"Really?" Sarah asked, her eyes bright. "Where's England?"

Maggie didn't want to think about England. Christopher loved her. He'd come all this way to tell her that he loved her just the way she was. And she certainly loved him. If living with him meant returning to stuffy old England, she supposed she could endure it.

"We'll tell you about England someday soon," Christopher promised. "Maybe we'll have a big bonfire one of these cold nights and tell everybody stories about England."

"Promise?" Sarah demanded.

"Promise. But right now Maggie and I have some business to see to. I hope you ladies don't mind if I steal her."

As Christopher lifted Maggie onto his horse's saddle and mounted behind her, she wondered what business he had in mind. Did he want to go over the books, or talk with Moss about the manager's plans for expansion? Was he that anxious to see what was the state of his precious land?

Christopher didn't turn his horse toward the house, though. He took a compass from his saddlebags, consulted it carefully, and then headed straight northeast. In twenty minutes' riding a line shack appeared on the horizon.

"I hoped this would still be here."

"A line shack? Christopher, what business do you have with a line shack?"

"I don't have business with a line shack, wife. I have business with you."

Maggie suddenly realized his purpose. Her heart jumped. "You must be crazy. It's freezing, and there's no heat in there."

He looked smug. "I came equipped with blankets, and I intend to make my own heat."

Christopher was as good as his word. They made heat enough that they scarcely needed the roll of blankets tied to the back of his saddle. Spread out on the packed dirt floor, the blankets made a bed cleaner than the straw mattress on the cot. Discarded clothes served as pillows, and a fire too long banked chased away the cold.

Christopher fought his own urgency. He'd not had a woman since Maggie left him, and his blood ran hot. For the whole Atlantic voyage and then the trip across the continent he'd lived in the shadow of a fierce need to make love to her, to put his mark upon her and shout to the world that Maggie Montoya Talbot was his woman and he was her man.

Now, in a cold line shack, the silky smoothness of her naked skin against his, the sweet warmth of her mouth, and the earthy woman-smell of her body drove him to desperate need. Within the same heartbeat he wanted to find immediate relief in her sweet womanflesh and also stretch their passion into a long, delicious time of loving.

It was Maggie who drove him over the edge. She refused to let him take his time with her. Her kisses were sweet agony, her eyes dark pools of desire that cast a spell robbing him of all control. As always, their joining was as much a battle as a love scene. He pinned her beneath him in an attempt to slow the pace of their escalating need. His mouth laid claim to hers while his hard-muscled thigh pressed between her legs in a slow rhythm that made her squirm to get more. She managed to wrap her legs around him. Her small hands found his buttocks and pressed him against her in sensuous temptation. Christopher gasped as her tactics sent a spasm of tortured delight through his body. Later there would be time for drawn-out, lingering hours of love. Now was the time for raw satisfaction.

"You are a bawdy little witch!" he whispered against her mouth. "The devil's own imp of temptation."

Her eyes twinkled up at him. "Maybe you should have married a lady."

"Maybe I shouldn't have." He taunted her by rubbing the hard tip of his sex along the hot, inviting groove of her femininity, and the mischief in her eyes flared to a bright blaze of desire. The fuse of his control burned down to nothing, and he thrust into her. Maggie's gasp of pleasure echoed in his head like a love song. The focus of his existence narrowed to the woman beneath him and the need to drive into her deeper, harder, faster. Her mewling sounds of desire urged him on. The pain of her fingernails raking his back only intensified his passion. He had never felt so powerful, so strong, and at the same time so tender;

and underlying every burning sensation—the certainty of wholeness, rightness, and love.

Maggie's sweet cry of release triggered his own climax. Every muscle in his body seemed to turn molten as he exploded within her. He could feel the contractions of Maggie's satisfaction as her legs gripped him like a vise. Suddenly, Christopher felt like a turbulent river that has finally found peace in the deep, quiet depths of the ocean; he had come home at last.

Maggie rode back to the house perched in front of Christopher on the saddle. Christopher had wrapped her securely in a blanket, but she scarcely needed it to keep the cold at bay; the new warmth in her soul would keep her toasty for many winters to come—as long as she had Christopher. She wondered why she had ever let her pride almost rob her of the man she loved.

She could feel his warm breath in her hair as she leaned back against the solid wall of his chest. A gust of that warmth tickled her ear as he leaned down to whisper:

"Tell me why you lied to me."

"What?" Those were not exactly the words of love she had expected to hear.

"Tell me why you lied to me in that miserable letter you left me when you escaped my clutches in England—which, by the way, is the last time you'll ever escape me. Were you so angry at me for being such a villain?"

"I wasn't angry at you at all. I was angry at myself for being such a fool over you."

"You weren't a fool."

"Yes, I was. I did everything but stand on my head to make you love me—or at least I tried. I couldn't do anything right. I made everybody unhappy, including you, and I thought you would never, ever come to love me.

The letter was to make you feel that you didn't need to worry about me or take care of me any longer."

His eyes caught hers and held them. "I loved you long before you left England, Maggie. I was simply too stupid to realize it and then too bloody stubborn to tell you."

"Is loving me such a tragedy that you fought it so hard?"

"Loving you is the best thing that's ever happened to me."

The warmth inside of Maggie solidified to pure, glowing gold. "If you truly love me, Christopher, I would go anywhere with you. I would even put up with your old dragon of a mother."

Christopher laughed. It was a deep rumble of a laugh, a more contented sound than any she'd ever heard from him. "I do truly love you, Maggie cat. But if you don't mind, I'd rather live right here. I'm afraid you've spoiled me for London Society. You are such a brilliant spokesman for your own world that I've decided to become a convert. Do you think you can teach me to become a cattle rancher?"

She attacked him with a hug. "No, but I'd wager that Moss Riley can."

"Then we'll give Mr. Riley a chance."

She propped her chin on his chest and looked up at him, her eyes sparkling. "Do you suppose a man could make love to a woman on horseback?"

One brow angled upward. "Not unless he wanted to get frostbite on a very sensitive part of his anatomy."

"I would make sure you didn't get frostbite," she purred.

She could see the idea taking hold as his eyes warmed. She cuddled closer against him and reached for the buttons of his trousers.

When they rode up to the house an hour later, Maggie

was smiling like a cat with cream on its whiskers and Christopher wore an expression that was a cross between bemusement and wonder.

Luisa greeted them tartly as they dismounted. "We were about to send out a search party."

"No, you weren't," Maggie scoffed. "You knew I was all right as long as I was with Christopher."

"It's almost sunset."

Maggie shot a surprised look toward the western horizon, where the sun rested in a slightly flattened red ball. "Oh. It is." She hugged herself, then dropped her arms in surprise as Peter Scarborough emerged from the house. "Peter!"

"Hello, Magdalena. Have you decided to give your jackass husband a second chance?"

Maggie flushed and shot a glance at Christopher. "Are you going to let him call you a jackass?"

Christopher just grinned. Peter chuckled. "I guess you are going to forgive him. The English charm must be irresistible. Not only has Christopher beguiled fair Magdalena into looking upon him with favor, but I have convinced beautiful Luisa to be my wife."

Maggie's mouth fell open. Christopher came up behind her and closed it with a finger on her jaw. "I'd say it's the ladies' charm that is irresistible."

Luisa smiled gently at Maggie. "I decided that if you can endure marriage to a stuffy Englishman, perhaps I can too."

"Oh, Christopher's not stuffy, it's just his—"

Christopher's hand clamped gently but firmly over her mouth. "Hush, my love. You'll ruin my reputation. Besides, Peter is much stuffier than I. Why do you think he's remained a bachelor all this time?"

"He won't be stuffy long when Luisa gets her hands on

him," Maggie said quietly as Peter took Luisa's arm and escorted her into the house.

Christopher pulled her away from the door and caged her against the wall with his arms. "You mean poor Peter might suffer the same fate I have?"

Maggie grinned. "Only if he's lucky."

He kissed her, closing the distance between them and pressing her against the wall so that his body molded into her. When he finally released her she was breathless. "Aren't you tired of me yet?"

"When I'm eighty years old I won't be tired of you."

"Is that a promise?"

"That's a promise."

They spent the evening sitting in front of the parlor fireplace with Peter and Luisa. The world seemed safe and very secure, even with a cold wind sniffing around the doors and windows and the threat of another storm in the air. Christopher and Peter both told stories on Maggie that colored her face bright pink. Luisa shook her head sorrowfully as she heard about Lady Christopher Talbot's wild ride through Hyde Park. Christopher smiled at Maggie as he told the story. She saw apology in his eyes—not for telling the story of her tantrum, but for having caused it.

"Magdalena never was one who thought much of rules," Luisa said.

Maggie sniffed. "That's not true. I can be as well behaved as anybody, but the English get upset by the least little thing, Luisa. If you let Peter drag you over there, you'll see what I mean. Nobody does anything useful. They spend all their time thinking up ways to keep people from having fun. Especially the ladies. The gentlemen sometimes cut loose and go hunting or gamble, but the ladies just sit around all day and talk about who's broken what silly rule."

She gave Christopher a narrow-eyed look. "Speaking of ladies, how is Miss Perfect Amelia doing now that she's duchess of Torrington?"

"She's taken to being a duchess like a duck takes to water."

"I'm sure she has," Maggie remarked sourly.

"And she rules Torrington House—and James—with a firm hand."

"Just what James needs."

"Amelia's not really so bad," Peter injected. "She's got Rodney on a strict allowance that has curtailed his drinking and gaming. Before the summer ends I predict she'll have him engaged to some strong-minded girl who will take him in hand. And she persuaded James to dower Catharine, which has improved that lady's temperament quite noticeably."

Maggie was only grudging in her approval. "What of Elizabeth? Luisa, you should meet Elizabeth, Christopher's sister. She's one of the sweetest girls you'd ever hope to meet, and she can draw and paint pictures so well, you'd think they were real."

"Elizabeth sends her love," Christopher said. "She said I was to thank you for teaching her that she should use and enjoy her God-given gifts. The portraits of the little Holloway girls turned out splendidly. She's received several other commissions as well—and an offer of marriage from Dr. Holloway."

"Oh! She's going to marry Dr. Holloway! How wonderful. I knew that man loved her the minute I saw them together. Are you pleased with the match, Christopher?"

"I don't think it would matter if I was pleased or not. Elizabeth has become quite an independent thinker since you infected her with your ideas, and little Rachel is following right in her footsteps, much to Catharine's dismay." He smiled at Maggie's frown. "But, yes, I'm very pleased. If anyone in this world deserves to be happy, it's Elizabeth."

"I bet your mother wasn't very happy about Dr. Holloway." She explained to Luisa. "Thomas Holloway is the nicest man, but I guess if you look at his family, he's almost as common as I am."

A wry smile pulled at Christopher's mouth. "My mother has discovered that there's more power in the heart than in the bloodlines, I fear. She hasn't said much about anything since Amelia has come to rule the roost. Amelia has persuaded James to renovate the dower house so that Mother can retire there and have some peace in her aristocratic life again."

Maggie thought for a moment on the irony that it was ladylike Amelia who had finally conquered the dragon duchess, not the brash commoner from America. Sitting in the security of her New Mexico ranch house, the Talbot family didn't seem nearly as intimidating as they had in England. She was surprised to discover that she wished them all well. Even the old dragon and sour Catharine. Maggie's world had suddenly become as close to perfect as a world could be, and she found it impossible to harbor animosity against anyone.

The next day, however, Maggie's world became a bit less than perfect when Todd Harley delivered several boxfuls of books for the school. As luck would have it, Christopher had stuck around the house that morning to go through the account books. He was sitting on the porch with Maggie drinking a cup of hot cider when Todd drove up in his wagon.

Maggie couldn't say which of the two men wore the blackest scowl when they recognized each other. Neither was pleased.

"Well . . . uh . . . hello, Talbot. Maggie told me you were in England."

Christopher stood, bristling like a dog scenting a skunk. "What are you doing here?"

"Just paying a visit on the lady. A woman alone sometimes needs a man's help."

"She bloody well doesn't need your help."

"Both of you quit it!" Maggie demanded. "Todd, quit making it sound like you're helping me with anything other than the school, and, Christopher, stop acting like a bull getting ready to charge. Todd has helped me get some books for the school. He has a friend in a publishing house. He's here to deliver our books, aren't you, Todd?"

The men glared at each other.

"Aren't you, Todd?"

Todd's scowl gradually faded. "The books are in the back of the wagon. Five boxes of them."

"Christopher, would you help us get them onto the porch?"

The men eyed each other warily as they unloaded the wagon.

"Here for a visit to check up on your investment?" Todd asked when they were finished.

"I'm here for good." Unmistakable challenge rang in Christopher's voice.

"Thought you were going to do your empire building from England."

"I decided I can build an empire from here just as well."

"You don't say."

"Christopher"—Maggie interrupted another exchange of glares—"Todd really has been very helpful to me in getting my school started. He's ranching the land south of here, and everyone says he's doing a fine job of it."

Todd spared Maggie a glance. His mouth relaxed momentarily in a smile. "The land's not as good as up here—and I don't have near as much of it as you do—but I'll make a go of it." He returned Christopher's stare with a level look. "I'm not a crook like my father was."

"Todd's our neighbor, Christopher. We have to be friends."

"We don't have to be friends with anyone who once held a gun on us. There's a lot of land between his house and ours."

Todd's face settled into an unreadable mask. "If that's the way you feel about it, maybe you should put an ocean between us again." He nodded toward Maggie and touched the brim of his hat. "Let me know if you need anything else. I'll be around."

When Todd's wagon rattled off, Christopher turned on Maggie. "Would you care to explain to me just why you think we can be friendly neighbors with Todd Harley?"

Maggie was suspicious. "You didn't seem that surprised to see him."

"Luisa wrote Peter that he'd bought the land south of here and was hanging around you like a fly around sugar."

"Is *that* why you came back? Because you learned that Todd was here?" Maggie's voice was sharp as a steel knife.

"I came back because I love you, dammit." His mouth pressed into a tight line. "And . . . because I feared Todd might still have his eye on this land . . . and he might hurt you."

For a moment Maggie considered being furious, but she couldn't really fault him for rushing to protect his investment. It would have been nice if Christopher had come back solely for her, but it was enough that he had admitted his love for her. She sighed. "Todd is harmless. It was his father who was the snake."

Christopher still fumed, in spite of Maggie's conciliatory tone. "Snakes generally breed little snakelets. He cooperated well enough with his father. If you hadn't hit him in such a strategic section of his anatomy, he would have delivered you to his father at gunpoint."

"I don't really think he would have." She smiled beguilingly. "I think you're jealous, Lord Christopher. Or is it Lord Dunbar now that James gave you the earldom?"

"Maggie! Don't try to sweet-talk me. I've a mind to give you a good tongue lashing for letting that piece of vermin anywhere near you."

"Ooooh! A tongue lashing." She dodged away when he reached for her in frustrated vexation. "That sounds interesting."

"Come back here, you minx! Dammit, Maggie!"

She allowed herself to be cornered in the alcove between the wall of the house and the root cellar. When Christopher grabbed her, she melted willingly into a grip that rapidly became an embrace. She pulled his head down and tempted him into a kiss. His hands traveled down her arms to grip her hips and press her closer.

"Dammit, Maggie! What were we talking about?"

"You were promising me a tongue lashing." She stood on tiptoe and traced a path up his throat with her tongue, purring in kittenish delight. "I think you should keep your promise."

"You are the most impossible woman I've ever met."

"Um-hm," she agreed while nipping at his ear.

"You win." He picked her up and strode with her toward the back door. Maggie buried her face in his warm shoulder, thoroughly enjoying the feel of being held in his strong arms.

A mere prick of uneasiness remained to mar her enjoyment, but she told herself that Todd Harley wasn't worth worrying about. The man wasn't dangerous. Not dangerous at all.

Twenty-one

Todd Harley was cursing as he pulled the team up to the corral. Neil Corcoran ambled out of the barn to help unharness, and Todd cursed Neil. He cursed the tired horses; he cursed the edge of the wagon wheel that caught his boot as he stepped down. When he walked into the house he was still cursing.

He walked straight to the cupboard that held his whiskey. One glass didn't suffice. Two managed to take the sharpest edges from his anger. Three mellowed him enough to make him realize that a setback didn't necessarily spell disaster. No poker game was lost until the last hand was played.

He looked around him and sneered. The stone house that he had constructed had only three rooms, a kitchen, a bedroom, and a front room. No carpets softened the hard plank floors; no curtains shaded the windows. A bed, a chair, several stools, a table, and a few storage cupboards furnished the place.

Every time Todd walked into the hovel he compared it to the house at Rancho del Rio. That was a house that a civilized man should live in—soft carpets, feather beds, comfortably upholstered chairs, fine china. But Todd Harley had never had the luck to make such a life for himself. He didn't have his father's talent at gambling, though he knew the tricks of the trade. Neither did he have the ambition to ranch—ranching involved too much hard work. So now he was stuck in this stone hovel he called a house, eating off tin plates, sleeping on a cot, walking on raw pine floors, and trying to build a ranch on land that had neither the grass nor water of the land up north—the Montoya grant, Maggie's Rancho del Rio.

He kicked a stool out of his path and headed for the room's one chair. Everything had been going so damned well, and now all his plans were spoiled by that cursed Englishman coming back. The whole purpose of purchasing this land had been to bring him within reach of Maggie Montoya Talbot. Maggie had been a bit standoffish, true, but that was because of his father's bumbling, not because of anything that Todd had done. Eventually he could have won her over; Todd had never met a woman whom he couldn't have eating out of his hand if he set his mind to it. Maggie would have come to realize that an absent husband—and a foreign one at that—deserved neither her loyalty nor her land. She would have obtained a divorce and fallen into Todd's waiting arms.

And thus he would have Rancho del Rio back—Rancho

del Rio and its fine house and fertile land and experienced hands that could run the place for him.

It had been an excellent plan, and it would have certainly worked had the Englishman stayed where he belonged. Because of Maggie's wretched husband Todd would have to stoop to obtaining Rancho del Rio by less honest means than seducing its mistress.

Almost reluctantly, Todd went to a drawer in the kitchen, moved a few utensils, and pulled out a bulging packet of papers. It wasn't his fault he had to play dirty, he told himself. He had hoped that he wouldn't have to use this alternative plan, but a man sometimes had to be flexible. When you were dealt losing cards, you discarded them and drew others. And when necessary, you stacked the deck in your favor.

First he would have to arrange for Maggie Talbot to pay him a visit.

Needlework was not one of Maggie's talents. She could hem a skirt or darn a sock, but the fine needlework required to make good clothes was beyond her patience. She was determined to learn, however. Now that she would soon be a mother, she needed to become more domestic, she told herself.

That thought was not sufficiently comforting when she stuck her finger for the fifth time.

"Dammit!"

"Maggie!" warned Luisa. "Wasn't it just this morning that you made a vow to never again curse?"

"It wasn't a vow; it was just an idea. A bad idea. Ouch! Damn! This needle is hungry for my blood."

"Your child will be fluent in profanity before it can say mama or papa. Is that the example you want to set?"

"The baby won't know what I'm saying. Besides, Christopher likes me just the way I am."

"Just the way you are, or in spite of the way you are?"

"You're as bad as the ladies in London. You should visit there after you and Peter get married. You'd feel right at home."

Luisa smiled at Maggie's vexation. "I prefer living in Santa Fe. That's why Peter's there finding us a house."

"Look at this embroidery! It's a mess! I hope the baby's a boy. I'll never be able to teach a girl to sew."

Luisa cocked a brow in Maggie's direction. "Speaking of the baby, don't you think it's about time you told Christopher he's going to be a father?"

"The time just hasn't been right." Maggie looked up from the chemise she was stitching and stared out the window. A tentative smile softened the line of her mouth. "It's something so special—having a baby. When I tell Christopher it must be at a very special time."

"I hope that time comes before you grow to twice your size. He may start to wonder why his wife looks like she swallowed a bale of hay."

Maggie made a most unladylike noise. "He hasn't taken the slightest notice that my waist is expanding."

"From the looks of you two together, he's too busy making up for lost time to dwell on such details."

Maggie smiled dreamily. "Maybe."

Just then young Toby Ross stuck his head in the front door. "Miz Talbot?"

"Yes, Toby."

"One of Mr. Harley's hands just rode in and asked me to give you this." He handed Maggie a piece of paper.

"Thank you."

"Yes, ma'am," he said as he left.

Luisa raised her brows. "What is this?"

"I guess Todd's afraid to make another appearance after the greeting Christopher gave him a couple of days ago." She read. " 'Another box of books arrived today—also a

new catalog with some things you might need for the
school. Reluctant to anger your husband by delivering
them. If you could pick up the books yourself you could
look at the catalog also.' "

"I wouldn't," Luisa warned. "If Christopher learned
that you'd gone to Todd Harley's place, he'd turn you over
his knee."

"Just let him try," Maggie said with an exasperated
frown.

Luisa's scowl only deepened.

"Oh, really, Luisa. Why shouldn't I go there on a perfectly honest visit? Todd's right. Christopher wouldn't be
happy to see him here. But you're starting school next
week, and if there's more books, we need to get them."

"Send one of the hands."

"I want to look through that catalog."

"Have him send the catalog along with the books."

"It's probably not his. The last catalog, his friend from
New York sent it out for him to look at but wanted it back
right away." She set aside her sewing. "I think I'll go right
now. Christopher's bound to be out with Moss for the rest
of the day, and with luck I can be back before he returns.
He won't even know I went."

Luisa shook her head. Maggie lifted her chin with a
hint of her old rebellion. "If I wanted to be told where I
could go and who I could talk to, I'd have stayed in London."

Maggie did make several concessions to caution, however. She persuaded Luisa to make the trip with her, and
the women took Toby Ross and Cleave Campbell, the
blacksmith, as escorts. Cleave alone, who could lift an
anvil one-handed, was enough to make Todd behave. The
smith could probably chase off a pack of renegade Indians
with just his scowl. He had a very impressive scowl.

Maggie didn't expect trouble from either Indians or Todd Harley, however. She was going to pick up her books, leaf through the catalog, and return home before Christopher returned. She had convinced herself that Todd was not a menace, but she hadn't yet convinced her husband. For a man who claimed to be a gentleman, Christopher could be as stubborn as a mule. Maggie acknowledged the same failing in herself, but this time she was quite sure she was in the right.

So Maggie was stunned when Todd refused to let her leave his little stone house. At first she didn't believe she'd heard him correctly.

"I appreciate the invitation, Todd," she said, flipping through the last few pages of the catalog. "But we really must be getting back. It gets dark so early these days. . . ." She looked up—right into the muzzle of a .44 caliber Colt revolver. Beside her Luisa stiffened.

Maggie felt the blood drain from her face. Only twice before in her life had she been face to face with a loaded gun—once when a customer at the Lady Luck had wanted her to expose her body rather than dance, and once when Todd Harley had gone along with his father's murderous scheme. Both times she had discovered that there was something very nightmarish about looking down the business end of a firearm.

"What is this?" she demanded.

Todd's voice was apologetic. "I'm sorry, Maggie. Don't worry, my dear. I don't mean you any harm. In fact, I've got only your good in mind."

"What do you want?"

"I just want your husband to come here for a little visit, but that man's got his mind set against neighborliness— you saw that for yourself the other day."

"Todd, this is crazy. Put the gun down."

Todd didn't answer. Instead, he turned to Luisa. "Mrs.

Gutierrez, you collect those two men who rode in with you and ride back home. When you get there, you tell that Englishman if he wants his wife back, he can come get her. Tell him he can come with two men—that's all— unarmed. And no tricks. I'm an honest man and a gentleman, but even an honest man can lose his temper and do things he might regret. You understand."

"I understand," Luisa said with stiff calm. She slanted Maggie a warning look. "You know, Todd, if you hurt her, Christopher will tear you limb from limb. Don't think he's a pansy just because he's an Englishman."

"I'm not going to hurt Maggie. Maggie and I are good friends."

Luisa gave him a disgusted look and left.

Maggie shut the catalog with an angry snap. She couldn't believe she had been so wrong. "You're no better than your father, Todd Harley. I don't know why I thought you were made from a different cut of cloth."

"I'm not my father," Todd replied testily. "I'm not a criminal."

"Then why are you standing there pointing a gun at me?"

"Because your husband came back, that's why. This is all his fault, you know. I was going to make you very happy, Maggie. You would be much better off married to me than that foreigner."

Maggie thought he might be a little crazy. For the first time she started to be truly afraid.

"It could still work, Maggie. Divorce Talbot and marry me. No one would think a thing of it. After all, he's a foreigner. And you came back alone from England. Everybody assumed that you had a falling out."

"Why would I be better off married to you?" Maggie tried to sound interested in his proposal.

"Because if you're not married to me, you'll lose Rancho del Rio altogether."

Maggie had trouble following her captor's reasoning. Carefully, she got up from the stool at the table and made her way toward the one chair in the room. The pistol followed her without wavering. "May I sit down?"

"Certainly. Make yourself comfortable."

"You know, Todd, I would feel more at ease talking about this if I weren't looking down the barrel of that gun."

He looked suspicious. "Are you going to behave?"

"There's not much I can do right now, is there?"

"No. There isn't." He lowered the gun, but didn't put it away.

"Todd, you realize if you kill Christopher, that won't get you the ranch. It would still be mine."

Todd chuckled, then shook his head. "Maggie, I keep telling you that I'm not my father. I'm not a criminal, and I'm certainly not going to kill your husband."

"Then why do you tell me that unless I agree to divorce Christopher and marry you, I'll likely lose the ranch?"

Todd simply smiled. "Wait and see, my dear. I think all along you've underestimated me. My father underestimated me also, but look where he is, and then take note of where I am."

"That didn't answer my question. If you expect Christopher to sign over Rancho del Rio just so you'll let me go, you're mistaken. If you make him choose between the land and me, he may very well choose the land."

"Wait and see. Wait and see. By the end of the evening you may have changed your mind about which one of us you want."

Luisa wouldn't have guessed that one of the English—a race noted for their cold-blooded calm—could be so furious. Christopher's fury would have put an angry bull to shame and made a full-grown grizzly stand to attention.

"That headstrong, naive, addle-witted, idiotic little imbecile! The wolf asks the lamb to visit him in his den and she goes! How could a grown woman be so senseless? Especially Maggie. She's not a sheltered little flower who doesn't know the pitfalls of the world. How could she have believed the blackguard?"

"Todd charmed her into believing he was harmless," Luisa said in Maggie's defense. "And with me and the two men along, she thought she was being careful."

"That little dimwit hasn't been careful a day in her life! She doesn't know the meaning of the word *careful!* She thinks she can do anything and conquer anyone. Dammit! Bloody goddammit!" He sent Luisa an apologetic glance for his language. "Sorry, Luisa, but that woman sometimes makes me mad enough to forget every claim to manners."

"That's quite all right, Christopher. She has done the same to me more than once."

"I should leave the little twit with Harley. It would serve justice better than putting the villain in prison. After two weeks with her he'd surrender and ask the judge to hang him."

A smile flickered over Luisa's face before she became serious once again. "Do you think Todd wants the ranch in return for her release?"

"Of course he does. What else would he want?" Christopher paced to the parlor window and stared into the night. The moonless dark seemed to hold a fascination for him, and Luisa grew uneasy as he made not a move and said no more. The land was important to him. In spite of their reconciliation Maggie still believed the land was of paramount importance to him. Luisa wished desperately that Peter had not chosen these last days to travel to Santa

Fe to find them a house. He might have known how to handle Christopher in this frightening mood. Luisa certainly didn't.

"Christopher, surely you're not thinking of refusing."

"Of course I'll refuse. I'm not in the habit of giving in to blackmail by thieves and scoundrels."

Luisa surged out of her chair. "Curse your damned English pride, Christopher! What about Maggie?"

"Maggie is my wife. What this misbegotten rogue fails to understand is that Englishmen hold very dearly to their possessions. This land is mine; the ranch is mine; and Maggie is mine. He threatens any of those at great risk to himself."

Luisa sat down again. She didn't like Christopher's tone. Maggie was the last on his list of possessions. Would he be willing to sacrifice her to keep the land if his back were to the wall? For a moment she considered telling him that Maggie was carrying his child, but she decided against it. Maggie wouldn't like thinking that she'd become Christopher's first priority just because she was pregnant. "What are you going to do?" she asked.

"Take her back," he answered simply.

Luisa looked skeptical. "With only yourself and the two men he said you could take—unarmed?"

"I'll think of a way before I get there." Christopher grinned, and Luisa thought that grin didn't belong on the face of an English earl; it belonged on the face of a wolf stalking its prey.

By the time Christopher, Cleave, and Moss arrived at Todd Harley's ranch house it was almost midnight, but the yellow glow of lanterns lit the house's windows. They were expected. Todd had guessed that Christopher wouldn't leave Maggie to spend the night as a prisoner.

A surge of anger heated Christopher's blood as he

thought of Maggie in Todd's hands. All through the ride anger and panic had eaten away at his control. In the army he had learned the value of thinking calmly, of reserving fury for the actual battle and employing cold reason to plan for victory. But fears for Maggie's safety interfered. Anger at her foolishness nibbled away at one part of his control while worry for what she might be suffering ate away at the other part. Overriding every other emotion was a deep, burning wrath directed at Todd Harley. If anything happened to Maggie, he vowed to strangle the villain with his bare hands. And when he got Maggie back, he might do the same to her.

They were met in front of the house by two of Todd's hands. The men behaved as though they were welcoming Christopher to a social affair rather than a kidnapping. Their smiles held more amusement than rancor.

"Go right on in, Mr. Talbot," one of them said. "Your men too. Mr. Harley is expecting you."

"I'll just bet he is," Christopher said under his breath. "Cleave, stay here with the horses, please. Moss, come with me." Todd Harley was more roundabout than a Frenchman. Christopher had thought Americans were supposed to be forthright even in their villainies.

Todd and Maggie awaited them inside, in a room that could be called a parlor only by the farthest stretch of the imagination. Three oil lanterns cast a greasy glow over a chair, several stools, and a table haphazardly arranged on a raw pine floor. A poorly vented fireplace provided the only heat.

Christopher spared only a quick glance for Maggie. Ascertaining that she seemed sound and unhurt, all his attention centered on Todd, who was leaning against the rough-cut fireplace mantel with studied nonchalance. Maggie's face plainly reflected her hurt at his lack of concern, but Christopher knew better than to reveal the worth of an item under negotiation. When she was safely back in his arms, then he would make it up to her—right after he strangled the little fool.

"Evening, Talbot. Glad you could make it." Todd waved to a bottle on the table. "Pour yourself a whiskey."

"Let's get on with this, Harley."

"Come, come. We're both men of the world. There's no reason for us to behave like peons. This is going to be a very civilized evening. I'm not like my father, you know. I don't ambush people or plot their demise."

"I scarcely consider kidnapping a woman and holding her hostage to be civilized."

"I certainly didn't kidnap anyone." Todd chuckled condescendingly. "Maggie came here on a friendly visit to pick up some more books. I merely extended you an invitation to escort her home." He went to the table and poured two glasses of whiskey. "Maggie, my dear, will you join us?"

"No," Maggie said. The single word could have frosted the whiskey glasses.

Todd shook his head as he handed one of the glasses to Christopher. "I fear that your wife is a bit put out with me at the moment. But then, you're probably not too pleased with me either. Or with her, I imagine. I do sympathize. Women are fools for the most part. Pleasant fools at times, but they do have a tendency to get a man in trouble. That's why I've never married." He downed his liquor. "Drink, man. Do you fear it's drugged? I promise I wouldn't be so crude." He pulled up a stool and sat down.

Christopher set his glass upon the table without drinking from it. He ignored Todd's irritated frown. "Let's get to the point, shall we? What do you want in return for Maggie's release?"

"You insist upon thinking of me as a villain," Todd said with a sigh. "Maggie is free to go anytime she pleases. If you object to her being here, you may assign one of your men to take her home. But she might find it entertaining to stay."

Christopher didn't want Maggie out of his sight, and he didn't trust Todd for one moment. "I take it that I am not free to escort her home."

"Certainly you may. Later. Right now I hope you'll stay for a few hands of poker. In fact, I insist."

"Poker's not my game, Harley."

"Such a pity. You Englishmen are so dull that I suspect you don't have a game." He grinned. "I'll teach you the nuances of play as we go."

"No, thank you."

"As I said before, I insist." Todd glanced at Maggie, then back at Christopher. "And, of course, being men of honor, we'll both abide by whatever wagers are made."

Christopher had no doubt what the stakes would be. "Why the complication of a poker game, Harley? You have Maggie. If you want Rancho del Rio that badly, you could demand it as ransom."

"Still don't believe me, do you? I'm not a criminal, Talbot. I do want the land, of course. But I'd rather win it honestly, as my father won it from your brother. I like the irony of it. Don't you? Your brother Stephen loses the ranch to Theodore Harley, and now you're about to lose the ranch to Theodore Harley's son."

"Are you so sure you'll win?"

"Maybe. Maybe not. We'll both have to pray to Lady Luck." He went to the table and picked up a deck of cards. "Pull up a stool, Talbot. We'll play a few hands for something inconsequential like money, just to get the feel of the cards. Then we'll get down to business."

"And if I refuse?"

"Don't make me become ungracious," Todd warned with a smile.

Christopher glanced at Maggie, whose face was pale and tense. Then he sat.

"Maybe you'd like that whiskey now."

Christopher suspected he was going to need a great deal of whiskey when this game was over. But he wouldn't stoop to drinking with Harley. "Deal the cards."

The game proceeded. Neil Corcoran, Moss Riley, and Maggie looked on. Todd wanted witnesses to tell the world that he had won the Montoya Grant fair and square. Christopher lost the first few hands to the tune of a hundred dollars. He'd done plenty of gambling in his life, and even played poker one evening in Santa Fe with Derek Slater and his friends. He had a knack for the game, but the cards weren't falling his way.

"Do you feel ready to play for real?"

Christopher saw the confidence in the other man's eyes. He wondered if his brother Stephen had felt a similar flood of anger when he had faced Theodore Harley. But no, Stephen had been drunk, the fool. And he had entered into the game willingly. Of course, in a situation such as this, even the strictest gentlemen wouldn't feel obligated to honor the wagers. But Christopher suspected that the force of Harley's ready gun was backing up the play. The man probably had transfer of title all made out ready for Christopher's signature.

"Do I have a choice?" Christopher asked.

Todd just smiled and dealt the cards. "Five card draw. Jacks to open. Deuces wild."

Christopher picked up his cards. He had a pair of fours.

"Openers?" Todd inquired.

"No."

"Neither do I. Redeal." He smiled. "Would you like to deal?"

Christopher didn't deal anything better. Not even a pair decorated his hand. Todd folded his hand as well.

"My deal," Todd said.

Christopher picked up two pair—queens and fives. He threw a wooden poker chip onto the table.

"Ah! We'll say that each of your chips represents one tenth of the grant—the part that borders my land. And I'll call your bet with a hundred dollars."

"Rather uneven bets, wouldn't you say?" Christopher commented, one brow raised.

Todd shrugged.

"Give me one card," Christopher said.

"And I'll take two."

Christopher drew a three. Useless. "Pass."

"Raise you another hundred. You may call with another tenth—about fifty thousand acres that would be. Or"—he grinned—"you can fold."

"Call."

Christopher won the hand with his two pair. Todd had bet on three of a kind.

Christopher lost the next two hands, but won the following five. He could see Todd's uneasiness growing. When Todd was five hundred dollars in the hole and Christopher still had all of the Montoya Grant, he decided to push his luck. "I think, since you want all this to be aboveboard, I should see some of this money you're betting."

Todd frowned, and Christopher felt a small bit of triumph.

"Don't you think that's the only fair thing to do?" he asked the witnesses.

Even Neil Corcoran agreed Christopher's request was only fair. No one extended credit in a poker game unless there was some surety offered.

"Maybe you should start betting your own land. But you have only twenty-five thousand acres, isn't that right? Worth about half a chip at the going rate."

Todd's mouth drew into a tight line. There wasn't much he could say after his protestations of winning the Montoya grant fair and square.

"All right. I told you I intended to be honest about this. I'm not a cheat like my father was. My deal. Five card draw. No openers. Jacks and deuces wild."

Christopher won with three queens. Todd was silent. He sat very still except for a rhythmic flipping of the cards with his thumb. "I have something else to bet. One more hand. All or nothing."

"You've already lost your land and five hundred dollars. What else do you have?"

A smile spread across Todd's face. "Neil. Moss. Take yourselves out to the messhouse. We don't need witnesses to this last hand. Maggie, you can stay. In fact, please do."

Moss hesitated. Neil sent him a menacing scowl. "Come on, Riley. We do like the boss says."

"Go on, Moss. Go find Cleave and tell him we'll be leaving soon."

When they were alone, Todd's smile grew. "Like I said. One more hand. All or nothing."

"I've retained the Montoya Grant and won your land besides. You're so insistent about this being a fair game. Suppose I'm not willing to risk an all-or-nothing hand?"

"But you are willing. Or you will be. You're going to want what I'll put on the table."

"Something worth all that land?"

Todd chuckled. "I suppose that depends on how much your wife means to you." He got up and walked into the kitchen. When he came back he threw a packet of papers on the table. "While I was in Denver after you threw my father in prison, I did some digging on sweet Maggie. I wanted to find anything that might prove her claim to this land false. I stumbled on a curious coincidence: Maggie wasn't a coddled lady who was living with friends in Denver. She was a saloon dancer at the Lady Luck, among other things, and she left her job quite suddenly—the day after a friend of hers was murdered. Arnold Stone. He owed her money.

"Of course, a coincidence doesn't prove anything. So I hired a private detective to investigate." He tapped the sheaf with a finger. "I've got enough evidence here to get little Maggie hanged for murder. Or maybe, since she's a woman, they'll just send her to prison. From what I've heard about the prisons in these parts, she might choose to be hanged instead. I'm rather fond of Maggie, myself. So I haven't brought this evidence to the attention of the law. It's what I'm betting against your land. If you win, you get the land and the evidence, and I'll keep my mouth shut. If you lose, I get the land. If you don't play, Maggie goes to prison."

Maggie felt as though she'd been hit with a log. Over a year had passed since that terrible night in Denver—so long, she'd thought she might be free of it. But here it was to haunt her.

Christopher looked at her. His face was carved from stone. She knew that she blazed with guilt. The killing itself hadn't been by her hand, but she was certainly guilty of instigating it.

Lordy! Why had she ever believed that she could escape so horrible a deed? She could point the finger at Luisa. That might defuse the situation. But that betrayal was beyond her. She couldn't do such a thing—not for her own sake, not for Christopher's precious land. Not for anything.

Christopher's silence stretched out. He seemed to be considering the value of the land against the value of his wife. Maggie wasn't sure which would win. Christopher had always been honest about having married her for the grant. She had come to mean something to him. Did she dare hope that she had come to mean more to him than the land?

Christopher cleared his throat. "Win or lose, Harley, that sheaf of papers goes into the fire. And if you go to the law about this, there won't be anywhere on this world that you can hide from me."

Todd paled at Christopher's tone. "I have no wish to see Maggie in prison. I just want the land. I'd take her with the land if I could get her. Maybe after you've lost it, she'll decide she'd rather be married to me."

"Maybe she will." He glanced at Maggie, but she couldn't read his expression. "But she's my wife, and she'd have a hard time getting loose from me. Deal the damned cards."

Maggie watched the game and wrestled with a warring set of emotions as she watched the game of five-card stud. Christopher was willing to risk everything he'd worked for to keep her; she had just won the most important victory of her life. Yet she was sick with fear that in winning Christopher, she had destroyed his dreams.

Two cards were dealt—one face down, one face up. Christopher's cards showed a three of hearts. Todd had a jack of spades.

"No need to bet," Christopher said. "We know what the stakes are, and neither of us is going to fold. Just deal out the rest of the cards."

Todd dealt three more cards face down. "Turn them."

One at a time they turned their cards. Todd turned a queen. Christopher turned a five of hearts. Todd turned a ten of clubs. Christopher had the jack of hearts. Todd followed with the nine of diamonds. He smiled, reading a possible straight. Christopher turned the ten of hearts. He cocked a brow. A possible flush.

They turned the last card together. Todd completed his

straight with a king. Christopher had a four of hearts. A flush.

Todd's face paled. His mouth drew into a tight line.

"You lose," Christopher told him.

Maggie let out the breath she'd been holding. She practically skipped around the table to get a look at Todd's cards.

"Omigod! You won, Christopher." She laughed. "You won!"

"Of course I won," Christopher said coolly.

"No. You didn't win." A pistol appeared in Todd's hand. "I had the flush, Talbot. You got the straight. A pity. Suddenly you're destitute."

Maggie didn't hesitate. She grabbed a stool and hit Todd from behind. Todd crashed to the floor and dropped his gun. As he picked himself up, Christopher grabbed the weapon and threw it out of reach. "Get out of the way, Maggie!" he ordered.

She was slow to obey. Fists doubled, she longed to give Todd the punching he deserved.

"Will you do as I say just once in your life?"

Maggie backed reluctantly against the wall.

Christopher clenched his fists. If he'd had a lick of sense, he would have kept Todd's gun, but he felt an irresistible urge to pound on the man. He'd had that urge ever since he met him.

"An Englishman shouldn't be hard to beat," Todd sneered. "What are you waiting for?"

Christopher raised his fists. Todd lunged. Christopher stepped aside and sent a hard fist into Todd's stomach.

"Ooof!" Todd clutched his middle, but seconds later he turned and charged again. His fist connected with Christopher's jaw, but Christopher's knee found a target in Todd's groin. Todd yelped.

Christopher didn't give the man time to recover. His

own blood was boiling. He grabbed Todd's shoulder and pulled him upright, then he sent his fist into Todd's face—once, twice. Todd's nose and mouth spouted crimson. Christopher felt a warm, wicked rush of satisfaction. He drew back his fist for another blow.

"Christopher!"

Maggie's voice penetrated the haze of rage. Todd looked at him cross-eyed.

"Christopher, please stop." Her hand landed lightly on his arm. "Please stop."

His blood calmed slowly to a mere simmer.

"Don't you think he's had enough? Todd, tell him you've had enough."

Todd agreed in a strangled voice.

"Tell him you'll never bother us again."

He shook his head eagerly. Blood spattered everywhere. Christopher released him.

"I'll be charitable," Christopher told him. "I'll give you a week to get off *my* land. You and all your hands."

Todd swayed. He staggered back against the wall.

"Do you understand?"

"Ye—yeth."

"Good. Just one more piece of business to attend to." Christopher took the damning packet of evidence from the table, tossed it into the fire, and watched for a moment as it burned. Then he shot a glare at Maggie. "Don't look so smug, wife. I've a few words to say to you."

Maggie sighed. Under her breath, she mumbled: "What a surprise."

On the slow ride home in the dark Maggie swayed on the front of Christopher's saddle. She leaned back against the solid wall of his chest, too exhausted for words; but when her husband sent Moss and Cleave ahead and out of earshot, she knew the time for words had come.

"What did that man do to you that you were forced to kill him?" was Christopher's first question.

Maggie's heart warmed for his assumption that the deed had been self defense.

"I didn't kill him . . . exactly." She spilled the whole story, leaving nothing out. Christopher was the only person in the world she would trust with Luisa's safety, not to mention her own.

Christopher was silent for a few moments when she was finished. "You could have told me this earlier," he said. "It might have saved us some trouble."

"I didn't trust you," she told him honestly.

"Yet you trust me now."

Maggie smiled. "You threw the evidence in the fire even before you had my explanation."

"So I did."

"And you bet the land to save me. Could it be, Your Mighty Lordship, that you put my safety above a fortune in land?"

Even in the moonless night she could see the gleam in his eyes.

"I knew I would win."

"No, you didn't."

"Of course I did. Talbots don't lose to scum like Harley. At least, not when we're sober."

Maggie laughed. "You're going to be a stiff English snob forever. I hope your son or daughter doesn't take after you."

For a moment Christopher didn't seem to have heard. Then he clutched her shoulder. "Son or daughter?"

"One of those. Probably in the late spring."

His teeth flashed white in the darkness. "Here I thought you were gaining weight. If we weren't in the middle of nowhere I'd take you down from this horse and pay that youngster a visit."

"And what would you tell him?"

"I'd tell him that I love his mother, even though she is a headstrong, idiotic little fool. And I'd tell him I hope he gets my common sense, because his mother doesn't have any. Be grateful that you're with child, Maggie. Otherwise I'd be tempted to turn you over my knee for allowing yourself to fall into Harley's trap." He tilted her face up toward his and gave her a brief, hard kiss that was a promise of passion to come. "But I suppose that will have to do, for now."

In June of 1884 Maggie gave birth to a son. Attending the mother at the birth were Luisa Scarborough, Jenny Slater, Lady Elizabeth Holloway, and her husband Dr. Thomas Holloway. Attending the anxious father were Peter Scarborough, Moss Riley, and several bottles of whiskey. Two hours after an easy birth Maggie was up and about, looking more sound than her husband. The baby was named Edward Ramón, after Christopher's father and Maggie's grandfather.

Todd Harley bought a saloon in Santa Fe using the money Christopher eventually paid him for his twenty-five thousand acres. Christopher had made him sweat a few months, but decided to give the blackguard a fair price for his land. A man with Theodore Harley for a father deserved a second chance, he told his wife. After all, fate had given Christopher a second chance. He had been well on his way to spending his life as a stiff English bore until Maggie turned him into a brawling, gambling New Mexican rancher with raw knuckles and an uppity wife who didn't know her place.

Maggie knew her place, she insisted. Her place was with him.